12/18/02 BTT $24.95

SIMON TOLKIEN

Final Witness

A NOVEL

RANDOM HOUSE

NEW YORK

Copyright © 2002 by Simon Tolkien

Library of Congress Cataloging-in-Publication Data
Tolkien, Simon.
Final witness: a novel / Simon Tolkien.
p.   cm.
ISBN 0-375-50882-1
1. Politicians—Family relationships—Fiction.   2. Mothers—Death—Fiction.
3. London (England)—Fiction.   4. Trials (Murder)—Fiction.
5. Teenage boys—Fiction.   6. Stepmothers—Fiction.   I. Title.
PR6120.O44 S84   2003   823'.92—dc21   2002021316

Printed in the United States of America on acid-free paper
2 4 6 8 9 7 5 3
First Edition

Book design by J. K. Lambert

THIS BOOK IS DEDICATED
TO MY WIFE, TRACY.
WITHOUT HER IT COULD NOT
HAVE BEEN WRITTEN.

Turning over and over in the sky, length after length of whiteness unwound over the earth and shrouded it. The blizzard was alone on earth and knew no rival.

When he climbed down from the window-sill Yura's first impulse was to dress, run outside and start doing something. He was afraid that the cabbage patch would be buried so that no-one could dig it up, and that his mother, buried in the open field, would helplessly sink deeper and deeper away from him into the ground.

—from *Doctor Zhivago*,
BORIS PASTERNAK

ACKNOWLEDGMENTS

I acknowledge with gratitude the help and encouragement that I have received from Tracy, Nicholas, Anna and Faith Tolkien, and from Ravi Dogra, Christine Groom, Elizabeth Sheinkman, Jonathan Karp, Margaret Wimberger, Rachel Calder and Beverley Cousins.

FINAL WITNESS

Chapter 1

My name is Thomas Robinson. I am sixteen years old. Today is Thursday, the sixth of July, and I am making this statement to Detective Sergeant Hearns of the Ipswich Police. I have made two statements already in these proceedings. Everything that I say is true to the best of my knowledge and belief, and I make this statement knowing that, if it is tendered in evidence, I shall be liable to prosecution if I have willfully stated anything which I know to be false or do not believe to be true.

I live in the House of the Four Winds, which is on the outskirts of the town of Flyte on the coast of Suffolk. The only other person who lives here now is the housekeeper, Jane Martin, who looked after me when I was a boy. My father never comes to visit me anymore.

My mother was killed in this house on the thirty-first of May last year. I described everything that happened in my first two statements. Two men came and murdered her. One of them had a ponytail and a scar behind his jaw. I was here too but hidden in a secret place behind the great bookcase at the top of the stairs. It was made for Catholic priests to hide in when the Protestants were searching for them hundreds of years ago. I hid there but my mother didn't. She couldn't because there was not enough time. That's why she died.

The men didn't see me, but I saw the man with the scar through the little spy hole in the bookcase. He was bending down over my mother, and I saw him when he got to his feet with something gold in his hand.

I remember his face more clearly than any face I've ever seen, although I only saw him for a second or two. It's like my memory took a photograph. Small, dark eyes, thin, bloodless lips and a thick scar that ran down from behind his jaw into his strong bull neck. You could see the scar because he had his black hair in a ponytail.

I'd seen the man before. He was with Greta in London. It was six weeks before he killed my mother. I only saw him from behind, but I know it was him. He had the same ponytail and the scar.

Yesterday evening at about seven o'clock I saw this man again. For a third time.

Jane Martin goes to the town hall in Flyte on Wednesday evenings for the Women's Institute, and so I was alone in the dining room eating my dinner. There are windows looking out to the front and toward the lane on the north side of the house. They were all open. I think I was listening to the sea and remembering things like I sometimes do.

I don't suppose I would have heard them come if the television had been on, but I felt that something was wrong as soon as I heard the car pull up in the lane. We use the lane to go down to the beach, but nobody else does. It's too far out of town and I wasn't expecting any visitors.

They came through the door in the north wall just like they did on the night my mother died. They must have had a key. I saw them coming down the lawn to the front door. They were moving quickly, and there was no time for me to get upstairs to the hiding place behind the books where I'd hid before. I ran instead to the old black bench, which is beside the door going from the dining room into the hall. It has a seat that opens up, and I got in there. There are carvings of Matthew, Mark, Luke and John on the front, and you can see out through the holes in their eyes. When I was small, I used to climb in there when I played hide-and-seek with my mother and Aunt Jane, but now I didn't fit very well and I was frightened, very frightened.

The police have installed a panic button in the house, and I pressed that before I got in the bench. It's connected to Carmouth Police Station and makes them come when I need them.

I was in the bench when they came in through the front door. There were two of them and they used a key. I'm sure of that. The one with the scar was in charge, but he didn't have his hair in a ponytail this time. He wore it long so I couldn't see the scar. He called the other man Lonny. They wore leather jackets and jeans, and Lonny was wearing a baseball cap. He was overweight and looked like a boxer. I'd never seen Lonny before. I'd say they were both in their thirties, but they could have been older.

They looked around the rooms downstairs for a while, but they didn't touch anything and they had gloves on.

Then the one with the scar said, "Lonny, watch the fucking road while I go upstairs. The kid's behind that bookcase where he was before. Greta told me how it works."

Lonny came and stood really close to where I was, but I couldn't see him because he was to the side of me, and the man with the scar went upstairs. It was really hard not moving, and I tried to hold my breath. That made it worse, and I thought Lonny would hear my heart beating. It sounded so loud to me.

About a minute later the man with the scar was back and I could hear anger in his voice, like he was getting ready to do something really bad. He wasn't shouting though; it was almost as if he was talking through his teeth. And I can't remember the exact words he used. All I can do is give the gist of them.

"Fucking kid's in here somewhere," he said. "Look, he was halfway through eating when we got here. He can't have gone far."

"Want me to turn the gaff over, do you, Rosie? I'll find him for you."

I could hear the eagerness in Lonny's voice, like he really wanted to break something.

"No, I fucking don't. I don't want you to touch anything, you moron. Just keep a fucking watch and leave it to me. And don't call me that again."

The fat man went to stand by the front door. It was half open.

"Lonny the loser," said the man with the scar. "He's a fucking loser, isn't he, Thomas?"

I couldn't see him but he wasn't far, and I almost answered because he said my name so suddenly and naturally, but I bit my tongue instead.

"I'm sorry about your mother, Thomas. Really I am. And I promise you that you'll be fine. Scout's honor, Thomas. Scout's honor. All we want is to take you on a little holiday. That's all. Until this trial is over and done with. Somewhere nice and sunny with plenty of foreign girls. Topless beaches. You'd like that, wouldn't you, Thomas? So why don't you be a good boy and come out and we can get acquainted."

I could hear him moving about opening doors and cupboards all the time he was talking in this mock friendly voice he'd put on, but now there was a pause. When he spoke again, the hard edge was back in his voice.

"Too scared to come out, are you, boy? Too fucking scared. Want to play fucking games with me, do you, you little runt?"

He stopped suddenly, his voice cut off by the sound of the siren, and a second later they ran out the front door. They must have waited in the lane until I buzzed the police in through the front gate and then driven away without anyone seeing them.

I would recognize both these men again, and I would also recognize the voice of the man with the scar. It was soft and he said the bad words slowly, like he enjoyed saying them over and over again. I think he would have killed me if he'd found me. I really think he would.

Like I said before, I have tried my best to give the gist of what the men said when they were in the house, but I can't remember all their exact words. However, I am sure about the names they called each other and I know that the man with the scar said about the hiding place that "Greta told me how it works."

When I went upstairs with the police officer afterward, the door in the bookcase was standing half open.

I confirm that I am still willing to attend court and give evidence for the prosecution in the trial of my stepmother, Greta Robinson.

Signed: Thomas Robinson
Dated: 6th July 2000

Chapter 2

_____

I N A TALL nineteenth-century house on a fashionable street in Chelsea, Lady Greta Robinson was getting dressed. She kept very still with her head slightly to one side as she considered herself in a full-length Victorian mahogany mirror positioned in the middle of the master bedroom. She was wearing a sleeveless black Chanel dress cut just above her knee, a pearl necklace and a thin gold watch on her left wrist. She stood five feet seven inches high in her stockinged feet.

Greta's short black hair matched her dress. It was swept back above her small ears and so exposed the full width of her cheekbones. There was something faintly Asiatic about her face, and her cool, green eyes accentuated an aura of detachment. However, this was contradicted by her full, red lips, untarnished by lipstick and always slightly parted as if she were about to tell you something that would change your life forever. Contradiction was the secret of her attraction. The boyishness of her face was in opposition to the fullness of her figure. With an easy motion she stepped out of the dress and looked at her nakedness for a moment with a half smile. Her full breasts needed no support, and there was no trace of fat around her hips or waist. There had been no child to change *her* contours.

Turning, she picked up a Christian Dior dress from where it lay draped across the back of a nearby Chippendale chair and put it on. It was black like the other, but it had sleeves, the hemline was longer and the neck was cut higher. Greta's eyes hardly blinked as they concentrated on the reflected image of their owner. There was much for her to admire, but it was not narcissism that motivated her scrutiny today. Appearance was vital. Her barrister, that wily old fox Miles Lambert, had told her that. She was about to go onstage. The men and women who would be gazing at her from the jury box day after day as she sat in the dock or gave evidence must learn to love her. Her fate would be in their hands.

Their lives were not glamorous. They had no titles, no designer dresses, no fashionable home to go back to after the court day was over. Nobody noticed what happened to them. She must not repel them. She had been, after all, just like them once upon a time.

She took off the necklace and replaced the gold watch with a simple one on a black leather band that matched her dress. Narrowing her eyes, she bestowed a half smile of approval upon her reflection.

"Showtime," she whispered to herself softly before she turned and padded over to the bed, where her husband lay sleeping. Looking at her at that moment, you'd have had to say that she was just like a cat. A sleek, well-cared-for white cat with a pair of glittering green eyes.

=

He looked good for his age, she thought. A full head of black hair with not too many silver flecks, a strong and wiry body; its outlines were clear and firm where he had wound himself up in his sheet during the long hot night. He had been sleeping badly for some time now, and she had often woken at three or four to see him standing by the open window gazing out into the night as if he could find some answer to his difficulties in the empty street below.

There had always been an inflexibility about the man, even before he was overtaken by disaster. He gave the impression of holding his features firm by an effort of will. It was apparent in the set of his jaw and the rigidity of his head upon his neck, but in the last year the lines on his forehead had become deeper and more pronounced. Recently he had formed a habit of passing his thumb and index finger along these furrows as if this was the only way of resting his piercing blue eyes, which never seemed to close. Except in his sleep, of course, like now, with little more than three hours to go before his second wife would go on trial for conspiring to murder his first.

Greta sat on the side of the bed and gently stroked her husband's cheek with the tip of her finger, feeling the bristly facial hair that had grown there during the night above the hard jawbone. "You don't know how to fight, do you, darling?" she whispered. "You're pretty good at conquering but not so good at fighting. That's the trouble. You can't step back and defend yourself; you just keep on coming until you've got nothing left. Nothing left at all."

"What's left?" asked Sir Peter Robinson, looking up at his wife in the confusion of his first awakening. "What is it, Greta?"

"Nothing. Nothing at all, darling. Except that it's nearly half past seven and it's time to get up and face the jury."

"Oh, Christ. Jesus Christ and all his saints. Christ."

"I agree we could do with some help, but perhaps that's asking too much. Come on, Peter. I need you today. You know that."

Sir Peter unclenched his fists with a visible resolve and got out of bed. Greta stood and stepped back into the middle of the room. She put her hands on her hips.

"How do I look?"

"Ravishing. Like, like . . ."

"I'm waiting."

"Like Audrey Hepburn in that movie. What was it called?"

"*Breakfast at Tiffany's*. Well, let's hope Judge Stranger likes old movies."

"Granger, Greta. Granger."

"Whatever."

====

Two hours later John the chauffeur was driving Sir Peter and Lady Greta along the side of the River Thames in the black Daimler with the darkened windows that insulated the minister for defense so successfully from the population that had reelected his party into government three years before. Two short years ago Sir Peter had been riding high with a beautiful wife in the country and a personal assistant named Greta Grahame, whose bright efficiency had made him the envy of all his colleagues in the Palace of Westminster. But today the Daimler did not stop at the House of Commons or at Sir Peter's offices in Whitehall but purred on toward an unfamiliar destination under the shadow of St. Paul's Cathedral: the Old Bailey, the Central Criminal Court built on the foundations of Newgate Prison. Less than fifty years ago men and women had been sent by the Queen's judges to death by hanging after being convicted of crimes just like that for which Lady Greta was about to be tried.

At the entrance to the courthouse the crews of photographers and journalists with their long, insidious lenses and soft woolly microphones were waiting for Sir Peter and his wife to arrive.

Against all the odds, the prime minister's support had kept Peter in his position for far longer than any of his friends or enemies had ever expected. But Peter knew that he could not continue to defy political gravity if the trial didn't go Greta's way. Everything he had achieved was hanging in the balance, threatened with imminent destruction. And who did he have to thank for this state of affairs? His son, Thomas. His own flesh and blood.

Thomas, who had had everything he ever wanted and was now repaying him with this. Thomas the little bastard, who was so determined to bring everyone down because of what had happened to his mother. God knows, he wasn't the only person who'd been hurt.

Sir Peter felt a surge of rage against his only child run through his body like electricity, and instinctively he gripped his wife's arm.

"God, Greta, I'm sorry."

"Don't be. It's not your fault," she replied, understanding that it was everything, the whole sorry mess that he was referring to and not the sudden grip, which had left a red mark on her slender wrist.

"Fucking little rat. That's what he is. A rat."

Greta did not respond. Instead she turned to look out the window. This was not a time to let their feelings show. The car had turned into the Old Bailey and was encircled by the swarm of reporters as it slowed to a crawl over the last 150 yards of its journey. She thought they looked just like people caught in a flash flood, holding their cameras high above their heads as if they were the only belongings they could hope to save from the rushing waters.

But that was wrong, of course. She was the one at risk of drowning. And as her husband had just said: all because of that boy. "The fucking little rat." Her stepson, Thomas.

Chapter 3

I T HADN'T ALWAYS been like this between Greta and Thomas. Three years ago everything had been fine, or as near to fine as it could be between them. Thomas was just thirteen, and she'd just started out working as Peter Robinson's personal assistant.

He was as dreamy a boy as she'd ever met. He had fair hair the color of summer straw, which he wore long so that it fell forward over his forehead. He had already developed a habit of brushing his hair away from his eyes with the back of his hand before he spoke, a habit that would stay with him all his life. It was part of a natural diffidence, which led him to speak in a tone of uncertainty even when he was sure of what he wanted to say. Yet underneath he had already developed the qualities of stubbornness and determination that were to become so evident after his mother's death.

He had inherited his mother's liquid, blue eyes and delicate mouth, which endowed his face with an attractive half-feminine quality. He also had her fine hands and long, tapering fingers, suggesting a future as an artist or a musician. Not a future that his practical-minded father wanted for his only son.

Peter had had such grand hopes for Thomas when he was small. On the boy's sixth birthday Peter got down the model airplanes that he and *his* father had made together when he was Thomas's age. He arranged them lovingly in squadrons on the nursery floor and told his son their names. But Thomas only pretended to be interested. As soon as his father had left the room, he picked up the book of fairy stories that he had been reading and left the Hurricanes and Spitfires to gather dust.

Two weeks later the dog pursued a ball into the corner and broke the model of the bomber that his grandfather had flown in over Germany fifty years before. That evening Peter packed all the model airplanes away in a box and took them with him when he went back to London. Already his political career was keeping him away from home during the week, and Anne would not hear of selling the House of the Four Winds. Peter felt it was not him but the house that his wife really cared about. Her house and her son.

Peter could sense the expectation in his son when he was about to leave at the end of each weekend. He grew to hate the way the boy seemed to cower when he spoke to him. There was no reason for it. Peter had done nothing to deserve such treatment. He had struggled all his life to make his own father proud of him, and there was not a day that he did not thank Providence for letting the old man live just long enough to know that his son had become the minister of defense. But Thomas didn't care what *his* father thought. He had no pride in his father's family, no interest in his father's achievements. Thomas's heart and mind belonged to his mother and to the house in which her family, the Sackvilles, had lived for generations.

As the years passed, father and son moved ever further apart. Thomas loved stories—he couldn't get enough of them—but Peter never read fiction. It was almost a matter of principle. His mind was fixed on the here and now, and he felt nothing but irritation on rainy days when Thomas lay reading for hours at a time. The boy would stretch himself out on the window seat in the drawing room with cushions piled high under his head so that he could see over the dunes to the North Sea, where great waves crashed upon the shingle beach. He would imagine the postman's knock on the back door as signaling the arrival of Long John Silver and his pirates come to claim their treasure from Billy Bones. Or when he was out walking the dog in the evening he would be looking for Heathcliff striding across the moors in search of a bloody revenge.

Thomas knew where all the wrecks were to be found off the coast. He had their locations marked with black crosses on a map on his bedroom wall, and he would swear on a stack of Bibles that he had heard the church bells of the lost city of Dunwich tolling bleakly in the small hours from their resting place beneath the waves. But such legends had no meaning for Thomas's father, who saw their only value as keeping up the local tourist trade.

==

Within only a few months of being hired Greta made herself indispensable to Sir Peter and so began to accompany him on his weekend visits to his family at the House of the Four Winds. For at least half of the time they would be working in either Sir Peter's study or the drawing room, with its French windows leading onto the garden where Lady Anne spent so much of her time planting and pruning and tending the rose walks for which the House of the Four Winds had become so famous in recent years. And Thomas would be out there too, wheeling a barrow or unraveling a hose. Always helping his mother. The two were inseparable.

Greta made a great effort to get on with Thomas, and by and large she succeeded, for a time at least. She was a good listener when she wanted to be, and she read as much as she could about Suffolk and its history so that Thomas began to come to her when he needed information for the stories he was always writing and reading to his mother in the evenings. Lady Anne raised her eyebrows and laughed in a disconcerting way when she heard of the assistance being given her son by her husband's P.A., but otherwise she said nothing. Greta, however, felt an obscure disapproval emanating from Lady Anne, a sense that the mistress of the house had found her out but chose to let events take their course without interference.

"I know who you are and you're not one of us," she seemed to be saying. "And you never will be one of us, however hard you try."

And so Greta cultivated the boy but remained at a distance from the mother. Sometimes when Lady Anne had one of her recurring migraines and lay upstairs silent with a white flannel over her head and her white bedroom curtains drawn against the sun, Thomas and Greta would walk on the beach and look for amber. Greta knew all about amber because she'd read a book about it.

Sometimes Sir Peter and Lady Anne would be invited out for lunch or dinner at the house of another well-connected family, and Greta, Thomas, and Mrs. Martin, the housekeeper, would remain behind.

It was on one such Saturday that the first trouble happened. It was the birthday of Mrs. Martin's sister, and the housekeeper was taking Thomas with her to the party in Woodbridge. Thomas enjoyed these visits. Mrs. Martin's brother-in-law owned a seagoing boat, and Thomas had already extracted a promise that he would be taken out night fishing when he'd reached the golden age of fifteen, only five months away.

By midday Greta was alone in the House of the Four Winds. She finished typing out the corrections to a speech that Sir Peter was to give at the party conference the following week and then went out into the front hall. There was not a sound anywhere except the murmur of the sea as she climbed the stairs to Lady Anne's bedroom and closed the door softly behind her.

Greta stood in the center of the room watching herself in the freestanding mirror as she slowly and deliberately undressed. It was the third time that she had done this, and each time it gave her greater pleasure. Now she carefully opened the top drawer of an antique chest and took out three or four pairs of Lady Anne's silk underwear, setting to one side a lavender sachet embroidered by the lady of the house. One by one she tried them on, pressing the white material against her body until at last she settled on the sheerest, thinnest pair of all and turned her attention to the closets containing Lady Anne's dresses.

Her green eyes sparkled as she passed the material between her fingers and raised it to her nose. As she breathed in deeply, it was almost as if she was holding Lady Anne close to herself. Turning, she laid out five of the dresses across the wide bed and slowly tried each one on. Her erect nipples visible through the fabric of each dress and the faraway look in her half-closed eyes told their own story. She was too absorbed to notice the sound of the front door opening down below, and she didn't hear the footsteps on the stairs as she pulled a lemon silk brocade dress over her head. She only knew that she was not alone when she looked in the mirror to admire herself and saw Thomas standing in the open doorway behind her.

=

One of Greta's greatest qualities as a personal assistant was her calmness under pressure.

"It's almost unnatural," Sir Peter had told his wife only the previous weekend when they were lying in the bed across which Lady Anne's evening dresses were now draped. "It's like there are all these boats being tossed about in some terrible tempest out there in the bay and she's in her own boat in the center and the storm's having no effect on her at all. She's one in a million, Annie. I bet that some of the other M.P.s would pay a king's ransom to get hold of her, but then, she's completely loyal. That's another of her qualities."

"Yes, I see what you mean," Lady Anne had replied. "It *is* unnatural. She must have worked very hard to become what she is."

Now, at this moment of crisis, Greta remained just as calm as her employer would have expected. Only a slight shudder indicated her awareness of the boy's presence. Thomas, however, stood rooted to the spot and his cheeks flushed crimson. His eyes were fixed on the reflection of Greta's full breasts in the mirror, with the rose-red nipples clearly visible as the buttons on the front of the yellow dress remained undone right down to the waist.

Greta looked evenly at the boy's reflection in the mirror but did nothing to hide herself.

"You're looking at my breasts, Thomas." There was a purring note in Greta's voice that the boy had not heard before.

"No, no. I'm not."

"All right. You're not." Greta laughed, pulling the front of the dress together. "My mistake."

"You're wearing my mother's dress. The one she said was like spring daffodils. And you're in her room. Why are you in her room?"

"Well, Thomas. If you sit down a moment, I'll try to explain it to you."

Greta picked up two of the dresses from the bed, and gestured for the boy to sit in the space that she had cleared, but he didn't move from the doorway.

"You shouldn't be in here. You don't belong in here."

"No, I don't. You're quite right. But Thomas, try to understand. I don't have beautiful clothes like your mother does. I can't afford them like she can. And I didn't think it would do any harm if I tried them on just to see what I looked like. It doesn't hurt anyone, does it?"

"It's not right. They belong to my mother."

"Yes, they do. But I wasn't going to steal them. I wouldn't be trying them on in here if I was going to do that, now, would I?"

"She wouldn't want you to have them on. She wouldn't want you in here. I know she wouldn't."

"All right, perhaps she wouldn't," said Greta, changing tack. "Perhaps she would be upset if she knew. And then she might get one of those horrible migraines. No one wants that, do they, Thomas?"

Thomas did not reply. His lower lip trembled, and he looked like he was going to cry. Greta pressed home her advantage.

"Wouldn't it be better if we didn't tell her? Then no one would get hurt. What do you say? It can be our secret. Just you and me."

Greta put out her right hand toward the boy, thus allowing the yellow dress to fall open again, exposing her breasts.

Thomas took a step backward, but Greta reached over and took his hand, pulling him toward her.

=

In the years that followed, Thomas always recalled this moment as one of the most significant of his childhood. It was a turning point of sorts. An end and a beginning. Certainly his memory chose to preserve the scene in extraordinary detail. Closing his eyes as an adult, he could recall his mother's room with the sea breeze coming in through the half-drawn curtains; the sun shining on the rich mahogany chest with its top drawer open; the mass of clashing colors on the bed where Greta had laid out his mother's clothes; the bright red sleeve of a gown that his mother had worn at Christmas cutting across the white of her pillow like a wound. And closer to him was his father's personal assistant: raven hair and green cat's eyes, yellow dress and full, exposed breasts with red nipples, which gave him a sense of urgency he'd never felt before. He was repelled and attracted all at the same time. And the mirror had been between them. They had seen each other in the mirror before she turned and began saying things. Things about his mother that he didn't want to hear.

She took his hand, and he felt sure that she was going to place it on her breast. The breast that he could now see again so full and close. And he knew that that would make a secret between them that he could never break.

Thomas dragged his eyes away from Greta and focused on the first thing he saw. It was the white flannel on the edge of the sink in the corner of the room, the one his mother used to cover her eyes when she had her migraines.

Thomas wrenched his hand away from Greta, and the force of his action took him out into the hall.

"No," he said, and all his being was concentrated in the one word.

Greta flinched, but whether from the hurt to her hand or the force of his response, Thomas didn't know. The shudder was certainly gone from her face as soon as it had appeared, and she laughed softly.

"I was only shaking your hand, Thomas. You certainly have got an active imagination. Your father's right about that."

There was no time for Thomas to reply. At the bottom of the stairs the front door was closing behind Mrs. Martin.

"What are you doing up there, Thomas? I told you the presents were in the kitchen. Come on or we'll be late."

Greta and the boy exchanged one final look, and then he turned and was gone.

===

If that bloody old housekeeper hadn't forgotten her sister's stupid presents and sent the boy back for them, I might not be here today, Greta thought to herself as she allowed her husband and the chauffeur to escort her to the courthouse door.

Thomas had waited until the weekend was over to tell his mother. And Greta had never had to discuss the incident with Lady Anne. It was Sir Peter who raised the subject with his personal assistant midway through the following week, and he did so in an uncomfortable, almost apologetic way that made her feel slightly sick. She, of course, had had time to prepare her response.

All morning her employer had been coming in and out of her room on one pretext or other. The ground floor of the London house had been converted into offices the year before, and Greta worked in the front room. A printer and fax machine stood on an elegant oak sideboard, while Greta sat at a circular walnut table in the center of the room amid computer screens and telephone lines. Her employer circled the table, nervously clearing his throat.

"What is it, Peter? Something's bothering you."

"Yes, it is. It's something I need to talk to you about, but it's damned difficult to know how to go about it. It's about Anne and that boy, Thomas. God, I wish I could understand him better."

"What about Thomas?"

"Well, he's told Anne something and she's told me. And, well, it's about you. She said I ought to talk to you about it."

"It's about your wife's dresses, isn't it?"

"Yes, that's it. Thomas says you were trying them on. Last weekend when we were out. I told Anne that the boy's made it up. Trying to cause trouble for everyone. He needs to be sent away to a good school. That's what he needs. But Anne won't have it."

"I did try them on. I shouldn't have done but I did."

"You did?"

"Yes. Because they're beautiful and I wanted to see what I looked like in them. I haven't ever had clothes like that, Peter. I'm not a rich girl, you know that."

"But couldn't you have gone to a shop? A boutique or something?"

"I suppose so. I do sometimes. It's just they never leave you alone. It's like they know who's got the money and who hasn't."

Sir Peter was defenseless against this turning of the tables. His dependence on Greta had increased with each month that had passed since she first came to work for him, and it was in his nature to be impressed by straightforwardness of all kinds. Greta's feminine attractions also had a more powerful effect upon him than he cared to admit.

"Well, you shouldn't have done it, but at least you've been honest enough to admit it, which is more than most people would have done. It's my fault in a way. I probably don't pay you enough."

And so Greta succeeded in turning the disaster with the dresses to her own advantage. Sir Peter spent more time with her after the incident and began taking her out for working dinners when they were in London during the week. They would often be seen at the Ivy or Le Pont de la Tour with their heads close together in animated conversation. And not only that: Sir Peter raised his personal assistant's salary by 50 percent, so that now she could afford designer dresses of her own to wear when she went out with her employer. As autumn faded into winter, Sir Peter commented to himself that Greta looked prettier every day. And there was nothing wrong in having a pretty P.A. He'd done nothing to be ashamed of.

Of course, the society tittle-tattles and gossip writers didn't see it that way, and stories began to appear in the tabloids and magazines, although they never made the headlines or even the front pages. The height of the publicity was a black-and-white photograph on page 21 of the *Daily Mail* of the two of them leaving a restaurant together under a caption that read, "Minister Out on the Town."

No word of all this reached the House of the Four Winds. Flyte might as well have been a thousand miles from London. Lady Anne didn't read tabloids or magazines, and none of her friends had the bad taste to raise the subject of Sir Peter's personal assistant in her presence. She visited London less and less often, preferring to concentrate on her garden and her son.

For his part Sir Peter no longer visited the House of the Four Winds every weekend as he had done in the past. He went there once or twice a month while Parliament was in session, and Greta continued to accompany him on these periodic visits, as his government duties made nonworking weekends an impossibility.

The atmosphere in the house was strained, but Sir Peter refused to admit it. Lady Anne was aloof, taking long walks with her son or shutting herself up in her room when Greta was there. The incident with the clothing lay between them unresolved. Lady Anne was embarrassed, and Greta interpreted her silence as condemnation.

=

A conversation at the dinner table one evening the following January brought matters to a head. Greta sat equidistant between Sir Peter and his wife at the long dining room table. The central heating had overcompensated for the inclement weather, and the room was hot and stuffy. The three diners were struggling to make their way through a dessert of cherry pie and custard.

Lady Anne had been talking about a rich northern industrialist called Corbett who had bought himself a stretch of coastline on the other side of Flyte. He had made a fortune manufacturing paper clips and was now building himself a mansion overlooking the sea. More than one of the Robinsons' neighbors had remarked in recent months on the similarity of this edifice to the House of the Four Winds, although it was clearly on a much larger scale.

"I expect they'll be sending their butler round to take photographs of the garden soon. Watch out for men in morning coats with stepladders and telephoto lenses," said Lady Anne.

"Oh, Anne, I'm sure it won't come to that," said Sir Peter. "You shouldn't be so sensitive." He had become increasingly impatient with his wife's preoccupation with this subject during dinner.

"I'm not being sensitive. It's the principle of the thing that's distasteful. People should be what they are. They shouldn't try to wear other people's things."

"Especially when they come from the north," said Greta, suddenly joining in the conversation.

"No, wherever they come from." Lady Anne suddenly stopped, realizing what she'd said. "Oh dear, I'm sorry. That wasn't what I meant at all."

"It's not your fault. You're a Lady and I'm not. People need to know their place. That's what you're saying, isn't it?"

"No. No, I'm not. I'm saying that people should be themselves and not try to be other people. That's got nothing to do with knowing your place."

"Well, if I'd stayed being myself, I'd probably have ended up working in a paper-clip factory," said Greta in a rush.

"My dear, I don't know why you're getting so agitated. I wasn't talking about you. I was talking about this man, Corbett. You shouldn't be so quick to take offense."

Greta said nothing but put her napkin up over her face. A series of visible shudders passed through her upper body, bearing witness to her distress.

Part of Lady Anne wanted to get up and put an arm around the girl. She was clearly upset, and it was rare for her to lose her self-control. But another, stronger part felt repelled. Greta seemed to cause nothing but trouble. It was Greta, after all, who had gone into her bedroom as a trespasser and put on her clothes like they were her own. It was Greta who had gotten Thomas so upset. Greta was the one who should be apologizing.

"Look, who's the injured party here?" said Lady Anne, unconsciously transferring her attention to her husband, who was moving about uncomfortably in his seat at the other end of the table. "I didn't go and try on *her* clothes, did I?"

"No, of course you didn't. She's got none for you to try on. That's the whole bloody point, can't you see that?"

"Yes, I do see that," said Lady Anne, getting up from the table. "I see it only too well. I'm going to bed. I think I've got a headache coming on. This home isn't London, you know, Peter. I'm not here to have political debates with you. Greta may be, but I'm not."

Lady Anne closed the door before Sir Peter could reply. Greta's face remained hidden by her napkin, but her shaking shoulders showed that she was in even greater distress than before. Sir Peter wound his own napkin into a ball and tried unsuccessfully to think of something to say to comfort her.

Eventually he got awkwardly to his feet and went over to stand behind Greta's chair. He shifted his weight irresolutely from one foot to the other and then put out his hand tentatively so that it came to rest on her shoulder.

"Please, Greta. Don't cry. She didn't mean it. She just got upset, that's all."

A few strands of black hair had fallen across Greta's face as she bent over the table, and Sir Peter pulled them gently back over her ear, stroking the side of her head as he did so.

Greta looked up toward him smiling through her tears, and he found himself staring down at the swell of her breasts beneath her simple white blouse. He felt a surge of sexual excitement.

"Thank you, Peter. I'm sorry I was so silly. You're so—"

But Greta didn't finish her sentence. Sir Peter pulled himself away quite violently and stood half swaying by the wall. Across the room a portrait of Lady Anne's father looked down at him with an expression of aristocratic contempt. It was a bad picture but a good likeness, painted in an era when family portraits were no longer in fashion. The artist had caught the aristocratic curl of his sitter's lip and the distant look in the half-closed eyes. Sir Peter remembered the old man's cool disapproval when he had come asking for his daughter's hand in marriage.

"Going places, Anne says. But which ones? That's the question, isn't it, young man? Which ones?"

"All right, you old bastard," Sir Peter whispered to himself as he stared up at the portrait. "I've done nothing wrong."

"What did you say, Peter?" asked Greta.

"Nothing. Nothing except that you're not the only one who's felt out of place in this damned house. I've got to go now. See if Anne's all right. You understand."

"Yes, of course," said Greta, wiping her eyes with her napkin.

Chapter 4

PETER TOOK the stairs two at a time but at the top he found his bedroom door locked. There was no reply when he knocked and called out his wife's name.

After a minute or two he walked despondently down the corridor to an infrequently used spare bedroom. The still heavy air of the evening persisted into the night, making it hard to sleep. Peter stripped himself naked, but still he felt his skin prickling and his heart beating too fast.

Getting up, he opened the old leaded windows as wide as they would go. Outside, the six thin yew trees at the front of the house stood completely still. Black clouds scurried across the sky, shutting out the pale crescent moon, and in the north over toward Carmouth jagged white lines of lightning rent the sky and were gone. There was a distant sound of thunder but no rain.

Peter remembered staying in this room when he and Anne had come to visit her father before their marriage. He'd lain on this bed listening to the sea, feeling the same anxiety mixed up with sexual frustration. Down the hall Sir Edward had lain snoring. Anne was in her room across the corridor, shut in with the stuffed bears and embroidery of her childhood.

"Got everything you want, young man?" had been his host's last words before they went upstairs. Said in a tone that implied he wasn't going to get anything more—like Sir Edward's daughter, for instance.

But he had. And now the old bastard was under the sod up in the Flyte churchyard and Peter was the knight of the house.

He was a knight because of what he'd done in his life. Not like his father-in-law, who had inherited his title. Peter's father had fought to defend his country and had instilled in his son a belief in duty and service. But all this counted for nothing with Sir Edward. The old man had lost no opportunity to make his feelings known. Peter wasn't the right class. He was a self-made man, a nouveau riche. Not what Sir Edward had in mind for his aristocratic daughter.

But perhaps the old man had been right to oppose the marriage, thought Peter bitterly. He and Anne had less and less in common now. Before there had been her beauty and his determination to win her against the odds, to make her choose him over her father. Peter was always most fulfilled when he was overcoming obstacles.

He had thought that he would be delivering her from a tyrannical father and a boring rural life, but as it turned out, that was the life she really wanted. She had an inner contentment entirely foreign to her husband. She was happiest growing her roses and listening to her son's stories. Far away from London and everything that mattered to Peter.

Thomas, of course, had driven his parents even further apart. He had made his father redundant, turned him into a visitor in the house, and in the last year, Peter had come to rely more and more upon his personal assistant for companionship.

The sound of the thunder came closer, answered by the crash of the waves on the shore. Outside in the corridor Peter heard footsteps. He pulled on his shirt and opened the door just in time to see a figure standing outside the master bedroom at the end of the corridor. The next moment his wife stood framed in the suddenly illuminated doorway before she reached forward and pulled Thomas inside.

His son hated thunder and lightning, and Peter had been woken many times on stormy nights to find Thomas in the bed curled up on the far side of his wife.

"He's got to learn to cope with it on his own, Annie," Peter would say. "He'll be frightened all his life if you carry on mollycoddling him like this." But his wife would not listen.

"You don't understand, Peter. You haven't got an imagination like Thomas or I have. I remember how frightened I was by the Suffolk storms when I was young. They made me think that the world was going to end."

The door of the master bedroom closed, and the corridor was plunged back into semidarkness. Peter felt a sudden stab of jealousy. His son was now lying in the bed where he should be. They made him feel like an intruder in his own home. They didn't want him and they didn't understand him. Only Greta did.

Peter remembered their first meeting. It had been at the time of the Somali crisis in late 1996, when the prime minister had sent in the SAS to rescue the British diplomats held hostage there. The mission had been a disaster. Most of the hostages were killed, and so were several of their would-be rescuers. The newspapers called it a national humiliation, and everyone blamed the prime minister. People said that the hostages would still have been alive if he hadn't been so impetuous. He should have tried harder to negotiate their release. But Peter didn't agree. He'd been to Somalia. The revolutionary government there had no concept of negotiation or compromise. There had been no alternative but to act.

In the aftermath, however, Peter had felt unable to do anything himself. He was paralyzed by the rumor and division swirling all around him. Every day the media talked openly about the prime minister as yesterday's man and speculated about his successor. Senior ministers smelled blood and jockeyed for position. The government's approval rating was the lowest in ten years.

Then one day everything had changed. Peter had agreed to be interviewed by a local newspaper about a hospital closure in his Midlands constituency, and a young reporter called Greta Grahame turned up to ask him questions. She was pretty and enthusiastic, and Peter took her out to lunch as a way of distracting himself from the political mess down in London. But the wine loosened his tongue, and he ended up telling her everything he thought and felt about the crisis. She listened while he drank the best part of two bottles of wine, and then she told him what to do. Her advice was so simple, but it hit him like a bombshell. "Speak out," she said. "Do what you think is right. Don't worry about other people or the future. If the prime minister was right, then he deserves your support."

Later in the afternoon, Greta interviewed Peter about the crisis, and by the end of the week the story had been taken up by all the networks. It was as if everyone had been waiting for someone to say what Peter had said. The political tide turned, and in the reshuffle that followed the prime minister's election victory three months later, Peter was made minister of defense. The conduct of future military rescue missions would be his responsibility.

Peter did not forget the young reporter in his moment of triumph. He gave her a job as his personal assistant, and he had never for a moment regretted his decision. She was always there for him. Not like Anne, who found politics boring and got a migraine every time she left Suffolk. Greta stayed up with him into the small hours drafting and typing his speeches. She encouraged him through the bad times, and she shared in his successes. Greta. Where would he be without her?

Peter thought of his personal assistant sleeping now on the other side of the corridor. It was extraordinary how she'd carried on coming down here even after what had happened with the dresses, particularly as Anne hadn't made it any easier for her. She came because he needed her. And Anne wouldn't even come to London for the opening of Parliament. She was too busy with her garden. With all those bloody roses.

Peter turned out the light, leaving the windows open in the vain hope of a breath of wind to circulate the fetid air in the room. Outside the thunder persisted but there was still no rain. He twisted and turned, and the wet heat made the sheet cling to his body.

Toward two o'clock he fell into an uneasy sleep. He dreamed that he was standing naked at the foot of his own bed here in the House of the Four Winds. The room was dark, but he could see by the light of the full moon, which hung outside the high open windows like a witness. In front of him a woman was lying facedown on the soft white eiderdown. She was wearing a white silk skirt with the hemline ending just below the knee. It was the same skirt that his wife had worn at dinner that evening. Above the waist the woman was naked, and she lay with her invisible face and forearms supported on a mass of white pillows. He couldn't tell if she was sleeping, and so he leaned forward and slowly traced two lines with the tips of his fingers down the back of the woman's calves, feeling the strength of the tightening muscles underneath.

As he reached her ankles, she drew herself forward, away from him, and raised her body up into a kneeling position. The skirt gathered up onto her thighs, and Peter followed her, kneeling at the end of the bed. Reaching out with both hands, he took hold of the skirt and folded it up onto the woman's waist, exposing her perfectly shaped buttocks.

And then it was as if time and movement were suspended. He knelt above the woman's body with every fiber of his being willing him forward to take hold of her. Yet nothing could happen unless she gave some indication of her consent.

It was a tiny wisp of wind that broke the moment. Some stealthy movement in the still air elicited a scarcely audible sigh from the naked figure beneath him. She pulled her knees forward and apart, raising herself up on her forearms so that Peter could see the swell of her breasts hanging down onto the white eiderdown. Everything was revealed to him, and with a cry of fulfillment he thrust himself forward and deep into the very center of the woman beneath him.

As he pulled himself back from the brink of orgasm and prepared to enter her again, Peter called out the name of this woman that he loved so much.

"Anne. Anne. I love you, Anne."

But the woman, who half turned her head toward him out of a mass of white pillows, did not have his wife's blue eyes. These eyes were green. Glittering green. How could he have mistaken that raven hair for the brown tresses of his wife? It was Greta beneath him on the bed. And someone was beating on the door trying to get in.

Peter woke with a start, sitting bolt upright in the strange bed with his body covered in sweat. It was not a knocking on the door that had woken him but the crash of the old leaded window against the casement. It had broken free of its catch and was swinging madly to and fro in the great storm that had burst over the house while he was asleep. A gray light showed that it was past dawn, although no sunlight penetrated the cloudy sky.

As Peter watched, the window crashed against the casement again and two of its leaded panes broke. The sill was awash with rain and shattered glass. Peter leapt from the bed and tugged at the window, forcing it back onto its latch but catching his elbow as he did so on a shard of broken glass. Blood dripped on his feet and on the apple-green carpet. Looking down, Peter saw that his penis was only now beginning to wilt. He stood still for a moment regarding himself with disgust tinged with a sense of ridicule before he crossed to the bed and wrapped the sweat-soaked pillowcase around his arm.

Outside, the previously statuesque yews were being blown in all directions by a screaming wind while the great rain beat against the House of the Four Winds with an unappeased fury. Beyond the yews the black gates stood open and Peter could see a small figure struggling up the drive toward the house.

Peter pulled on his clothes as fast as he could and ran down the wide curving staircase to the front door. Dropping the pillowcase tourniquet from his arm, he turned the key in the lock and opened the door. Mrs. Marsh from the cottage across the road was dimly recognizable beneath her raincoat as she struggled to make her way up the steep steps to the yew-tree terrace. Sir Peter hurried forward and pulled her into the house.

"What is it, Grace? You look white as a sheet. Has something happened?"

"No, it's all right, Sir Peter. It's just that my Christopher's a volunteer on the lifeboat and they got called out just before midnight. He usually keeps in touch with the shore by radio when the boat's out and so I can phone them to see that everything's all right, but our telephone line's gone down and so—"

"You can't. And so you need to use ours. Come into my study, and you can take your coat off."

"Thank you, Sir Peter. I'm sorry if I got you up."

"You didn't. The storm woke me. Broke the window upstairs. It seems like quite a gale."

"It is. I haven't felt the wind like this since the storm we had here ten years ago. I just hope that Christopher's all right. I don't know what I'd do—"

"It's all right, Grace, everything's going to be fine," said Sir Peter with a conviction that he did not feel as he picked up the telephone on his desk. He had heard the underlying panic in her voice.

"Damn. It's dead too. Look, Grace, I'll drive you down to the harbor. It won't take a moment."

Mrs. Marsh weakly protested, but Peter remained firm. There was nothing in fact that he wanted more at that moment than to get out of the house and put a space between himself and the events of the night.

The trouble with Anne, the debauchery of his dream, the blood on the floor.

=

"There, I've written a note telling Anne where we've gone. I'll just get my coat, Grace. I won't be a minute."

When Peter came back, he found that Grace Marsh was no longer alone. Greta had put a coat over her nightdress and was sitting beside Grace on the old black bench in the hall, the one with the four evangelists on the front. As she turned toward him with a look of concern, Peter felt himself plunged back into his dream and it was only with a supreme effort of will that he fought down a sudden, almost overwhelming urge to take her in his arms.

"What? You're up as well." Peter blurted out the first words that came into his head.

"Yes, I want to come too. Please let me." Greta's green eyes glittered.

"All right. But mind yourself on the steps. That wind'll blow you into the road if you let it. Grace, you hold on to me. I'll have you down at the harbor in less than ten minutes."

=

Peter held the steering wheel of the Range Rover almost in his lap as he craned forward onto the dashboard in order to pick out the turns in the narrow road that wound down to the harbor alongside the seawall. He was conscious of Grace Marsh straining forward just like him, as if willing herself closer to the harbor and news of her husband.

Going out on the sea now would be like signing one's own death warrant, thought Peter to himself as he glanced out to the foaming mass of furious high waves beating against the shore.

"I'm sure everything's going to be all right," he said, summoning as much conviction into his voice as he could. "Everyone on the lifeboat is very experienced." The harbor came into view through a sloping wall of rain.

"I know. Thank you, Sir Peter. It's just there's not been a storm like this one since 1989. And that was when . . ."

Grace's voice trailed away. Peter knew why. The storm of '89 had not only uprooted the great chestnut tree in the Flyte churchyard planted in honor of Queen Victoria's Golden Jubilee. It had also ended the lives of two Flyte fathers swept from the deck of the lifeboat as it went to rescue a sinking fishing boat out in the bay.

In the back of the Range Rover Greta gazed out at the sea. She felt electrified by the storm. Never had she seen such violence. She heard nothing of the anxious conversation being carried on in the front.

Peter parked beside the Harbour Inn and walked down the unmade road to the harbormaster's hut in search of news.

"They had them on the radio about half an hour ago," he told the others when he returned to the car. "They're expected back at the harbor mouth in the next ten minutes."

"But what about my Christopher?" asked Grace Marsh. "Did they say anything about him?"

Peter sensed the rising hysteria in her quavering voice and tried to inject a note of reassurance into his answer.

"Nothing one way or the other, Grace. But that's good, I think. They'd have said something on the radio if anything was wrong."

Peter did not mention the atmosphere of gloom and foreboding that he'd found in the hut. More than a dozen men in there, and no one saying anything except in brief answer to his inquiry. The radio communication that he had told Grace about had been cut off halfway through.

The minutes passed without any sign of the lifeboat, and the storm began to die away. On the opposite bank of the Flyte River the landscape took shape. Tethered boats rode high on the churning water, and beyond the harbor, fields of waving reeds and grasses rose toward Coyne Church. Several trees stood twisted at crazy angles.

Like men broken on the rack, thought Greta, standing now beside Peter and Grace Marsh at the back of a small group at the water's edge. Everyone had their eyes fastened on the mouth of the harbor where the Flyte River begins and the North Sea ends.

It was just after the bells of the two churches, Flyte and Coyne, had finished tolling the hour of seven that a boat came into view, plowing its way slowly downstream.

"Black flag!" shouted a man at the front, who had the advantage of a pair of field glasses. "There's a black flag on the mast." A shudder ran through the crowd, and Peter caught Grace Marsh as she stumbled forward in a half swoon.

Soon everyone could see not only the black flag but also the bright yellow caps and raincoats of the crew moving about on deck. They tied up at the end of a long wooden jetty and came ashore almost immediately.

It was easy to distinguish the shivering rescued strangers plucked from the murderous sea by their rescuers, men of Flyte whom Peter recognized from their other lives as bank tellers or fishmongers or churchwardens. Their faces, however, were haggard, drained by the struggle with a force so much more powerful than themselves.

Peter kept an arm around Grace Marsh and watched the silent men coming up the jetty in the hope of seeing his neighbor. A minute passed and the last man reached the bank. There seemed to be no one left on either the boat or the jetty.

"Where's my husband?" cried Grace in the voice of the about-to-be-bereaved. "Where's my Christopher?" As if in answer, Christopher Marsh and another yellow-coated man appeared out of the boat's cabin carrying a third man in their arms. A drowned man. Peter could tell from the way that they carried him, as if it were a duty rather than an act of love. Their shoulders sagged with their load and their failure.

"He was on the other side of the boat. Drowned before we could get to him, poor bastard," said Abel Johnson, bank teller turned lifesaver.

He finished his sentence with a mute cry of protest as Grace Marsh pushed him aside in her rush toward her husband.

"Christy. I thought you were dead, Christy. Oh God, I don't know what I would have done."

"It's all right, Grace," said her husband, who had had no option but to deposit his burden on the ground at the end of the jetty as his distraught wife threw her arms about him. "You mustn't take on like this. How did you get here?"

"Sir Peter brought me. In his car."

"Well, thank you, sir. It's a kindness. Grace takes it hard when we go out at night."

"Perhaps you shouldn't do it anymore, Christopher. Find someone to take your place."

"Well, I don't know, sir. It's like a duty. My father was on the lifeboat and his father before him."

As the two men talked, Greta stood looking down into the face of the drowned man. Blue jeans and a thick black sou'wester jersey. A black beard flecked with white, and thick black curly hair. A big, strong, sea-faring man, and now just a corpse. A thing to be disposed of in an appropriate way. Morgue meat.

The man's blue eyes were like glass. There was nothing behind them, and the last of the rain pattered down on his upturned face, causing him no discomfort. His hands hung limp at his sides. Five hours ago they would have been wiping the water from his eyes. From his blue, far-seeing eyes.

Life and death. Everything over in a moment as the drowning man's lungs collapsed and he floated facedown in the sea. His whole huge life was gone, and now he lay discarded on the ground while people talked about the weather and a man embraced his wife.

It was this that struck Greta most of all: the extraordinary insignificance of the fisherman's death. A man from the lifeboat was cupping his hands in a practiced gesture to light a cigarette. The landlord of the Harbour Inn was sweeping the water from his doorstep with a broom, and the dead man lay untended on the muddy ground.

Christopher Marsh gently disentangled himself from his wife's embrace, and he and the other man from the lifeboat bent to pick up the corpse. Wearily they shuffled along the uneven road toward the harbormaster's hut.

Peter turned to Greta. There was a faraway look in her green eyes as she gazed out toward the sea. He thought that she looked quite extraordinarily beautiful at that moment but also inscrutable. He had no idea what she was thinking.

=

It was the end of January 1999. It would be four months before another person died of unnatural causes in Flyte—and that would be murder. A cold-blooded murder that would be talked about in houses the length and breadth of England. A murder to put this sleepy fishing town forever on the map. Sir Peter's own wife, the beautiful Lady Anne, gunned down in her own home by armed robbers while her son hid behind a bookcase less than ten feet away.

Chapter 5

THE SOUND of the clicking cameras and the reporters' unanswered questions ceased suddenly as the doors of the Old Bailey closed behind Sir Peter and Lady Greta. Security men watched impassively as they emptied their pockets and passed through a metal detector. Then up two wide flights of stairs and into a great open area, which made Greta think for a moment that she had arrived on the concourse of one of Mussolini's North Italian railway stations.

I am on a train journey though, she thought to herself wryly. I am but Peter isn't, and I can't get off the bloody train. It goes really slowly, stopping at all the stations along the way as the witnesses give their evidence, and all the time you don't know where it's going to end. Barristers and relatives and reporters get on and get off, but at the end they all go away. And then it's just me. Just like it's always been. Just me.

"Are you all right, darling? You look pale. Is there something I can get you?"

Peter stood looking concerned but impotent at the side of his wife, who had halted, swaying slightly in the middle of the great hall.

"No, it's nothing. I was just feeling a little faint, that's all. Getting here is quite an ordeal, isn't it?"

"Yes, it's ghastly. Those reporters are just like bloody parasites. Sit down a moment and get your strength back. There's plenty of time."

They sat on one of the tan leather benches that were positioned at regular intervals through the hall. There was no adornment on any of the walls apart from a clock that had stopped. The morning light penetrated weakly through dirty net curtains hung over the high windows.

All around them barristers were moving to and fro. Their long black gowns billowed out behind them, and their patent leather shoes clicked on the marble floor. The eighteenth-century-style horsehair wigs that were part of the barristers' required dress would have seemed absurd if their owners were not wearing them with such apparent confidence. Greta was suddenly filled with a sense of being out of her element. How could she control what happened here if she didn't know the rules? She got up from the bench hurriedly. Sitting still only made things worse.

"Come on, let's go and find court nine. That's where we're supposed to be meeting Miles."

Greta injected her voice with a sense of purpose that she was far from feeling.

A small crowd was waiting outside the bank of elevators, and Greta glimpsed the squat figure of Sergeant Hearns, the officer in the case. He smiled lugubriously when he saw her, and Greta couldn't decide whether it was a greeting or a spontaneous expression of pleasure at seeing the object of his investigation inside the courthouse at last. In any event, she didn't respond, turning suddenly on her heel and calling to her husband.

"Come on, Peter, it's too crowded. Let's take the stairs."

Peter turned obediently to follow his wife. He was determined to stand by her, but there were some places, of course, where he could not follow. She would be alone in the dock. Alone when she gave her evidence. Alone when the jury came back with their verdict.

He worked his fingers into the wrinkled furrows on his forehead and hid his face momentarily behind his upturned hand.

==

Four floors above them at that very moment Miles Lambert, counsel for the defense in the case of *Regina* v. *Lady Greta Robinson,* was buying two cups of coffee in the barristers' cafeteria. One white with two sugars for himself and one black with none for his opponent, John Sparling, counsel for the prosecution.

Miles Lambert was sixty-six and single. Forty years of drinking fine wines and eating rich food with other successful lawyers had earned him a florid complexion and a rotund figure that he kept encased within expensive, tailor-made suits, complete with waistcoat and gold watch and chain. Court etiquette required him to wear a wing collar and starched white neck bands, but outside court he was known for extravagant ties of wildly clashing colors that matched the handkerchiefs that poured from his breast pocket when he was not using them to dab his sweating brow. Although in recent years "Lurid Lambert" had given way to a new nickname of "Old Lurid," opinion in legal circles was that Old Lurid might be sixty-six but as a defense lawyer he was at the height of his powers.

Miles's pale blue eyes looked out on the world from behind a pair of gold-framed half-moon spectacles, and those who knew him well said that the eyes were the key to understanding Miles's character. They were small and shrewd, and if you studied them carefully, you would see that they seemed to become more quiet and watchful as Miles became more exuberant. It was as if they took no part in his loud laughter and extravagant gestures. They remained detached and attentive, watching for weaknesses, waiting for opportunities.

John Sparling was as different from Miles Lambert as it was possible to be given that they were two successful lawyers of roughly the same age dressed in approximately the same way. He was tall while Miles was short, and thin while Miles was fat. He wore no glasses, and his large, gray eyes looked out coldly on the world from above a long, aquiline nose. His mouth was small, with thin, straight lips, and he spoke slowly, forming his questions with careful decision and always pausing after the witness had answered for the extra fraction of a second that was enough to tell the jury his opinion of what had just been said. He was fond of telling juries that they must put pity and sympathy aside in their search for the truth. Sparling's enemies said that this was something that he had no need to do himself, as he had had all pity and sympathy excised from his character at an early age.

John Sparling never defended, and Miles Lambert never prosecuted. They were polar opposites, and yet in a strange way they liked each other. You could almost say they were friends, although they never met outside the courthouse, where they spent their days in an unending struggle over the fate of their fellow human beings.

If pressed, Sparling might have described himself as an instrument of justice. It was an article of faith for him that nobody should escape the consequences of his actions—least of all the wife of a cabinet minister. Sparling had been looking forward to this case for weeks, but then so too had his opponent. For Miles Lambert, criminal law was not so much about justice as about winning. It was something the two men had in common. They both hated to lose.

"So, Miles, you've got Granger," said Sparling. "Her Ladyship must be pleased." His lower lip raised slightly, the nearest he ever got to a smile.

"Haven't talked to her about it yet," replied Miles Lambert as he vigorously stirred the sugar into his coffee. "But yes, I'd prefer old Granger to one or two of the death's head judges that sit on the first floor. Defense'll get a fair crack of the whip at any rate." He would have liked to have ladled four spoonfuls into the cup, but his doctor had set strict limits on coffee and sugar since Miles had suffered a minor heart attack two years before. The instruction to reduce stress by taking on fewer cases, however, had fallen on deaf ears.

"He'll like your client, I expect," said Sparling. "Old Granger's always been one for the ladies, hasn't he?"

His Honor Judge Granger was known as a fair judge with something of a defense bias. Miles was secretly very pleased to have gotten him, although it wouldn't do to gloat.

"It's not the judge that matters," he said diplomatically. "It's the jury."

"Hoping for a few priapic jurors too, I expect."

Miles smiled broadly, but behind his cup of coffee he was registering a slight surprise. It was unlike John Sparling to be so cynical about the legal process. Something must be bothering him. Miles needed to find out what it was.

"You're exhibiting an unhealthy preoccupation with sex, if you don't mind me saying so, John," said Miles in a bantering tone. "Not what you need on a Thursday morning."

"Don't be ridiculous, Miles. Have you got those further statements?"

Miles's smile gave way to a grin. It was the return of the killers to the murder scene the previous week that had gotten under his opponent's skin. It was too much of a good thing.

"Yes. I got them on Friday evening through the fax. The policeman at the scene, follow-up investigation by the omnipresent Sergeant Hearns. And the boy, of course. Your star witness."

"My star witness."

"Uncorroborated to the last."

"All right, Miles. We'll let the jury form their own opinion about that."

"Oh, yes. The priapic jurors."

Sparling gave another of his smile imitations. He looked determinedly tolerant.

"Yes, the priapic jurors," he said. "But it wasn't them I was asking you about."

"No," Miles acknowledged. "You want to talk about the statements, don't you, although I can't imagine why. I've got them. You've got them. You're calling these witnesses. What else is there to discuss?"

"I want to call the boy last. Hearns says he needs time to get over what happened last Wednesday."

"If it happened."

"All right, Miles. I've read the police statements too, you know."

"No trace of any intruders whatsoever. No one saw the car come. No one saw the car go."

"It happened in the evening. The place was deserted."

Sparling sounded defiant, but this only encouraged Miles to goad his opponent more.

"You've got no forensic evidence at all. Admit it, John."

"I do admit it. But the prosecution still says that Thomas Robinson is a witness of truth, and there's no reason to change that."

"Maybe not. But I reckon you could have done without his latest contribution. Lonny and Rosie. I wonder where he dreamed them up from. He's been watching too much television."

"Not when they drove up, he wasn't."

"No. Very convenient."

Miles finished his coffee and put on his wig. He'd enjoyed his precourt skirmish with John Sparling even more than usual. The wily old prosecutor would never admit to being unhappy with his case, but

Miles would have bet good money that the new statements had not been welcome arrivals in Sparling's chambers at the end of the previous week. The Crown's case depended too much on the unsupported evidence of young Thomas already. This latest development made the case positively top-heavy, thought Miles, patting his own bulk contentedly.

Certainly the defense had more to gain than to lose from the new statements. He'd seen Lady Greta in conference on Saturday morning and obtained her assurance that she knew nobody called either Lonny or Rosie and that she had not told anyone about that hiding place in the House of the Four Winds.

"I'm going to find my client," said Miles, getting up. "I'll take her instructions, but I can't see us objecting to you calling the boy last. Better make sure he turns up, though. Statements are one thing, evidence is another."

Miles was gone in a swirl of wig and gown before John Sparling could think of a suitable response.

=

Peter and Greta were waiting outside court 9 with Peter's lawyer, Patrick Sullivan, a handsome Irishman who bore more than a passing resemblance to Liam Neeson. Patrick and Peter had been at university together, and it had been a natural development for him to become Peter's lawyer when Peter had started to need one. The work had taken up more and more of Patrick's time since Peter had become a minister, and Greta's trial had made it virtually a full-time occupation.

Patrick was no criminal lawyer, but he had given Peter and Greta vital support in those nightmare days after Greta was first arrested. He had conveyed a sense that he was truly on their side, that he believed in them, and that was what Peter had craved more than anything else.

Greta, unsurprisingly, had retreated into her shell as the police began investigating Thomas's allegations against her, and Patrick seemed to restore some of her confidence. Later, after Greta was charged, Peter had asked Patrick to find a top criminal barrister to take on her case. He appeared to have succeeded admirably. Everyone that Peter spoke to agreed that Miles Lambert was one of the best in the business.

"I've reminded Peter that he can't be in court during the trial," said Patrick.

"That's right," said Miles. "Not until after you've given your evidence. But Patrick's told me he's going to be here most of the time and so Greta won't be on her own. No need to worry about that."

He smiled encouragingly. They'd been over this many times already, but it was better to be safe than sorry. He'd had witnesses before who had disbarred themselves from giving evidence by sitting in court during the trial.

"How are you feeling, Greta?" he asked solicitously. Trial for murder was a terrible experience for anyone to go through, and Miles knew that waiting for it to begin was one of the worst parts of the process.

"All right, I suppose. It's not easy, though. I felt like I was in a zoo when we got out of the car." Greta's normally even voice shook, and Peter took hold of her hand and squeezed it. Not being able to be with his wife in court and share her ordeal was almost more than he could bear.

"I know," said Miles. "I'm sorry about that. But look, the important thing to remember is that you're not going to need to say anything until the middle of next week at the earliest. It'll probably be the end of next week, in fact. The prosecution has got a lot of evidence to get through, and they're calling Thomas as their last witness. They say he needs time to get over whatever happened last Wednesday."

"Nothing happened," Peter interjected. "He's made it up just like everything else. He just can't stop. Ruining our lives and his."

"All right, Peter," said Greta. "Not now." She drew a great deal of support from Peter's anger against his son, but this was not the time for any loss of control.

"Is this a problem?" she asked. "Thomas going last?"

"No, I don't think so," replied Miles. "It'll make the jury see how little the prosecution has got without him."

"Yes. Yes, I see that."

Greta smiled, but this only made the tension in her face more visible. She looked perfect, Miles thought. She'll make the jurors who aren't priapic come over all parental when she touches her eyes with that little white handkerchief she's got in her bag.

"That was the usher," said Patrick, returning to the group and breaking the momentary silence. "We're wanted inside."

"I'll be here at lunch, Greta," said Peter. "I love you."

"I love you too," replied Greta as she turned to follow the lawyers through the swinging doors of the courtroom.

"It'll be all right," he added. "Just you see." But she did not reply. The doors had closed behind her, and he could not follow.

Chapter 6

THE FIRST THING that Greta was aware of on entering the court-room was the sound of many voices suddenly becoming still. The benches on the left of the court were thronged with the same reporters who had surrounded her outside. There was to be no escape from them, although the cameras and sound equipment were absent.

Before her arrival the court had been just another room, but now there was the beginning of drama, the certainty of action to come. Everything was lit by bright artificial light because this was a place removed from the outside world. There were no windows, and the soundproofed walls were bare except for the extravagant lion-and-unicorn emblem behind the judge's empty chair.

Miles Lambert came to a halt beside the dock. This was a dark wooden enclosure at the back of the court, which Greta had had to oc-cupy once before when she came to court in the spring to plead not guilty. Now a security woman with cropped black hair and a sallow face bent to open the low wicket gate and stood aside for Greta to enter the enclosure. The latch of the gate clicked behind her.

"Now, Patrick'll be watching to see if you need anything," said Miles in a soothing tone. "Have you got plenty of paper and pens? You can pass me a note if you think of something important, although I doubt we'll get much beyond the prosecution's opening statement this morn-ing, and you don't need to worry about that. It's not evidence."

Greta nodded and bit her lip. As if paper would help her. With all these people looking at her and strangers deciding her fate.

"We ought to get a jury fairly soon. Remember not to look at them directly. They don't like that. But let them look at you. There'll be a bad minute or two with the photographs of the body. I can't stop Sparling showing them those, but it won't last long. The judge'll see to that. Granger's all right. We could have done a lot worse."

Greta smiled wanly. She was grateful to Miles Lambert for trying to make things easier for her.

The security woman tapped Greta on the shoulder, interrupting the conversation.

"You need to surrender to custody. It's the rules."

"But haven't I just done so?"

"No, I've got to search you. Check your bag."

"Oh, all right," said Greta, offering her handbag up for inspection.

But this wasn't enough.

"It's through here," said the woman, touching Greta's arm this time as she guided her through a door in the side of the dock out into a small holding area. The once white walls were covered with obscene words and pictures drawn by rapists and murderers raging against their fate. Greta thought how strange it was that such a place should exist within a few yards of the judge, sitting in all his pomp and glory. But neither the graffiti nor the stale smell of urine emanating from a lavatory cubicle with a seatless toilet in the corner really bothered Greta. She'd seen worse.

It was the staircase in the far corner that sent a shiver down her spine. She couldn't see more than the first three steps from where she stood near the door to the court, but it was enough to know that they went down and not up. Down to the cells below, from which there would be no escape. One word, one little word from the jury, and she'd be stumbling down those stairs with guards holding her elbows. Greta felt that it was like having the chance to see the scene of one's own death before it happened. She was suddenly gripped by a wave of nausea and sat down on the bench that ran the length of the room as if she'd just been punched.

"Come on now," said the security woman with a note of irritation creeping into her voice. "You can sit on your arse in court all day. But right now I need to search you. It's the rules."

Greta held herself rigid while the woman's hands patted down her body. Shoulders, breasts, stomach, thighs; with each touch Greta felt herself being claimed by a system that was too big for her. Too impersonal. She kept her eyes fixed on the whitewashed ceiling until the search was over, never allowing her gaze to stray for a moment to the staircase in the corner.

"All right, you're fine," said the woman, holding open the door to the dock.

Back in the courtroom, Greta breathed deeply. She took out her handkerchief and held it to her nose. The fragrant Chanel perfume allowed her to imagine the cool interior of the drawing room at home. The chandeliers and the rich hangings. With an intense effort of will she forced the holding room and the descending staircase out of her consciousness. Then, opening her eyes, she ran her hands through her perfectly layered black hair and settled back into her chair as she began to take in her surroundings.

The reporters had gone back to talking amongst themselves, and in front of her the barristers were unpacking heavy files and law books onto the long tables at which they worked. To Miles's left a tall, distinguished-looking man in wig and gown was listening to the police officer, Detective Sergeant Hearns.

They made a strange pair, thought Greta. Hearns in his ill-fitting suit and kipper tie standing almost on tiptoe to whisper what he wanted to say to the barrister, who leaned slightly to his left, allowing Greta to see his profile: the long, thin face and the aquiline nose. This must be the man that Miles had told her about, John Sparling, counsel for the prosecution.

As usual Hearns was waving his crude, stubby-fingered hands about for emphasis. Greta remembered this irritating habit from the interview that she had had to undergo with him before she was charged.

"I put it to you, madam, that you're the brains behind this conspiracy," he had said then.

"The éminence grise, Mr. Hearns?" Greta had asked, resorting at last to sarcasm.

"Don't bandy foreign words with me, madam," he'd countered. He had always addressed her as madam; never Greta or Miss Grahame. Perhaps that was something they'd taught him at the training college. Interrogation techniques for aspiring detectives.

"This is a very serious allegation, madam. A lady is dead and I'm putting it to you that you're responsible."

"And I'm putting it to you that you've been reading too many detective stories."

And so it had gone on. Hour after hour in the dingy police station in Ipswich. At least she wouldn't have to hear all the interviews played back. Miles had managed to agree with the prosecution that a summary would be read to the jury at the end of their case.

Greta pulled her mind back to the present. Hearns had finished putting whatever he had to put to Sparling, and as the lawyer turned back to his papers, his eyes met Greta's for a moment. She could not read his expression. It was distant but knowing, cool but penetrative. She shivered.

A loud knocking on a closed door to the right of the judge's chair brought everyone in the court to their feet. Immediately the door opened and His Honor Judge Granger swept in, preceded by the court usher. He was an old man with only a year or two left before his retirement, and yet he carried himself ramrod straight. His threadbare wig was perched forward on his head above a pair of bushy eyebrows. His face was very lined and his cheeks were sunken, but his bright gray eyes told a different story. They seemed as if they belonged to a much younger man as they darted around the room taking in everybody and everything before he gathered his black robes about him and sat down heavily in his high-backed chair. There was a shuffling and scraping as everyone else in the courtroom including Greta followed suit, but she was only allowed to remain seated for a moment.

The clerk of the court, dressed also in wig and gown, rose to his feet. "The defendant will stand."

Greta did so.

"Are you Lady Greta Robinson?"

"I am."

Greta tried to keep her voice up, but the words that came from her lips sounded small and distant. Not how she wanted them to sound at all. She needed to remember what her elocution teacher had taught her before she came south. "Projection," it was called. She hadn't worked as hard on that part of the course, as her attention had been focused on changing her accent—losing the thick northern vowels and replacing them with the long *a*'s and *o*'s of the British ruling class.

The judge had heard her answer, at any rate. He treated her to a half smile and gestured downward with his hands.

"Sit down, Lady Robinson. Sit down." His voice was surprisingly high, and its almost feminine tone was accentuated by the courtesy with which he always spoke. Loudness and rudeness formed no part of Judge Granger's judicial vocabulary.

"Now, Mr. Sparling."

The counsel for the prosecution got slowly to his feet. "Yes, my Lord."

"What about bail?"

"There are conditions of residence and reporting, my Lord."

"Reporting, Mr. Sparling?"

"Yes. On Wednesdays and Saturdays to Chelsea Police Station."

"Well, I don't think we need persist with that now that the trial is under way. Residence should be quite sufficient."

"Very well, my Lord."

"Now, there is one other matter that I want to raise with you both at this stage, gentlemen. I've been looking at these photographs."

"Of the house, my Lord?" asked Sparling. "Or the victim?"

"Of the victim. There are five, I believe. Showing these very dreadful wounds. Now, I can't see any need for them to be shown to Lady Anne's son. The medical evidence is agreed as I understand it. Death occurred as a result of two gunshot wounds to the shoulder and the head, with the second shot being fired at close range."

"That is correct, my Lord," said Sparling. "The photographs will be given to the jury during my opening statement this morning, but the Crown will not show them to Thomas Robinson, who will by agreement be giving evidence last."

"Oh, why is that, Mr. Sparling? He should surely be your first witness."

"Ordinarily, yes, my Lord, but the Crown wishes to give him the maximum time to recover from the events of the fifth of July. Your Lordship has seen the new statements?"

"Yes, I have. Well, I suppose that does seem sensible in the circumstances. Now, Mr. Lambert, about these photographs."

"I won't show them to Thomas Robinson, my Lord," said Miles Lambert, rising from his seat and pushing the table back a few inches as he did so in order to make room for his ample stomach.

"There is one matter of admissibility on which we will need your Lordship's ruling," added Miles, "but that is perhaps better done before Detective Sergeant Hearns gives his evidence."

"Yes, Mr. Lambert, I agree. Let's press on. Miss Hooks, we're ready for the jury now."

This instruction was directed at the court usher, a diminutive lady less than five feet tall. She looked out on the world distrustfully through an enormous pair of black-framed glasses with thick lenses that seemed to cover almost half her pinched little face. Her black gown fell almost to the floor, and Greta feared for a moment that she might stumble over it as she moved as quickly as her small legs could carry her toward the door in the far corner of the courtroom behind which the jurors were waiting.

=

The strangest thing about the jury was their lack of strangeness, Greta reflected, as each of the twelve stood in turn to swear or affirm that he or she "will faithfully try the defendant and give a true verdict according to the evidence."

Here were her judges. A motley assortment of men and women plucked at random from the capital's population. An Indian man with a turban and another without. An Italian in an expensive suit, who she caught out of the corner of her eye giving her an admiring glance. Two middle-aged ladies with big hair and large busts on either side of a young man in a crumpled T-shirt with a picture of Kurt Cobain on the front. An Asian girl with a tiny voice, who had to be made to take the oath twice because nobody could hear her the first time round. Four other men of nondescript appearance, who would hopefully have Greta's pretty face well in mind when it came to reaching their verdict; and finally a woman in her forties, who looked exactly like Margaret Thatcher might have looked at that age if she'd had short black hair and worn a trouser suit. She took the oath in a determined voice that made everyone in the courtroom sit up while she held the Bible above her right ear, in the manner of a president on inauguration day.

The names of the other jurors had flown past unnoticed, but Greta caught this one as it was read out by the clerk: Dorothy Jones. Greta thought that there was nothing Dorothy-like about her at all as she extracted a black pen from her clutch handbag and tapped it menacingly on the table in front of her.

In the well of the court John Sparling allowed a half smile to momentarily crease his thin lips. Here was a juror who wouldn't have trouble obeying his instruction to put all pity and sympathy aside in her search for the truth. She'd be like a hound on the trail of a wounded fox when it came to that task.

To Sparling's left, Miles Lambert moved his bulk uneasily about on his chair as the Indian man without the turban stood up to take the oath. He didn't like the look of the woman in the trouser suit. The rest seemed all right, and he'd gotten what he wanted with eight men to four women, but the Margaret Thatcher look-alike would no doubt try to take over and get herself elected as forewoman before the day was out.

Miles knew the type, and he thought nostalgically of the good old days when the defense had the right to get rid of up to three jurors for no reason at all. Now there was nothing one could really do unless the jurors knew the defendant or one of the witnesses. It was one area in which Miles felt that the American system was decidedly better. He'd have liked nothing better than to cross-examine this Jones woman about her beliefs and prejudices, but still it wasn't to be, and she was only one of twelve. Perhaps the men would rebel and elect the youth with the grungy T-shirt to chair their deliberations.

"All sworn, my Lord," said the usher in the shrill voice of those who go through life suffering from an incurable doubt that people won't hear what they are about to say.

The jury settled themselves in their chairs and looked up expectantly at the judge, but it was the clerk of the court who claimed their attention. He rose to his feet holding up a piece of paper.

"The defendant will stand."

It was the second time the clerk had said these words. The third time would be for the jury's verdict.

Greta stood, holding herself steady with her hands resting on the brass rail of the dock.

"Members of the jury, the defendant stands charged on indictment 211 of the year 2000 with one count. That between a date unknown and the thirty-first day of May 1999 she did conspire with persons unknown to murder Lady Anne Robinson. To this charge she has pleaded not guilty, and it is your task having heard the evidence to say whether she is guilty or not."

Guilty or not. Guilty or not. Guilty or not. Greta held hard to the rail as the courtroom suddenly swirled in front of her and the words echoed in her mind. Her trial had begun.

Chapter 7

J UDGE GRANGER allowed his eyes to travel down the two rows of jurors as they shifted in their seats, still trying to adjust themselves to
the formality of the courtroom and the stress of taking the oath.

Lord knows what petty prejudices they brought into court with
them, thought the old judge. What colored spectacles they used to
view the evidence. He was glad he wasn't able to hear the discussions
that they would have shut up in their jury room, as it would only have
made him want to interfere. And he had learned over the years that the
best way to a fair trial was to interfere as little as possible. Juries weren't
infallible, but they were better than lawyers or civil servants, and they
must be allowed to reach their own verdicts.

The judge turned his head toward the counsel for the prosecution
and nodded imperceptibly.

John Sparling got slowly to his feet and gathered his gown about
him.

"Good morning, members of the jury. Let me begin by introducing
myself to you. I am John Sparling, and I am appearing for the prosecution in this case, and on my right is Miles Lambert, who is representing
the defendant. She is sitting in the dock."

Sparling paused after the word *dock,* on which he had laid a heavy
emphasis, as if he wished to imply that that was where the defendant
should be.

"Members of the jury, I am now going to open this case to you, and that has nothing to do with keys and doors." Sparling laughed gently, eliciting the same response from several of the jurors. He knew the importance of making contact with the jury, and he never made the mistake of talking down to them, treating them instead with an unwavering courtesy. "No, the opening is designed to help you."

Miles Lambert grimaced. Sparling always used this trick of portraying himself as the jury's assistant helping them to reach the only possible verdict: guilty as charged.

"To help you to understand the evidence by giving you a framework within which to place it. This is particularly necessary because the Crown's most important witness will be giving evidence last."

Sparling did not say why. He did not tell the jury that Thomas Robinson was too traumatized to come to court to give evidence today. Instead he made it seem as if this were the Crown's decision. To save the best for last.

"And so, members of the jury, let me tell you what this case is about. It is about an old house and the people who lived there. The House of the Four Winds was built in the sixteenth century and is famous for its rose gardens and an ornamental staircase that curves up from the front hall to the first floor above. The staircase is important, and I shall come back to it later.

"The house is on the outskirts of a fishing town called Flyte on the coast of Suffolk. The Sackville family have lived there for generations. Lady Anne Sackville was born in the house, and her mother had no other children. At about nine-thirty on the evening of the thirty-first of May last year she was murdered in the house by two men, who have not to this day been identified. The hunt to apprehend them continues.

"Lady Anne married Peter Robinson. You may have heard of him, members of the jury. He is now Sir Peter Robinson, and he is the minister for defense in the present government. They had one son, Thomas, who is now aged sixteen. You will be hearing from him next week.

"Sir Peter had a personal assistant, who is the defendant. She has now become his second wife, and the Crown says that that is part of what she hoped to achieve when she entered into a conspiracy to murder Lady Anne Robinson.

"It is clear that Sir Peter came to depend heavily on the defendant's assistance, and he would take her with him on his weekend visits to the House of the Four Winds. I will leave it to the witnesses to describe to you how the relationships between the family members and the defendant developed in the ensuing two years, but it is right to say that by the spring of 1999 the defendant and Lady Anne were certainly not friends.

"I come now to the day of the murder. The thirty-first of May 1999. The housekeeper, Mrs. Martin, left at five o'clock, as she was going to stay with her sister in Woodbridge. This was something that she almost always did on a Monday evening, but on this occasion she was accompanied in her car by Thomas. Mrs. Martin was giving him a lift to a friend's house in Flyte, where he was due to spend the night. You will hear evidence from the mother of this friend that it was the defendant who made this arrangement. This had never happened before, members of the jury, and the Crown says that it is highly significant. It shows that the defendant wished Lady Anne to be alone in the house later in the evening.

"Before she left, Mrs. Martin checked that the windows and doors in the house were secure, and she also checked that the east and west gates and the door in the north wall were locked. This was her custom, and she did not deviate from it on the afternoon of the thirty-first of May."

Sparling paused and drank some water. He appeared to hesitate and then picked up some documents from the table in front of him as if coming to a decision.

"I have spoken of doors and gates, and before I go any further I need to explain the layout of the house and its grounds. There are photographs and a plan."

Again Sparling paused while the diminutive usher with the long gown distributed copies to the jury. His opening was going well. Sparling could see that. The eyes of all the jurors were fixed upon him. He had their undivided attention.

"You will see the points of the compass in the corner of the plan, members of the jury. To the east of the house is the sea and to the west the main road connecting the coastal towns of Flyte and Carmouth. To the south are the grounds of another property, and to the north is a small, unpaved stretch of road that runs from the main road down to the beach alongside the north wall of the property, and it was here that the two killers parked their car at about half past nine that evening.

There were tire marks found in this lane, which are consistent with a car turning at speed.

"They parked their car and then entered the grounds through the door in the north wall, which was unlocked. The police found footprints on both sides of the door, but there were no signs that the door had been forced or that the lock had been picked. It was unlocked at half past nine, but at five o'clock Mrs. Martin had left it locked. The Crown says that it was unlocked by the defendant before she left the house at half past seven with Sir Peter Robinson in order to drive down to London, where Sir Peter was to attend a government meeting early the next day.

"Turn now to your album of photographs, members of the jury. You can see the lane and the door in the first two photographs, and then there are pictures of the outside of the house. Notice the wide lawn that the killers had to cross to get to the house from the north wall."

\=

Greta sat in the dock listening to Sparling even though she would have preferred not to. She could see how the jurors were hanging on the loathsome lawyer's every word as he slowly set the scene and painted in his characters. All of them had names, of course, except her. She was the defendant.

And now there were photographs to look at. They were supposed to help the jury imagine what the place was really like, except that the small police photographs could convey nothing of its reality, thought Greta. The reality of the murder, perhaps, but not the haunted beauty of the House of the Four Winds. The leaded windows set in the old stone weathered by thousands of North Sea storms. The symmetry of the six ancient yew trees standing guard over the front approach and the wide lawns shimmering under the elm trees. All of it encircled by the high stone wall covered by generations of lichens and mosses.

Greta pictured to herself the two wooden doors in the wall, each bearing an inscription in faded early-nineteenth-century gold lettering. Beyond Lady Anne's rose gardens to the right of the house was "the South Wind," and that opening onto the lane was "the North Wind." Greta did not know if there had once been west- and east-wind doors set in the walls at the front and the back of the house, but if so, they were now long gone, replaced by black wrought-iron gates of intricate design.

Greta had never seen the south door open. Over the years it had become half obscured by a rampant rambling rose, which flowered brilliant white in the summer. However, the north door was in constant use, as it was the most frequently taken route from the house to the beach. It was opened with a huge key that hung from a nail in the back hall, and Greta well remembered the part played by the old key in the games that a younger Thomas used to play when she first visited the house with Peter more than three years before. It was the key of the castle, and seeing it as she came down the back stairs from her bedroom in the mornings, Greta had caught herself wondering more than once what it would be like to be the mistress of the House of the Four Winds.

=

"The two killers crossed the lawn and came to a halt in front of the study windows." Sparling had finished showing the jury the exterior photographs and had now resumed his account of the night of the murder.

" 'Fuck,' said one of them. 'They're all fucking closed.' "

"He said this because he expected at least one of the windows to be open. You will recall that Mrs. Martin checked the windows before she left at five o'clock and they were secure, but when Thomas came home unexpectedly at eight-thirty he discovered that the window facing onto the north lawn was open. He closed it before he went up to his bedroom. The Crown says that it was the defendant who left that window open.

"Thomas Robinson came home because he had found that it was the defendant who had arranged for him to spend the night at the house of his friend in Flyte and he had been unable to get his mother to answer the telephone. On his return he found her asleep, and there is agreed medical evidence that Lady Anne took a sleeping tablet that evening. Her son did not wake her but went himself to his bedroom at the end of the corridor overlooking the north lawn.

"He had turned out his light but was not asleep when he heard a car drive up and park in the lane. Going to his window, he saw two figures crossing the lawn and then come to a halt in front of the study window below where Thomas was standing. It was then that Thomas heard one of the men say those important words: 'Fuck. They're all fucking closed.'

"Foul language, members of the jury. Foul language and foul play.

"Within seconds the men began to smash out the glass in one of the study windowpanes. It is possible that the butt of a handgun was used for this purpose. One of them then leaned in and opened the window latch. Either at this point or as they climbed into the study, one of the men cut himself slightly on the broken glass, and the small amount of blood that was left on the windowsill was sufficient to yield a DNA profile. Unfortunately, however, no match for the profile has been found on the police national DNA database.

"Once inside the two men made their way through the study into the main entrance hall. You can see the layout of the ground floor on the plan, members of the jury. By this time Thomas had gone to his mother's room and shaken her awake. It was his idea to go to the hiding place that is situated at the top of the front stairs, and he pulled his mother along after him. She was wearing a long white nightdress and no slippers.

"This hiding place is almost as old as the house, members of the jury, and you can see it in your photographs. It was made for Catholic priests to hide in when the Protestant government was searching for them in the sixteenth century, and it is clever but simple as the best of these priests' holes are. There is a wide bookcase at the top of the stairs, which turns on its axis when a certain set of books is pressed. Behind them is a lever, which operates the mechanism.

"Thomas and his mother could hear the breaking of glass and the men moving down below. They got to the bookcase just as the men arrived in the hall. The men heard the movement at the top of the stairs when Thomas opened the bookcase, and they shone their flashlights up the staircase. He heard one of them shout: 'There she is. She's up there. Look, she's up there.' And then he felt the bookcase close so that he was shut in the hiding place alone. His mother had shut him in to save him. She knew that they had seen her, but her son was already inside and she hoped that they would not see the bookcase close. She was right. She did save her son, but she could not save herself.

"They shot her twice. The first bullet was fired upward from the bottom of the stairs and hit her in the shoulder as she stood in front of the bookcase. She fell down screaming, and then one of the two men came up the stairs and shot her again. Shot her in the head and killed her while her son was no more than ten feet away. Less than the distance that I am from you now, members of the jury."

Sparling stopped. He had achieved his purpose. He could see anger in the eyes of the jurors. Surprise and horror but above all anger. Now was the time to show them the final set of photographs.

"Here is the murdered woman lying on the carpet with the bookcase behind her. Thomas would have been invisible behind that. And here is the staircase curving up from the hall below. One shot fired from there and then another from point-blank range at the top of the stairs. You can see the wounds. These men came to kill. This was no robbery gone wrong. They came to kill *and* to rob. And who sent them, members of the jury? Who sent them? That's the question."

Sparling stopped, allowing his gaze to move slowly from one juror to the next. The answer, he seemed to be saying, is to your left. Sitting in the dock with her head bowed because she doesn't want to look you in the eye.

The judge looked up and cleared his throat. Sparling was going beyond the boundaries of an opening address. It was time to move on.

"Yes, Mr. Sparling," he said, allowing a note of irritation to creep into his voice.

"Yes, my Lord. I'm sorry," said the counsel for the prosecution as he closed the album of photographs with visible reluctance.

The moment was past, but it had been just as unpleasant as Miles Lambert had warned Greta it might be. The photographs were bad. She knew that. They made people angry, seeing all that beauty destroyed by lead bullets. The home invaded. The boy hiding in the dark only a few feet from his mother. There were sacred principles here that had been transgressed, and someone would have to pay. That was the problem. Miles had told her that. The need to make someone responsible. Otherwise the photographs were unbearable.

"They left her lying there, members of the jury, and went into her bedroom and ransacked it. They took their time because they believed there was no one else in the house. They broke into the small safe concealed behind the portrait of Lady Anne's grandmother and took the jewelry that Lady Anne kept there. Necklaces, rings and bracelets of enormous value. Heirlooms that had been handed down through generations of Lady Anne's family, the Sackvilles, going back as far as when the House of the Four Winds was built more than four hundred years ago.

"Then they left, stepping over the body of Lady Anne to go down the staircase. There is a spy hole in the wall of the hiding place, and Thomas was able to see the faces of the two men in profile as they went past. One of them had a ponytail and a scar behind his right jawbone. Thomas had seen a man with a ponytail and a similar scar with the defendant in London six weeks before, and he believes that the two men are one and the same, although he only saw the man in London for a short time and from behind. It will be for you to weigh up the strength of that evidence when you hear from Thomas Robinson, members of the jury.

"However, two other matters are significant with regard to the man with the scar. First, neither he nor his companion were wearing masks. They wore gloves but no masks, and the Crown says that this is because they did not care whether Lady Anne saw them or not. Their intention was to kill her, and the dead can tell no tales. They cannot give evidence or attend identification parades.

"Second, Thomas saw the man with the scar bend down out of sight for a moment as he crossed from the bedroom to the stairs. Thomas could not see the body of his mother, but he knew where she had fallen, and when the man got up Thomas could see him putting something in his pocket. He could see the glint of gold, members of the jury.

That glint of gold is vitally important. The Crown says that it was a locket that the man with the scar had torn from the dead woman's neck, leaving a scratch mark there as he did so. That locket subsequently found its way into the possession of the defendant, members of the jury. Into her desk in her husband's house in London."

The jury turned to look at Greta, and she involuntarily bit her lip. That bloody locket, she thought to herself. To be having to sit here exhibited like an animal in a zoo because of a trinket. She turned away, resolved to shut her ears to the rest of Sparling's speech. That was what Miles had half-jokingly suggested she should do when they had talked about the case in his chambers on Saturday.

"It's not evidence, Greta. It's the evidence we need to worry about. Leave old Sparling to me."

She should have taken his advice.

"The prosecution has the first word, my dear, but we have the last. Remember that. We have the last."

Greta smiled. She had a lot of faith in Miles.

Chapter 8

ONE HUNDRED and twenty miles to the east of the Old Bailey the boy who was figuring so prominently in John Sparling's opening address was standing at his bedroom window in the House of the Four Winds looking out over the broad expanse of the north lawn. It was a bright summer's day, and the sun shone down through the branches of the elm trees, creating a fantastic play of shadows on the newly mowed grass.

One hundred yards from where Thomas was standing, the north gate of the property stood closed and locked. Thomas shivered as he looked at it even though his room was warm, even hot. As had happened so often in the last few months, Thomas could not stop his mind from going back to the previous summer, to the night of his mother's murder.

In his imagination, Thomas saw the man with the scar and his sidekick pulling up in the lane in the dark. The sidekick would have been driving, Thomas thought, with the other giving directions in his soft, cruel voice. Pushing through the unlocked door in the wall, Thomas imagined that they must have hesitated for a moment while the man fingered the scar running down behind his jaw and let his eyes run over the house, visible in the pale moonlight. Thomas thought of him in that moment as if he were a cat enjoying the defenselessness of what he was about to destroy before he set off across the lawn with the gun hard and metallic in his pocket. He knew where he was going, and nothing would deflect him from his purpose.

Just as it had done a thousand times before, Thomas's mind flew to his mother, sleeping so peacefully in her bed with the moonlight shining down through the half-drawn curtains. Sleeping in the same room where her parents had slept. Where her father had died looking up at the portrait of his wife on the wall. Where Thomas had often slept himself, driven by the Suffolk storms to find comfort beside his mother in the small hours. Life and love and death going on through the generations of the Sackvilles, until Greta came.

Hardly anyone had been in the room since Lady Anne's death. Sir Peter never came, and it was only Jane Martin who went in there once a week to dust, and she didn't stay long. She had not yet been able to face the task of disposing of Lady Anne's clothes. The dresses still hung in the closets just as they had before their owner's death, as if nothing had happened.

Thomas kept his distance. He had been determined from the outset to remain in the House of the Four Winds. He was his mother's heir. To leave would have meant defeat, and he honored her by remaining, but at a cost. Everywhere he went reminded him of her. He tried to help himself by avoiding the front stairs and his mother's bedroom, but he often found himself standing outside his own bedroom as he was now, gazing down the corridor to the closed door at the end, remembering his failure.

Over and over again he'd replayed it in his mind. He'd had to shake her so hard to get her to wake up, and there'd been no time. He could hear the men downstairs. Perhaps if he'd been quicker or made her go in front, then she'd have gotten inside the hiding place and the man with the scar would never have seen her, never have shot her, never have taken her away. Put her in a black, wet hole in the Flyte churchyard.

Suddenly Thomas felt violently sick. His legs went weak and he was barely able to make it into the bathroom before he threw up, kneeling on the tiles with his arms hugging the cold porcelain of the toilet bowl. He retched again and again until he had nothing left.

Back in his bedroom Thomas tried to think of something good. The trouble was that the past was his mother and her death had destroyed it all. Made it unbearable. He looked out the window again and tried to reclaim the north lawn for his own. It was across the lawn to the north gate that he would go with Barton at his side almost every morning of the holidays for as long as he could remember. Walking barefoot with the Labrador padding after him, making a path through the glistening dew on their way to the beach. There Thomas would break off a piece of driftwood and throw it high and far and the dog would rush headlong across the sand and into the sea, grasping it miraculously from the clutch of the waves before bringing back the prize to his master.

At night there was a ritual. The word *bedtime,* said by Lady Anne even in the softest voice, would transform Barton into a wolf. He would growl menacingly and push Thomas up the back stairs toward his room. Protests were useless. The growls would redouble in volume and even turn into snarls until Thomas reached his door, whereupon the dog would spring onto the bed and curl up in contentment.

Thomas loved the Labrador passionately, and Barton loved him. The two were almost inseparable. When Thomas wrote stories about being marooned on a desert island, he never imagined himself alone. Barton was there to keep him company, protecting him from the wild animals that tried to attack their camp after the sun went down. If Thomas was a knight of the Round Table dressed in the helmet and breastplate that Jane Martin had given him for his tenth birthday, then Barton would be his black charger dressed up for the tournament in one of Lady Anne's most beautiful silk handkerchiefs.

Time passed and Barton grew older. He could no longer always catch the sticks that Thomas threw out into the waves. The dog would stand at the water's edge looking puzzled as the tide took his prize away, and the sleek black tail that had always crashed from side to side with the joy of being alive now hung still. Thomas put his arm around Barton's warm neck and went to tell his mother.

The vet in Flyte listened to Barton's heart and shook his head a fraction.

"There's a murmur. Give him these tablets and don't let him strain himself. He's an old boy now, Thomas. Nearly ninety in our years."

Nearly ninety? Barton wasn't ninety. He was three years younger than Thomas. "But dogs don't live that long, darling," said Lady Anne in the car on the way home. "We must enjoy them while we can."

Two months later Barton could not get up the stairs. Thomas picked up the old dog and carried him up to his room. He slept on the bed all night, but toward dawn he began to whimper and Thomas fetched his mother.

In the morning Barton was no better, and they called the vet.

"It's not fair to Barton to make him carry on," said Lady Anne to her son. "He's hurting inside, Tom. You can see that."

"But I don't want him to die," cried Thomas with his pajama-clad arm wrapped around the old dog's neck.

Barton looked up at his master and tried to get to his feet, but the effort was too much and he laid his head down on the floor again.

"He's trusting us. Trusting us to help him. You have to understand that, Tom." And Thomas did. Love worked both ways.

He kissed the dog and held his paw while the vet prepared the injection. And then it was all over in an instant. It was something that Thomas never forgot: the thinness of the line between life and death.

He and his mother buried Barton in the garden under the old elm tree that stood by the north gate so that Thomas could see the grave from his bedroom window. They held hands and said a prayer thanking God for Barton's life, and the next day Thomas made a wooden cross with Barton's name and dates and dug it deep into the soil.

=

Lady Anne had thought of buying a puppy before Barton died so that Thomas would have another dog already there when Barton was gone. However, she ended up not doing so. It wouldn't have been fair to the old dog to see a puppy rushing about as he lost his strength and couldn't compete for Thomas's attention.

Lady Anne took care also to allow her son enough time to properly mourn his friend. Thomas and she would pick the wildflowers that grew on the edges of the marsh and bring them back to lay on Barton's grave, but Lady Anne soon came to realize that these walks were only making things worse. Thomas would forget what had happened and look up expecting to see Barton bounding toward him across the dunes, only to realize that the Labrador was gone for good and nothing would bring him back.

After two weeks Lady Anne decided that it was time to act. Breakfast was over, and Thomas was sitting on the front step watching the early sun make patterns on the hall carpet as it shone down through the yew trees. A paperback copy of *Robinson Crusoe* lay face up beside him, but in truth he hadn't read anything since Barton's death. The sea was quiet, and as Thomas looked down over the lawn to the front gate and the houses beyond the road, he felt an enormous desolation settling over the world. There seemed to be nowhere to go and nothing to do.

The voice of his mother calling to him from the top of the stairs startled him out of his lethargy.

"Come on, Tom, we need to get packed."

"Packed. Why?"

"Because we're going to London. This afternoon. Everything's arranged."

"London. Why are we going to London?"

"For a holiday, Tom. For a change of scenery. To put some color in your cheeks so you stop walking around looking like the Carmouth Ghost."

"I don't look like the Carmouth Ghost. She was a woman who killed her husband with a steak knife, and I'm a—"

"You're a fourteen-year-old who's been having a terrible time and doesn't know what to do with himself."

"But Mum, you hate London. You know you do. That's what you always say to Dad when he wants you to go up there for one of his political things."

"I'm not going up there for them. I'm going to London to spend time with you."

"And Dad?"

"Yes, of course. He's promised to take time out to be with us. He knows you're having a bad time at the moment. That's why he wrote you that letter."

"Not exactly a letter. Five lines. 'I was sorry to hear about Barton. Here's ten pounds. Buy yourself something at the shop.' "

"He's very busy, darling. He meant well."

"No, he didn't. If he cared, he'd have come down here last weekend."

"He couldn't. There was a conference he had to go to. You know that."

"I know that he doesn't care about me. Or you. That's what I know."

"That's not true, Thomas."

"It is true. Spending all his time with Greta. Green-eyed Greta."

"She's his personal assistant, Tom. And the fact that she's got green eyes has got nothing to do with it. She's very good at her job, and we must try to like her for your father's sake."

"Everything is for his sake. Nothing is for ours," said Thomas, becoming visibly angry. He kicked his book to one side and went and stood at the top of the steps leading down to the drive.

Behind him he felt his mother approaching, but he did not turn his head even when she came to stand beside him. He fought to hold back the tears that were starting in his eyes and bunched his hands into hard fists.

Lady Anne worried for her son as she stood beside him between the yews. He was so rigid and unbending as he fought to control emotions of anger and grief that threatened to overwhelm him. She thought of the old beech tree by the south gate, broken by the great storm in January when the fisherman had drowned in the bay. It had been too rigid, unlike the yews that swayed in the wind.

Peter had been here that night. With Greta. Driving Gracie Marsh down to the harbor. Lady Anne didn't like Greta. She had formed that opinion long before her son had found the woman trying on her clothes. She had seen Greta watching everyone, insinuating herself into their lives, but Anne had held her peace because Greta had done nothing wrong and it was clear that Peter needed her so much for his work.

Anne could tell that Greta had changed her accent, and she felt that the girl was watching her in order to imitate her. It sometimes almost seemed as if Greta was trying to become her.

"She's not one of us," she had once caught herself saying to her husband in an unguarded moment, but she had accepted his retaliatory accusation of snobbery as just. Forgiveness was part of the code of manners by which Lady Anne lived her life, and she had forced herself to accept Peter's explanation for why Greta had tried on the dresses. She had money and Greta didn't, and if she'd been nicer to her, then perhaps Greta would have felt able to ask to borrow a dress or two.

Thomas, of course, didn't see it that way. It was ironic, given all the efforts that Greta had made to get on with him. All those books she'd read about Suffolk. Lady Anne didn't know how she'd found time. It was as if something more had happened in her bedroom when Thomas found Greta trying on her clothes, but there was no point in asking her son. He'd found it difficult enough to tell her about the dresses.

"Let's not talk about Greta or your father, Tom. I know things aren't easy at the moment with what's happened with Barton, but you shouldn't try to make them worse. You're not the only one who misses Barton. Jane loved him and so did I. What we both need is a change of scenery. London'll be good for us."

There was a note of appeal in his mother's voice that Thomas could not resist. He loved his mother and could not bear to make her anxious or distressed. That would lead to one of the terrible migraines that hurt her so badly. The long afternoons when his mother lay on her bed with her face covered by a flannel sighing with the pain were the worst days of his childhood. Afterward she would be weak for days, sitting in the rocking chair by the kitchen door in her dressing gown, drinking the cups of peppermint tea that Aunt Jane made for her in a special teapot.

"Yes, Mum. I'm being silly. I'd love to go with you. I'll go and get packed."

"Jane's washed your shirts. They're in the laundry room. And you'll need to take your blazer for the theater."

"The theater? What are we going to see?"

"*Macbeth*. At the Globe. I've got tickets for Thursday night. Just you and me."

"*Macbeth!* Oh, Mummy, I love you! It's the one I've always wanted to see." Thomas ran up the stairs, taking them two at a time, and hurried to his room to get ready.

Lady Anne smiled. What a strange boy he was! It was the first time in two weeks that she'd heard real happiness in his voice, and what was it that had caused this change? A tale of ghosts and bloody murder, treachery and treason.

==

They drove with the top of the Aston Martin down. It was a beautiful car that Lady Anne had had since she was in her twenties. The garage in Flyte that had looked after her father's Rolls-Royce had done the same for the bright red sports car that he had given her for her twenty-first birthday. Driving it made her feel young again. The world that flew by in a blur of fields and haystacks seemed full of possibility. She was a fool to have shut herself and Thomas up in the house for so long.

Thomas also felt exhilarated. He loved to watch his mother drive. Her beautiful hands laced themselves around the spokes of the steering wheel, which was small like in a racing car, as she sat back in her tan leather seat and allowed the wind to blow her brown hair over her shoulders. She was wearing a white summer dress with an open neck, and Thomas could see her favorite gold locket glinting in the sun where it lay heart-shaped on her breastbone. His father had given it to his mother on their wedding day, with a picture of them both shut inside.

On her finger Lady Anne wore a blue, square-cut sapphire ring. The stone had been brought back from India by Thomas's great-grandfather just before the First World War. There was a family rumor passed down through the generations that old Sir Stephen Sackville had stolen it from its native owner, who had then cursed him and his descendants, but no one believed the story. The jewel seemed so pure and magical, and the portrait of Sir Stephen hanging in the drawing room at the House of the Four Winds was of a kindly old man, saddened by the early death of his daughter, Lady Anne's mother, in a riding accident. She had only been forty when she died, the same age that Thomas's mother was now, and Thomas had often come into his mother's bedroom to find her sitting at her dressing table gazing up at the portrait of her mother hanging on the wall above the fireplace.

"I'm wearing the ring for you," said Lady Anne, sensing her son's attention to the sapphire. "I know it's your favorite."

"Grandmother's wearing it in the portrait, isn't she?" asked Thomas, who loved family history. "I was looking at it yesterday."

"Yes, she always wore it. Her father gave it to her when she was twenty-one. There's that old story I told you about it. About where it came from in India. I've got a letter about it somewhere. I'll have to dig it out. The sapphire's so very beautiful. Wearing it makes me feel close to her. It's silly, I know."

"No, it's not."

"You're right. It's not." Lady Anne smiled at the certainty in her son's voice.

"I do so wonder what she was like, Tom," she went on after a pause. "My father used to say that she was a daredevil. Always getting into scrapes and running up huge debts that old Sir Stephen had to pay off. But everyone forgave her because she was so pretty and full of life. Then suddenly she was dead. Killed by a horse, of all things."

"How old were you, Mum?"

"When it happened? Five. I'd just turned five."

"It must've been awful. Really awful." Thomas suddenly wished that he'd not brought up the subject of his grandmother.

"I don't know, to be honest," said Lady Anne. "I mean, yes, it must have completely traumatized me, which is why I can't remember anything about it except one image, which may have nothing to do with her death except that I feel sure it does. It's seeing my father sitting on the front stairs. I can't remember if he was crying or not, but I know that he never sat anywhere except on a chair and there he was sitting on the stairs."

"The front stairs?"

"Yes. And for many years I couldn't remember anything about my mother at all. I would look at the old photograph albums, but they didn't mean anything, and curiously it was that painting that you like that gave me the strongest sense of her. It used to hang in the hall, and I'd gaze at it for hours until one day a memory came back to me.

"I was in a park on a swing. It must've been like a children's playground, and I've never been able to work out where it is, although I can see a grove of big green Christmas trees nearby. Anyway, there's someone pushing the swing, and I go up, up, up in the air so high that my little patent leather black shoes are right above my head."

"But where's your mother?" asked Thomas.

"She's pushing the swing. I can't see her but I know she is. And that's why I'm so happy. Going so high but feeling so safe because she's pushing me. That's my memory of her."

Lady Anne stopped talking and wiped a tear from her eye. Unlike many boys his age, Thomas was not repelled by emotion. He had the quality of empathy, and so he leaned across the hand brake and kissed his mother on her wet cheek.

"Thank you, Tom. You're a good boy."

This did upset Thomas, who didn't feel he was a boy at all. He moved uncomfortably in his seat, but Lady Anne didn't seem to notice. She was still thinking of her mother.

"So anyway, after my father died and I moved into the big room with Peter, I took the portrait up there with me and hung it over the fireplace."

"Was the safe already there?" asked Thomas irrelevantly.

"No, that was your father's idea. He wanted me to put all the jewelry in a bank vault because it was much too valuable to be left lying around. You know what he's like. Practical, unlike me."

"Yes." Thomas responded with feeling. Practicality had always been his father's code word for what he felt was missing in his son.

"But I wouldn't have it. What's the point in having beautiful things if they're shut away where no one can ever see them? And so we compromised. Your father installed his big, ugly safe, and I hung your grandmother's portrait over it."

"Looking after her jewels," said Thomas.

"Yes, in a way; but for me the important thing about having it over the fireplace is that I can see it in the morning when I wake up. The picture makes me feel close to her."

"She looks funny in it, I think," said Thomas, searching for the right words. "Not funny peculiar but two-things-at-once funny. Like she doesn't care about anything except that she really loves people too."

"Yes, you're right. She seems so free. Unlike me. That's the result of losing your mother when you're young, I guess."

Lady Anne caught the look of anxiety creasing her son's brow as she parked the Aston Martin in front of the house in Chelsea.

"I'm sorry, Thomas. I don't know what I'm thinking of. I bring you to London to cheer you up and spend half the journey talking about my mother. It's awful of me."

"No, it's not. I just hate it when people die young. That's all."

"Well, you don't need to worry about me. I'm as fit as a fiddle."

Lady Anne smiled at her son and rummaged in her bag for the key to the house. As she did so, the sun came out from behind a nearby tall building and shone down suddenly on her sapphire ring. The jewel glowed midnight blue and Thomas shivered in the sun.

Chapter 9

━━━━━━━━━━━━━━━━

I T HAD BEEN a long time since Thomas had stayed in the house off
the King's Road, and he enjoyed running up and down the staircases
and opening the doors to the various rooms.

Greta had an apartment in the basement, while the ground floor had
been converted to a suite of offices where Sir Peter conducted his government business and held important meetings. All the rooms were
empty now, however, because both Peter and Greta were away from
home on the weekly visit to Peter's constituency in the Midlands. They
were expected back the following evening, so Thomas had the place to
himself for more than twenty-four hours.

The house was tall and narrow, with a small walled garden at the rear.
Sir Peter had bought it twelve years before when he was first elected to
Parliament, and it had always been very much his house, in contrast to
the House of the Four Winds, which bore the stamp of Lady Anne and
her Sackville ancestors.

The rooms were expensively but sparsely furnished, and they contained almost nothing personal. The only two photographs in the house
were a studio portrait of Lady Anne and one of Thomas, both displayed
in heavy frames on a bookcase in the living room. The books were all
biographies of statesmen and treatises on economics and foreign policy.
Thomas looked without success for a novel on the shelves.

Everything was clean and tidy. Decorative objects stood at exact right angles to their neighbors, and the cushions on the armchairs and sofa were plumped up as if nobody had ever sat on them. Thomas noticed that almost every room except his own contained a clock.

Lady Anne was having a rest after the journey, and the tall house felt cold and unfriendly to Thomas. He unpacked everything in his suitcase and draped his clothes over the furniture in his bedroom on the top floor, but this did nothing to fill the underlying emptiness. It was the sort of place, thought Thomas, where you could die and nothing would happen. Nobody would notice.

Outside everything was different. It was a warm spring day in Chelsea, and the young and the beautiful vied to fit themselves into outfits that revealed more of their breasts and legs than Thomas would have believed possible. It all filled him with a random lust of which he felt ashamed in the presence of his mother, who took him shopping at Harrods in the afternoon.

Later they ate dinner on the other side of the river at a little French restaurant with a view of Big Ben and the Houses of Parliament. Thomas thought of his father and felt glad that he was away from home. About Greta his feelings were more ambiguous. Not a day went by that Thomas did not remember the sight of her breasts as she stood half naked in his mother's bedroom and pulled him toward her. The girls that had passed so close to him on the sidewalks during the afternoon had made the memory more vivid than ever, and yet at the same time he almost hated Greta. He'd seen the way she looked at his mother and his father like she was greedy for something they had, but then he remembered the way she looked at him when she said: "You're looking at my breasts, Thomas." The way she laughed when he denied it.

=

Back at the house in Chelsea Thomas lay awake in bed listening to the passing voices of the late-night revelers. Someone somewhere was playing David Gray's *White Ladder*, and the songs filled Thomas with a sense of longing for people and places he didn't yet know.

Toward midnight he fell into an uneasy sleep. He dreamed that he was once again in his mother's bedroom in Flyte watching Greta in the long mirror, but this time she seemed unaware of his presence in the doorway. She stood with her hands on her hips, wearing the same lemon silk dress of his mother's that she had worn on that day the previous October, but now Greta had brought it in at the waist with a thin black snakeskin belt that matched her raven hair.

Slowly her hands moved to the buckle of the belt and eased open the fastening. She held the two ends for a moment and then let go. In Thomas's dream the belt fell slowly to the floor but he didn't hear it land. It was a dream without sound, but unlike other dreams he'd had, it was full of will. Greta did as she did because he willed it. If he did not will it, then she would stop. No, more than that: she wouldn't be there at all.

Slowly her hands moved to an invisible zipper at the back of the dress just below the nape of her neck. She had it in her fingers, and slowly, with exquisite deliberation, she pulled it down. He could feel the movement as if he were tracing the line of her spine with his finger, and he knew that she only did it because he willed her to. The effort made him sway and catch hold of the side of the door, but she didn't seem to notice. Instead she pulled her arms free of the dress and stepped out of it closer to the mirror. The dress was a discarded pool lying on the floor between them.

Her body was perfect. Thomas could feel the strength of it, the muscle tone of the thighs below the rounded hills of her buttocks. He imagined running his hands slowly up the inside of her legs, and as if in answer to his thought Greta slowly moved her legs apart, arching herself forward as she did so.

In his dream Thomas stepped out from the shadow of the doorway and fell to his knees. Groping forward almost blindly, he took hold of Greta's naked sides, pulling her close so that his fingers soon had hold of her hard nipples as she pushed her breasts down toward him. Almost at the same moment his tongue found the wet softness between her legs and he went forward into a dark, unconscious ecstasy.

Thomas tossed and turned on the bed, throwing the hot duvet onto the floor as he did so, but he did not wake. The dream would not let him go. He felt Greta's hands on his shoulders pushing him toward his mother's bed.

He staggered to his feet, asking for release, but as his knees landed on the bed and he arched his back ready to thrust himself deep inside her, he looked down and saw his mother's sapphire ring glowing midnight blue on Greta's finger, and his mother's gold locket hanging from her lovely neck.

He cried out in his sleep, waking as he came, and then lay on the bed like someone pulled half drowned from the sea while the sound of fire engines' sirens passed the house and then faded into the distance.

=

Thomas stood washing himself at the sink in the bathroom at the top of the stairs. He was flushed with a confusion of feelings, self-disgust and sexual excitement contending with each other for dominance. Looking down at his body, he felt almost frightened. It was as if he had no control over its workings.

His inner clock had been set to the unchanging rhythms of Flyte. Year after year, nothing changed there except the weather—until Barton died, of course, which was why his mother had brought him to London, where everything was different. The girls in the street, the music after dark, the sound of the sirens. Anything could happen here, and Thomas suddenly felt imprisoned by his father's house, with its anonymous rooms and high staircases. He needed to get out and walk, breathe the air, if only for five minutes.

He dressed hurriedly and went down the stairs almost on tiptoe so as not to wake his mother. In the hall the grandfather clock gave the time as half past twelve and Thomas realized that he couldn't have been asleep for more than an hour before the sirens had woken him up.

He opened the front door and looked out. The main road to his left seemed as deserted now as the little side street on which his father's house stood. The music had been turned off and almost all of the windows that he could see were in darkness. Only one or two passing cars broke the stillness of the night.

Thomas took a deep breath of the cool air and then walked down the steps, shutting the door behind him. The house was only three away from the main road, and Thomas turned immediately into it, heading toward the bridge over the River Thames. He had driven across it with his mother earlier in the evening when they were coming back from the restaurant. It had been covered with tiny white lights, and they'd stopped on the other side to look at it properly because it was so pretty. The Albert Bridge it was called. Named for the husband of Queen Victoria, the Prince Consort. The one who'd died young and broken the Queen's heart.

However, Thomas didn't get as far as the river. Two young men with baseball caps turned back to front appeared suddenly, coming toward him up the street. One was walking half in the gutter, and the other was running a beer can along the black railings of the houses so that Thomas realized he would have to pass between them. He could not turn back, as he was too close to them, and there was no one else in sight. He accelerated to get the moment over with, but just before he drew level they both moved into the center of the sidewalk, knocking his shoulders so that he almost lost balance.

Nothing else happened, however. Behind him, Thomas could hear them laughing as they carried on down the street.

"Stupid little cunt," one of them said. "Did you see the look on his face?"

Thomas didn't hear the other reply. He carried on, walking slowly down the street, cursing himself for his stupidity in going out so late. His mother had told him to be careful, that London was a dangerous place, and she hadn't even been talking about walking deserted streets after midnight. He hoped that the noise of the beer can on the railings wouldn't wake her up, send her into his room to find him gone, but soon it had faded into the distance and he felt safe to turn around and head for home.

He'd gotten almost as far as the little side street when he saw them at the top of the road. They were coming back toward him. They were still walking but quicker, more purposefully than before, and Thomas felt desperately in his pockets for the house key. His mother had given it to him when they first arrived, and he was sure that he had brought it with him when he came out.

They were closer now, and Thomas could see their faces. They were laughing, and one of them was punching the fist of one hand into the open palm of the other. They could see him too, feel his fear.

"Got lost, have you, cunt?" said one. "Why don't you come here and I'll give you some fucking directions."

The other one laughed.

"Got any money?" he asked. "Got a phone?"

Panic had momentarily paralyzed Thomas as they approached, but when the second youth spoke he felt his strength return. He dashed suddenly to his right down the little side street, and in two seconds he was trembling by the streetlight outside his house.

There was clearly no time to lose. He could hear them coming toward the corner. It was obviously worse than pointless running up the front steps if he had no key, and the thugs would catch him if he ran on down the side street. They were three or four years older than him and a lot quicker. He took his only chance and ran down the stone steps into the basement area by the front door of Greta's apartment.

He'd noticed the house trash cans down there earlier, but when he got to the bottom of the steps they were nowhere in sight. Someone must have moved them since the afternoon. A second later he saw where they'd gone. They were just inside the open entrance to a vault under the sidewalk. Thomas dashed in, taking care not to make any noise. In normal circumstances nothing would have frightened Thomas more than going into a pitch-black vault, but now he went right inside without hesitation, grateful for the enshrouding darkness.

He was not a moment too soon. The two youths had stopped on the sidewalk just above his head.

"He's gone down in one of these fucking basements. That's where he's gone," said the one who'd offered to give Thomas directions.

"No, he hasn't," said the other. "We'd have seen him if he'd done that. I'm not fucking blind, even if you are. Come on, we'll catch him if we're quick."

Thomas heard the sound of them setting off at a run down the side street. He wiped the sweat from his face with the sleeve of his shirt and pressed his hand hard against the left side of his chest, covering the pain of his racing heart.

Breathing deeply, he stepped out of the vault into the basement area so that he was standing outside the front window of Greta's flat. It was less than five feet away. The bottom half of the window was open, raised no more than six inches from the sill. It had been shut earlier in the day and the curtains had been half open, whereas now they were closed. Thomas noticed the difference because he'd been down in the vault after lunch—part of exploring the house with no risks attached because his mother had said that his father and Greta would be away until the following evening. He'd looked in through the window and seen the gas fire and the two armchairs and behind them a table and chair and a bookcase. Everything neat and tidy. He couldn't see into the room now, but he could hear voices. One was too soft to make out, but the other was close and Thomas recognized it almost immediately as Greta's.

"You'll just have to be patient. It's not that difficult."

Thomas couldn't hear if the other voice replied, but a moment later Greta was speaking again. She seemed to be just on the other side of the curtains.

"No, you listen to me. You can wait a little longer. That's what we agreed."

Another pause and then her voice came again. It was farther away this time.

"Can't you see I haven't got it yet?"

Or was it "him yet"? Thomas couldn't be sure. The words were indistinct, and he couldn't make any sense of them. What was she talking about? And to whom? Why was she home when she was supposed to be in the Midlands with his father until the following evening?

Thomas stood motionless and preoccupied in front of the window, revolving the unanswered questions around in his head, and he would have been entirely visible to the two youths coming back up the street if they hadn't chosen to advertise their approach. They were talking even more loudly than before, as if to assert their defiance of the rich neighborhood around them. Thomas had just enough time to retreat back into the vault before they stopped outside the house.

"It's a fucking waste of time," said the one who'd voted for going on down the street. "He didn't look like he had anything on him anyway." But his friend didn't agree.

"He looked like a fucking little rich kid to me. With a wallet full of Daddy's money in his back pocket, and he went down in one of these fucking basements. I saw him. I told you that before!"

"All right. So what if he fucking did. He probably lives there."

"Maybe. But I bet the little cunt was hiding. Probably still is. He went down this one or the one next door."

"Well, I'm not fucking going down after him. We'll end up in the nick for burglary."

Thomas heard the sound of one set of footsteps going off toward the main road. The other youth was still standing by the gate at the top of the steps.

"Cunt," he said. "Fucking gutless cunt." He kicked the gate hard so that it hit the wall behind. Then he ran away into the night.

Thomas waited a moment before he came back out of the vault heading toward the steps. Just as he did so the curtains in front of him opened and he instinctively crouched down under the windowsill where he could not be seen.

As he bent over, the house key fell out of his shirt pocket and hit the concrete with a loud clink. Thomas froze, certain that Greta or who-ever it was on the other side of the window must have heard the noise. He wondered how he could explain his presence bent over underneath her window and then gave up the attempt. He was eavesdropping and he couldn't deny it. How he got down into the basement was ir-relevant.

It was soon clear, though, that neither Greta nor her friend had heard the key hit the ground. The sound must have been drowned out by the greater noise of the sash window being lifted up as far as it would go. Thomas could now hear her voice inches away from his head.

"I can't see anyone, but that doesn't mean anything. There've been burglars up there before, and I'm not having them stealing my com-puter. Mrs. Posh won't hear. She takes sleeping tablets. And the boy's at the top of the house."

If Greta could have leaned out far enough, she would have touched Thomas, but the bars on the window prevented this. He was safe until she opened the door of her apartment, but from the sound of it that was precisely what she was about to do.

Thomas did not hear any reply from the other person in the room because the next moment Greta pulled the window down. There didn't seem to be enough time to get away before the door opened, but he had to try. Picking up the key, he turned and crept up the steps with his back against the wall. There was no sound from below.

At the top he had no choice but to run in front of the house under the streetlight so that anyone looking out of the basement window could not have failed to see him. But when he stopped to fit the key in the lock with a trembling hand, he still heard nothing. It seemed like a miracle.

Thomas pulled the front door shut behind him and stood in the dark hallway trying to fight back the panic that was once again turning his legs to jelly. Afterward he realized that it was this moment of inactivity that had saved him from discovery. Turning on the light would have given him away, but as it was, Greta came through the door at the end of the hall to find everything in unsuspicious darkness, and Thomas had time, while she turned the key in the lock, to escape into the room she used as an office. He half closed the door behind him.

There were tiny red lights twinkling on the computers and the other machines in the room, but they didn't illuminate it sufficiently to enable Thomas to see any hiding place other than behind the thick curtains drawn across the tall windows. He moved slowly, taking care not to trip over any wires or bump into the circular table in the center of the room that he remembered from his afternoon tour of inspection. It seemed an eternity away now.

Thomas realized as he stood by the curtains in the office that he was more frightened than he had ever been in his life. Clearly his experience with the youths in the street had shaken him, but it was Greta's strange words, the invisible second person inside the basement flat, and the closeness of their presence that had unnerved him so badly.

Outside in the hall Thomas heard footsteps, so he ducked behind the curtains and stood up against one of the front windows. On the other side of the room the owner of the footsteps—Greta it must be—turned on the light. She wasn't moving, but Thomas could sense her standing in the doorway looking into the room. Involuntarily he turned his head away to look out into the street and in the same instant clapped a hand over his mouth to strangle a gasp that had risen in his throat. There was a man standing under the streetlight with his back to the house. Thomas did not know why he knew with such certainty that this was the person whom Greta had been entertaining in her flat two minutes before. He just knew.

The man was wearing tight blue jeans and a white, collarless shirt. He had a belt too, thick and black, and Thomas had a sudden vision of the man taking it off his narrow hips and holding it above his head like a whip. There was something about his body, about his posture, that suggested violence. Thomas could sense the strength of the man's muscles as he rocked back and forward on his heels like a boxer or a dancer even. He felt the man's quickness. The stranger's black hair was long, tied back in a ponytail. Without the ponytail Thomas wouldn't have seen the scar that ran from behind the man's right jawbone down into his strong bull neck.

Thomas was terrified. He didn't know how long he stood there with Greta behind him on the other side of the curtain and the man in front, who had only to turn his head for a moment to see Thomas in the window. In reality it was only a few seconds before Greta turned out the light and closed the door, but it seemed forever to Thomas as he fought to hold his breath and willed the man with the scar not to turn around. And he didn't. He remained standing by the streetlight. Several times he looked to his right up toward the main road, but he never looked back at the house. Not while Thomas was standing at the window.

When he heard the door to the basement close behind Greta, Thomas stepped back into the room and the thick curtain fell into place behind him, shutting out the streetlight and the man standing beneath it.

He began slowly to grope his way across the dark room. He put his hands out in front of him to feel for obstacles and felt them trembling until they met the sideboard, which took him step by faltering step out into the hall.

Thomas was only halfway up the stairs before his legs gave way under him outside the door of his mother's room. He could hear her even breathing, but he did not go inside. Not too long ago he would have gotten into the bed beside her seeking comfort from the Suffolk storms, but now everything was changed. This was London and he was no longer a boy, whatever Greta Grahame might say to the contrary.

Thomas brushed the tears from his eyes and took hold of the banister. At the top of the house he washed his face and then lay down on his bed. But sleep didn't come until long after the bells of St. Luke's Church had tolled three, and then it was troubled by dreams of faces at the window and hands behind the curtains.

Chapter 10

THOMAS WOKE at ten o'clock in a pool of sunshine and for a moment did not know where he was. There were no trees like there were outside his bedroom window at home in Flyte. Here the view was of the roofs of the neighboring houses and in the distance towers and high spires. Through the open window he could hear the endless noise of the passing traffic. London had been awake for hours.

After breakfast he went for a walk down to the river. The sidewalks were thronged with people, and he had to wait two or three minutes at the embankment before the traffic lights brought the stream of cars and trucks to a halt and he could cross over onto the Albert Bridge. It was just as pretty during the day, thought Thomas, even without the twinkling lights. There were golden portholes in its bright white sides and a canopy of curving metal girders overhead. Thomas stood in the center of the bridge, leaning over the parapet, and followed the line of golden sunlight glittering on the water that drew his eyes toward the east, toward Westminster and the Tower of London invisible beyond the next bend in the river. He felt suddenly excited by the great city stretching out all around him. The events of the night seemed as if they had taken place in another country. Children on bicycles were crossing the bridge on their way to Battersea Park, and it was hard to imagine being frightened in these sunlit crowded streets.

Back at the house, Thomas leaned over the railings and looked down into the basement area. The curtains on the front window of Greta's apartment were open, and there was no sign of life. After a minute or two he got up his courage to venture down the steps and peer in at the window. Everything was as it had been the previous afternoon. There were no glasses on the table, no papers left lying around, nothing to suggest that anyone had been home last night.

Thomas's mother was up when he returned, writing letters at an old oak bureau in a corner of the drawing room. She looked up when she saw her son and smiled.

"Hullo, Tom. How did you sleep?"

"All right, I suppose."

Thomas was surprised by his mother's question, and he lied almost without thinking. He'd hated himself for telling his mother about Greta trying on her clothes last autumn. Nothing good had come of it, and he wasn't about to confess to being an eavesdropper now.

As for the trouble with the two youths, that had been his own fault and he wasn't intending to wander the streets in the small hours again. There was no point in worrying his mother with what had happened now that it was over and done with.

"I suppose?" Lady Anne turned her son's answer back into a question.

"Yes, I slept fine. Why? Didn't you?"

"Yes, I did, but I've got my sleeping tablets. I was only asking because you've got big black circles under your eyes."

Thomas glanced at himself in the mirror over the fireplace. His mother was right. He looked like death.

"Bad dreams, I suppose," he said with a half laugh.

"Do you remember them?"

"No, I don't."

This time Thomas lied with conviction. He was not about to provide his mother with a blow-by-blow account of his wet dream even though he could remember much of it in Technicolor detail.

"Stop interrogating me, Mum," he added for good measure.

"Sorry. It's just you look so strange. Black circles under your eyes and now your cheeks have gone bright red. Are you sure you're okay?"

"Yes. Absolutely sure. If you won't leave me alone, I'm going to go out again."

"No, don't do that. I've got a table booked for lunch. I'll go and get ready soon."

Thomas stood in the doorway with his hands thrust deep in his pockets. He looked irritable and morose.

"Come here, Tom," said Lady Anne apologetically. "I'm sorry if I've offended you. Look, there's something I want to show you."

Thomas shuffled across the room and came to a halt on the other side of his mother's desk. He hoped that she wasn't just making an excuse for more cross-examination.

"Don't look like that. I won't show you if you're not interested. It's a secret."

"A secret what?"

"Wouldn't you like to know?"

"Come on, Mum. Tell me. You've got to now."

"All right. But you're not to tell anyone else. Your father might be upset if he knew that I told you."

"Told me what?"

"About the drawer. Come round here and look. I'll show you how it works."

Thomas leaned over his mother's shoulder while she reached into the bureau. He saw that there were two sets of three tiny drawers on either side of a recess in the center, which appeared to extend to the back of the desk. As Thomas watched, Lady Anne gently pressed the two tiny brass knobs on the bottom drawers on either side of the recess, and suddenly the back of it opened, disclosing a small, hollow cupboard.

"But there's nothing inside," said Thomas, sounding disappointed.

"That's not the point, silly. It's the mechanism. Don't you think it's clever?"

"Yes, but there should be something inside it. There's no point in having a secret cupboard if you don't keep something secret in it."

"Well, we haven't got anything in the priest's hole at home. Nothing secret anyway."

"That's different. It's bigger and everyone knows about it."

"Oh, well, I'm sorry to disappoint you. Personally I'm rather glad that your father isn't hiding any guilty secrets. Not that I suppose he'd keep them here if he did have them. He never seems to use this bureau much."

"How long has he had it?"

"Oh, I don't know. He had it when we were first together. Inherited it from his mother, I think. He showed me the secret cupboard ages ago and made me promise not to tell. I don't know why. Perhaps he just wanted to make a mystery out of it. Anyway, don't tell him I told you."

"I won't," said Thomas, his mood brightening with the knowledge that his mother had shown him the secret even when his father had told her not to.

"When are we going?"

"Ten minutes. There's a taxi coming. I'll see you downstairs. I'm going to go and get ready."

=

They ate lunch in a restaurant in Covent Garden and then walked back to Westminster Pier and took an excursion boat down to the Tower of London.

Thomas could hardly contain his impatience as the boat slowly chugged along the river. He had a book about the Tower in his bedroom back home in Flyte and thought it was the most wonderful building in the world. Once they had gone under London Bridge, the Tower's high battlements came fully into view.

"That's where they put the heads of the executed prisoners," said Thomas, pointing behind them. "On spikes on London Bridge. I read about it in my book."

"Were there pictures?" asked Lady Anne mischievously.

"No, of course not. And it's not the same bridge. They sold the old one to the Americans."

The boat's pace got even more sluggish and there were signs of people getting ready to disembark, but Thomas kept his mother beside him looking out over the rail. He was waiting for the boat to pass its final landmark, the highlight of the journey.

"There it is!" he cried suddenly, pointing toward the Tower. "Look, Mum. The Traitors' Gate. That's where they brought the prisoners. Through there on their way to die."

Lady Anne shivered in spite of herself. The gate's name was chiseled into the stone above the portcullis, and the gray river water lapped against the black gates below. Sunlight did not penetrate this entrance to the Tower.

"God, Thomas, you're ghoulish," she said with a note of real concern in her voice. Her son's preoccupation with darkness and death troubled her. It was something she needed to talk to Peter about. Anne found herself wishing not for the first time that Thomas was not so imaginative. She felt that nothing good would come of it.

Inside the Tower they did the full tour of dungeons and places of execution before waiting in line for over half an hour to see the Crown Jewels, but once inside Thomas was strangely disappointed. The huge jewels in their bulletproof cabinets held no meaning for him in contrast to the echoing stony interiors of the White Tower and the Bloody Tower, where Thomas could imagine the lives of the prisoners who had suffered there.

His mother felt the same. About the jewels at any rate.

"That's why I wouldn't let your father put our family jewelry in a bank vault," she said. "Just like I was telling you yesterday in the car. If you take something out of its context, out of its history, then it stops having any meaning. For me at any rate."

They headed for the exit.

=

In the evening they went to the Globe Theatre and saw *Macbeth*. Thomas was enthralled. He knew the story, but only now, under the open night sky, did the characters really come alive for him.

At first Thomas remained aware of the other spectators and his mother, wrapped up in a shawl on the seat beside him, as Macbeth met the three witches who hailed him as the future king. But soon he lost all sense of his surroundings as Macbeth began to argue with his wife about whether to kill King Duncan while he slept in the guest bedroom of their castle.

Thomas loved Macbeth, the brave chieftain who spoke so magically, and he willed him not to commit the crime even though he knew that Macbeth could not escape his fate.

Then at last the stage became almost completely dark and a hush fell over the evening as Macbeth crept into the King's room and stabbed him through the heart. Now Thomas hated Macbeth, and he hated him more as Macbeth went on to kill all those who stood in his way. Then at last King Duncan's son, Malcolm, returned to Scotland with an army, and Thomas's heart went out once more to the murderer, Macbeth, as he faced up to his own death with courage.

As the play ended with a fanfare of trumpets and the characters turned back into actors bowing to the audience's loud applause, Thomas felt almost drunk with the roller coaster of emotions that he had endured during the preceding two hours.

"Oh, Mum, wasn't it extraordinary?" he said suddenly in the taxi on the way home as his enthusiasm overflowed.

"Yes, I suppose so," replied Lady Anne coolly. *Macbeth* was not one of her favorite plays, and she'd had quite enough blood for one day.

=

Back at the house they found Sir Peter and Greta sitting upstairs in the living room with files of papers on their laps and glasses of red wine in their hands. Work never seemed to stop for his father, thought Thomas, as he dutifully bent down and kissed him on his upturned cheek. These greetings always seemed to Thomas to have nothing to do with affection and everything to do with acknowledging his father's superior status in the family. There was something quasi-military about them.

"So, have you had a good evening?" asked Sir Peter.

"Yes, we saw *Macbeth* at the Globe," replied his wife. "I got a little cold toward the end, but Thomas enjoyed it. Didn't you, darling?"

Thomas nodded. Words couldn't describe the wonder of his experience.

"Oh, you're so lucky," said Greta, joining in the conversation with sudden passion. "It's my favorite play. I love Macbeth. The character, I mean. Not just the play."

"Do you?" said Lady Anne frigidly. She already had her doubts about whether the Tower of London and *Macbeth* had been the best way to entertain Thomas when he was already so clearly in such an excited state. The last thing she wanted now was a ringing endorsement of Macbeth's murderous qualities from her husband's personal assistant.

But Greta failed to be put off by Lady Anne's forbidding tone.

"I remember when I first saw the play. I was at university, and I'd never seen anything like it before. Macbeth has the most amazing lines. Do you remember when he sees the imaginary dagger in the air before he goes off to kill the King?"

Greta held her hand up in front of her as if to take hold of a weapon and started to recite:

"Is this a dagger which I see before me,
The handle toward my hand? Come, let me clutch thee.
I have thee not, and yet I see thee still.
Art thou not, fatal vision, sensible
To feeling as to sight? or art thou but
A dagger of the mind, a false creation,
Proceeding from the heat-oppressed brain?"

Greta spoke the words well, conveying Macbeth's final uncertainty before he murders Duncan, and Thomas warmed to her. She seemed to him at that moment like a kindred spirit. He felt that he'd misjudged her in the past.

However, her performance had the opposite effect on Lady Anne, who could not hide her irritation. Coming upon Peter and Greta sitting so intimately together in the living room had brought all her suppressed resentment to the surface, and now she wanted to lash out, put green-eyed Greta in her place.

"Grand words," she said in a tone that implied she thought the opposite. "They're all very well, but you can't hide behind them. Macbeth killed the King, who was a guest in his own house. Stabbed him in cold blood with a real dagger. Isn't it hard to think of anything more mean and cowardly?"

"His wife drove him to it," said Greta. "His wife and the witches."

"You're just looking for excuses. He was a bloodthirsty little man, who got exactly what he deserved."

"Maybe, but why then does the audience sympathize with him at the end and not with boring Malcolm?"

Thomas longed to say how much he agreed with Greta, but he held his tongue. He instinctively realized that there was more at stake between his mother and Greta than two different interpretations of Shakespeare.

It was Sir Peter who intervened in the argument. He seemed to have no idea of his wife's underlying resentments.

"You're a revolutionary, Greta," he said. "That's what you are." There was an unmistakable note of fondness in his voice, which irritated Lady Anne still further.

"I sincerely hope she isn't," said Lady Anne. "I don't hold with revolution. People ought to know their place."

Immediately Lady Anne wanted to apologize, to take the words back, but something inside prevented her from doing so. It was the same resentment and anger that had possessed her in the House of the Four Winds three months earlier, on the night when the fisherman drowned in Flyte Bay and Peter took Greta down to the harbor to find Christopher Marsh. Not her but Greta. Always Greta.

She'd said almost the same thing then, she remembered. It was as if those words, "know your place," were always lurking there just beneath her consciousness, ready to fly out. As if she knew that they would be the most likely to inflict the deepest wound on her enemy. Judging from Greta's twisted expression, it looked to Lady Anne as if she had more than succeeded this time.

There was an awkward silence, which no one seemed able to fill until Lady Anne spoke again, this time to her husband: "How were your constituents?"

"Okay, although I could've done with Greta being there. She always has all the difficult ones eating out of her hand."

Lady Anne frowned. Her husband had as usual found a way of expressing his support for his personal assistant rather than his wife.

"I thought you were going up there together."

"No, Greta had to change her plans. Her mother was unwell and so she had to go and stay up in Manchester for the night."

"I'm sorry, Greta," said Lady Anne. "Is she okay?" There was real concern in her voice. She felt guilty now about lashing out.

"Yes, she's fine, thank you," said Greta. It hadn't taken her long to recover her self-possession. "It's just the arthritis. She gets depressed and a visit cheers her up."

"I'm sure it does," said Lady Anne, getting up from the sofa. "Well, I'm for bed; and Thomas, you better go up too. You've got another long day ahead of you tomorrow, and you need your sleep. I don't want you looking like you did this morning again."

"What was wrong with him this morning?" asked Sir Peter.

"Great black circles under his eyes. I don't think he slept a wink. Too excited about being in London, I imagine. Come on, Thomas. Bedtime."

Thomas went over to his father, provided him with another dutiful kiss, then hesitated in the middle of the room. He didn't know whether to kiss Greta or not.

She made his mind up for him, getting up from her chair and walking over to him. She kissed him warmly on the cheek, resting her arm on his shoulder for a moment as she did so.

"Good night," she whispered, and as Thomas turned to go, summoned again by his mother to follow her up to bed, she added, "I'm glad you liked the play."

=

Fifteen minutes later Thomas lay in bed gripped by a turmoil of conflicting emotions.

Greta had lied about where she had been the previous night. She hadn't been hundreds of miles away like she'd said, tending to her sick mother in Manchester. She'd been downstairs in the basement entertaining a strange man who wore his hair in a ponytail and had a scar running down under his ear. She'd told him to be patient, to wait a little longer. Wait a little longer for what? Thomas wondered, as he had done off and on ever since he'd gotten back up to his bedroom the night before.

There were so many unanswered questions. Who was the man? Why had Greta lied? What was she waiting for?

Thomas put his hand up to his cheek and gently ran the tips of his fingers over the spot where Greta's lips had placed her good-night kiss. He remembered how pretty she'd looked when she'd spoken those lines from the play, and then, with a rush, he remembered his dream.

Chapter 11

━━━━━━━━━━━━━━━━

T HE NEXT MORNING Thomas waited at the top of the stairs leading down to the kitchen. He could hear his mother talking to his father, who was clearly about to leave—Thomas could see his briefcase out in the hall with a raincoat draped over it—and his natural instinct was to avoid his father if he could. But he also wanted to hear what his parents were saying—he knew they were talking about him, because they kept using his name.

"You need to spend more time with the boy. Either that or he's going to need some outside help." Thomas could hear the anxiety in his mother's voice.

"I will. I told you I will." Peter sounded irritated. "I'm taking him out today, aren't I? It's your fault for keeping him down in Flyte all the time. He needs to go away to a good school. That'd make him grow up."

"He *is* going to a good school. We've been over all this, Peter. I don't agree with you about English boarding schools. I never have and I never will. All they do is turn out emotional cripples with a taste for sadomasochism."

"But tying him to your apron strings isn't doing him much good either, is it? We wouldn't be having this conversation if Thomas was an emotional success."

"No, we wouldn't. He's obviously got some sort of a death fixation.

You don't have to be a psychiatrist to see that. And it's gotten a lot worse since his dog died."

"Dogs do die," said Peter brutally. "It's part of growing up."

"For you, maybe. But you should have seen him yesterday. His imagination's completely out of control. I mean, he's a world authority on executions. He could take the tourists round the Tower of London himself, telling them how many axe blows it took to dispatch Anne Boleyn, *and* what they did with her head afterward. And then *Macbeth*—he was practically jumping out of his seat."

"Well, that's your fault. You shouldn't have taken him to the bloody play if he's got this problem."

"I know I shouldn't. But he's not the way he is because of going to the theater. You know that, Peter."

"All right, I get the point. What do you want me to do about it?"

"I want you to spend more time with him. Take him out in the world a bit."

"How? You stay down in Suffolk all the time, and I'm trying to be a cabinet minister."

"Well, we'll both have to try harder, that's all. We are his parents, you know. I'll bring him up to London more, and you can take him out when I do."

"Okay, it's a deal. Starting today. After I've dealt with these Arabs. They want to buy a whole lot of fighter aircraft to use on each other. Have him meet me at twelve. I'll be free by then."

Thomas's parents came out into the hall, and he ducked back behind the banister. As they kissed each other good-bye on the front doorstep, they looked just for a moment like a normal middle-aged couple at the start of a working day, instead of two people who only saw each other two weekends each month.

=

After the door shut, Thomas waited a minute or two before going down to join his mother in the kitchen.

"You look better, Tom," she said brightly. "It's wonderful what a proper night's sleep will do for a tired boy."

"I do sleep well. Why do you keep on going on about how weird I am?" he asked irritably.

"I don't. Where do you get that idea from?"

Thomas didn't reply. He wanted to know what his mother had meant by outside help, but on the other hand, he didn't want to own up to eavesdropping.

"Where's Dad?" he asked.

"He had to go early. Something came up with his work, but he's still taking you out to lunch and showing you round Parliament."

"Oh, God, Mum, do I have to?"

"Yes, of course you do. Don't be so mean, Thomas. You should be proud of your father and all he's achieved."

"Well, he's not proud of me. Any chance he gets he's on about how hopeless I am. Doesn't play cricket. Doesn't play rugby. How can I when they don't even play rugby at my school?"

"I know. He needs to get to know you; spend some time with you. That's why I'm so pleased about today. You're to meet him in the lobby of his office building at midday."

"What? In Whitehall? Will I need a pass?"

"No, of course not. You're only going into the reception area. You might need one later, I suppose, when he takes you on the Parliament tour, but he'll organize all that."

"Do you think we'll see the prime minister?" asked Thomas, suddenly shaking off his lethargy as the full possibilities of the tour opened up to him.

"I don't know, but you'll need to be dressed smartly if you do. You can wear your blazer and the trousers we bought at Harrods the other day. And you better take a coat as well, in case it rains."

=

Lady Anne was going to the hairdresser and then on to her dressmaker, so Thomas was alone in the taxi as it went past Big Ben and the Houses of Parliament. He felt confused by his emotions. He was still smarting with resentment at the offhand way in which his father had talked about him earlier, but he was also curious about what he was going to see. Not every boy was the son of a cabinet minister. More than anything Thomas felt nervous as he got out in front of the tall gray stone Victorian office building with the gold plaque on the side of the high doorway bearing the legend MINISTRY OF DEFENSE. He became almost tongue-tied as he tried to explain his business to a porter who seemed to consider it part of his employment contract to wear an unvaryingly dubious expression when dealing with members of the public, whatever their age.

Thomas waited for nearly five minutes, wilting under the porter's withering stare, until Greta appeared at the top of a flight of red carpeted stairs. She looked different today. In Flyte and again on the previous evening she'd been dressed casually, but now she was wearing a dark gray business suit over a plain white blouse. The material was soft and beautifully cut to display her figure to the best advantage, and the hemline of the skirt was high above the knee, revealing the perfection of her long, tanned legs. Thomas's head swam for a moment as his recent dream of Greta returned to him with sudden intensity.

She came running down the stairs carrying a picnic basket. She put down the basket and kissed him on the cheek, just like she had the night before, resting her arm on his shoulder so that he felt her breasts for a moment brushing against his chest.

"Been looking after our young guest, have you, Mills?" she said, turning with a mock serious expression toward the old porter, who grunted in response from behind his desk. Not even Greta in a miniskirt seemed capable of changing his dubious exterior.

"Miserable Mills we call him," whispered Greta, bending toward Thomas so as not to be overheard.

"I can see why," he whispered back, but his voice came out louder than he'd intended and he was sure that Miserable Mills had heard them. He looked suddenly quite warlike, gripping a stapler on his desk with apparently ferocious intent.

"Bad news, I'm afraid," said Greta, ignoring the outbreak of militancy behind her. "Your father can't make it. There's been a semi-disaster this morning. The Saudis are threatening to cancel a big defense contract."

"Why?"

"The usual thing. Somebody's said something rude about their legal system. I must say it gets bloody difficult at times pretending it's perfectly all right to stone women for adultery and cut people's heads off in the town center. Anyway, it's not his fault he can't be here, and he is really sorry. I hope you don't mind having me as a substitute."

As she spoke, Greta was shepherding Thomas out of the building and into a taxi she'd hailed just as they set foot on the sidewalk.

"It's not far, but I don't feel like dragging the picnic around with us if we can avoid it. I thought that we could have it by the river after we've done the Houses of Parliament."

Thomas was touched. His feelings about Greta were as confused as ever. The evident antipathy between her and his mother made him feel that a day spent with Greta would be seen by his mother as an act of disloyalty, but what choice did he have? His father had let him down, and his mother had gone out for the day. It was kind of Greta to take the time out and bring a picnic. She didn't need to do that. Thomas took it as a compliment, and sitting beside Greta in the taxi he felt his skin tingle as he anticipated the day ahead.

It was the Easter recess and Parliament was not sitting. The long green leather benches in the House of Commons did not interest Thomas much even when Greta pointed out the government front bench and the microphone where his father would stand when making a statement to the House. Thomas felt let down by his father but at the same time relieved that he didn't have to spend the day with him. He could imagine how boring his father would have made it, whereas Greta told racy anecdotes about prominent politicians, prefacing each disclosure with an injunction "not to breathe a word or I'll get into terrible trouble with your father."

The sun was shining high in a cloudless sky when they got outside into Parliament Square just after one o'clock, and they walked down to the park carrying the picnic basket between them. There was a blanket on top of it, and Greta spread it out on the grass near the river.

"We went on a boat yesterday," said Thomas, making conversation while Greta unpacked the rest of the picnic. "Me and my mother. We went from here up to the Tower. Past Traitors' Gate."

"God, it's a grisly place," said Greta. "I haven't been there since I first came to London."

"Why grisly?"

"Well, where do you start? The Princes in the Tower. Anne Boleyn. Catherine Howard."

"Yes, we saw where they were executed."

"By that bastard, Henry the Eighth. The most disgusting old man in history. Marries pretty girls a third of his age, and a third of his weight too, and then he kills them when they have an affair. What did he expect?"

"But they didn't," said Thomas eagerly. "Not Anne Boleyn anyway.

Thomas Cromwell told the King she did, but she didn't." Henry VIII and his six wives was one of his favorite historical subjects.

"Well, I'm sorry to hear that. I know what I would have done if I'd been married to that old goat."

Thomas did not respond. Greta's reference to her own sex drive made his heart beat fast. He felt the blood rushing to his cheeks and turned away.

"Come on, let's not talk about people getting executed. It's much too nice a day for that. I don't want to get blamed for you having another sleepless night."

"What do you mean? I slept fine."

"That's not what your mother said last night, Thomas. She said you had dark circles under your eyes, that she didn't think you'd slept at all."

"Oh, you mean the night before."

"Yes, that's right."

Greta looked at Thomas expectantly. She hadn't asked any question, but it felt to Thomas exactly as if she were waiting for an answer. When he didn't give her one, she pressed the subject further.

"It must be strange being in London after the quiet of Flyte. It takes awhile to adjust, doesn't it?"

"I guess so."

"The traffic can be noisy too. Even when it's way past midnight. It often keeps me up."

"Well, I didn't have a problem. Not the first night and not last night either. I don't know what my mother was talking about."

Greta smiled. She seemed to visibly relax suddenly, and Thomas felt as if he'd given her exactly what she wanted. He knew he should have been pleased; the last thing he needed was for Greta to suspect that he'd been spying on her and her mysterious friend. However, he also felt the old sense of disloyalty stirring within him. He couldn't even be with Greta anymore without feeling that he was treating his mother badly, and there were other things that he knew he shouldn't forget. Like the man with the scar, and the lie she'd told his parents last night about being with her mother in Manchester.

Thomas knew that he needed to be on his guard, but it was hard when Greta was so attractive and was making such an effort to be nice to him.

"I've got white wine," she said. "A little won't hurt you, but don't tell your parents."

This secret didn't require any oral agreement. Taking the polystyrene cup from Greta's outstretched hand was quite sufficient to seal Thomas's complicity, and the alcohol made everything glow in the warm afternoon sunlight.

"God, I wish I was wearing something more comfortable," said Greta as she took off her jacket and unbuttoned the top two buttons of her blouse. She had already kicked off her high-heeled shoes when they sat down.

"Not enough room in the picnic basket for cushions, I'm afraid. Look, I can't use this jacket, Thomas. I need it for work. Do you mind me using your legs? As a pillow, I mean."

Thomas nodded. He couldn't trust himself to speak as Greta stretched her legs out on the blanket and positioned her head on his thigh. She closed her eyes and sighed with apparent contentment.

Thomas was lying on his side with his head resting on his elbow, and soon his arm began to ache, but he didn't move. Concentrating all his attention instead on slowing down his breathing and his heartbeat, he moved his other arm until it came to rest just by where the mane of Greta's raven hair was spread out over the pale cotton trousers that his mother had bought him the day before.

He hesitated for what seemed like an age with his hand suspended above Greta's head before he began gently to stroke her hair. After a moment she turned her head slightly so as to move herself more fully onto his legs, and looking down, Thomas could see the rounded beginnings of her breasts. He felt himself hardening against her, but he was powerless to do anything about it. He was certain that Greta couldn't help but be aware of his excitement. However, she did not move away from him. Instead, without opening her eyes, she began to talk in a sensual, half-sleepy voice that aroused him even more.

"You know I like you, Thomas. I always have. You're so unlike your father, and yet you remind me of him as well."

"I like you too," whispered Thomas.

"Your father and a boy I knew in school years ago," Greta mused. "You remind me of him as well." Thomas didn't know whether she had heard him or not. "Pierre, he was called. Always quoting poetry; telling crazy stories. His father was from somewhere in France and hated it in

Manchester. Maybe Pierre got it from him. His romantic nature, I mean."

"What happened to him?"

"Pierre? He left school. Came south. Got lost in London somewhere. We kept in touch for a while, but I haven't heard from him in ages. The last time we spoke he was working somewhere in France. I don't know if he stayed there. He's probably got a wife and two-point-five children by now."

Greta broke off. A note of annoyance had crept into her voice, and a frown creased her wide forehead down to her black eyebrows. Thomas tried unsuccessfully to smooth it away with the back of his hand.

"Do I look like him?" he asked, trying to return the conversation to its previous intimate footing.

"No, not really," said Greta irritably before she added in a softer voice: "I'm sorry, Thomas. It's the past. I don't like talking about it. It's not your fault."

She smiled up at him, but the afternoon's spell was broken. Big Ben struck three, and Greta pulled herself up to a sitting position.

"Come on," she said. "Time to pack up. We've got to be home in twenty minutes."

"Why?" asked Thomas, shaking his arm about in a vain attempt to rid himself of the cramp, which was now transforming itself into a painful attack of pins and needles.

"I'm meeting your father there. On the way to the next set of meetings. Let's hope he's managed to sort out the Saudis."

"Sort out who?"

"The Saudis. The ones with the Islamic sensibilities. Don't you remember anything?"

Thomas didn't answer. He did dimly remember the reason that Greta had given for his father's absence, but it didn't seem important. His father was always absent, always letting him down. What mattered was the afternoon with Greta: the sun and the white wine, her head resting on his thigh, his hand in her hair, and now it was all going to be over. Why? Because of his father and his stupid work. Thomas wished that he didn't remind Greta of his father at all, but perhaps that was what she liked about him. He felt he couldn't win.

They were on the sidewalk for less than a minute when a taxi pulled up. Greta seemed to attract them like a magnet, Thomas thought bitterly as they sped off down the road by the river toward Chelsea. There was hardly any traffic to hold them up, and every one of the signals seemed to turn to green just as they approached.

Greta was checking the voice-mail on her mobile phone as she sat beside him in the back of the taxi, and Thomas felt as if she'd already moved on to the next part of her day, leaving him and their picnic far behind. Thomas thought that it might be weeks before he saw Greta again. She and his father had not been down to Flyte in over a month, and it might be just as long before they came again, and then there was always the possibility that Greta might not come at all, given the hostility that Thomas's mother so clearly felt toward her.

Thomas was too young to cope with the violent emotions that had taken such a firm hold on him. He was like a boat in a storm that had broken free of its moorings and was now tossed about rudderless in uncharted waters. He forgot his loyalty to his mother and his suspicions of Greta. All he wanted was to say what he felt before his time with Greta was over. Before the taxi got them home.

At last a traffic light turned red. They were by Chelsea Bridge, and Thomas knew it was now or never.

"Greta," he said, and his voice came out in a whisper, contradicting the power of the emotion that had led him to break his silence.

Greta heard him, however. She'd put her mobile away in her bag and was gazing half wistfully at Thomas's profile when he spoke her name.

"Yes, Thomas. What is it?" The sensual sweetness was back in her voice, and it gave him the courage to continue.

"You know how I feel about you."

"How do you feel about me, Thomas?"

"I feel that you are so beautiful."

Greta heard the longing in Thomas's voice, and she didn't know how to respond.

"You're very sweet," she said lamely.

"No, I'm not," he said with sudden vehemence as his voice broke through his earlier whisper. "You are beautiful. I've never met anyone as beautiful as you are."

"But you will, Thomas. I promise you, you will."

"Don't say that," he said. "I love you, Greta. Can't you see that? I love you. Not anyone else. You."

"You mustn't say that, Thomas. It's not right."

"Don't you feel anything about me at all?"

"I like you. No, more than that. I'm very fond of you. But that's all it can be. I'm too old, Thomas. Too old for you."

Tears had formed in the boy's eyes, and they now began to trickle down his cheeks. Greta put her hand under his chin and turned his half-resistant head toward her. Then, leaning forward, she kissed him on the forehead.

"Don't cry, Thomas," she said. "Don't spoil our wonderful afternoon."

Thomas did not reply. There was no time. The taxi drew up in front of the house, and he could see his father on the doorstep waiting impatiently for his personal assistant to get out. Thomas hung back for a moment before he followed Greta out onto the sidewalk. He did not know in that instant whether he loved or hated this mysterious green-eyed woman with whom he had become so obsessed.

Looking up at the house as he got out of the taxi, Thomas caught sight of his mother standing framed in one of the high windows of the drawing room on the first floor, and he never afterward forgot the look of infinite sadness on her face. It was as if she knew that she had less than two months left to live.

Chapter 12

A ND NOW, with your Lordship's leave, I will call my first witness,"
said John Sparling, turning his attention away from the jury and
focusing on the old judge above him, who was busy sharpening a set of
colored pencils.

Sparling felt his opening had gone well. The jury had stayed attentive and seemed suitably upset when shown the murder photographs.
Now was the time to build on that effect, and who could be better for
the purpose than the crime-scene officer? Detective Constable Butler
would keep the jury concentrating on the appalling circumstances of
Lady Anne's death, and the more the jury thought about that, the more
they would want to find someone responsible for it. The more they
would be prepared to follow Sparling's lead down the paths of circum-
stantial and uncorroborated evidence that led to the defendant.

Sparling had no doubt in his mind that Lady Greta had conspired to
murder her husband's first wife, but proving it was quite another matter, particularly when he had Old Lurid Lambert to contend with. He
did not underestimate his opponent; he'd lost too many guilty defendants to Miles over the years to allow himself to do that.

Detective Butler came into court preceded by Miss Hooks, the
diminutive usher, who looked no more than half his height as he tow-
ered above her in the witness box and read the oath from the card that
she held up in front of his solar plexus.

He must be six feet six. Detective Giant, thought Greta as she looked across at the crime-scene officer and imagined the back pain that he must endure bending over to examine floors and recesses for tiny bits of forensic evidence.

"I arrived at the House of the Four Winds at ten fifty-five P.M., having been called to the scene by the two officers who had attended in response to the original 999 call," said Detective Butler, adopting the impersonal voice of the professional witness.

"It's agreed, members of the jury, that that was made by Thomas Robinson from the house of a neighbor, Christopher Marsh," said Sparling, speaking across his witness. "He'd gone there to raise the alarm."

"Yes, that's correct," said Butler. "The officers had entered the house through the open side door by which Thomas Robinson had exited. They had climbed the back stairs and discovered the body, and they had afterward gone through the rooms in the house in order to ascertain if there were any other persons present."

"Any intruders, you mean?"

"Yes. They found nobody, and they did not disturb the scene of the crime. I was satisfied that upon my arrival it was in the same condition as when Thomas Robinson had left the property to raise the alarm."

"Why would he have needed to do that?"

"Because the telephone cable on the outside wall of the house by the side door had been cut. It is my opinion that a pair of garden shears were used for the purpose, although none were recovered from the scene."

"What else did you find in that area?"

"The side door was open, as I have already said. There was a key in the lock on the inside of the property, suggesting that it had been unlocked from the inside. There is a study room to the left of this side entrance with two windows that look out over the north lawn."

"Please refer to the plan if it assists, Detective Butler," said Sparling. "The jury have copies."

"Thank you, sir. One of the panes in the window on the left had been smashed."

"Using what?"

"I can only say that a blunt, hard object with an even surface would have been used."

"Could it have been the butt of a handgun?"

"It could have been. The window was open, and I found some wet earth and debris in the study room and the front hall area, which suggested that the intruders had entered through the study window and had then gone through these rooms and up the front staircase. I believe that that was their exit route as well, since there was no debris on the back staircase."

"It was at the top of the front staircase that the body of Lady Anne was found?" asked Sparling.

"Yes, that is correct."

"You can assume that the jury have already seen the photographs, Detective Butler."

"Thank you, sir. She was lying as shown midway between the top of the stairs and a large bookcase, which was turned so as to disclose a hiding place behind."

"Again we have the photograph. Did you find anything in the hiding place?"

"No forensic evidence, sir, except that the carpet near the center of the bookcase was stained with urine. This was subsequently found to match a sample given by Thomas Robinson."

"Did you find any forensic evidence to assist with identification of the perpetrators of the crime?"

"A small amount of blood on the study windowsill from which a DNA profile has been obtained but not one that matches any suspect on the database. Otherwise there are only the intruders' footprints and the car tire marks in the roadway known as the lane."

"We'll return to them later. Are you able to say whether or not the intruders wore gloves?"

"They must have done, sir. There is no fingerprint evidence."

"Thank you, Detective Butler. Please continue."

"The electric lights in the upper corridor and on the back staircase were on, and so was the lamp beside the bed in the master bedroom. These were the only lights on in the house. The telephone by the bed had been unplugged, and the bedroom had been ransacked. However, none of the other rooms in the house showed any sign of having been searched. As I have already said, the grass and earth debris were only found in the study, the front hall, and in the master bedroom."

"What do you mean by the word *ransacked*, Officer?"

"The pictures were all removed from the walls and were lying on the floor. The glass in several of them was broken. The drawers in a high chest positioned between the two windows were all pulled out and their contents strewn over the floor."

"The curtains?"

"They were drawn, sir. There was also a safe over the fireplace, and it was empty."

"Had it been broken into?"

"It had been opened, sir. It's impossible to say whether the person who opened it already knew the combination or not."

"Thank you. Now let me ask you about the body of the deceased."

"I have already indicated her position, Mr. Sparling."

"Yes, I know. I still need you to describe what Lady Anne was wearing, however. For the record."

"She had on a white nightdress and no slippers. She was not wearing any underwear."

"What about jewelry?"

"She had on her wedding ring. Otherwise no jewelry at all. And no watch."

"And the injuries?"

"There were two bullet wounds. One to the right neck-and-shoulder area. The other to the side of the head."

"Anything else?"

"There was a small scratch on the left side of the deceased's neck."

"Thank you. Now, if we may turn to the exterior of the property. Can you assist us as to the intruders' route of entry?"

"Yes. It began raining shortly after nine P.M. that evening, and the intruders' footprints were preserved by the north gate and, to a certain extent, on the north lawn, which they crossed to reach the house."

"Upon which sides of the north gate did you find the footprints?"

"On both sides. There were two sets of prints, which enabled me to establish that there were two intruders."

"What about the north gate itself?"

"It is in fact a door in the wall. It was closed but unlocked. The footprints in the doorway showed quite clearly that the intruders came through the door rather than over the wall and left by the same route."

"Did you inspect the lock, Officer?"

"I did. There were no signs that it had been forced. It is my opinion that it was unlocked using a key. The lock is modern and resistant to being picked from the outside. Picking would have left some scratches inside the lock itself, and there were none found."

"I see," said Sparling. "Now, you referred earlier to tire marks in the lane. Please would you tell us about them."

"Yes, sir. They were distinctive. They were of a type usually fitted a Mercedes C-class vehicle, which had been turned at some speed in the roadway outside the north door before being driven away."

"Were any of the other exterior entrances to the property open?"

"Only the main gates at the front of the property. They had been left open by Thomas Robinson when he went over to Christopher Marsh's house."

"To raise the alarm?"

"Yes, sir."

"Good. Thank you, Detective Butler. If you wait there, my friend here may have some questions for you."

"Just a few, Officer," said Miles Lambert, getting slowly to his feet. "Just a few. We wouldn't want to keep you from your duties unnecessarily."

Butler did not respond. He'd sworn to tell the truth, and that was what he was going to do. However, that did not extend to exchanging unnecessary pleasantries with the other side's counsel. He kept his eyes fixed on a point just above Miles Lambert's head and waited.

"Ransacking, Officer. A strong word."

"Yes, sir."

"Implying that those who did the ransacking did not know what they were looking for?"

"I can't say, sir. I wasn't there."

"Yes, Detective Butler, that's right," interrupted the judge. "Mr. Lambert, stick to questions please. Don't make points."

"I'm sorry, my Lord. Let me ask you about the bed, Officer. Had it been slept in?"

"The one in the master bedroom?"

"Yes, the one in the room that was ransacked, as you put it a minute ago."

"I'd say it had been slept in. Yes."

"And what about the one in Thomas Robinson's room?"

"That had more the appearance of having been laid on rather than slept in."

"I see. Now the north door of the grounds. You believe it was un-locked using a key."

"Yes, sir. After close examination of the lock, I feel sure of it."

"Did you find the key?"

"Yes. It was hanging inside the side door of the house. With various other keys, sir."

"Thank you. Now, you told Mr. Sparling earlier that it began raining that evening shortly after nine P.M."

"Yes, sir. There was a thunderstorm. It rained for about half an hour."

"And the rain would have washed away any footprints that were there before?"

"Where, sir?"

"In the lane and by the north door and on the lawn."

"Yes, sir."

"And the weather before it started raining. Was it hot or cold? Can you assist us with that, Detective Butler?"

"It was a warm evening, sir. Quite warm, as I understand it."

"Understand it from whom?"

"From the meteorological office. There's a report in the case papers."

"Yes, I have it. Now, you've told us about the smashed window in the study, but what about the windows elsewhere in the house? Were any of them open?"

"The one in the boy's room. In Thomas Robinson's room. That was slightly open, but I don't recall any others."

"Thank you. Now, that's all I want to ask you about the night of the thirty-first of May. I do, however, want to move you forward a little more than a year. To last Wednesday evening in fact. The fifth of July."

"Yes, sir." Butler looked unperturbed. He'd expected this line of questioning.

"Now, it's right, isn't it, that you were called to the House of the Four Winds again last Wednesday? To act as a crime-scene officer."

"Yes, sir. I was called by Detective Sergeant Hearns, and I attended the scene at just before eight P.M."

"Who was there when you arrived?"

"Thomas Robinson and two officers from Carmouth Police Station. Sergeant Hearns was also present."

"You spoke to Thomas Robinson about what he said had happened?"

"Yes, sir."

"Tell us in outline what he told you, Officer. Just a thumbnail sketch."

"He said that he had heard a car pull up in the lane and that he had seen two men enter the property through the north gate and cross the lawn to the front door. That he had hidden in a bench in the hallway while the two men searched the house, and that they had left when they heard a police siren in the road outside. Thomas had called the police earlier when he first saw the men."

"So he said. Now, Officer, you naturally searched all the areas in the property where Thomas said the men had been?"

"Yes, sir."

"Looking for clues. For forensic evidence. For fingerprints, DNA, things like that?"

"That's right."

"And did you find anything like that, Officer? Anything like that at all?"

"No, sir, I didn't."

"On your visit to the house on July fifth you found nothing to suggest that anyone had gotten in. Isn't that right?"

"Nothing to suggest they had and nothing to suggest they hadn't."

"Well, let's examine that, shall we? Beginning on the outside and working in. Let's start with the lane. Did you find any tire marks there?"

"No, sir. But it didn't rain that night and it hadn't in fact for some time before, and so I would not have expected to find tread marks unless the car was driven or turned at speed."

"As it was on the night of the murder. But on this occasion Thomas Robinson told you that the intruders left because they heard the police siren. They ran from the house."

"That was my understanding, sir."

"I see. And the lack of rain explains the absence of footprints."

"That's right, sir. I wouldn't have expected to find footprints if the intruders kept to the path."

"Which they failed to do on the night of the murder."

"It was dark then, sir. On this occasion it was still light when I arrived."

"A strange time for breaking and entering."

"Don't answer that, Detective Butler," interrupted Judge Granger.
"Stop making points, Mr. Lambert. I've already told you once."

"I'm sorry, my Lord. Now, about the door in the wall, Officer. Was it
open or closed?"

"It was shut."

"Locked or unlocked?"

"Locked."

"No sign of the lock having been picked?"

"No, sir."

"And what about the front door of the house?"

"Thomas Robinson told us that the intruders left the front door
open when they ran off, sir."

"But he also told you that it had been locked earlier on and that the
intruders had used a key to gain entry. Yes?"

"Yes, sir."

"I see. Well, thank you, Detective Constable Butler. You've been
most helpful."

Miles Lambert sat down heavily and dabbed his cheeks with a crimson handkerchief. He felt pleased with his afternoon's work. Just as he
had hoped, Butler had had to give him exactly what he wanted. There
wasn't a scrap of real evidence that Thomas had had any visitors on that
Wednesday evening, other than Butler himself and his fellow police officers. All the prosecution had was Thomas's word for it, and Miles felt
confident that that wouldn't be worth much by the time he'd finished
with young Master Robinson. Miles rubbed his pudgy hands together.
He had a feeling that he was going to enjoy this case.

Sparling, however, looked even more morose than usual as he got to
his feet to reexamine his witness.

"Just one more question before you go, Detective Butler. You agreed
with Mr. Lambert that you searched all the areas in the property where
Thomas Robinson said that the men had been last Wednesday."

"That's right."

"Well, did you search upstairs?"

"Yes. I did."

"And did you find anything?"

"The bookcase hiding place was open, sir. Like it was on the night of the murder."

"Like it was on the night of the murder." Sparling repeated the words slowly and then smiled at the crime-scene officer.

"Thank you, Detective Butler. That's all. No more questions."

Sparling resumed his seat, and Detective Constable Butler was gone with the swing doors of the courtroom closing behind him.

Judge Granger's bright gray eyes did a circuit of the courtroom, taking in the jury, Greta, the barristers, and Miss Hooks, who was standing by the witness box waiting for orders.

"I think that's enough for today, gentlemen," he said. "We'll meet again at half past ten tomorrow."

"All rise," commanded Miss Hooks in her shrill voice, but Miles Lambert had not yet made it to his feet by the time Judge Granger had gathered his papers and walked out the door to the left of his chair.

Chapter 13

O N FRIDAY the court did not sit until half past eleven. The Indian
juror with the turban had had an unspecified problem that prevented him from getting to court on time, but he seemed entirely unperturbed as he took his place beside the Margaret Thatcher look-alike
in the front row. His expression remained just as inscrutable as the day
before. Mrs. Thatcher's, however, looked even fiercer.

A witness called Margaret Ball was the first to give evidence. She'd
traveled up to London from Flyte on the train, and it looked as if it was
the first time she'd ever left home. It was certainly the first time she'd
ever been in a courtroom. She peered about herself shortsightedly and
answered John Sparling's questions in an almost inaudible voice, which
soon brought an intervention from the judge.

"Speak up, Mrs. Ball. We all want to hear what you have to say. I
know it isn't easy, but do speak up."

The judge spoke kindly, but his urgings made Mrs. Ball unable to go
on at all and there had to be a short adjournment while Miss Hooks re-
vived the witness with several glasses of water and a tissue.

Eventually, with much prompting from Sparling, she got her evidence out. She was the mother of Edward Ball, who used to go to the
same school as Thomas Robinson: St. George's, Carmouth. She was
very happy that her Eddy had a nice boy like Thomas for a friend. On one
or two occasions Eddy had been to stay at Four Winds House, as she
called it, and yes, Thomas had also been to stay with them in Flyte.

She did remember an evening in late May of the previous year when Thomas came to stay. How could she forget it? That was the night that those crazy men killed poor Lady Anne. No one in Flyte had had a proper night's sleep ever since. It was terrible when you couldn't feel safe in your own bed.

It was Sir Peter's personal assistant who rang up to make the arrangement the day before. Sometime in the early afternoon. Mrs. Ball was sure of that. She'd never met the lady, but she had said who she was: Greta somebody. Wanted to know if Thomas could come and spend the night with them, and no, she didn't say anything about acting on Lady Anne's instructions. Mrs. Ball assumed she was. Naturally.

It was Jane Martin, Lady Anne's housekeeper, who dropped Thomas off. It would've been sometime between five and six. She couldn't be more precise. Jane was driving her car. One of those small foreign ones. A Renault or something like that.

Why did Thomas go home? Well, he got anxious when he heard that it was this Greta who had made the arrangement. Mrs. Ball had asked him about who she was. That was how the subject came up, and then Thomas rang his mother and there was no answer, even though he let it ring for ages and ages. He seemed upset, and so Mrs. Ball had offered to run him home. She couldn't say when they got there except that it was quite a bit after eight o'clock, as that was when her husband called to say he would be late coming home.

She left Thomas at the front gates, and yes, she knows she shouldn't have done. There's not a day gone by since that she hasn't thought about it. It's just Thomas was so insistent. Said his mother was definitely at home but maybe she'd unplugged the phone in her bedroom or something like that.

"Were there any lights on in the house when you dropped Thomas off?" asked Miles Lambert, getting to his feet to begin his cross-examination and bestowing on Mrs. Ball one of his sweetest smiles.

"I don't think so. I didn't really look, to be honest."

"And you can't be sure of the time except that it was after eight o'clock?"

"When my husband called. That's right."

"Did he call before or after Thomas rang his mother?"

"Oh, I don't know. It's a long time ago now."

"That's all right, Mrs. Ball. It's understandable. You can't remember all the details, but you'll be able to help me with this. The drive from your home to the House of the Four Winds takes how long?"

"About ten or fifteen minutes. Longer after dark. I drive slower then."

"Was it dark when you drove Thomas home?"

"No. But the light was going."

"Was it raining?"

"No, I don't think so."

"On the drive back?"

"No."

"Good, now just one more question about that evening, Mrs. Ball. How long would you say it was between Thomas calling his mother and you getting in the car to take him home?"

"Oh, I don't know. It's difficult to remember."

"Try, Mrs. Ball. Please try."

"Well, I remember we talked about it. About why she wasn't answering. Speculating a bit. And I don't know; maybe it was then that my husband called."

"At eight o'clock."

"Yes."

"So there might've been a good ten or fifteen minutes between Thomas calling his mother and leaving in the car?"

Mrs. Ball didn't answer. She looked uncertain.

"Could that be possible, Mrs. Ball? We need your answer."

"Yes, I expect so."

"Thank you, Mrs. Ball. That's all."

=

"You're sure about these late-evening walks that Lady Anne used to take, Greta?" asked Miles Lambert.

The judge had given the jurors a coffee break, and Miles and Greta were closeted in an interview room discussing the evidence.

"Yes, she'd always go down to the beach. With the dog. It was like a ritual."

"The dog was dead, though."

"Dogs," corrected Greta.

"Sorry, yes I forgot," said Miles. "Place was a canine disaster area. No doubt we'll be hearing about that in a minute from Mrs. Martin."

"Shriveled-up old shrew," said Greta.

"Yes, but let's hope she helps us with these walks. I'll try and take her by surprise. The last witness set it up nicely, I think. Probably about eight-thirty that Thomas returned home. Butler said it didn't start raining until after nine, and Mrs. Ball doesn't remember any rain."

"What's so good about him getting back then?" asked Greta. Miles's musings often frustrated her when she didn't know what he was getting at.

"It gives us the time for Lady Anne to go for a walk in the beautiful warm evening. Down to the beach and back."

"And forget to lock the north door on her return," added Greta excitedly. Now she was seeing where Miles was going.

"Yes," said Miles. "And good Mrs. Ball has been generous enough to allow us at least thirty minutes between Thomas's phone call and his arrival back at the house. Consistent with what I shall tell the jury. She didn't answer the phone not because it was unplugged but because she was out walking, setting off soon after you and Peter left the house at seven-thirty. Detective Butler has already told us it was a warm evening before it rained, which explains incidentally why you opened the study window, Greta, and then forgot to close it before you left. If Thomas opened his bedroom window when he got back, then it makes sense for you to have opened the window in the study three hours earlier.

"So anyway, Lady Anne walks down to the beach to admire the waves, and then, while her son's debating with the Ball family about what to do, she comes back through the north gate and forgets to lock it behind her. She crosses the lawn to the house and hangs up the key by the side door. Then she goes up to bed, takes her sleeping tablet, unplugs the telephone so that she won't be woken up and is fast asleep by the time Mrs. Ball arrives outside the front gates. Half an hour later the rain starts and washes away all her footprints."

Miles finished his long speech and blew his nose on a bright yellow handkerchief. He looked very pleased with himself.

"What about the phone call that I made to arrange Thomas's visit?" asked Greta. "Isn't that a problem?"

"No, *you* can explain that when the time comes. Lady Anne asked you to ring up. No reason you should have had to spell it out to Mrs.

Ball. No, so far so good, my dear. Let's see how we do with Mrs. Martin. What did you call her?"

"A shriveled-up old shrew," said Greta, emphasizing each word.

"Well, let's see if I can tame her," said Miles, smiling.

=

Jane Martin had dressed in black for her day in court, a simple black dress above a pair of sensible patent leather shoes. Her only concession to female vanity was an ebony comb, which kept her almost white hair in place above the nape of her neck.

Miles Lambert thought that she must be over seventy, but she was strikingly well preserved for her age. It was as if she had spent many years growing into her angular face and now wore it comfortably, with no attempt to hide the multitude of tiny lines that crisscrossed its surface. She didn't look shriveled-up at all, he thought. As to whether she was a shrew, only time would tell.

She chose to sit down to give her evidence with her small bony hands folded over the clasp of her black leather handbag, but this did nothing to diminish the imposing presence that she brought with her into the courtroom. As the morning wore on, Miles Lambert was struck more and more by the defiance of the old housekeeper, her refusal to be intimidated by either the court or its officials. She sat with her small, hard chin jutting forward and made sure that she always gave as good as she got.

Miles Lambert was secretly rather impressed with Mrs. Martin. She was not what he had expected. There was something almost admirable about her, and he wondered to himself about whether he should be benevolent or aggressive in his cross-examination. Benevolence might be interpreted by the jury as weakness, but aggression might lose their sympathy. There was still plenty of time, however, for Miles to study the Robinsons' housekeeper before he had to ask her any questions. John Sparling had plenty of his own to ask this witness.

"How long have you known the defendant?" he asked once Mrs. Martin had taken the oath and given her name.

"About three years. Maybe a little longer."

"How would you describe the relationship between your former employer, Lady Anne Robinson, and the defendant during that period?"

"Reasonable at first but then it got worse. By the end I'd say that they hated each other."

"What led you to form that view?"

"That they hated each other?"

"Yes."

"It was what happened when the little dog died. What they both said."

"I see, Mrs. Martin. Now I think we're going to need some background here. Whose dog are we talking about?"

"Thomas's. My Lady gave her to him for his fifteenth birthday just after they got back from London. The old Labrador, Barton, died at the beginning of April, and Thomas was heartbroken. Mattie was supposed to cheer him up."

"Mattie being the new dog?"

"That's right. She was a sweet little thing. A little Highland terrier with a wet, black nose. Always getting into things. Running about."

"Thank you, Mrs. Martin. We're not going to need a detailed description of the dog." Sparling was eager to get to the meat of the story.

"Thank *you,* sir, but I think we are," said the housekeeper tartly, causing almost everybody in the court except Sparling and the juror who looked like Mrs. Thatcher to burst out laughing.

"It was Mattie's running about that caused the problem," she added.

"I see," said Sparling with a half smile. "Please explain." It had only taken him a moment to swallow his irritation and decide to let Mrs. Martin tell it her own way. He knew better than to cross swords with his own witness, particularly when she was as vital to his cause as this one.

"Mattie had to be kept in for the first couple of weeks until she was trained. If she went out on the grounds, it had to be on a leash. Everyone had to remember to check that she was shut up before they went outside.

"Well, Sir Peter and Greta, the defendant that is, hadn't been down to Flyte for over a month. They usually came together, and my Lady was very disappointed when Sir Peter did not make it down for Thomas's birthday on April 30. Anyway, she rang him up, and he agreed to come on the following weekend."

"How long had Mattie been there then?" asked Sparling.

"Just over a week. Well, they both came down late on the Friday evening. Everyone had gone to bed, and the little dog was sleeping on Thomas's bed. The next morning Sir Peter got up early and went off in his car."

"How do you know that?" asked the judge.

"I know it because I saw him come back in it. I was cleaning the front windows in the drawing room, and I heard him open the gates and drive up. Mattie must have heard him too because she was at the front door making her normal commotion: leaping up, barking, scratching and the like. Next thing I knew, Greta was at the front door too and had let the little thing out. I didn't have time to tell her not to. Well, Sir Peter couldn't have stopped the dog even if he'd tried. She was going faster than a greyhound. Down the steps and out the gates. It was just bad luck that there was a car coming. They drive so fast on that road, and the little dog didn't have a chance."

Mrs. Martin stopped to open her handbag and produced a white lace handkerchief with which she dabbed at her eyes, although there was no evidence of any tears there. The jury looked unanimously appalled.

"Mr. Sparling," said the judge in an authoritative voice. "I am a little concerned and I am sure that Mr. Lambert is too. The defendant is not charged with murdering a Highland terrier, is she?"

"No, my Lord."

"And there is in fact no evidence as I understand it to suggest that she knew that she would be endangering the dog's life by letting her out the front door. That's not your case, is it, Mr. Sparling?"

"No, it isn't, my Lord. Not at all."

"Good. Well then, I understand your wish to allow Mrs. Martin to tell things her own way, but please ensure that it's done properly."

"Yes, my Lord. Now, Mrs. Martin, where had the defendant come from?"

"She'd been in the dining room having her breakfast. On the other side of the hall from me."

"Thank you. What happened next?"

"Sir Peter brought the dog up to the house. She was obviously dead, poor little thing. He laid her out on the settle in the hallway."

"What settle is that, Mrs. Martin?"

"It's like an old black bench that opens up. There are carvings on the front. It's been in the house for as long as I have."

"I see. Please carry on."

"Well, that was when Tom came down. He was in a terrible state. He'd only had the little dog for just over a week, and to see it all dead like that was horrible for him. I remember him touching her side and then he had blood on his hand. It'd have been better in a way if Sir Peter hadn't brought her in, but I don't know what else he was supposed to do.

"Anyway, when Tom realized what had happened, that Greta had let the dog out, he really lost his temper."

"Who told him?" asked Sparling.

"I think I did. He asked and I told him."

"I see. So what did Thomas do when he lost his temper, Mrs. Martin?"

"He went for her. Greta, I mean. I don't know if he hit her or not because it all happened so quick, but I know that she pushed him back."

"Pushed him where?"

"In the chest. With both hands. He fell back onto the settle and knocked the little dog off it onto the floor. The whole thing was really horrible. There was a lot of crying and shouting."

"Who by?"

"Tom first of all, and then everyone joined in. My Lady was at the top of the stairs. I could see her from where I was in the doorway of the drawing room, and when Greta pushed Tom back onto the settle, she, my Lady that is, she got really angry. I'd never seen her like that before, and I'd been with her since she was just a girl."

"What did she do?"

"She came rushing down the stairs like the house was on fire, shouting to leave her boy alone, and then she gave Greta a piece of her mind. Quite right too, if you ask me."

"Mr. Sparling didn't, Mrs. Martin," said the judge firmly. "Please do not give us your opinion of how people behaved. Just tell us what happened."

Mrs. Martin turned away from the judge even before he'd finished speaking to her and pursed her pale lips. There was a defiant look in her eyes, a determination to stand her ground.

"Please tell us what Lady Anne said to the defendant," asked Sparling, injecting a placatory tone into his voice.

"She told her she was common and that she didn't belong in the house."

"Did she swear?"

"Who?"

"Lady Anne. Did she use abusive language to the defendant?"

"My Lady never used foul language. Never. Not like that Greta."

"We'll come on to that in a moment, Mrs. Martin, but we do need you to tell us everything in the right order. Now, you've told us what Lady Anne said to the defendant. What happened next?"

"Well, that was when Sir Peter got involved. He got between my Lady and the defendant, and he was telling my Lady not to talk to Greta that way. That she was being unfair. I mean, I couldn't believe it. He was attacking his wife when he should have been defending her."

"Mrs. Martin," said the judge. "I won't warn you again."

Again the housekeeper pursed her lips and looked defiant, but this time she didn't need to be asked to continue.

"Well, that's what my Lady told him, so it's not just my opinion. And what did Sir Peter do? He turned round and walked out the front door. We didn't see him for more than an hour after that. I don't know where he went."

"What about everyone else in the hallway? What did they do?" asked Sparling.

"My Lady told Greta a few other home truths."

"What did she say, Mrs. Martin?" asked Sparling when the housekeeper did not elaborate.

"I can't remember everything, but I know my Lady said that Greta had turned her husband against her and given Thomas bad ideas. She told her she was poisonous. That was the word she used. Poisonous like a snake."

"I see. Did the defendant respond, say anything herself?"

"No, it was funny, that. She didn't say anything at all. Not until my Lady had gone off with Thomas and she thought she was alone."

"Why did she think that?"

"Because I'd stepped back into the drawing room when all the fighting and shouting started. It wasn't my place to be standing there in the middle of all that."

"But you heard something that the defendant said after the others had gone?"

"Yes. She was still in the hall and she said . . ."

Mrs. Martin stopped in midsentence, hesitated and then looked up at the judge.

"Do you want me to say all the words?" she asked. "She used disgusting foul language, like I've said before."

"Yes, Mrs. Martin," replied the judge. "All the words please."

"Well, she called my Lady 'a fucking stuck-up bitch,' and then she said, 'You've fucking had it now, Mrs. Posh. Just you wait and see.' Those were her exact words. And she spoke in this hard, coarse accent that I'd never heard her use before. It was like she was talking through her teeth. Like her true character was coming through."

"Mrs. Martin, I have had to remind you over and over again to tell us what you saw and heard and not what you thought about what you saw and heard," said the judge. "Your refusal to abide by my instructions is soon going to have a prejudicial effect on this trial. I am going to adjourn now slightly earlier than I had intended for lunch so that you can think about what I have said, and when we resume I will want your assurance that you will do as I have asked. Very well. We will meet again at two o'clock."

Judge Granger was out of the courtroom well before Mrs. Martin had had any chance to formulate a reply, even if she had wished to do so.

Chapter 14

GRETA LEFT the courthouse by a side exit and walked down to Blackfriars Pier. Peter was at an unavoidable meeting and she was glad to be alone, even though it was her husband that she was thinking about as she stared into the gray water lapping against the platform where she sat. It wasn't the sea, but the river helped her remember that morning the previous summer when she had followed her employer, as he then was, down to the beach at Flyte.

She'd run out of the front door wanting to put as much space as possible between herself and the dead dog lying on the floor in the hall. She must have gone past that sour old shrew Jane Martin, in the drawing room, without knowing she was there.

Outside she'd turned to her right—God knows why!—and caught sight of him just as he was going through the north door into the lane. The same door that Miles was getting himself so worked up about. And then she'd followed him. Again she hadn't any idea why. She just did. Through the door and down the lane to the beach. She'd come up to him where he stood almost at the water's edge skimming stones into the sea.

He looked so sad and out of place, and when he spoke, his voice came out all tangled up and choked like it belonged to someone else. Not Peter at all.

"I'm sorry about what she said, Greta. I really am. She should never have said that to you."

"It's all right. I don't mind. I'll live." She was nervous and said the first words that came into her head.

"I don't know what's gone wrong with this family," he said after a while. "It's something about this place. I've never been happy here and I never will be. It's so bloody lonely and desolate, and this sea's so cruel. Do you remember that dead fisherman lying on the ground down at the harbor? And that dog today?"

"It's a coincidence."

"No, you belong here or you don't. That's what she said to you, wasn't it? But she could just as well have been talking about me. My life is in the city with things I can understand, things I can control. This place defeats me."

"Nothing defeats you, Peter. Nothing." She said it like it was a statement of belief, an article of faith.

"But you're wrong," he replied just as certainly. "This house does, and yet Annie loves it so much. More than anything else in the world, I think, except Thomas. It's in her blood I suppose. I have tried, God knows I've tried to make it work. Long walks on the marsh, sailing on the river, shivering down by the harbor, but every time I come here I feel more alien with my city suit and my city brain. Look at me today. I had to go into Flyte as soon as I woke up to get the newspapers. Came back and killed the bloody dog."

"It's just bad luck, Peter, that's all," said Greta soothingly.

"No, it's more than that. I don't belong here. I guess that's why I want Thomas to go away to school, because I don't feel like he's my son as long as he's living here."

"He's a good boy. He's just a little frightened of you."

"I know. You're always so perceptive, Greta. That's what I like about you. You understand me. Nobody else seems to."

"You can count on me, Peter. You know that."

Peter did not reply, and Greta didn't know if he had heard her own soft response above the noise of the breaking waves. However, she said no more. Peter's silence commanded her own, and after a little while she left him standing by the sea and walked back up the lane to the house to face his family.

Overhead the Suffolk sky had been gray and overcast. Just like today, thought Greta as she turned to walk away from the river.

Crossing Fleet Street on her way back to the court, Greta put a hand up to her face to brush away the rain that was now falling fast. But there were tears in her eyes too. She was crying not for herself but for Peter and the fractured soul that he had first begun to reveal to her on that beach the year before. She thought of it as a precious gift that this intensely private man should have opened himself up to her. And now he depended on her completely. Anne was gone and Thomas had turned on his father like a viper. She had to win this crazy trial. For Peter's sake as much as for her own.

Greta's life had not been easy, and Peter's need for her had given her a sense of purpose that she had never felt before. It made her feel powerful and whole, and it filled her with determination. Greta clenched her fists and held her head up high as she walked past the reporters into the courtroom and took her place in the dock.

=

Less than five minutes later, the old housekeeper was back in the witness box with her handbag on her knees.

"Are you ready to proceed, Mrs. Martin?" asked the judge, looking down at her from his high chair.

"I am."

"On the basis that I made clear to you before lunch?"

Mrs. Martin replied with a curt nod.

She won't keep those lips buttoned for long, thought Miles Lambert. Not if I have anything to do with it.

But John Sparling had a long way to go yet.

"Now, Mrs. Martin, I want to move on to the day of the murder; the thirty-first of May last year. Where were you on that afternoon?"

"I was at the house until just after five o'clock, when I left with Thomas in my car."

"Where were you going?"

"To my sister's in Woodbridge. I often go there on a Monday evening and stay the night. Tuesday's my day off."

"Was Thomas going there too?"

"No. I dropped him off at the house of a friend of his in Flyte. He was going to stay the night there."

"Did you have anything to do with the making of that arrangement?"

"No. Greta told me that Mrs. Ball, the mother of Thomas's friend, had rung her up and invited Thomas. I offered to give him a lift."

"Did you discuss the arrangement with Lady Anne?"

"No. I assumed she knew about it, obviously."

"What did you do before you left the house with Thomas?"

"What I always do. I checked the doors and windows to see that everything was secure."

"Which doors?"

"The doors of the house and the door in the north wall as well. I also checked the east gate, the one above the beach, and then I drove out through the west gate and locked it after me."

"That leaves the door in the south wall. What about that?"

"No, it's hardly ever used. There's Lady Anne's roses growing over it. I never check the south door."

"I see. Now tell us about the door in the north wall."

"I already did. I locked it just before I left and I put the key in the back passage, just like I always do. When I went, all the doors in the house were locked except the front door. I left that open."

"What about the windows?"

"They were all shut. Upstairs and downstairs. Except for the drawing room where my Lady and Sir Peter were."

"Where was the defendant?"

"In the study, working on her computer."

"What about the windows in the study?"

"Shut."

"Moving on, Mrs. Martin, can you tell us what time you arrived at the Balls' house?"

"Sometime before five-thirty. I remember Thomas was complaining all the way over there about how he didn't want to go. My Lady had got one of her headaches, and I think he wanted to stay home with her."

"But you said that you had left Lady Anne with Sir Peter in the drawing room?"

"That's right. She was lying on the sofa. She used to do that sometimes rather than go up to bed, and I suppose she wanted to have the time with Sir Peter before he left."

"When was he leaving?"

"Later in the evening. With Greta. He had to get back to London for some business meeting early the next day."

"Thank you, Mrs. Martin. I want to move on to a different subject now. You were familiar with Lady Anne's jewels?"

"Yes, I was. I looked after the jewelry for thirty years. I knew every stone in every necklace, and now they're all gone. Emeralds, rubies, and diamonds. Beautiful things."

The housekeeper's hard voice softened as she remembered the jewels, and Miles Lambert had a sudden picture of the old lady passing the bracelets and necklaces through her bony fingers, licking her pale lips as the glittering stones went by.

"And you have prepared this list of the items that were taken from the safe in Lady Anne's bedroom on the night of her murder."

Sparling handed a document to Miss Hooks, who handed it on to the witness. The housekeeper did not read it immediately but instead opened her handbag and took out a pair of small, black-framed reading glasses. After she had put them on, she snapped the spectacle case shut and then snapped the clasp of the handbag as well. Snap, snap. Miles thought the old lady looked very pleased with the two uncompromising noises, as she held the jewelry list close to her distrustful nose and passed her bony index finger down its list of contents.

"Everything there?" asked John Sparling a little impatiently.

"Yes, that's my list," said Mrs. Martin decisively. "Lovely things they were. I remember my Lady wearing the ruby necklace when she first came out. It was a ball at St. James's Palace, and she looked so beautiful. Her tawny brown hair done up high and diamond drops in her ears—"

"Thank you, Mrs. Martin," interrupted Sparling. "I don't mean to be rude but we must press on. It's an agreed list, my Lord, and there are copies for the jury with an insurer's statement of valuation attached. You will see that the net value of the pieces stolen is in excess of two million pounds."

"Yes, very well, Mr. Sparling," said Judge Granger, ignoring the half-suppressed gasps of astonishment that the figure had elicited from several of the jurors. "The jury can have these."

Mrs. Martin kept her glasses on while Miss Hooks distributed the copy documents to the jury. She stared at John Sparling over her oval lenses as if seeing him properly for the first time and registering just how thoroughly nasty a specimen of humanity he was. She was clearly not about to forget the rudeness of his most recent interruption.

Sparling, however, was undeterred.

"It's also agreed that none of the items on this list have been recovered, with one exception," he went on. "That is this gold locket, prosecution exhibit number thirteen: I'd like you to have a look at that now, Mrs. Martin, please. Do you recognize it?"

"Yes, Sir Peter gave that to my Lady after their wedding. There's a picture of them both inside it."

"When did you last see that locket, Mrs. Martin?"

"Well, I can't be absolutely sure, but I think that my Lady was wearing it on the day she died. She had on a blouse and so I couldn't see the locket, but I remember noticing the gold chain on her neck when we were eating lunch. She was very fond of the locket. She used to wear it a lot."

"Thank you, Mrs. Martin. That's all I want to ask you."

Miles Lambert got to his feet, pulled his gown around his shoulders and smiled at his adversary. Mrs. Martin swiveled her head toward him in response with a movement that made Miles think of a tank commander redirecting his gun as a new enemy came into view.

"The first thing I want to ask you, Mrs. Martin, is about your late employer's walking habits."

"What?"

"Not what but where and when is my question. She liked to walk, did she not?"

"Yes, she did. Every day she'd go for a walk. Nothing wrong with that." The housekeeper didn't like questions like this; she didn't know where they were going.

"Nothing wrong at all, far from it," said Miles, who walked as little as he possibly could in spite of his doctor's orders to the contrary. "Walking must be very enjoyable in a beautiful place like the coast of Suffolk," he went on musingly. "Lady Anne must have loved going out on warm summer evenings. Isn't that right, Mrs. Martin?"

"I suppose so."

"And Lady Anne would usually go down to the beach to walk, would she not?"

"That's right."

"Through the north door and down the lane. I expect that sometimes she may have forgotten to lock the door when she came back in. Isn't that possible, Mrs. Martin? On particularly beautiful evenings."

"Oh, I see what you're up to. You're trying to say my Lady left the door unlocked for those men to come through. Well, you can forget it; she didn't."

"But you don't know, do you, Mrs. Martin? You'd already left. At just after five o'clock. That's what you told Mr. Sparling."

Miles spoke quickly, having thrown off his lazy air like an unwanted mask, and then moved on giving the housekeeper no time to respond.

"I want to go back to what you were telling us about before lunch, Mrs. Martin. To the events following the death of that unfortunate dog. Now, let's be quite clear. You're not saying that my client knew that the dog had to be kept in."

"I don't know one way or the other. I didn't tell her about it. I had as little conversation with her as I could."

"Mr. Lambert, we've already been over this," said the judge.

"Yes, my Lord. I just wanted to get things clear. Now you say that Thomas went for my client. That must mean that she was only doing the minimum to defend herself when she pushed him back."

"He was just a boy. She shouldn't have touched him."

"But what choice did she have if he was attacking her?"

The housekeeper transferred her attention from Miles Lambert to the ceiling but didn't otherwise respond.

"Well, I shall assume that you don't have an answer for that, Mrs. Martin. Perhaps you will agree, however, that my client showed remarkable restraint when Lady Anne came downstairs and attacked her. She'd done nothing wrong, after all."

"She had. She'd got the little dog killed and then afterward she said those things behind my Lady's back that made my hair stand on end. I don't call that restraint."

"She didn't, Mrs. Martin. She didn't say those things."

"She did. As God is my witness, she did."

Mrs. Martin half shouted her answer with her hands now gripping the wooden edge of the witness box in front of her. The black leather handbag had fallen with a thud to the floor.

Miles Lambert smiled.

"You believe my client committed this offense, don't you, Mrs. Martin?"

The old lady had her eyes fixed on the defense barrister now. She nodded once.

"You hate her for it, don't you?"

"I do."

"You've always hated her, haven't you?"

"No, I hate her because of what she did."

"She acted superior to you, didn't she? You'd been the housekeeper all those years, and then she came down and treated you like a servant. That made you angry, didn't it?"

"No, it didn't surprise me. She was just like a lot of these young people nowadays. They aren't brought up to respect their elders like we were."

"Badly brought up and putting on airs. Is that right, Mrs. Martin?"

"If you say so," said the old lady. She was visibly trying to keep her emotions in check.

"It's not what I say; it's what you say that matters. You didn't like the way she tried to get Thomas away from you either, did you?"

"He saw through her in the end. It just took him a bit longer."

"You hated her from the first," pressed Miles, allowing the witness no time to think, and this time the old lady could no longer resist his challenge.

"She's poison!" she shouted.

"You want her convicted, don't you?"

"I want justice. For my Lady. For Thomas."

"At any cost. You'd do anything to get what you want, wouldn't you, Mrs. Martin?"

"I don't know what you're talking about."

"Yes you do. I'm talking about giving false evidence. My client never said, 'You've fucking had it now, Mrs. Posh.' She never said that."

"Yes she did. She wouldn't have done if she'd known I was there, but she didn't. More fool her."

The old lady positively spat these last words out at Miles, who responded with one of his most pleasant smiles.

"Well, Mrs. Martin, I'm sorry to see that you're getting so upset. Let's move on a bit and see if we can shed any more light on what happened. Now, where did my client go after this little speech that you say she gave?"

"Out the front door. Same way Sir Peter had gone."

"I see. And when and where did you see her again?"

"She was in the study a bit later on."

"How much later on?"

"Later on in the morning. I don't know more than that. She must have come in through the side door. I was in the kitchen on the other side of the hall when I noticed she was back."

"How did you come to notice my client's presence in the study, Mrs. Martin?"

"Because my Lady went in there to talk to her. She had Thomas with her, and she wanted to make things up. She was like that, my Lady was: too good for the rest of us, but she should never have done it if you ask me. She should have left that Greta to pack up and be off. That's what she should have done."

"I see. And did you offer your Lady this advice, Mrs. Martin?"

"No, of course I didn't. It wouldn't have been my place. I told her what that Greta had said, though."

"In the hallway?"

"That's right."

"And this would have been before Lady Anne went into the study to make things up with my client."

"It would."

"Isn't that rather unlikely, Mrs. Martin?"

"What?"

"You tell Lady Anne that my client has just called her a 'fucking stuck-up bitch' behind her back and Lady Anne goes straight into the study to make things up with her. It doesn't make much sense, does it?"

"You didn't know my Lady."

"It doesn't make sense because it's not true, is it, Mrs. Martin? You're lying again."

The old housekeeper went white with anger, but instead of venting it on Miles, she turned round in her seat and looked up at the judge.

"Listen, Your Lordship or whatever you call yourself, I want you to stop him talking to me like that," she said. "You've had a go at me; now you deal with him."

"Mrs. Martin, I'm sorry if you feel that Mr. Lambert is being rude to you because I don't think that's his intention," said the judge. "He's got to put his case to you and examine your evidence, and that's what he's doing. Now please answer his questions."

"Thank you, my Lord," said Miles. "Now, Mrs. Martin, I want to ask you about what happened in the study. Did you hear everything that was said?"

"I did."

"You must have gone out into the hallway then."

"I may have done."

"To listen. Well, I'm sure that that was very natural. You say that Lady Anne went in to make things up. Does that mean that she apologized to my client?"

"She did. I couldn't believe it. It was that Greta who should have been doing the apologizing. Down on her knees, she should have been."

"And did my client accept Lady Anne's apology?"

"Of course she did. She must have thought it was her lucky day. She didn't want to have to leave."

"And so they made up their quarrel and they were friends. Yes?"

"No, they most certainly weren't. My Lady apologized because she thought it was right, not because she liked Greta. She didn't like her any more than I did. And Greta, she hated my Lady. I know she did. I saw the way she used to look at her, *and* I heard what she said in the hall."

"Well, we've already dealt with that, Mrs. Martin," said Miles. "Can you move on now and tell us about Thomas?"

"What about him?"

"Did he and Greta have any conversation in the study?"

"Oh, yes. She was saying how sorry she was about letting the dog out and how she wished she'd known. She probably was sorry. She was always after Thomas. My Lady always felt like Greta wanted to take him away from her. Not that there was much chance of that."

"And how did Thomas react to Greta saying she was sorry?"

"He was very upset, but he didn't seem so angry with her as he was before. He always liked Greta, until he found out what sort of person she really was. Teenagers can be blind like that sometimes."

"We'll let the jury be the judge of that," said Miles, turning to a new page in his notes. "I want to talk to you about this locket now. Lady Anne was very fond of it, was she not?"

"Yes, it was one of her favorite things."

"And so you would agree with me that she took it to London with her when she went up for the Chelsea Flower Show on the Thursday before she died."

"She may have done."

"You helped her pack, didn't you?"

"Yes."

"And the locket was in the suitcase?"

The old lady didn't answer.

"Come on, Mrs. Martin. Lady Anne took jewelry with her to London, didn't she? You helped her choose it, didn't you?"

"Yes."

"And the locket was one of the pieces she took."

Again no answer.

"Wasn't it, Mrs. Martin?" Miles spoke louder this time, with more urgency in his voice, and the housekeeper finally gave way.

"Yes, she took it but she brought it back too."

"How do you know?"

"Because I saw it on her neck the day she died. I said that already."

"You saw the top of a gold chain. That could have been the gold chain to some other piece of jewelry."

"I don't think so."

"And you've never mentioned this bit of gold before today, have you? It's not in your statement."

"I didn't know it was important when I made the statement. That was before Tom found the locket."

"You've never made a statement since he found it, though, have you? And so we can no doubt safely assume that you've never told the police about it."

"I didn't know I had to."

"The locket was found more than nine months ago, Mrs. Martin. You've had all that time to come forward and say something, and yet you wait until today to do so. Isn't that because you only thought of it recently? On one of those long evenings that you've been spending with Thomas Robinson down on the coast with nothing to do except talk about this trial."

"I've got plenty to do. I've been running that house single-handed since Lady Anne died."

"Have you talked to Thomas about the locket, Mrs. Martin?"

"I may have done."

"Of course you have, and that's why you've come up with this story, isn't it? Because he's told you how important it is that somebody else should say that they saw the locket on Lady Anne after she came back from London. Isn't that right, Mrs. Martin?"

"I don't know what you're talking about."

"You don't know what I'm talking about. I see. Well, let me ask you a general question about the jewelry. Lady Anne liked talking about her collection, didn't she?"

"She was proud of it, yes."

"And she made no secret of the fact that she kept the jewels in the house, did she? It was well known among people who knew her, wasn't it?"

"It was well known to her," said the old lady, pointing toward the dock. "Greta knew. That's why she sent those men."

"All right, Mrs. Martin. Let's talk about that. Let's move on to the day of the murder. You say that my client told you that Mrs. Ball had invited Thomas for the night."

"That's right."

"When did she tell you this?"

"The day before, I think—the Sunday, unless it was the morning of the day it happened. I'm not sure."

"You're not sure. And do you remember where you were when this conversation took place?"

"No, I don't. It's more than a year ago now."

"That's right. You don't remember where or when you spoke to my client, so how can you be so sure of what she said?"

"I know what she said."

"But why should you remember it, Mrs. Martin? Surely it wasn't the issue of who came up with the idea of Thomas going to Edward's that would have been significant to you. What was important was that you could give Thomas a lift."

"So who made the arrangement if it wasn't Mrs. Ball?" asked the housekeeper, trying to turn the tables on the defense barrister.

"Lady Anne asked Greta to ring up Mrs. Ball. Greta didn't tell you that because she had no reason to. She simply told you about the ar-rangement."

"My Lady would never have asked Greta to do that. She'd have asked me."

"But you were out on the Sunday afternoon, weren't you, Mrs. Mar-tin? Out and inaccessible."

"What's Sunday afternoon got to do with it?"

"Because that's when the call was made. Mrs. Ball has told us that."
Miles's tone suggested that he felt he had won this particular argument.

"Let's go on to Monday afternoon. You say you checked all the doors
and windows before you left."

"All except the door in the south wall."

"It's the one in the north wall that concerns me. Are you quite sure
that it was locked?"

"Positive. I remember walking across the lawn and turning the key in
the lock."

"I see. And what about the windows?"

"All shut except for the ones in the drawing room."

"And that would include the window in Thomas's bedroom?"

"Yes. All of them."

"It was a warm afternoon, wasn't it, Mrs. Martin? That's why Sir
Peter and Lady Anne had the window open in the drawing room."

"I expect so. It was a summer's day."

"Yes. Now, one last question about that day, Mrs. Martin. We know
that Lady Anne took a sleeping tablet in the evening. It was normal, was
it not, for her to do this?"

"Yes. She always had trouble sleeping, poor love. Ever since she was
a girl."

"Thank you. Now finally, Mrs. Martin, I want to ask you about what
happened at the House of the Four Winds nine days ago. On the evening of Wednesday July fifth, to be precise."

"What about it?" The old lady suddenly looked suspicious and distrustful.

"You went out at about six o'clock to the Women's Institute meeting
in Flyte. Is that right?"

"Yes. About that time."

"Before you left, you checked the doors and gates, I expect. All except the one in the south wall."

"I did."

"And the door in the north wall, was it locked?"

"It was."

"You're as sure about that as you are about it being locked on the
night of the murder?"

"I am."

"What about the doors of the house? Were they also locked?"

"Yes, they were. Tom had the keys if he wanted to open them."

"And when you came back from the Women's Institute, there were policemen in the house?"

"Yes, there were four of them. Looking in everything, turning the place upside down. Those men had come again. That's what Tom told me."

"Ah, yes, unless of course he was making it up."

Miles Lambert sat down suddenly, leaving the old housekeeper high and dry in the witness box.

Chapter 15

===========

"HOW WAS IT, honey?" asked Peter.

He was sitting in the back of the Daimler with Greta. John the chauffeur was driving them home from court. London went by smoothly outside the car's black tinted windows.

"It was good, I suppose," she replied. Her voice was tired and came as if from far away, even though she was sitting right beside her husband, leaning against his shoulder. It was like the voice of a soldier who'd come back from the front, he thought: shell-shocked.

Peter felt the anger rising in him again like it had a thousand times before, invading his throat, making his temples throb. He couldn't get used to the unfairness, the injustice, and he fought for self-control. He didn't speak until he had unclenched his fists and got sure of his voice again. Peace and calm were what his wife needed now.

"Who were the witnesses today?" he asked.

"There was a policeman and then Mrs. Ball from Flyte and Jane Martin. It's incredible how that woman hates me. It's like she won't be satisfied until she sees me hanging from a tree. A tall tree."

"Don't talk like that."

"She kept pointing at me. Looking at me. Saying I was poison. Things like that."

"I should have dismissed her ages ago. It's just I didn't know what to do about Thomas."

"It's not just her. I feel like some caged animal in there. A caged animal who everyone's got a license to mistreat."

"I just wish I could be there with you. Perhaps I should talk to Miles."

"No," said Greta, and her voice was suddenly firm. "I don't want you to hear those things they're saying, and we must do what Miles says. He's good, you know. He made Aunt Jane look just like the nasty bit of work she is."

"Well, that's something," said Peter. He took her delicate hand in his and gently stroked the back of it with the tips of his fingers, mapping all the tiny bones that radiated out from her thin wrist. It was something that he'd often done with Anne in the early years, before they grew apart.

"What about the other witnesses? How did Miles deal with them?"

"All right. He's made it so it's perfectly possible that Anne took a walk down to the beach after we'd gone and then left the door unlocked when she came back."

"Which door?"

"The one in the north wall. There would've been time for her to do that and go to bed before Thomas came back. She'd have been out when he telephoned."

"Well, that's good," he said, trying to sound a note of encouragement when it was the opposite of what he really felt.

Not for the first time Peter was aware of a tiny pinprick of doubt on the outer edge of his consciousness. He remembered Anne lying on the sofa in the drawing room with her face knotted in pain. She didn't look like she was about to go for a walk, but perhaps she felt the air would clear her head. Peter fought down his momentary feeling of unease almost without thinking.

"I won't need you again today, John," he said to the chauffeur as he helped his wife out of the car. "Lady Greta and I will be staying in tonight."

"Very good, sir," said the chauffeur, touching his peaked cap. Peter could not read his expressionless features. Perhaps he was looking for another job. Scandal does not sit well with men in high places.

=

Later, lying in bed, Peter could not sleep. Greta was turned away from him with her knees brought up almost to her stomach. She had slept in this fetal position for weeks now, and he could feel the tension in her back even without touching her. Sometimes she cried out strange words and names that made no sense, and he would be struck with how little he really knew his wife. She seemed to have no real friends or relatives; just the half-disabled mother in Manchester that she traveled up to visit every few weeks. Greta's solitude in the world made Peter even more painfully protective toward her than he might otherwise have been. The trial made him feel that he was letting her down even though he knew that there was nothing he could have done to prevent it. He contrasted the way in which Greta had helped him over the years with his inability to help her now.

He closed his eyes and remembered how she had been there for him when Anne died. It had been just about this time—eleven at night—when the telephone had rung beside the bed and he had answered it, waking blearily from sleep to hear the news that shattered his life. The same telephone was there now less than a yard from his outstretched hand sitting pale and silent in the half darkness.

It was Hearns who made the call. He must have been standing in the drawing room where Peter had been sitting with his wife only four hours before.

"You don't know me, sir. I'm Detective Sergeant Hearns of the Ipswich Police. I'm afraid I've got some bad news. It's your wife . . ."

Peter could still remember the exact words Hearns had used. It was like a tape recorder had been turned on in Peter's brain when he answered the telephone. He could remember Hearns's tone too. The intrusive, pressing quality of it that he later got to know so well as the policeman pulled his net around Greta, although he couldn't have closed it without Thomas. Nothing would have happened without Thomas, thought his father bitterly.

Disbelief was the first thing he'd felt after talking to Hearns. Peter remembered how the news seemed to bear no relation to reality. There was no violence in the ordered bedroom where he was standing in a pair of clean pajamas. There were no shouts or screams coming from the quiet street below. Everything was normal, and yet 130 miles away this event had happened. There would have been no call if it hadn't. He dialed the House of the Four Winds and a policeman answered. Another policeman. Peter put the phone down and felt the panic beginning in his chest, spreading down into his legs as the news seeped through into his brain, overwhelming the pathetic defenses that it had tried to throw up against the horror.

Peter sat down on the end of the bed. He did not cry, but his upper body shuddered convulsively. As he steeled himself against these tremors, a thought came into his mind. It was the thought of Greta. He needed help, he needed not to be alone. He picked up the telephone again and dialed her number.

"Please hold. The person you are calling knows you are waiting," said the operator's mechanical voice, once, twice, three times. He put the phone down and the shudders began again. Two minutes later she called him back.

After that it was a blur. He didn't remember getting dressed or much of how he told Greta or of her reaction. He remembered that her phone had been engaged, though, and he wondered not for the first time who she'd been talking to so late at night.

She'd brought the Range Rover round to the front of the house and insisted on driving. It didn't seem as if they'd even discussed whether or not she should go; he had just assumed it.

At the last moment he got out of the car and went back into the house, returning a minute later with a half-drunk bottle of whisky. It was almost empty by the time they passed through Carmouth at quarter to two. The little seaside town was deserted, but the lights were on in the police station.

A uniformed policeman with a flashlight stood outside the front gate of the House of the Four Winds. Not that he needed the flashlight. The house was ablaze with lights and Peter could also see spotlights set up away to his left by the north gate and over on the north lawn. There were men in white overalls moving back and forth.

All this, however, was at a distance, seen through the bars of the gate where Greta and he were told to wait. They sat saying nothing, gazing up at the house and the six old yew trees standing in front of it like sentinels. Ineffectual sentinels they had proved to be, Peter thought bitterly.

Two minutes passed and he got out to remonstrate with the policeman.

"I'm sorry, sir. I've got orders not to let anyone in. I've told Detective Sergeant Hearns you're here. He won't be long."

Peter was too exhausted to be angry. He was just a young man doing his job.

"Where's my wife? Can you tell me that?" he asked, trying to summon up the voice that he used at work, the voice of a man used to getting his way.

"We've moved her, sir. She's gone to Rowston. You can see her tonight if you want to. I can phone ahead."

Sergeant Hearns's voice came out of the darkness beyond the gate, followed immediately by the man himself. He was dressed in a cheap suit that was too small for him. Peter was aware of the stomach pressing against the belt and the sweat from the constricted underarms trickling down the inside of the polyester shirt into the detective's clammy palms. Peter felt it transmitted onto his skin as he shook Hearns's hand, and he resisted a sudden urge to wipe his palm on the side of his trousers.

"I'm sorry to meet you under such distressing circumstances," continued Hearns in the same soft but insistent voice that was already grating on Peter's overstretched nerves. He had questions himself—he was overflowing with them—but the detective seemed to give him no chance to speak.

They walked back to the open passenger door of the Range Rover and Peter sensed Hearns registering the smell of alcohol on his breath and connecting it with the empty whisky bottle on the floor. Connecting, noting, filing observations, impressions, conversations away in some dirty corner of his mind for later consideration back at the station or in whatever neat little house on the outskirts of Ipswich Hearns called home.

"Hullo, I'm Detective Sergeant Hearns, Ipswich Police," he said, pushing his clammy hand across the vacant passenger seat in the general direction of Greta's left breast.

She took his hand, she had no option, and he held it until she'd given him her name and explained her relationship to Peter. He looked at her quizzically for a moment, half raising his thick eyebrows as if wondering to himself why a minister of defense should want to bring his attractive personal assistant to the scene of his wife's murder. Then he gave her a lugubrious smile that exposed two long yellow teeth in the middle of his mouth and turned back to Sir Peter.

"I'm sure that you'll want to see your son. He's with Mr. and Mrs. Marsh across the road. They have been very kind. He went there to raise the alarm after the . . ." Hearns hesitated, searching for the best word. "The men left. He has been through quite an ordeal, I'm afraid. He was hiding, you see, when they killed Lady Anne. Very unpleasant."

Peter was trying to digest this new horrific information when he was distracted by a sudden gasp from inside the car. It was Greta. All the color had gone out of her face, and her eyes were open wide and frightened.

"Oh my God, is he all right?" she cried. "Did they hurt him?"

"They?" repeated Hearns, making the word into a question.

"The killers. You said men a moment ago, and so I assumed there was more than one."

"Ah," said Sergeant Hearns. Greta's explanation made sense. It was the need that she felt to give it that was interesting.

"No, I'm pleased to say that Thomas is physically fine," he added. "The men didn't know he was there. He stayed hidden while they ransacked the bedroom. They took all your wife's jewelry, I'm afraid. His mental state I cannot, of course, answer for. Shall we go?"

Hearns addressed his invitation to Sir Peter, but Greta didn't wait to be asked herself. She opened the door of the Range Rover and caught up with the detective and her employer by the time that they were halfway across the road.

"I know it's a bad time, sir," Hearns was saying, "but perhaps you could help me with just a couple of questions. It's just so our forensic boys know to look in all the right places."

"Very well, but make it quick," said Sir Peter, refusing to slow his pace to match that of the detective. "I want to see my son."

"It's that door in the wall, sir. The one leading to that little roadway."

"The lane."

"That's right. Was it locked, as far as you know, when you left?"

"Yes, Mrs. Martin would have locked it. I didn't go through there after she left. What about you, Greta?"

"No."

"Thank you, sir. Just one other question. The windows in the study. Did you happen to leave one of them open before you left?"

"No, I was in the drawing room with my wife. Why?"

"It's just that your son has told us that he found one of them open when he came home at about eight-thirty."

"Well, it wasn't me. It could've been Greta, I suppose. She was working in there, I think. Wait a minute. I'll ask her."

Greta had walked on ahead, and Peter quickened his pace to catch up to her. She was almost at the Marshes' front door.

"Greta, did you leave the study window open before we left? The detective needs to know."

She turned around to face him. She looked terrible, he suddenly thought. As if the full force of the tragedy had only just hit her. It was the detective who pressed the question in the insistent voice that Peter found so grating.

"Can you help us, Miss Grahame?" he asked.

She looked cornered, uncertain of what to say, and then, after a moment's hesitation, she blurted out her answer: "I don't know. I may have done. It was a warm evening."

"It certainly was, madam," said Hearns, moving past her to knock on the door. "A fine summer's evening."

The detective did not wait for the door to open but instead turned back toward them. It was Peter he addressed now.

"I'm going back up to the house, Sir Peter. We're still busy with the forensics, but come and ask for me at the gate when you're finished here. I can ring forward to the hospital at Rowston, like I said before. I'm very sorry, Sir Peter. Very sorry indeed."

Peter walked through the open door of the cottage, but he was hardly aware of the man greeting him in the hallway. Christopher Marsh was wrapped up in a dressing gown, making inarticulate sympathetic noises. Nothing could have prepared him or his wife for what had unfolded since they had been woken from sleep four hours earlier by a terrible knocking at the door and had come down to find Thomas crying on the step.

Peter moved past his neighbor, bending at the waist to avoid hitting his head on the low lintel of the living room doorway.

He found Thomas sitting on the sofa next to Grace. She'd thrown a blanket around his shoulders even though it wasn't cold, and he was holding a mug of tea between his shaking hands. He got awkwardly to his feet just after his father came through the door and spilled half the mug's contents onto the hearth rug at his feet.

"Tom, I am so sorry," Peter said, then stopped in midsentence, suddenly aware of the inadequacy of his words to match the significance of the moment in both their lives. He wanted to leap across the ten feet of carpet that separated them and take the boy in his arms, but something held him back. It was as if they didn't know each other well enough.

And there was no time. Greta came in behind Peter. Lacking the English reserve that afflicted her employer, she took a step toward Thomas, holding her hands out as she did so.

"Oh, Tom, Tom!" she cried, and there were tears in her green eyes.

He stepped back, half falling into the sofa behind him, and then coming forward again almost immediately, he threw his mug at Greta. Perhaps he would have hit her if he hadn't been off-balance. There was no doubt that that was what he had intended to do. As it was, the mug exploded into fragments as it smashed against the edge of the Marshes' fireplace, and all that came into contact with Greta was a little of the warm tea splashing out of the mug as it flew past her through the air.

Peter reacted instantly, rushing forward to put himself between Greta and his son, just as he had gotten between Greta and his wife a few weeks earlier. He had no difficulty reacting to violence; it was emotion that held him back.

"Get her out! Get her out!" Thomas screamed the words over and over again, full in his father's face. Peter felt he would have carried on until his lungs burst if Greta hadn't backed away out of the door, edging past Christopher Marsh as she did so.

"I'm sorry, Miss Grahame," said Christopher, following her out onto the front step. "The boy's not himself. He'll get over it."

"No he won't," she muttered, pulling her coat up above her shoulders and turning her haggard face away as she walked out into the road. "No he won't."

=

With Greta gone, Thomas fell back onto the sofa, leaving his father standing over him. Grace had moved to the fireplace and begun picking up bits of the shattered mug. She was very fond of Thomas, whom she had known all his life, but her concern for the boy was battling with a longing for all these people to go. She was by nature a timid woman, and the boy's act of sudden violence had terrified her. She was tired too; it was nearly two-thirty in the morning.

"Why did you do that, Thomas?" His son's full name came far easier to Peter than the affectionate Tom that he had used when he first came into the room. He persisted when the boy did not answer. "What's Greta got to do with it? She's only here to help."

"She sent that man. He killed my mother."

"What man?"

"He's got a scar. I saw him through the hole in the wall."

"What wall?"

"The bookcase wall when he killed Mummy. When you were in London with *her*."

"Yes, Thomas. A man has killed your mother. I don't know what to say to you. I wish it wasn't true. I wish I'd been here for her, and for you, but I wasn't. I just don't understand what it's got to do with Greta."

Thomas breathed deeply and then looked up at his father. It was as if he had time for one final effort at communication before he was sucked back down into the seeping black quagmire into which he'd been pushed.

"I saw the man with the scar before. In London with Greta that first night I came up with Mummy. Greta lied about it. She said she was with her mother, but she wasn't. She was with that man. I heard them talking down in the basement. She was telling him to wait."

"Did you see them together? Greta and this man with a scar."

"He was standing in the street when she came upstairs. He'd have seen me if he'd turned around, but he didn't. I saw him, though."

"From behind?"

"That's right. I could see the scar. And tonight she arranged for me to go and stay with Edward so Mummy would be alone, and then she left the window open. It must have been her."

Thomas's voice started to break just after he said his mother's name, and he finished speaking in a rush, his voice halfway between a cry and a scream.

"Have you told the detective all this?" asked Peter.

"No, I haven't. I haven't spoken to anyone at all except Christy and Grace."

"He was too upset, Sir Peter," said Christopher Marsh, who had come back in from outside. "The detective came to the door a couple of hours ago and wanted to know where the men went in the house. Master Thomas told me that he closed the window in the study, and I passed on that and the other details. Sergeant Hearns wanted to make sure the police were looking in all the right places. That's what he said anyway."

"Thank you, Christy. You and Grace have been good friends to us tonight. Thomas, I'm going to go and talk to Greta about what you've told me. You wait here, and try and get a hold on yourself," Peter added as he went out of the door.

He found Greta sitting in the Range Rover. She'd moved it away from the gate of the house so that it was now parked farther up the road, away from the lights.

"I need to talk to you, Greta," he said. They both sat looking forward into the darkness, and he felt the empty whisky bottle under his foot like a reproach. He needed a clear head now more than ever.

"Thomas says that he recognized the man who came to the house tonight. The man who shot Anne. He says that he saw you with him in London." Peter spoke in a monotone, fastening his eyes on the dark road ahead.

"He's wrong. It's not true, Peter. He must have made a mistake. You know me."

Peter felt the pressure of Greta's hand on his arm, but he steeled himself to continue.

"Listen, Greta. I've got to ask you about this. Try and help me."

"How can I help you? He's crazy. You saw him."

"All right, help me with this. Thomas says he saw you in London, in the house on that first night he was up there with Anne. I was in my constituency, and you had to go up and stay with your mother. Is that true, Greta? Were you in Manchester or were you in London? I need to know."

There was silence in the car. Peter sat very still waiting for Greta to answer. When eventually she spoke, her voice was soft and sad, regretful almost.

"Yes, Peter, I lied. I wanted to keep it a secret from you, but I shouldn't have done. I see that now."

"Keep what a secret?"

Peter turned to look at Greta, but she kept her eyes fixed on the darkness ahead.

"When I was at school in Manchester I met some bad people. I wasn't like I am now. I'd lived with my parents all those years, and I wanted excitement. I wanted to test things, see how far they would go. I did something I shouldn't have done, something I feel ashamed of."

"What was it?"

"I don't want to tell you, Peter. You wouldn't respect me anymore if I did, and I couldn't bear that."

"That's crazy, Greta. I wouldn't turn my back on you because of something that happened in the past, before you knew me. What do you take me for?"

"A good man. You're a good man, Peter. I'm not saying you'd turn your back on me; it's just you wouldn't like me anymore. You don't know how important you are to me."

Peter wanted to give in. He was tired and half drunk, and he longed for unconsciousness, some time when he wouldn't have to feel this pain inside. It was under his ribs, trying to get out. But he couldn't leave it: not after what Thomas had said. Not with his wife dead, lying in a hospital mortuary under a white sheet. Dried blood and the cold, fierce light of the postmortem; the gleam of the pathologist's scalpel and the photographer waiting in the corner with the witnesses: all these images and more flashed across Peter's brain and made him go on.

"You've got to tell me, Greta. My wife is dead and I have to know."

"You don't know what you're asking."

Peter could feel Greta's tension. Her knuckles were white where her hands gripped the steering wheel.

"No, I don't know, but you still have to tell me. Was it something criminal?"

"Yes."

"Could it have something to do with what happened here tonight?"

"No!" Greta's voice exploded in the car like a pistol shot. "What do you take me for?"

"I don't mean you sent the man. Just that he might have found out about the house, about the jewelry, through you. That's all."

"How could you think that? I've never talked to anyone about the jewelry, and besides, I don't know any man who would do a thing like this."

"So who were you with in London? Thomas said he heard you talking with a man in your flat. Late at night."

"He's blackmailing me. I've been paying him for years. I saw him because he wanted more money. I shouldn't have done it, I see that now."

"Blackmailing you over what? You have to tell me, Greta."

"Over what happened after I left school. He's the only one who knows about it."

"About what?"

"If I tell you, I'll be in your power. Do you want that, Peter? Do you want that responsibility?"

Greta spoke as if she were playing her last card, making her last appeal, but Peter had gone too far down the road with her to stop now.

"I have to know. There's no choice."

"All right," said Greta. Her voice was dull, and she had slumped back into her seat. It was as if all the fight had finally been knocked out of her.

"I'll tell you but only if you promise to say nothing, to do nothing, to keep it to yourself."

Peter was silent thinking of his wife lying on the sofa as she had been only eight hours earlier. She had had her slippers on, he remembered. Little gold slippers that looked like dancing shoes. He hadn't kissed her properly when he left.

He felt Greta's hand on his arm, her breath on his cheek requiring complicity.

"If it has nothing to do with Anne, I promise," he said. "You'll have to satisfy me of that."

"All right, that's fair," she said, releasing him. "It's simple, really. Most bad things are, I suppose. I took drugs. Everyone did then. I even got a conviction for it. I couldn't afford to buy enough, and so I sold them too. Only a few times, but that was enough. I sold some pills to a girl and she died. I didn't know they were bad. I swear I didn't."

There was bitterness in Greta's voice, and she spoke quickly, allowing no time for Peter to respond.

"This man was with her. He felt he had a claim over me."

"A claim?"

"He wanted me. Sexually."

"What did you do?"

"I let him a few times. It was only sex, and I thought it didn't matter, but then I realized it did."

"Why?"

"Because the girl had died. Because I hadn't. I stopped taking the drugs, and it cleared my head."

"So what happened?"

"I refused to do it anymore. We fought, but he seemed to accept it in the end. He took money instead, and then I didn't hear from him for a while. Not until recently. He'd seen my picture in the paper, coming out of a restaurant in London with you, and he wanted more money, a lot more. I had to give him some. I had no choice. He kept threatening to go to the police. He said he'd tell you too."

"Bastard," said Peter. "*You* should have told me, Greta."

"No, I didn't want to. I didn't want you to know. I arranged for him to come to the flat when I was sure that you would be away. I didn't know that Anne and Thomas were coming until it was too late, too late to put him off. I showed him what I earned—pay slips and everything. I told him I couldn't pay him all he wanted, and then he wanted to touch me. I don't know what got him going; maybe it was me being P.A. to a minister and being in your house, but it made him start all that up again."

"Did he?" Peter could hardly get his question out. There were too many burning emotions inside of him fighting for release. The grief and the guilt and now anger against this unknown stranger demanding money, pawing at Greta in his house. Beneath the anger was another unacknowledged emotion: Peter was gripped by sexual jealousy. He felt it in his loins.

"Did he what?"

"Have sex with you?"

Peter blurted the words out. His heart was beating painfully inside his rib cage, and pictures flooded into his exhausted mind that he could not control. His wife dead, Greta naked with this man above her. He wanted to take hold of her, feel her full breasts encompassed in his wide hands. He thought of them like they were life when all around him was death and emptiness. In the early-morning darkness a cold breeze was blowing off the sea.

"No, I wouldn't let him," she said. "He's frightened of me when I'm angry. It's strange; it's like he always wants to get me to that point, and then he backs away."

Peter sighed. The constriction in his chest lifted, and Thomas's accusations blew back into his consciousness.

"Greta, I understand about this man, and why you invited him. Thomas said that he heard you telling him to wait, and so that makes sense, given you were talking about the money. But that wasn't all he told me. He said he recognized the man, that he was here tonight, that he killed Anne. Killed my wife, Greta."

"It's not the same man. I swear it isn't. He knows nothing about this house, and even if he did, he wouldn't do it. He's a sneak, not a murderer."

"Thomas says he saw him in the street outside the house when you came upstairs."

"So he didn't see him with me?"

"No."

"Well, he could just have been a pedestrian then, couldn't he?"

"Standing outside the house at midnight?"

"Why not? Was he looking in the house?"

"No, Thomas says he wasn't. The man had his back to him."

"How can he be sure it was the same man then?"

"I don't know. He said he had a scar."

There was doubt now in Peter's voice, and Greta pressed home her advantage.

"That's not enough. You know it's not enough, Peter. Anyway, the man that was in my flat had no scar. Thomas has too much imagination; that's the trouble. He's heard me tell a lie and he's seen a man in the street, the back of a man in the street, I should say. After dark. And now he's crazy with shock and grief and he's decided it's the same man because he wants to blame me for what happened."

"Why should he do that?"

"Because he knows Anne and I never got on. Because he feels guilty about liking me when his mother didn't want him to. Because he has to make someone responsible other than himself."

"What do you mean? How can Thomas be responsible?"

"He's not. Of course he's not. He just feels it like you do. He probably feels it because he was there and you feel it because you weren't."

It made sense. Peter wanted it to make sense, and so it did make sense. It was like when Greta tried on Anne's clothes. He talked to her about it, and afterward he felt closer to her. It made him feel responsible for her, and he did not forget what she had said to him on the beach. There wasn't anyone else in the world who loved him, who understood him like Greta did, now that Annie was dead.

Annie was dead. The words came unbidden into Peter's mind. He had tried to keep them at bay, but now he was suddenly confronting the terrible reality of what had happened. She was no longer in the world. Her life had not been as happy as it should have been because he had let her down. Insisted on his career and his life in London. Not been the father to Thomas that she wanted him to be. Not been the husband that she deserved.

Peter did not know how he could cope with all this. He needed strength, he needed help, he needed Greta.

As if in answer to his unspoken thoughts, she leaned over and kissed him chastely on the cheek where the bristly early-morning hair was beginning to grow.

"Go and talk to Thomas," she said. "He needs you. I'll wait for you here."

Chapter 16

THEY GOT TO Rowston with the dawn. It was the hour when the tint of the sky changes subtly with every minute, and the birds had begun to chatter haltingly overhead. Peter felt feverish and wound down the window to let the cold morning air into the car. Greta drove without saying anything, staring into the new day, which was taking her away from Flyte forever.

In his head Peter could hear voices, a commotion of voices from yesterday and today all talking to him at once: Thomas yelling, "Get her out!" and Greta whispering secrets about a past that seemed to bear no relation to who she was. The grating, insistent voice of Sergeant Hearns: "Please let us know where you are both going to be," with the emphasis on "both" containing just enough insinuation not to be offensive. Then Thomas's voice again when he had gone back to the Marshes' cottage. No words this time. Just screams, terrible screams, until the boy had finally fallen asleep and Jane Martin had arrived from Woodbridge to take care of him. Peter wished that the Marshes had called her earlier; the boy needed somebody he felt comfortable with, but he couldn't criticize them. Christy and Grace had been good neighbors, the best.

There was one other soft voice asking to be heard that Peter still kept blocked out of his conscious mind. He would hear it soon enough. At the bottom of the road Rowston Hospital came into view: a silver-and-glass building glimmering in the first rays of the June sunshine like an alien arrival. Outside the entrance a police car was waiting. Arrangements had already been made for the first ceremony of the murdered dead: the identification of the body.

"Do you want me to come with you?" asked Greta.

"No," he almost shouted. Anne and Greta had to be kept apart, he saw that clearly. He needed Greta more than ever, but outside this horror, somewhere distant where he could go when it was over. After the hospital she would go back to London on the train and wait for him there while he did what had to be done.

"I'm sorry, Greta," he added after a moment, speaking softly now, tenderly even. "You've helped me more than I can say, but this is something I have to do alone."

Inside the hospital he followed the policeman's heavy-duty shoes as they beat a tattoo on the linoleum floors of the corridors. Turning right and left a dozen times, guided by black signs on white walls, they came eventually to a pair of doors that did not swing open like the others. Knocking was required here at these gates of the modern underworld.

While they waited, Peter noticed that the bottoms of the doors were scuffed, no doubt by hospital orderlies kicking them open so that they could bring in the dead. They could do with a lick of paint, Peter found himself thinking irrelevantly just before they opened.

At least they did it properly, Peter thought afterward. There was no drawer pulled out of a high steel filing cabinet and no row of silver metal tables to walk down while the doctor counted until he reached the right number. Instead he was taken to a room marked PRIVATE with a picture of a watery blue landscape on the wall and a vase of carnations on the windowsill. Peter wondered if they were real, but he didn't touch them to find out.

"This won't take a moment, sir," said the policeman. "Just the identification and then you can have time alone with your wife."

There was a kindness in the man's voice that Peter was grateful for. He appreciated the description of the body under the white sheet as being his wife rather than the deceased or some other impersonal medical term, and when the mortuary attendant pulled back the sheet, he had no difficulty in recognizing her. The second bullet had done its damage at the side of the head, not the front.

It was Anne, but he didn't feel she was there at all. It was her absence that hurt. The dead body made him realize its permanence. He wanted to say he was sorry, to make amends, but Anne was not there to hear his confession, to forgive him his sins. She was gone somewhere he could not follow, and he was left with this empty face wearing an expression that he couldn't read. There was fear there but also something else; it almost looked like joy.

Peter felt heartbroken. He thought of all the times that he had stayed in London, the gentle reproach with which she had spoken to him so often on the telephone and the way she'd looked up at him from the sofa in the drawing room when he had gotten up to leave the evening before: "Do you have to go so soon, Peter? It's like you've barely arrived."

That was what she'd said. He couldn't remember if he'd replied, done more than kiss her lightly on the cheek on his way upstairs to pack.

It was just after he'd bent down to place the last ritual kiss on his wife's cold brow, just after he'd turned away from her that the memory came floating unbidden into his numbed mind. He thought of it later as Anne's last gift to him, and he tried to remember it whenever he thought of her afterward.

It was a summer's morning just like this one that he remembered, but it was fifteen years ago and he was waking in their bed at home. Thomas was two or three months old, and Peter had been up with him in the night. The baby wouldn't stop crying, and so he'd walked him up and down in the corridor at the top of the stairs singing some silly song that he remembered from his own childhood. Now he reached out toward Anne and found her gone, even though the bed was still warm where she had been sleeping with Thomas beside her in his cot.

Peter opened his eyes, blinking against the sunlight flooding into the room through the high open windows. To the east was the sea breaking blue and white on the sandy beach below the house, and to the south were Annie's roses, multitudes of them staked out in the gardens and climbing on the old perimeter wall up toward the sun.

Standing in the south window looking out were Peter's wife and son. Thomas's hair was curly and golden, and his cheeks were fat and red and round above a little dimpled chin. His unbelievably tiny fingers were twined in his mother's long, brown hair, and he seemed to gurgle with delight as she held him up to the light. Peter smiled at his son, and just at that moment Anne turned to him with eyes that were liquid blue and sparkling.

"Oh, Peter," she said. "I am so happy. I can't tell you how happy I am."

=

Peter dropped Greta at the railway station and watched the first train of the morning take her off into the distance. Then he drove the Range Rover slowly back to Flyte and took a room at the Anchor Inn. He was more exhausted than he had ever been in his life, and he fell on the bed without bothering to undress and slept until the afternoon.

He woke because the phone was ringing. It stopped and then began again, on and on until he finally answered. It was Thomas, but his voice sounded different. There was a desperate determination in it that Peter had never heard before.

"I need to speak to you, Dad. Aunt Jane does too."

"Where are you? Are you all right?"

"We're in Woodbridge. At Mary's house."

"Whose?"

"Aunt Jane's sister. It's twenty-eight Harbour Street. Will you come?"

"Yes, of course I will. I'm glad Jane's taken you there. I should have thought of it myself." Then, just as Peter was about to replace the receiver, Thomas's voice came again.

"Has she gone, Dad? You have to be alone. I can't see you otherwise."

"Don't worry, I'm alone," said Peter, and hung up. He'd said no more than the truth; he'd never felt more alone than he did now.

=

"What are you going to do, Dad?"

"About what?"

"About Greta. She killed my mother."

"No, she didn't. She had nothing to do with it, Thomas. You've got this fixation in your mind, and it's doing neither of us any good."

They were sitting in the front room of the little house in Harbour

Street surrounded by a lifetime's collection of bric-a-brac. Coronation mugs and ships in bottles jostled for space with china cats and dogs. Their owner, Jane's sister Mary, had made them cups of milky tea and then left them sitting around a heavy 1930s oak dining table—Jane and Thomas on one side and Peter on the other.

Part of Peter realized that all this was wrong. He should be the one with his arm around his son, not the old housekeeper, but Thomas's obsession with Greta divided them and Peter felt powerless to do anything about it.

"All right, Dad, listen to what Aunt Jane has got to say," said Thomas, controlling his impatience with visible difficulty.

"She said bad things about my Lady, Sir Peter," said the housekeeper.

"When?"

"The day the little dog died. After you left the house. She said she was going to make my Lady pay."

"A lot of people said bad things that day. The important point is that everyone said they were sorry afterward. Didn't they, Thomas?"

"She left the window open, and I heard one of the men saying that they were all closed," said Thomas, ignoring his father's question.

"She left the window open by mistake. It's easily done on a warm evening like yesterday was. Why would she have admitted leaving it open if she'd done so deliberately?"

"Because she didn't know I'd recognized him then."

"Someone you saw from behind in the street at midnight. She shouldn't have lied, Thomas, but she had her reasons."

"Why did she arrange for me to go to Edward's, then? What about that?"

"I don't know, Thomas. I haven't got the answer to everything. I'm sure this is wrong though. I know Greta, and she'd never have had anything to do with something like this."

"Yes, she did. You know she did. You're just protecting her because you're screwing her."

Thomas pushed his chair away behind him and stood leaning over the table toward his father, resisting Jane Martin's ineffectual efforts to pull him back.

"You're screwing her and my mother's dead because of her. I hate you, I hate you, I hate you!"

Thomas's voice rose to a hysterical scream, which was suddenly cut off when his father leaned across the table and smacked him hard on the cheek with the back of his hand.

Peter stood up, facing his son. Thomas had a hand over his face, but his father could see the fury in his eyes. It was the sort of rage from which a lifetime of hatred is born.

"I'm sorry, Thomas," he said. "I wish I hadn't done that, but you shouldn't have said that to me. It's your decision what you tell the police, but think before you speak. You might regret it otherwise."

Peter had retreated to the doorway and now stood there, hesitating for a moment. Neither his son nor Mrs. Martin said anything, and he felt as if he had no option but to go. To stay would only enrage the boy more, he told himself, so without another word he turned and let himself out the front door.

Outside he sat in the Range Rover, gazing at the motionless net curtains hung across the front window of the little house. He longed to get out of the car and walk back up the path to the front door, but he didn't do it. Instead, after a couple of minutes, he started up the engine and drove slowly away. There was no way back.

=

Four days passed before the police said that the family could return to the House of the Four Winds. Sir Peter remained at the hotel in Flyte making arrangements for the funeral, and Aunt Jane thought that she and Thomas should stay on with her sister in Woodbridge, but he insisted on going home at the first opportunity. The House of the Four Winds had been his mother's life, and walking in her garden made him feel that she still existed in the world.

He sat on an old bench as the sun set and looked up at the window of his mother's bedroom through a curtain of white roses imagining that she might appear there at any moment, calling him to come in. Trudging back to the house in the semidarkness brought a renewal of his pain, but these moments in the garden when his mother seemed so close were part of what kept him going. The rest was the thought of revenge: the need to make those responsible pay for what they had done. He knew what his mother had thought of Greta; Aunt Jane sat with him in the kitchen almost every night and told him all the things that his mother had said. Lady Anne had often used the old housekeeper as a shoulder to cry on, little realizing that all her words of frustration and resentment were being remembered so faithfully by the old friend she had known since her childhood.

Thomas felt ashamed now, remembering his dreams about Greta. He bitterly regretted the declaration of love that he had made to her in the taxi, linking it in his mind with the sadness in his mother's face as she looked down at him from the first-floor windows of his father's house in London.

Lying in his bed at night he thought of killing Greta, of plunging a knife into her chest, but then he remembered his mother lying at the top of the staircase with the pool of red sticky blood behind her head and her eyes full of nothing at all. There was another way of making Greta pay—a cleaner way, the way his mother would want. He knew what his father had said about talking to the police, but his father was with Greta just like he always had been. Thomas remembered the sting of his father's hand on his face and made his decision.

Early the next morning he telephoned the police and made an appointment for Sergeant Hearns to come and take his statement in the afternoon. He needed to have it over and done with before his mother's funeral the next day.

==

It rained on the morning of the funeral. A slow Suffolk rain that fell heavily on the heads of the congregation as they stood around the newly dug grave in the corner of the Flyte churchyard.

Thomas had sat between his father and Aunt Jane in the church. He had no more wish than Sir Peter to advertise the divisions in the family, but by the graveside he shrank away from his father's protective arm and gripped hold of Aunt Jane's hand instead.

The wet dirt clung to Thomas's black, polished shoes and the rain plastered his long, fair hair to his head. He wiped it from his eyes and wondered why he wasn't crying. Aunt Jane wasn't either. The old lady bit her lip and stared angrily up at the overcast sky, looking like a veteran about to go into battle. Thomas loved the old housekeeper; now that his mother was gone, she was the only person he really trusted in the whole wide world.

Thomas kept his face turned away from his father and tried not to look down into the obscene hole in the ground into which the undertaker's men had lowered his mother's body. He could hear the rain pattering on the wooden coffin lid and the vicar's voice louder than it had been before, straining to be heard above the rumblings of thunder in the sky.

"Man that is born of a woman hath but a short time to live, and is full of misery. He cometh up, and is cut down like a flower . . ."

Yes, thought Thomas. The words were right. His mother had never been happy. How could she be when his father had deserted her? And she had not lived long enough. She had been cut down like one of her roses when she was the most beautiful, the most vital, the best of women in the world.

Thomas suddenly began to weep not just for himself but for his mother too. For what had been taken away from her. She would never see another summer; she would never know what he might become.

"O holy and most merciful Savior, deliver us not into the bitter pains of eternal death," asked the vicar, but the grand words felt hollow to Thomas. His mother's death was eternal. That was what this funeral meant. She would never be again. He would never again see the smile that lit up her face when he came into the room; never feel her hand as it brushed his long hair back away from his forehead in a gesture of affection that had lived on past his childhood. Thomas did not know why he was still in the world when she was not. How could he live when she didn't?

"O holy and merciful Savior, thou most worthy judge eternal, suffer us not, at our last hour, for any pains of death, to fall from thee."

Thomas thought of his mother's last hour, and the memory came to him as it had so often in recent days of their last moment together at the top of the stairs. He'd pushed the books and the hiding place had opened. He'd heard the voices at the bottom of the stairs and sensed the light of the flashlights. He'd stepped forward, stumbling into the darkness of the priest hole, and lost hold of the side of his mother's white nightgown. He'd replayed it in his mind so many times, but still he couldn't say whether he had let go or his mother had pulled away. All he knew was that as he turned back to her in the darkness, he felt the bookcase close behind him. She must have stood with her back to the books pushing the shelves back into place until the first shot took her and she fell to the ground. But by then she had succeeded in her purpose. She died knowing that he was hidden.

Her last act was to preserve his life, and suddenly Thomas realized what this meant. He had to continue living because she had saved him. He was not cut off from her because he knew precisely what she wanted. She was not shut up in that dark brown box in the ground on which his father was at that moment throwing his farewell flowers. She lived on in him. It was not "earth to earth, ashes to ashes, dust to dust." He would see that it was not.

Thomas looked around him. The graves of generations of Sackvilles and their retainers stretched back toward the old gray stone church, past the trunk of the great chestnut tree that had blown down in the storm of 1989. Some of the moss-covered graves had sunk into the ground so far that it was not now possible to read the name of the Sackville whose bones lay under the turf.

The church and the graveyard had not changed in 350 years. Buried here were the same men and women who had screamed lustily in the font at their baptism and glowed with the promise of life as they signed their names in the leather-bound Register of Marriages that was now gathering dust in the church vestry. Eighteenth- and nineteenth-century vicars had walked down this same gravel path between the graves and read the same words from the *Book of Common Prayer.*

Thomas suddenly had a profound sense of the significance of the dead who lay all around him. People who had walked the old narrow streets of Flyte and fought against the same cruel sea. Sackvilles who had inherited the House of the Four Winds and passed it on intact to the next generation. Thomas's father was alien to all of this, but he, Thomas, was inseparable from what had gone before and what was still to come. He looked up at the friendly, sympathetic faces of his neighbors; men and women whom he had known all his life, and he smiled at them through his tears. He was not alone, and as if in answer to his thought, the rain slowed and then stopped and the sun came out weakly overhead.

Chapter 17

A FTER THE FUNERAL, Peter stood beneath the portrait of his father-in-law in the dining room of the House of the Four Winds,
talking in turn to each of the friends, neighbors, and distant relatives
who had come to pay their respects.

His training in politics had made him skillful at this type of event.
He remembered almost everybody's name and spoke to each of them
for just the right amount of time, accepting their sympathy with just
the right amount of gratitude.

All the time that he was talking, however, he was also looking for his
son. Thomas had disappeared after the funeral, and no one, not even
Jane Martin, seemed to know where he had gone. Peter had been very
conscious of how the boy had shrunk from his side in the graveyard,
and he wanted to try to bridge the gap between them before he had to
go back to London.

Not a day passed that Peter did not regret hitting his son, although
he knew himself well enough to realize that it was not something that
he could have chosen not to do. Thomas had provoked him too far
when he said those terrible things.

Most of the guests had gone when Jane Martin told Peter that Greta
wanted him on the phone. He extricated himself politely from a conversation with the Flyte harbormaster and took his glass of red wine
into the study where he stood looking out through the newly repaired
window as he picked up the phone.

"Hullo, Greta," he said, but there was no response. Just a hubbub of voices above which he could hear a drunken man shouting that he wanted to go home.

"Greta!" he shouted into the phone. He could feel something was wrong, although he didn't know what it was.

He heard her voice just before he was about to hang up and try to call back.

"Peter, thank God you're there. They've arrested me."

Peter dropped his glass of wine on the floor. It did not smash, but the red wine spread out over the pale carpet and Peter turned away. It looked too much like blood.

"Where are you?" he asked.

"I'm in Ipswich with this Hearns man. They brought me here from London."

"Are you all right?"

"I don't know. There's a lawyer here. He says that Thomas has made a statement saying it was me that sent those men to kill Anne. I don't understand how he could say that to them, Peter. Not after all the time that we've spent together."

"Greta, I'm coming. I'll get you out. I promise."

"Make it quick, Peter. Please."

As he put down the phone, Peter saw his son come through the north gate and walk toward the house across the lawn. Peter ran outside to intercept him. They met under an old elm tree, and Peter pulled his son behind it so that they wouldn't be visible from the dining room window.

"What is it, Dad?" Thomas was alarmed. His father was breathless and had still not let go of the lapel of his suit jacket.

"Where've you been?" It was not the question Peter wanted to ask but he needed time to find the right words.

"I went down to the beach. I was trying to make some sense of it all. You can help me, Dad."

"Help you?" Peter laughed harshly. He could hear the wine in his voice. He'd drunk too much at the wake or whatever the dismal gathering inside was called. It wasn't just today, of course. He was drinking too much every day and every night trying to cope while his son went off to that pushy policeman and stuck a knife in his back.

"Help you after what you've done to me!"

"What, Dad?"

Thomas sounded frightened now. His father had hold of both his lapels and was shaking him as he spoke.

Abruptly Peter let go. It was as if an electrical current inside him had suddenly been switched off.

"They've arrested Greta. Just like you wanted them to. You've got what you wanted now, Thomas."

"It's not what I want, Dad. It's what's right. That man was with her in London. I know he was."

"There's no point arguing with you, Thomas. You've gone down your own road now, and I can't follow. I just think I deserved better from you. That's all."

"Oh, Dad." Thomas began to cry. All the sense that he had started to make of things at the graveside and down on the beach began to crumble inside him.

"I'm sorry, Thomas. Perhaps you should have waited to make your revelations until after your mother's funeral."

Peter knew he was being cruel. Somewhere inside he even dimly realized that he was quite wrong to speak to his fifteen-year-old son like this on the day of his mother's funeral, but uppermost in his mind was the thought of Greta in the police station among all the drunks and lechers. Stuck in the back of the police car coming down from London, with Hearns beside her sweating onto the stained upholstery, and now sitting in a cell feeling sick and scared.

"It's true, Dad. Why can't you believe me?" Thomas begged his father through his tears.

"Because it's not true. It's delusion. You're sick with delusion, and you're making innocent people pay for it." The urgency was back in Peter's voice. "I've got to go now, Thomas."

"Where?"

"Where do you think? To Ipswich Police Station to get Greta out, and then I'm taking her back to London."

"When will I see you again, Dad?"

"I don't know. I've got to go back to work. Jane'll be here to look after you, and then we'll see. You need to go to a good school and learn something. That's my opinion."

Thomas turned away. There was no point in talking to this man who understood him so little. Just like his father hadn't understood his mother.

Thomas started to walk slowly toward the house. His shoulders sagged and his back bent like he was carrying a burden way beyond his years.

"Pull yourself together, Thomas," his father called after him. "There are still people in the house."

=

Peter drove fast, checking in his rearview mirror to see that none of the reporters at the gate had followed him. The road was empty, and beyond Carmouth he wound down the windows and tried to make some sense of what was happening.

Above all he felt guilty about having left Greta alone in London. She had offered to come to the funeral, but he had told her to stay away. He hadn't wanted any more conflict with Thomas after what had happened in Woodbridge, but he should have seen this coming. There was a craziness about his son that afternoon that should have given him fair warning, although there was obviously nothing he could have done once Thomas had decided to point the finger at Greta. Injustice must take its course, like justice. Except that he might have been there with her when they came for her; he might have been able to get to the police station sooner, get her a good lawyer. She needed someone strong to protect her from Hearns with his probing questions and dirty insinuations.

Greta was still being interviewed when he got to the station. He paced up and down in the front office, watched indifferently by a uniformed constable behind the desk.

"How long will it be before I can see Sergeant Hearns?" he'd asked over and over again, only to get the same reply each time.

"He knows you're here, sir. He knows you're here."

It was past six o'clock, and Peter was debating whether or not to go to the nearest pub and drink some whisky when Hearns came out.

"I'm sorry to have kept you waiting, Sir Peter."

"No you're not," Peter countered rudely. "Couldn't you have waited until after the funeral?"

"I'm afraid not. We have to move quickly, otherwise evidence might be destroyed."

"Who by?"

Sergeant Hearns did not reply, other than to raise his shaggy gray eyebrows. He looked as if he was wearing the same suit and tie that he'd worn on the night of the murder.

"Can I ask you a question, Sir Peter?" he said after a moment. "Why are you so angry about us pursuing this investigation? It is *your* wife that has been killed. I would have thought you would want us to find the culprit."

"The right culprit. I don't want you chasing up blind alleys. Persecuting my assistant."

"She's not been persecuted, Sir Peter. She's been interviewed."

Hearns's studied politeness enraged Peter even further.

"You have no right!" he shouted. "She's done nothing wrong."

"Then you have nothing to fear," said the detective. "It does seem strange to me that you should be so concerned about us interviewing Miss Grahame, Sir Peter. I hope that you're not concealing anything. That would not be sensible."

"What the hell do you mean? How dare you talk to me like that! Do you know who I am?"

Peter felt himself losing his temper, but his anger seemed to have no effect on Hearns's maddening equanimity.

"You're an important minister in Her Majesty's government, and to be honest with you, I don't know if we've ever had a minister in this police station. We don't get too many VIP's down in our neck of the woods. I should get you to sign our visitors' book before you go."

Peter was speechless. Hearns clearly had a real talent for being rude while pretending to be the opposite.

"The point is, Sir Peter, it doesn't matter who you are. You could be the prime minister, and it wouldn't stop me doing my job. There's evidence pointing toward your assistant, and it's my duty to investigate it."

"What evidence? A ridiculous identification and a window she's left open by mistake. You're trying to build a case for which there's no foundation, when you should be out trying to catch the real killers."

"I am trying to catch them, Sir Peter, and I won't allow you or anyone else to stand in my way."

"Don't be ridiculous. I want to take Greta home with me now. Have you finished with her?"

"Yes, just about. There are a few formalities. It won't take long."

"So you're not charging her. I thought as much. You're not charging her because you haven't got any evidence."

"There is evidence, Sir Peter, but at present there is no charge."

Hearns smiled as if pleased with the succinctness of his response, and once again Peter was treated to a sight of the detective's yellowing teeth.

"I will have Miss Grahame join you in just a few minutes," he said.

=

Greta slept on the way back to London. Peter drove fast, glancing repeatedly at her profile. The smooth, soft skin of her face and the groomed black hair tucked behind her delicate ear made his heart beat fast. He hadn't realized until now how much he'd missed her. He felt determined to protect her from a hostile world, whatever the cost might be.

In Chelsea he stood at the top of the railings while she went down to the basement and opened the door. A minute later he heard her scream. Inside the apartment, drawers were pulled out everywhere and papers lay all over the floor. There was no cupboard or recess that had not been searched.

"They must have carried on after Hearns took me to Ipswich," she said. "I didn't know it was going to be like this."

"Oh, Greta, I wish I could do something," he said. "I feel so responsible. I didn't want you to come back to this."

"You are doing something. You're being here."

They were in the kitchen and Greta was moving about, straightening her possessions, making coffee, and bringing out a glass and a bottle of whisky for Peter.

"Have some too, Greta," he said. "You'll feel better."

"No, I won't. I'll feel worse," she said, laughing suddenly. "The coffee's enough, and I'll have some toast. I didn't touch anything in that filthy police station."

"Was it really bad?"

"It was squalid. Full of human misery like those places are. They put you in a cell, give you a taste of it to soften you up before they start asking you questions."

"I've never been in one."

"Of course you haven't, Peter. You haven't got a rich past life like me.

Sorry, *poor* would be a better word." Greta spoke harshly. There was a bitterness in her voice that Peter had not heard before.

"What are they going to do, Greta?"

"Oh, they gave me a date to go back. 'Bail to return' it's called, but nothing'll happen. They're grasping at straws."

"I know. That's what I told Thomas."

"It's because of him that they're doing it. You know that, don't you, Peter? He's so convinced that I'm the person behind it that he's got Hearns convinced too. And the best part is that he didn't even see the face of the man that I'm supposed to have been with. God, I wish I hadn't lied. It's too late now, of course."

"Don't blame yourself, Greta. I understand why you had to. What else have the police got?"

"The window that I forgot to close. The arrangement with Mrs. Ball that Anne asked me to make, and now they've got sweet Aunt Jane saying that I was standing in the hall talking to myself about how Lady Anne 'had fucking had it now.' Mrs. Posh I'm supposed to have called her."

"Jane told me something about this. It was the day after it happened, and I went over to Woodbridge to talk to her and Thomas. Everyone got angry."

"Well, I know why she's said it. To back up Thomas, because that's his problem. He needs someone else to say something."

"You mean she's lying."

"Of course she's lying. She's always hated me."

"I'll dismiss her then."

"No, don't do that. It'll just make things worse."

"No, you're right. I can't leave Thomas there on his own."

"On his own?"

"I can't see him. Not after what he's said to me. Not after what he's done."

"What did he say to you?"

"He said I was protecting you because we're, we're . . ." Peter flushed and looked away, busying himself with pouring out another glass of whisky.

Greta sat down beside him at the table and took his other hand in hers, knotting their fingers together.

"Look at me, Peter," she said. "That's why Thomas is doing this. I didn't want to tell you before, but things have gone too far now. You need to understand."

She was very close to him, and he sat captivated by her glittering green eyes.

"He wanted me, Peter. He told me that I was beautiful, that he loved me."

"When? What did you do?"

Peter felt a rush of panic as if she'd suddenly taken a knife out of the drawer and put it to his throat.

"It was in the taxi on the way back here after we had a picnic in the park. The day that you couldn't make it, you remember."

"What did you do?"

"Nothing. What do you think I did? He was fourteen and I'm twenty-seven. I told him that he was very sweet but it wasn't right. What else was I supposed to say?"

"Nothing. You did right. He must be crazy."

"He's a teenager who has never had a girlfriend. He's thinking about sex three times a minute just like other boys his age."

"I didn't."

"That's not the point. The reason I'm telling you all this is so that you'll understand why he's got it in for me. I rejected him and he's got to hate me for that. Then he thinks that I'm having sex with you, which makes him hate me even more because I've taken you away from him and because he's jealous. Then his mother's killed and he feels guilty about having wanted me when I wasn't Lady Anne's favorite person. It's a poisonous brew."

"Did he touch you, Greta?"

The thought of his son's hands, of anyone's hands holding Greta had engulfed Peter. He suddenly felt sick with jealousy.

"Of course he didn't, Peter. Don't be ridiculous."

"I don't want anyone to touch you."

"They're not going to."

She smiled and reached out her hand so that it touched his cheek. Her red lips were open, and he could see the tip of her tongue between her perfect small white teeth.

He took hold of her hand and kissed it. He meant his touch to be gentle, but instead it was hungry and his breath came in short, sharp bursts.

She stood up, and for a moment he thought she was going to leave but she did not pull away. Instead she took his other hand, unlacing it from the whisky glass, and brought it up until it covered her breast.

She looked dreamily at the wall through half-closed eyes as he cupped her breast in his palm and felt with his fingers for the hard nipple through the thin black material of her dress.

She was feeling behind her back for the zipper, grimacing in frustration when she could not reach it, but she did not speak. Instead she pulled his other hand round behind her, pressing herself forward into his body while she guided his fingers upward.

A moment later and he had found it. He pulled down and suddenly he felt the flesh of her back. He pulled apart the bra strap so that he could feel the hard bones of her shoulder blades and below that, a second later, the parting of her skin, the cleft above her buttocks.

As Peter's hand descended, Greta threw her head back, exhaling deeply. The black dress fell away from her, and his face was crushed into the soft center of her breast. He opened his mouth and searched with his tongue for the nipple. It was hard and thick between his teeth, and he held her breast in both his hands, feeling in his fingers the soft size of it, the weight of it in his palms.

But she would not stay still. Instead she was pushing the dress down over her hips as she straddled him in the chair. Reaching out he cupped his hands under her strong buttocks so that he could guide himself deep into her.

Later they made love in Greta's unmade bed, ignoring the chaos of the ransacked room around them. He moved slowly inside her with his eyes wide open so that he could experience every facet of her nakedness; the pink aureoles, the cleavage between her high breasts, the rich, thick blackness of her pubic hair.

"I love you, Greta," he whispered and she smiled.

"He loves me, he loves me not," she said as she rocked backward and forward above him, but he knew that his time for choice, if there had ever been a time, was now over.

Six hours earlier he had watched his wife being lowered into the wet ground, and now here he was having sex with his assistant for the second time. He was disgusted with himself; he smelled the whisky on his breath and the sweat on his body, but at the same time he rejoiced. Greta was more beautiful than he could ever have imagined.

==

At half past one the telephone rang. Just once, but it was enough to wake Peter up. He had been sleeping badly for the last week anyway. The whisky gave him insomnia, and any disturbance shattered his uneasy dreams.

He lay on his side facing the window and listened to Greta's whispered conversation.

"Do you know what time it is?" she said angrily, and then after a moment she added: "Wait, I'm going to go in the other room. I'll call you back."

He felt her get out of bed and put on a robe. She went out into the hall and put the light on and then came back to stand on his side of the bed looking down at him for a moment. He kept his eyes closed and breathed evenly. He didn't know why. It was almost as if he felt it was the polite thing to do, to pretend to be asleep.

She pulled the door to behind her without closing it fully, and he sat up in the darkness wondering who it could possibly be, who would call Greta like this in the middle of the night. He thought of the blackmailer Greta had told him about on the night of the murder. Had he come back? Perhaps he wanted more money. That's what usually happened. It wasn't just Greta's problem now, Peter realized. It was his too. Peter needed to tell Greta that she could count on him. He groped around on the floor for his clothes and pulled on his shirt and trousers. Then he walked purposefully down the hallway to the door at the far end and paused with the handle in his hand. Greta's voice was audible on the other side of the door and Peter suddenly felt that he would be intruding to walk in on her. He knew he ought to go back to bed, but her words kept him rooted to the spot.

"Look, you've got to leave me alone." Greta sounded angry like she had been in the bedroom.

A pause, then her voice came again, louder this time: "Don't call me that. I'm not your Greta Rose. Not anymore."

Another pause and then: "You've had what we agreed. You got it all. Now leave me alone."

Peter felt like a spy. He had to go forward or back, and he went forward. He needed to know what it all meant.

As he opened the door, he was just in time to hear her last words before she put down the phone.

"I've got just as much on you now as you've got on me. Remember that."

Greta looked shocked to see Peter standing in the doorway.

"I thought you were asleep," she stammered.

"I was. I heard you get up. Who was that calling you? Was it that man?"

"Yes, yes it was. He won't call again."

"Why?"

"Because I've got something of his. I made him give it to me when he had the money. You heard what I said."

"What have you got?"

"I don't want to tell you, Peter. You don't need to know. Isn't it enough that I tell you he's going to stop?"

Greta held her arms out toward Peter and her robe fell open, exposing her body. But he remained by the door. His forehead was creased with anxiety.

" 'I'm not your Greta Rose.' What does that mean, Greta? I need to know what it means."

"You were listening outside the door, Peter. You were spying on me."

Peter ignored the accusation. He needed an answer.

"Tell me what it means, Greta."

"It means nothing. Greta Rose is my name; that's all. Everyone used to call me that up in Manchester. Rose was my grandmother. I don't know where they got the Greta from. Unless it was Greta Garbo, but she was a bit before my mother's time, I think."

Greta smiled but Peter was still not satisfied.

"I've never heard you called Greta Rose."

"That's because I dropped the Rose when I left Manchester. I wanted to make a clean break with all that life, start afresh. I told you that before."

"Why did you say you weren't *his* Greta Rose?"

"Because I'm not. You know what I told you. He likes me. He tried it on that last time he was here, but I didn't let him."

Peter's head swam. The thought of this stranger's hands on Greta had the same confusing effect on him that it had had when she had told him about the blackmailer a week before. Except that now the sight of Greta's naked body and his experience of it only hours earlier redoubled his anger and lust.

Greta could see the effect of her words and pressed home her advantage.

"Perhaps I should have let him. It would have been easier."

"No." Peter almost shouted the word as he crossed over to Greta and took hold of her hands in a fierce grip.

"I didn't because of you," she said softly as he pushed the robe back from off her shoulders and laid her down on the floor.

This time he came almost immediately and lay exhausted with his head upon her breast. She had pulled a cushion under her head and lay naked on the carpet, making no effort to cover herself. She stared dreamily up at the ceiling with a faraway look in her green eyes. A smile played across her red lips as she stroked the thick black hair of her lover.

Chapter 18

"THE NEXT WITNESS, my Lord, is Matthew Barne."

"Barne or Barnes?"

"Barne, my Lord," said John Sparling. "Without the *s*."

It was Monday morning and the courtroom was once again full. The benches reserved for the press were packed, and there was a sense of expectancy in the air. All the jurors were alert, and Greta noticed that the Margaret Thatcher look-alike had moved into the seat nearest the judge, where the foreperson of the jury goes when it's time to deliver the verdict. It looked as if it would be a forewoman this time.

Matthew Barne came in accompanied by his mother, who took a seat close to the witness box while her son took the oath.

He had red hair and freckles and pale blue eyes, which fluttered from person to person as he stumbled over the words on the oath card that Miss Hooks held up in front of him.

He was dressed in a double-breasted suit, which looked as if it had been bought for the occasion, and his school tie was tied in a big knot over a shirt collar that seemed to be a size too small for his bulging neck. He had a gift-wrapped appearance, and his discomfort showed in the way that he answered questions. He spoke in stops and starts, sometimes saying too little and sometimes too much so that his audience felt as if they were only catching periodic glimpses of his true personality. He constantly brushed his bangs off his forehead in a habitual gesture that reminded Greta of Thomas.

"How old are you, Matthew?" asked the judge.

"Sixteen, sir."

"I think you'd be more comfortable if Mr. Sparling and Mr. Lambert here called you Matthew rather than Master Barne or anything formal like that. Is that what you'd prefer, Matthew?"

"Yes, sir."

"And I suggest you sit down to give your evidence. It's not easy for someone of your age being in court, and you should tell me if there's anything I can do to make it less difficult for you."

"Thank you, sir."

Matthew managed a nervous smile as he sat down and turned his buttoned up neck toward John Sparling. "Matthew, do you know Thomas Robinson?" asked the prosecution barrister.

"Yes, I do. He goes to school with me."

"Which school is that, Matthew?"

"Carstow School, sir. It's in Surrey."

"How long have you known Thomas?"

"Since last September. We both started together."

"Tell us about your relationship."

"He's my best friend. All the other boys in our class had already been there two years when we got there, and so we were sort of in it together, if you know what I mean."

"I see. Now, have you ever been to five St. Mary's Terrace in Chelsea, London?"

"Is that where Tom's dad lives?"

"Yes. Have you been there?"

"Yes. Yes, I have."

Matthew suddenly sounded very nervous and looked up at Judge Granger, swallowing visibly as he did so. The judge did his best to calm him down.

"Just answer the questions, Matthew," he said gently. "You have nothing to fear. Have some water if you need to."

"Thank you, my Lord," said Sparling. "Now, Matthew, when did you go to Sir Peter Robinson's house?"

"Near the end of October last year. It was at the weekend. On a Saturday."

"Who were you with?"

"With Tom. It was his idea."

"I see. Now tell us in your own words, Matthew, what the idea was. Why did you go to the house?"

"Because the girlfriend of Tom's dad had her stuff there. Tom read in the paper the weekend before that his dad was going to Paris for some political thing, and Tom said his dad's girlfriend goes everywhere with him because she's his assistant too."

"So they'd be away. What was the significance of that?"

"So that Tom could go through her stuff. He thinks she was behind his mum getting killed, and he wanted to find something to prove it. Because that's what the police told him. That they needed more evidence."

Miles Lambert had caught Judge Granger's eye while Matthew was talking, and the judge now leaned forward to speak to the prosecution barrister before he asked his next question.

"I know it's difficult, Mr. Sparling, but please try and cut out the hearsay. Thomas Robinson can tell us about his motives when he gives his evidence. We don't need Matthew here to do it for him."

"No, my Lord," said Sparling. "I hear what you say. Matthew, tell us what time you got to the house."

"It was in the afternoon. About half past four. Tom had a key to the front door, but he rang the bell first. We watched to see if anyone answered, but they didn't. He did the same downstairs in the basement. Then when we were inside, there's a door that goes downstairs in the hall, and he went through that."

"How?"

"There was a key in the door. He was down there for quite a while."

"Where did you go?"

"I stayed upstairs. There was a room off the hall with a whole lot of computer equipment, and I sat in there. I didn't touch anything."

"What happened next?"

"Tom came back, and then he went through the stuff in the computer room."

"What stuff?"

"He looked in the drawers and he turned on the computer and went through the files. He didn't find anything though. We were there for ages and I wanted to go but he said we had to go upstairs. He said that his dad and his assistant were living together and so she'd have personal stuff in the bedroom."

"Mr. Sparling," said the judge in a warning voice.

"Yes, my Lord. Matthew, try to stick to what happened and don't tell us what Thomas said. Okay?"

"Yes, sir."

"Right, tell us what happened upstairs. Did you go up there too?"

"Yes, but I only stood in the doorway while Tom went in. She did have stuff in there like Tom said she would, but he didn't find anything to do with his mother in any of her clothes or her drawers or anything like that, and so we started to go back downstairs. Tom was really upset. He was frustrated at not finding anything when he'd been going on about how he was going to get Greta all the way up on the train. He—"

"Yes, Matthew," interrupted Sparling. "We do need to focus on what happened in the house. You said you were going downstairs. Tell us what happened next."

"Well, we were one floor up from the computers. On the landing. And there was a door open into this big room."

"The drawing room?"

"I guess so. Anyway, Tom saw this old desk in the corner, and he was saying that his mother used to use it when she was in London and that it had this really neat secret drawer. That was where he found the locket."

"He showed it to you? You saw it up close?"

"Yes, sir. It was gold with a chain, and there was a little photograph inside. Tom said it was his parents. In the photograph I mean."

"Thank you, Matthew. Now I'd like to show you one of our exhibits. It's number thirteen, my Lord. Do you recognize that, Matthew?"

"It looks like it. Yes, I'd say it's the same as the one Tom found."

"Thank you. Now, Matthew, please tell us what happened after Tom found the locket."

"He was really excited. Talking a lot and everything. I guess that's why we didn't hear the door open downstairs. We didn't hear anything until she was on the stairs."

"Who? Who was on the stairs?"

"Greta. She . . . she's over there." Matthew pointed at the dock where Greta was sitting forward in her chair watching him intently.

"What happened next?"

"Tom was in the doorway, and I think she saw him first. She was really angry, shouting at him, using all this really bad language."

"We need you to tell us everything she said, Matthew," said Sparling in a fatherly voice. "I know it's not easy, but we need to know even if the words are bad."

"She called Tom a fucking little sneak. I remember that. It was scary. Tom backed away into the room and almost knocked me over. I was behind him. Tom was holding up this locket thing in front of her saying, 'Look what I've found' or something like that. He was really angry too. They were both shouting."

"What was Greta shouting, Matthew? Help us with that."

"She said, 'Give that to me. It's mine.' That's what she said. She made a grab for it but she missed. Tom pulled it away and then he pushed her back. I don't know what she was going to do. Scratch him or something I guess."

"What happened when he pushed her back, Matthew? Where did she go?"

"She was on the floor and Tom was standing over her and he was like shouting down at her."

"What did he shout?"

Matthew's brow furrowed as if he was concentrating hard to remember something exactly.

"He said, 'No, it's not. It's my mother's. That bastard took it from her and he gave it to you. He gave it to you.' And then just after that, Tom's dad came in."

"Sir Peter. What did he do?"

"He was really upset. It's not surprising really. I mean we weren't supposed to be there, and there was his girlfriend lying on the floor and Tom shouting at her."

"Was Thomas shouting when his father came into the room?"

"I don't know. It all happened really quick. Tom backed off when his dad came in. I remember that, and then his dad got Greta up off the floor and put her on the sofa. She was crying. I don't know if she got hurt when Tom pushed her over."

"Yes, I see. Carry on, Matthew. What happened next?"

"Tom's dad asked Greta what happened, and she said how Tom had pushed her. She said Tom had attacked her, and then it was like this guy was going to hit Tom. I know he's done that before because Tom told me. He had his fists clenched and he was going toward Tom, and that's when Tom showed his dad the locket. He was holding it up like it was some magic charm or something and telling his dad where he'd got it from. He said that Greta must have gotten it off the man who killed his mother."

Matthew's words had come slowly at first, but now he spoke in a rush with sentences tumbling into one another until at the end he seemed to have entirely lost control of the torrent of words falling from his mouth.

"All right, Matthew, I think we've all got that," said Sparling, "but please try to go a bit slower from now on; calm down a little; take your time. Now, how did Greta respond to what Thomas said?"

"She didn't at first. She was crying, like I told you before, but then she said that it wasn't true; that she'd found the locket in the bathroom a day or two after Tom's mother got shot and that she'd put it in the secret drawer to keep it safe. That's when Tom started asking her all these questions and she was answering them too. It was like she realized she needed to give some sort of explanation."

"To whom?"

"I don't know. To Tom and to Tom's dad too, I guess. Tom was the one asking the questions, though."

"Okay. Then tell us what they said, please, Matthew."

"Tom was asking what she was doing in the bathroom because it was like near the top of the house, when Greta works on the ground floor where all that computer equipment was; and she said that the cleaner was in the downstairs loo and so she'd gone upstairs. Then Tom said that the basement would've been nearer. It was going back and forth like that, and then he asked her why she'd put it in the secret drawer in the desk. Greta said something about it being Anne's desk and so it was a natural place to put it. Something like that."

"Did Thomas's father, Sir Peter, ask anything?"

"Yes, he wanted to know why Greta hadn't given him the locket, and she said that she hadn't wanted to upset him and then she'd forgotten about it. She seemed to have an answer for everything."

There was a pause while John Sparling looked for something in his notes. Miles Lambert turned round to his client and smiled. The witness's last comment had been a gift.

"Was anything else said, Matthew?" asked Sparling.

"Tom's dad seemed to believe what Greta was saying, and he got really angry with Tom and with me too. It was scary. He said we were to get out and go back to school or he'd call the police."

"Yes, Matthew, but was there anything else that anyone said before Sir Peter told you that? Have you left anything out?"

Matthew looked blank and Sparling tried again.

"What happened to the locket, Matthew?" he asked.

"Oh, yes, Tom showed it to his father again and told him what Greta had said about it before his dad came in."

"What was that?"

"That it was hers. She denied saying it even though I knew she did. I heard her."

"Yes, Matthew. Now you've said that Sir Peter told you to get out. Did you do so?"

"You bet I did. I ran down the stairs so fast that I almost fell over. Tom caught up to me outside. He didn't run like me. I was really scared that his dad would write to my parents, get me expelled or something like that, but nothing happened. Not until the police came to see me."

"When was that?"

"A couple of days later. It was Mr. Hearns and he said I'd done really well, which was the opposite of what I expected to hear. It was really weird."

Matthew gulped and then smiled at the memory. The smile transformed his face and made him suddenly attractive, so that he was no longer a nervous schoolboy in an ill-fitting suit but rather a real person with a strange story to tell. Several of the jurors smiled too, and Sparling realized instinctively that he'd reached the high point in his examination of his witness. The high point was the point at which to stop; Sparling didn't need to be told that.

"Thank you, Matthew," he said as he sat down, with something closely resembling a smile playing across his usually funereal features.

"I think we'll take a ten-minute break there," said Judge Granger before Miles Lambert could get to his feet. "You can have a chance to stretch your legs, Matthew, and the jurors can have a cup of coffee."

=

In his room Judge Granger sat in an easy chair facing out toward the London skyline and drew deeply on an unfiltered cigarette. The room filled with blue smoke as he exhaled so that Miss Hooks appeared as if out of a cloud when she arrived with his cup of morning coffee.

"Everything all right, Miss Hooks?" he inquired as he always did once the cup of coffee had safely been passed over. The judge had never rid himself of an anxiety that Miss Hooks would stumble over her floor-length black gown at the vital moment and fall down on him in a rain of scalding black coffee, but it hadn't happened yet.

"Yes, your Lordship. Jury are in their room," replied Miss Hooks, just as she always had done, except for that memorable day two years before when a younger juror had given Miss Hooks the slip and escaped from the building in midtrial.

Miss Hooks was a creature of routine, and to Judge Granger she was as much a part of the courtroom landscape as the barristers' wigs and gowns and the old clock that kept the time above the defendant's head. He'd never had a meaningful conversation with her, and to the extent that he had ever thought about it, he assumed that she did not pay attention to any of the evidence after she'd gotten the witness seated and sworn in. That wasn't her department. The old judge imagined what a good job she'd have made of placing the black cap on his head if capital punishment were still in force. She'd probably have a little iron in the ushers' room, where she could get the cap nicely pressed in anticipation of a guilty verdict.

Judge Granger did not believe in God, but he thanked him anyway that he had never had to sentence anyone to death. There were always cases where he did not feel sure. Like this one for instance. She was a strange fish, this Lady Greta Robinson. He had sat opposite her for two days now, making sure not to catch her glittering green eyes, and he still didn't know what to make of her. She was obviously clever, as well as pretty, and she had nothing in common with the usual listless defendants fidgeting in their chair as incomprehensible legal arguments droned on in front of them. The judge had watched the way she balanced her notebook on her knee, looking at each witness intently and occasionally passing notes to Miles Lambert. He certainly seemed to believe in her.

John Sparling kept producing all these bits of evidence like they were links in a sturdy chain, but they didn't feel like that to the judge. An un-locked gate and an open window. The victim could have left the gate unlocked herself, and the window might not be sinister at all. The de-fendant had admitted leaving it open after all, and it had been a summer evening. What else? A few angry words muttered in a hallway; an iden-tification from behind, and now this locket. Would this clever young lady really have kept such a dangerous trophy? And what did she need a trophy for when she'd gotten the husband and the money? So much seemed to depend on this boy, Thomas. It certainly wasn't usual for the chief prosecution witness to testify last, but of course there was a reason for that. Sparling said the boy had been traumatized by the return of the killers a week before the trial began. If this had happened, trauma would be too mild a word for the boy's experience. But had it hap-pened? What was it the statement said: the killer had looked for him in the house but hadn't found him because he was hidden in a bench, and so this "Rosie" had gone away, but not before he'd implicated Greta, the defendant, by name. There was something all too convenient about this reappearance; something that just didn't feel right.

The judge shifted in his chair and stretched out his long legs, enjoy-ing the last of his cigarette. There were rumors that the courthouse would soon be a smoke-free zone, although he'd probably be retired by then. He dreaded his approaching compulsory retirement to the same degree that Mrs. Sybil Granger back home in Richmond-upon-Thames was looking forward to it. She'd long ago made clear what she had in mind. The annual holiday down in Bournemouth would be-come a permanent arrangement. They had so many friends there, after all, and the judge could play a little golf and maybe join a society or two. He couldn't say no after all the years that he had kept his wife in Lon-don, and the thought crossed his mind, as he got up stiffly and posi-tioned his threadbare wig on the top of his bald head, that the best solution might be for him to die. Death or Bournemouth? It was a tough choice.

Still, he didn't need to think about death right now. Old Lurid had had a sly look on his face toward the end of this Barne boy's evidence. Perhaps he had something up his sleeve. Judge Granger approached the door of the courtroom with something almost approaching a spring in his step.

=

"Matthew, are you okay to continue?" asked Miles Lambert solicitously.

"I'm all right." Matthew sounded more confident now, as if he'd gotten used to the courtroom and the barristers in their wigs and gowns.

"Good. Now, I want to read back to you a little bit of your evidence so that you can have a chance to think about it some more. You told Mr. Sparling that Thomas Robinson held up the locket in front of Greta saying, 'Look what I've found' and that they were both shouting. Do you remember that?"

"Yes."

"Good. Then Mr. Sparling asked you what Greta was shouting, and you told us that she said, 'Give that to me. It's mine.' Do you remember telling us that?"

"Yes, I do."

"But did she really say that, Matthew? Are you sure you've got it right?"

"Yes, I'm sure."

"I see. Well, why didn't you confirm it to Sir Peter when he asked you if she'd said it?"

Matthew swallowed but did not reply. He was nervous again now.

"Come on, Matthew. You know what I'm talking about. You gave evidence that Thomas showed the locket to his father and told him what Greta had said about it and that she then denied saying it. You remember telling us that, don't you, Matthew? Mr. Sparling was so anxious that you should remember that bit of your statement that he asked you all those questions until you did."

"Yes, I remember."

"Good. The point is, though, that you didn't tell us what Sir Peter said after that. I'm not criticizing you, Matthew. Mr. Sparling didn't ask you."

"What's the question, Mr. Lambert?" asked the judge, moving restlessly in his chair.

"The question is this, my Lord. Did Sir Peter ask you whether Greta had said it? Yes or no, Matthew."

"Yes. Yes, he did."

"And what was your answer?"

"I didn't answer. I ran down the stairs. I told you that already. I was scared."

"But you're not scared today?"

"What do you mean?"

"Just that you've been prepared to tell this jury something today that you weren't prepared to tell Sir Peter Robinson nine months ago."

"I was scared nine months ago. He was really upset. I thought he was going to hit Tom. He'd done it before."

"You said earlier that you weren't surprised he was upset, Matthew?"

"No, I wasn't."

"Because you'd gone into his house without his permission and been through private files and papers?"

"I didn't. Tom did."

"He went through all Greta's clothes too, didn't he? You were watching from the bedroom doorway, I think you said."

"Yes. I wanted to go."

"Did he go through her underwear, Matthew?"

"I suppose so."

"I see. It wasn't the first time you and Thomas Robinson had done something like this, was it, Matthew?"

"I'd never been there before. I swear it."

"That's not what I mean, Matthew, and you know it isn't. It wasn't just your day out in London that made you think you might be expelled, was it? You were both already in trouble at Carstow. Isn't that right, Matthew?"

The boy's pale blue eyes remained fixed on Miles Lambert, but he didn't reply. The movement of his Adam's apple as he repeatedly swallowed showed the extent of his anxiety.

"All right, Matthew, let me help you. You've already told us that Thomas Robinson and you started at Carstow at the same time in September of last year, when you were both fifteen. Yes?"

Matthew Barne nodded.

"And everyone else in your class had already been there two years so that you and Thomas were like outsiders. Was that difficult, Matthew?"

"A bit."

"Did the other boys let you join in with their activities?"

"Not at first. No."

"No. They said you had to prove yourselves first, earn their respect. Isn't that right, Matthew?"

"Something like that."

"Do a dare. Is that the right word for it?"

The boy nodded.

"What was the dare, Matthew?"

"Going into the headmaster's room and taking something. Showing it to the rest of them and putting it back."

"And that something was a paperweight, wasn't it, Matthew? Quite a distinctive one."

"Don't answer that for the moment, Matthew," interrupted the judge. "What is your source of information for all this, Mr. Lambert?"

"A letter sent by the headmaster to Thomas Robinson's father after the event, my Lord. I can prove the evidence later if the witness disagrees with it."

"What's its relevance?"

"It's relevant to the witness's credibility, my Lord."

"Very well, but let's not stray too far, Mr. Lambert, and please make sure that you remember the witness's age. I will not allow him to be bullied."

"That is not my intention, my Lord."

"All right, but keep it in mind. Don't get carried away. Now Matthew, Mr. Lambert was asking you about a paperweight."

"Yes, it was a paperweight," said the boy.

"Did you take it, Matthew?" asked Miles.

"No, I didn't. Tom did."

"I see. The same setup as in London. What did you do?"

"I stood outside while he went in, and then the headmaster's secretary came by and asked me what I was doing."

"That would be Mrs. Bradshaw?"

Matthew nodded. He'd stopped swallowing and started to speak quickly again as if he wanted to make a clean breast of what had happened and get it over with as fast as possible.

"She wanted to know what I was doing, and I told her I was waiting to see Old Lofty."

"Who's Old Lofty?"

"Sorry. The headmaster. It's just a nickname."

"His real name is Mr. Lofthouse. Is that right?"

"Yes. And he's tall too so . . ." Matthew laughed nervously without finishing his sentence.

"You were lying when you told Mrs. Bradshaw that you were waiting to see the headmaster. You accept that, don't you?"

The boy nodded.

"That's a yes, is it, Matthew? For the record. The tape won't pick it up if you just nod."

"Yes."

"Thank you. Now what did Mrs. Bradshaw do when you told her this lie?"

"She didn't believe me. I don't know why."

"Perhaps because you're not a good liar, Matthew."

"Mr. Lambert," said the judge crossly. "I've warned you about this. Let the witness say what happened without interrupting him. Go on, Matthew. Tell us what Mrs. Bradshaw did."

"She went in the study and found Tom in there and then she called the headmaster and he made us empty our pockets and that's when he found the paperweight. Tom had it in his pocket."

"He'd stolen it. Yes?" asked Miles.

"We were going to put it back afterward. I already told you that," replied Matthew defensively. "Lofty believed us. That's why he only wrote to our parents and didn't expel us or do anything like that. He was quite decent, really."

"Yes, he certainly was," said Miles. "Now, I've only got a few more questions, Matthew, and the first one is this: have you talked to Thomas Robinson about your evidence?"

"We've talked about the case at school. Everyone has."

"Have you talked about what everyone said in the drawing room? Greta and Thomas and Sir Peter?"

"I suppose so."

"Word for word."

"Not word for word. No."

"What about what you say Greta said: 'Give that to me. It's mine.' Have you talked about that?"

"I don't know. Maybe."

"Maybe," repeated Miles musingly, and then he suddenly opened up at Matthew Barne with all guns blazing. "Not maybe, Matthew. Definitely. Greta never said that. Thomas Robinson has told you to give that evidence, and you've done so even though you know it's untrue. You're lying, Matthew. That's what I'm putting to you. You're lying to this jury."

"No, I'm not. I swear I'm not," stammered Matthew with tears in his eyes, but Miles Lambert had already sat down with a satisfied look on his red face.

Chapter 19

POLICE CONSTABLE Hughes arrived in court in full uniform other than his police cap, which he held in his hands while he gave evidence, periodically turning it over as if inspiration might be waiting for him under its brim.

John Sparling had very little to ask, and it was soon his opponent's turn. Miles Lambert tried to set the Carmouth policeman at ease with an anodyne first question: "Am I right in saying that you were the first officer to arrive at the House of the Four Winds on July fifth?"

"Yes, sir. There was an emergency call from the occupant, Thomas Robinson. Police Constable Jones and I attended in response. We were the nearest mobile unit at the time."

"Do you have a note of the time of the emergency call?"

"Yes. It's down on the computer printout as being received at seven-oh-six P.M."

"Thank you. Now, which of you was driving?"

"I was."

"It was a marked police car?"

"Yes."

"And did you have your siren turned on?"

"Yes, sir. We were responding to an emergency call."

"I understand. Where did you park?"

"Initially outside the front gate, sir. It was locked and so I got out and pressed the buzzer on the wall. Thomas Robinson answered and I identified myself as a police officer. He then buzzed the gate open. It works by remote control."

"What did Thomas say when he answered?"

"He just asked who I was. That's all, sir. Then he opened the gates."

"Without saying anything else?"

"That's right."

"Now, Officer, could you see the front door of the house when you were outside the gate?"

"No, sir. I was able to see it once I drove in and parked the car but not before."

"Was the front door of the house open or closed when you first saw it?"

"It was open. Thomas Robinson was at the top of the steps about four or five yards from the door when I first saw him. There are six quite distinctive trees in front of the house, and he was standing between the first two of them. He seemed quite distressed, sir."

"Was he crying?"

"No. He was agitated though."

"What was said?"

"Officer Jones and I got out of our car, and I asked him what had happened."

"How did Thomas respond to your question?"

"He told us that two men had entered the house through the front door and that he recognized one of them from the night of his mother's murder. He said that he had seen them approach the house from the direction of a lane, which he pointed to. It was across a wide lawn on the north side of the house."

"Yes, you will see that the lane and the house are shown on the plan that the usher is placing in front of you."

"Yes, sir. Thomas said that the intruders had left by the front door moments before."

"What did you do when you had obtained this information, Officer?"

"I left Officer Jones with Thomas and drove round into the lane. I went up as far as the door in the north wall of the grounds, but there was no sign of the intruders."

"Did you try the door?"

"Yes. It was locked, sir."

"Did you see any footprints?"

"No. It had not been raining, and I would not have expected to find any footprints at this time of year."

"Did you see any other sign of intruders?"

"No, but I didn't make any close examination of the area, sir. I left that for the crime-scene officer. Detective Constable Butler arrived about one hour after Officer Jones and myself."

"I see. What did you do after you checked the door in the lane?"

"I returned to Officer Jones. He had gone back inside the house and Thomas Robinson was showing him an old black bench in the hall where he said he had hidden from the intruders."

"You also located the key to the front door, did you not?"

"Yes, sir. Thomas showed it to me."

"You asked him about it?"

"Yes. It was hanging on a nail in the hall. Thomas said that the intruders had opened the door using a key and that they had run out the same way when they heard our siren."

"Thank you, Mr. Hughes. I've got nothing else."

"Any reexamination, Mr. Sparling?" asked the judge.

"Just one question, my Lord. Officer, you've said that you parked outside the front gate. Could you see the exit from the lane from where you were?"

"No, sir. The gate is set back from the road a little way, and there's a row of trees between the wall and the curb. We wouldn't have had a view from where we were parked, sir."

"Thank you, Officer. That's all."

Police Constable Hughes put on his cap and headed for the door on his way back to Carmouth and obscurity.

=

The day wore on. At one o'clock everyone broke for lunch. John Sparling wasn't hungry but made a concession to the time of day by picking at a green salad, which he washed down with a glass of mineral water in the barristers' canteen upstairs.

Miles Lambert, however, took his bulk round the corner to a little Italian restaurant where Dino kept him a table in the corner. A glass of thick red wine and a plate of Dino's mother's special lasagna fortified him for the afternoon. Afterward he ordered himself a cup of sweet

Turkish coffee and sat back in his chair wearing an expression of heavy contentment.

Miles felt well pleased with how the trial had gone so far. The prosecution's case was not standing up to cross-examination, and he could hardly wait to get at their main witness. It was obvious that Thomas had gotten the old housekeeper and his schoolfriend to back up his story. And he'd also made up the Lonny and Rosie characters, for whom there was not a shred of evidence outside of his statement.

Miles knew that he could rely on his client to put on an Oscar-winning performance in the witness box when her turn came. Every day he grew more confident of an acquittal, and he felt sure that that would be the right verdict in this case. Miles had decided long before the trial began that Lady Greta was the most beautiful client he had ever had. Now, having seen Sparling's witnesses, he had no doubt of her innocence.

Detective Sergeant Hearns had, of course, precisely the opposite view of the defendant, and he ruminated on her guilt in the police room as he chewed the big cheese-and-pickle sandwiches that he had brought down with him from Ipswich.

At two o'clock he fastened his double-breasted jacket over a pickle stain in the center of his polyester shirt and went down to court to begin giving his evidence. It was a hot day and the jurors were sleepy. Sparling asked questions to which they felt they already knew the answers. It was only when Miles Lambert got to his feet and asked for them to be sent out of court that they really started paying attention.

"Will this take long, Mr. Lambert?" asked the judge.

"No, my Lord. Not long."

The jury filed out looking perplexed, and Miles waited to speak until the door had finally closed behind them.

"It's about my client's character, my Lord," said Miles. "You will see that she has one minor indiscretion recorded against her from nearly eleven years ago but nothing since."

"A conviction, Mr. Lambert. Not an indiscretion."

"Yes, my Lord, but it is only for possession of a very small amount of drugs."

"Cocaine, Mr. Lambert. A class-A drug."

"Yes, my Lord, but she was a juvenile at the time."

"What's your application?"

"For my client to be treated as a lady of good character. The conviction is old and not serious in nature."

"What do you say, Mr. Sparling?"

"I'd say that possession of cocaine is not minor, my Lord. Mr. Lambert does not need to raise the issue of his client's character, but if he does so, the jury should know all about her. Of course your Lordship has discretion."

"Yes, I do, and I shall exercise it in favor of the defendant on this occasion. The conviction is indeed old and it is not for violence or dishonesty. Lady Greta may be presented as a lady of good character, Mr. Lambert."

"Thank you, my Lord."

=

"Sergeant Hearns, I want to ask you about a conversation you had with my client outside the House of the Four Winds," said Miles once the jury was back in place.

"I've only ever had one conversation with her there, sir, and that was when Sir Peter drove down with her after I told him about the murder."

"That's the one. Now you'd already spoken to Thomas Robinson."

"No, sir, I hadn't. He was too upset. I spoke to Christopher Marsh, who spoke to Thomas. I did that because I needed to know where the perpetrators had gone in the house. And the grounds, sir," the policeman added as if it were an afterthought.

Sergeant Hearns's lugubrious smile was set in place above the big tie and the bulging stomach. He was clearly determined not to let the lawyer set the pace of their exchanges.

"All right, you'd spoken to Christopher Marsh and you had discovered that Thomas had found the study window open on his return to the House of the Four Winds."

"At about half past eight. Yes, sir."

"Now, you asked my client about whether she was responsible for leaving the window open, did you not, Sergeant?"

"No, sir."

"No?"

"No, I asked Sir Peter. He said that he had not been in the study, and then Sir Peter asked your client and she said that she *may* have left the window open."

"She didn't refuse to answer, did she, Sergeant Hearns? She didn't say Thomas was lying. She freely admitted leaving the window open."

"She said she didn't know but she may have done. She looked anxious at the time, sir. Very anxious."

"Like Sir Peter?"

"No, he looked more determined than anxious. Your client had gone on ahead of us, sir."

"Perhaps she was anxious to see Thomas?"

"Perhaps, sir."

"Did she not also say that she'd left the window open because it was a warm evening?"

"Yes, she did say that, sir."

"Now, you didn't arrest her that night, did you, Sergeant, even though you knew she'd left the window open?"

"No, I did not, sir. I arrested your client after I had taken statements from Thomas Robinson and Jane Martin. It was only then that she became a suspect."

"You took the statements on Saturday, the fifth of June. Five days after the murder. Is that right?"

"Yes, sir. That was the first occasion that Thomas felt able to talk to me about what had happened."

"And you arrested Greta Grahame, as she then was, the next day. The Sunday. The day of the funeral?"

"Yes, sir. In the morning. We went to her apartment in Chelsea at seven twenty-five A.M."

"And you searched the premises."

"Yes, we had a warrant."

"I don't doubt it. Did you find anything?"

"Nothing relevant to the allegation. No, sir."

"Then you took Miss Grahame to Ipswich and interviewed her."

"Yes. She denied the allegation."

"And then you released her without charge, didn't you?"

"She was bailed to return. Pending advice from the Crown Prosecution Service."

"And they advised that she should not be charged because there was no realistic prospect of conviction. Isn't that right, Sergeant Hearns?"

"They advised that she should not be charged, sir."

"Yes. No charge even though you had the window that she'd admitted leaving open and the unlocked north gate. You had the arrangement for Thomas to go to the Balls and his identification of the man outside my client's apartment with the killer. You had all that and the statement of Jane Martin, but you still didn't have enough to charge. Because it didn't amount to anything very much. Isn't that right, Sergeant?"

Miles had loaded his gun, taken aim, and fired, but Sergeant Hearns dodged the bullet. The lugubrious smile remained in place as he turned to the judge.

"Do I have to answer that, your Lordship? I don't think it's for me to give an opinion."

"No, you're quite right; it's not. Mr. Lambert, please don't play games with the witness. Stick to the facts."

"Yes, my Lord. Now, Sergeant, we can take it that your efforts to find Rosie and Lonny have drawn a complete blank."

"There have been no arrests so far, sir. But it's not been for want of investigating. The trouble is that the killers left so few clues. We've got the car and the footprints and the bullets but not much else, sir. There's no match for the DNA from the blood sample on the database."

"What about the jewelry?"

"Nothing there, sir. The jewels could have been reset, of course."

"Leaving aside the locket, you have found no jewelry of Lady Anne's on either of the occasions you have searched my client's apartment?"

"No, sir."

Miles paused and cleared his throat loudly to ensure that the jury was paying attention to his next question. "My client, Lady Greta Robinson, is a lady of good character, is she not, Sergeant?"

"That's right, sir."

"Good. Now I want to ask you about your visit to the house of my client's mother in Cale Street, Manchester. You've told Mr. Sparling that you found these pictures of Lady Anne in one of the bedrooms."

"Yes. They were in a scrapbook of press clippings dating from the late 1980s."

"There were in fact quite a number of these scrapbooks, were there not?"

"Yes, sir. They were in the bedroom that Mrs. Grahame said her daughter had used before she left home."

"How many scrapbooks, Sergeant?"

"Eight or nine. Perhaps more."

"And they contained over two thousand pictures, did they not? Lady Anne's were just two among more than two thousand?"

"Yes, sir. They were pictures of ladies of fashion."

"Taken from society magazines like the *Tatler* and *Harpers & Queen*."

"That's right, sir."

=

What must they think of me? thought Greta, looking over at the impassive faces of the jurors. Their eyes traveled from lawyer to policeman and back again with metronomic regularity, like those of an audience at a tennis match.

It had been years since she'd last looked at them, but she still vividly remembered those scrapbooks, which she'd lovingly assembled in those lost teenage years, crouching in front of the gas fire on winter evenings with scissors and paste while her mother watched the telly and a pot of tea got cold on the table. Her mother had stopped sewing by then, forced to give it up by early Parkinson's, which had now—fifteen years later—reduced her to a shaking wreck.

But perhaps it wasn't Parkinson's, reflected Greta. Perhaps it was just the fear of her husband, George, that made her mother's hands tremble in her lap on those distant winter evenings.

They'd have the news at six on. Her mother didn't really watch it but instead just let it pass over her. Floods and famines, earthquakes and volcanoes, economic highs and lows soothed Greta's mother. She liked that nice Mr. Baker who read the news, and when he'd finished she'd say in a comforted voice: "Terrible. It's all just terrible. Those poor people. We should be grateful for what we've got, Greta."

But Greta wasn't grateful. She pasted the pictures into the big black scrapbooks because they made her believe that there was a different world out there where women wore beautiful clothes and walked on thick carpets in perfect high-heeled shoes. Somewhere it didn't smell of boiled cabbages and disinfectant.

After the news came the program about local events—a Manchester school opened, a Manchester woman raped—and Greta's mother wasn't soothed anymore. George would be home at just after seven expecting his dinner on the table—unless he stopped at the pub of course, but that just made it worse.

Sitting in the dock now, Greta tried to think of a time when her father hadn't been the way he was, returning from the factory full of dust and rage. There must have been another time because otherwise he wouldn't have affected her the way he did, filling the horizons of her imagination long after he was gone from this world. But she couldn't remember, however hard she tried. It was too long ago.

Her father was a man who had done so many bad things that there was no going back. He'd pressed down and down, harder and harder, smothering the light deep inside himself until all that was left was a greedy darkness. Darkness and the need for more darkness.

There was no going back for Greta's mother either. Perhaps it was her very lack of spirit, her cow's eyes, that a younger George had found attractive back in the days of evening dances at the Manchester Empire, when his coal-black hair and sharp, chiseled features gave him the pick of the local girls. Greta would have bet good money that her mother never once thought of leaving her husband. It would have been like questioning the will of God.

They'd gotten married in the rain; Greta remembered the picture in her mother's old photograph album gathering dust on the bookcase in the front room at home. One of the guests was holding a sodden newspaper over her parents' heads while they stood at the top of the church steps waiting to be recorded for posterity. Her mother smiling nervously for the camera and her father looking defiant.

The dusty bookcase was all that posterity had to offer that wedding. Greta wondered if Hearns had had a look through the old album during his nasty, prying search for evidence. He probably had. God knows he was thorough enough. She imagined him leafing through the snapshots, turning the pages with his stubby fingers before he replaced the album between *Casserole Cooking* and an AA Road Atlas from 1966.

It was upstairs that he'd found prosecution exhibits 18 and 19: the newspaper clippings of Lady Anne dressed in a shimmering Dior gown for some gala function with her young husband on her arm and a caption that said he was destined for high places. "Summer 1988," she'd written on the front of the scrapbook. They were just a couple of photographs among two thousand. As exhibits they were ridiculous. Greta didn't even need to listen to Miles making the obvious points at the expense of Detective Sergeant Bloodhound.

The scrapbooks mattered, though. They had allowed her to dream, to believe in a world beyond the poor smoky Manchester suburb where she grew up, beyond the reach of her father's calloused hands. He was always angry, burning with an eternal sense of injustice. No year went by without him being passed over for a better job because some snot-nose twenty years his junior had a piece of paper in his pocket, some qualification or diploma that the company was too cheap to pay for him to get. Perhaps her father had a point. He'd been made ugly by his resentment and the ugly do not attract fair treatment, but at home Greta never thought about whether life was fair or just. She just tried to survive, pasting photographs of aristocrats into scrapbooks and whispering the names of fashion designers to herself like a religious mantra: Balenciaga, Christian Dior, Givenchy, Chanel. Greta wore her black hair like Coco Chanel and hung a picture of the queen of fashion beside her bed at just the right height to cover up a tear in the fading wallpaper.

As she grew older, her father's power over her diminished. He drank more, ranting down at the pub at the injustice of it all until the regulars turned their backs on him and the landlord told him he'd outstayed his welcome. He couldn't afford pub prices anymore either. The company had laid him off, and he'd spent most of the severance pay the first year standing drinks to those who would listen.

At home he sat in his battered armchair grinding out cigarettes in a black plastic ashtray and drinking cans of Special Brew. Greta's mother still cooked the same stodgy meals, but he ate less and less, and after a while he stopped hitting her anymore. He was just too weak. He sat and watched the telly, using what energy he had to hate the people who passed across the screen. There was always someone to hate—someone who was younger than him, richer than him, more successful. Like the boy next door. He moved in when George Grahame had been out of work a year and Greta had just turned seventeen. The boy's mother was an invalid, and there was no sign of any father, which explained a lot, according to George. The boy wore tight black leather trousers and kept a thick wad of twenty-pound notes in the breast pocket of his shirt. More money than George used to earn in a month down at the factory. And yet the boy was only a couple of years older than Greta.

George waited six weeks and then called in the police. He accused the boy of pushing drugs in the town center. How else could somebody that age have gotten all that money? But the police told George that he shouldn't waste their time. If he did it again, he'd be committing an offense.

From then on the boy began to goad Greta's father, tuning his motor-cycle up in the street outside every evening so that George couldn't hear the television and the beer cans vibrated in his hand. George called the council, but they did nothing. It was just like the police, he said. The boy next door had bought them all off with a few bills pulled con-temptuously from the wad in his shirt pocket. But George had paid his taxes all his life, and where had that gotten him?

Greta thought about the boy next door just as much as her father, but the roar of the motorcycle in the dark didn't make her angry. It sang to her of freedom and escape. She dreamed about the boy's narrow hips and the tight muscles in his legs and arms. She longed to hold him hard against her as he drove them far away into a new world.

And the boy watched her. She could sense him staring at her as she walked down the street in the morning on her way to school. It made her cheeks burn and her legs heavy. She felt hot and cold all at the same time.

He took the longest time to ask her out, so that when he did, she ac-cepted too quickly and felt stupid afterward. It was as if the boy always had an advantage over her. Everything he did was a challenge, and if she didn't accept, she'd be right back where she started.

She slept with him because she knew that he didn't think she would. And the sex wasn't lovemaking; it was more like fighting. She reveled in it. At night she slipped downstairs after her parents had gone to bed and let herself soundlessly out the front door. She stepped over the privet hedge that separated the two front gardens and waited for him to pull her into his house.

He told Greta not to worry about his mother, and so she didn't. His living room at midnight was an entire world lit by candles, and their en-twined bodies cast fantastic shadows on the canary-yellow walls.

And then for the first and last time in her life, Greta got pregnant. The baby had been growing inside her for two months by the time she went to the doctor. Back in the waiting room afterward she panicked. She couldn't have the baby and she couldn't kill it. She didn't know what to do, and so she told her mother; and her mother told her father.

With a sudden return of his old strength, George Grahame slapped his daughter across the face and called her a bloody whore. Greta wanted to hit him back, but instead she told him who the father was.

George threw his black ashtray weakly in her direction and told her to get out.

It was so easy to go. She tossed a few of her clothes in a suitcase and shut the front door behind her with a bang. She allowed herself one backward glance at her childhood home—just enough to catch a glimpse of her mother peeking out anxiously from behind the dirty net curtains hung across the window of the front room.

Greta never had the baby. She miscarried in the sixth month and ended up in the Memorial Hospital with complications, and an Indian doctor telling her she was going to be all right if she didn't take any more crazy drugs. He didn't know where she'd been getting them from, but they'd almost killed her as well as the baby.

"You'll get used to not being able to have children," he said. "It's not the end of the world. You've got your whole life in front of you."

And really she hadn't allowed herself to think about it until much later. There was no time. Three floors down and a wilderness of corridors away, her father was lying in one of the hospital's terminal wards struggling to stay alive.

It was as if he had always had cancer. It's just it was mental before it became physical, and by the time it was diagnosed he was long past any hope of cure. Greta winced as she remembered the hospital ward with its rows of metal beds each tenanted by a dying man in concentration-camp pajamas. Flowers didn't last long in the hot, humid air, and they kept the television on all day to drown out the sound of the coughing.

She should have gone there to gloat over his death, but she didn't. It made her desperate, it made her want to cry, but she couldn't. He clung to her like he clung to life, and it was as if he'd forgotten all that he'd done to her. The anger and the envy were gone from his eyes, leaving only the fear that had been lurking there behind them all the time. An awful naked fear that made him fight death for weeks, long after the doctors had predicted that his bed would be free for the next terminal patient to take his place.

Greta hated the fear. It seemed to be telling her that she would never get out, however hard she tried. She'd always be sucked back into the smoke and failure in which she'd grown up. She blamed her mother for it. In those long days in the hospital when her father hung on, refusing to die, Greta grew to hate her mother. She hated her trembling fingers and her pale blue deer-in-the-headlight eyes. She hated her lifeless hair and her shapeless figure, and above all she hated her mother's acceptance of things. Her "its all for the best" view of the world.

She understood why her father had always been so angry. He'd just not been clever enough to make something of his rage. Greta swore to herself softly that she would be different, and all the time he held her wrist and gazed up at her even when he could no longer speak.

The other men in the ward who were not so far gone spoke to her, asking her to come over in shouted whispers as she went past their beds, but she ignored them. She wished that she could afford a private room so that she could watch her father die in peace.

Peace for her, not peace for him of course. He would never feel peace. Not while he was still alive. Greta's mother talked of getting a priest, even though neither she nor Greta's father had been inside a church since their wedding day, but Greta wouldn't hear of it. There was no forgiveness for her father's sins; it disgusted Greta that her mother should even think of it. He wasn't going to hell; he'd been in it all his life. George Grahame knew more about hell than anyone that Greta had ever met.

That much is certain, she thought to herself as she looked out at the courtroom and thought how smug and self-satisfied all the people looked. Contented with their dingy lives and their second-rate marriages. Even the old judge in his wig and gown looked pathetic. He could sit up there grandly while everyone called him "my Lord" and bowed and scraped, but at the end of the day he probably had to go home to some nagging wife and badly cooked food.

Greta closed her eyes. The droning voice of Sparling as he read out witness statements evaporated from her consciousness, and she was back in the hospital on the day her father died. Her memory had recorded it, taken a photograph, just like Thomas had done when his mother got killed. She felt it coming in the grip of her father's hand on her wrist. Suddenly he was holding her tight, not just touching her, and his hand felt strong again like it had when she was a child. He opened his green eyes wide, and it was as if she could see Death reflected there, coming at him like a runaway train. Black and huge and total and gone in a second.

Greta's mother missed it, of course. She was downstairs in the cafeteria getting a cup of tea, and when she came back she had no difficulty bursting into tears, crying for the loss of a man who had beaten her and made her life a misery for twenty-eight years. She cried at the funeral too, and the rain and the tears made her inexpertly applied makeup run down her fat cheeks. She looked so awful that the other mourners had visibly to overcome their aversion to approach her and offer their condolences, but Greta didn't cry. Not then and not later.

Her father's death changed everything. Greta realized that now. It filled her with a determination to start over, to leave Manchester behind. She'd finished with boyfriends and relatives. She wanted a new life in a new town.

She got a job as a reporter on a newspaper in Birmingham to pay her way through college and found she liked the work. She had the rare gift of making people believe in their own importance. Perhaps it was the concentration in her liquid green eyes or the half-suppressed enthusiasm in her low-pitched voice, but even the most taciturn of her interviewees ended up telling her all she wanted to know and more. Afterward they wondered about what they had or hadn't said, but by then, of course, it was too late.

And she wrote well too. Greta's articles were punchy. They brought their subjects alive. As time passed, she was often promoted to the front page. The owners gave her more money and hoped that one of the big papers down south wouldn't snap her up. But it didn't happen. Because instead, one October day in 1996, the local member of Parliament walked into her life.

Peter was at a crossroads, and she pointed him in the right direction. It was obvious that he should come out in support of the prime minister over the hostage crisis in Somalia and forget about what everyone else was saying. Peter was just too far inside the problem to see its solution. It was all so simple. Except that he was unlike anyone else she'd ever met. He had a driving ambition that wouldn't give him any rest, and he allowed her to glimpse for the first time a new world of power politics. Afterward she couldn't rest until she'd made that world her own. She could no longer bear her small-town existence, and when Peter's call came after the election, she didn't ask for time to think. She took the job as his personal assistant and everything that came with it. It was the easiest decision she'd ever made.

And what did come with the job? Long hours and a sense of being close to the beating heart of government. The happiness of knowing that Peter depended on her, and the pleasure that came from the time she spent with his son. It was the only aspect of her employer's character that Greta couldn't relate to. He neglected the boy, and Greta couldn't understand it. At first she tried to get Peter to change, but the subject of Thomas always made him irrationally angry. He seemed to blame his son for not loving him, when he had given the boy no chance to do so. Greta soon came to realize that there was nothing she could do except give Thomas her own affection. And he warmed to her in response. They spent hours walking together on the beach at Flyte exchanging stories, while they held themselves steady against the rush of the wind off the sea. Thomas appealed to Greta's imaginative, dreaming side—the side that Peter could never know.

In the early days, long before the murder, Greta had often wondered at her growing attachment to Thomas. Eventually she had come to the conclusion that it must be, in part at least, a long-delayed reaction to her own infertility. Certainly there was a sense in which she thought of Thomas as the child she would never have. She cared for him without showing it too much, because she knew what the boy's mother thought of her. Lady Anne resented anyone becoming close to her son, especially a factory worker's daughter from an industrial town up north.

Then suddenly Anne was murdered and everything changed. Greta could never forget Thomas's searing hatred when she had rushed to comfort him in Christy Marsh's cottage. She had somehow gotten through that terrible drive up from London with Peter getting drunk on whisky in the passenger seat, but then Thomas had thrown his mug at her and screamed for her to get out. He'd been like someone possessed.

She had gotten out. Left on the train and stayed away just like they'd all told her to. She'd been questioned and searched and questioned again by that pig Hearns until she couldn't bear it anymore, until finally she'd had enough. On the first weekend in October she drove down to Carstow School to see Thomas.

=

Perhaps it would have been better if Greta had planned out what she was going to say. But the only way she could get to Carstow was on a wave of emotion, so she drove fast down the motorway and opened the windows all the way. The big wind blew away all her mixed-up thoughts like cobwebs.

She'd dressed carefully. After much debate, she'd finally selected the dark gray business suit that she'd worn on that magical spring day in London when they'd had the picnic together in the park. She wanted to remind Thomas that there was another time before his mother's murder, when she'd meant something very different to him.

Greta didn't tell the woman in the school office her name, because she thought that Thomas wouldn't come if she did. She just said that she was a friend of the family, and then sat down on a hard-backed chair to wait.

She felt hot in the suit and wished that she'd worn something more comfortable. Beads of sweat trickled down her arms, but she kept her jacket on and drummed her fingers on a school prospectus. The minutes ticked by, and Greta felt stifled by the waiting room. She allowed her head to drop and lost all sense of time and place. She looked up bemused when someone said her name. Thomas stood facing her in the doorway.

For a moment she didn't recognize him. He was thinner than when she had last seen him, and the school had given him a military haircut. It allowed Greta to see for the first time that Thomas had inherited the set of his father's head. She recognized Peter's rigid determination in his son's forehead, and for a moment she quailed.

At least Thomas didn't turn and leave. He didn't go forward or back. Greta couldn't read his expression. He seemed resolute and vulnerable all at the same time, and she was stirred by a great longing for the past. She stood up, putting her arms out toward him, and there were tears in her eyes.

The effect on Thomas was instantaneous. "Get away from me!" he screamed, putting his hands up in front of him to make a barrier.

"Thomas, don't get upset. I only want to explain. You've got it all wrong. You know you have. What happened to your mother had nothing to do with me."

Greta spoke in a rush as if she knew that he would only give her a little time.

"You liar!" he shouted. "You sent them. I know you did."

"No, I didn't. I swear I didn't. I wouldn't do anything to hurt you, Tom. I care about you, can't you see that?"

Greta waited a moment for an answer, but there was none. Thomas remained hidden behind his hands.

"You need me," she said. "You know you do."

"I need my mother." The words escaped from Thomas with a cry, as if they had been pulled out of him by brute force.

"Of course you do. But she's not here anymore, Tom. I am. I'm here for you."

Greta moved toward Thomas again and took hold of his hands, pulling him close just like she had done on that afternoon in his mother's bedroom a year before. And perhaps he would have given in if they hadn't been interrupted. But their raised voices had brought the school secretary to the door asking if everything was all right, and her question broke the connection between them forever.

"Get away from me!" Thomas shouted. "I'm in hell because of you. I hate you."

The venom in his voice forced Greta back. The color drained from her cheeks, and the words dried up in her throat. When Thomas spoke again, his voice was cold and quiet. Not like she'd ever heard it before.

"I'm going to make you pay, Greta," he said. "There's nothing you can do about it. Nothing at all."

Thomas turned on his heel, leaving Greta behind. She did not try to follow.

Two weeks later he went to London with his friend Matthew Barne and found the locket in the secret drawer of his father's desk.

Chapter 20

O N THAT SAME Monday afternoon, the third day of the trial, Thomas roamed restlessly from room to room in the House of the Four Winds, unable to settle down to any occupation. He could hear the murmuring voices of Aunt Jane and the detective from Carmouth coming from behind the half-closed door of the kitchen, but he did not try to make out what they were saying. He knew that Aunt Jane would be talking about the trial down in London; she'd talked about nothing else since she'd gotten back to Flyte the previous evening until Tom didn't want to hear any more about Greta's fat barrister and his tricks and the jury that watched everything and said nothing. Thomas knew that he would have his turn the next day. For now he didn't want to think about it.

He stopped his pacing and stood in the center of the wide hallway midway between the open front door and the staircase behind him. He looked out beyond the yew trees into the hot summer's day, and suddenly it was as if there were voices all around him, snatches of conversation drifting in and out of earshot like specks of dust on the air.

Thomas recognized some of the voices or thought he did, but they were gone before he could be sure. He thought he heard his mother saying something about a dress, but it was his mother younger than he had ever known her, with an eager voice that had no awareness of responsibilities. Then there was a voice behind him that was like his mother's but richer, talking about a horse. Thomas turned but there was nothing, only the sound of a man crying and the name Sarah wrenched from somewhere deep down inside.

The voices were above Thomas now: a man talking in clipped tones about India and another voice, an older woman's cursing. Her words came from very far away, and Thomas could barely make them out.

He stood rooted to the spot, unable to tell if the voices were real. They had been calling him to climb the stairs, which he had avoided for so many months. At the top he could see the bookcase where he had hidden, but he couldn't get to it without crossing the place where his mother had died. They had taken up the carpet and laid a new one since, but he knew where the bloodstains had been. He'd had to step over her when he ran to Christy Marsh's cottage.

Thomas closed his eyes and realized his mistake. The voices hadn't been calling to him from the hiding place at all. They were coming from somewhere else. Slowly he began to climb the stairs and the voices came down to meet him. The older woman and the military man were arguing about a present.

"It's mine, I tell you. It's mine. To do with as I please."

"Stephen, Stephen," came the woman's querulous voice, but again it faded away on the air, replaced by the voice of his mother speaking to him in the car on the way to London the previous year when he had struggled to hear her above the sound of the wind: "I do so wonder what she was like, Tom. I do so wonder what she was like."

Curiously Thomas felt his fear and anxiety leave him as he climbed the stairs. He had not been this way in over a year, but his mother's death was far from his mind as he passed over the place where she had died. He knew where he was going now and turned toward the bedroom without a glance at the great bookcase on his left. He wondered for a moment if Aunt Jane would have locked the door, but the handle turned easily and he went in.

Thomas knew that some of the paintings in the bedroom had been damaged by the men when they ransacked the room looking for the safe, but the portrait of his grandmother had been restored to its former position over the fireplace. She was as he remembered her. Flashing eyes and a flashing smile, a face full of energy and freedom, although there was love in her dark eyes too. Thomas stared up at her, this Lady Sarah Sackville whom he had never known. He felt an overwhelming sense that the portrait had something to tell him, but he could not fathom what it was. His grandmother looked out on a world he knew nothing about. Artist and sitter were long dead, leaving behind this picture, a relic to gather dust.

It was just as Thomas turned away toward the windows that he realized what it was he had been looking for in the portrait. It was the ring on his grandmother's finger glowing midnight blue, just like it had on that day in the car when his mother had worn it and he had shivered in the sunlight.

Her words came back to him as if they had been spoken only yesterday: "She always wore it. Her father gave it to her when she was twenty-one. There's that old story I told you about it. About where it came from in India. I've got a letter about it somewhere. I'll have to dig it out . . ."

As far as Thomas knew, his mother had never dug it out. London and *Macbeth* and Greta had driven it out of their minds, and then had come the murder. Lady Anne was gone as far away as her mother now. Both dead at forty, leaving only whispers behind.

Thomas looked about him. His mother's clothes still hung in the dressing room, and it came to him that nobody would have gone through her little walnut wood desk in the corner of the bedroom if the killers had not done so. Sir Peter had stayed away from the House of the Four Winds since the funeral, and Aunt Jane had a horror of anything involving documents.

Thomas crossed to the desk and opened it. The contents were undisturbed. He thought back to that defining moment with Matthew the previous autumn when he'd remembered his mother's voice telling him about the secret drawer in the desk in London. He'd gone into the drawing room and opened that desk almost as an afterthought. All that time searching in the basement and on the computer and then upstairs in his father's bedroom before he stopped on the first-floor landing and remembered his mother calling him: "Come here, Tom. . . . There's something I want to show you. . . . It's a secret."

He'd pressed the knobs on the bottom drawers gently just like she'd shown him until the recess opened and he found the locket. He remembered it all: holding it up, opening it, showing it to Matthew, moving across the room to the doorway and seeing Greta on the stairs with that crazy look in her eyes.

Thomas shook himself, banishing Greta and the locket from his mind. They could wait until tomorrow. Greta's fat barrister would no doubt have plenty of questions to ask about his visit to the house in London.

Thomas returned his attention to his mother's desk. There was no secret drawer here. Just letters and papers neatly filed into the pigeon-holes or tied up in rubber bands. On the top was an unfinished letter to a garden center in London ordering a rose with an extravagant Latin name. It was dated May 31, 1999: the day of his mother's death.

Thomas hardly knew what he was looking for as he unpacked the papers onto the floor so that he soon became a human island in a sea of documents. In the end he found it in the bottom drawer: the letter folded round a small black jewelry box. Thomas knew what would be inside the box before he opened it, but the perfection of the dark blue stone still shocked him. The sapphire glowed in his hand, drawing his eyes down into its dark mysterious interior like a magnet.

Why had his mother not put it in the safe with her other jewels? Per-haps the paper might provide a clue. It was folded four ways, and Thomas opened it carefully. The once white vellum writing paper had turned yellow with age, and for a moment Thomas was filled with a su-perstitious fear that the black ink would disappear in the sunlight or that the paper would crumble to dust in his hands.

It was indeed a letter, written under the heading "The House of the Four Winds" and dated November 28, 1946. It was signed "Daddy," but Thomas soon realized that the writer was his great-grandfather, Sir Stephen Sackville, whose portrait hung downstairs in the drawing room. Sir Stephen had lived the longest of the modern Sackvilles, and the portrait had been painted in honor of his eightieth birthday. He would have been fifty-eight when he wrote this letter to his daughter, and she would have just turned twenty-one.

My dear Sarah,

You asked me to tell you a little about the Sultan's sapphire, as the jewel that I gave you for your twenty-first birthday is called. It does indeed come from India, where it was owned by a nawab in one of the wild northwestern provinces near the Afghan frontier. I know noth-ing of the Sultan that once owned the jewel and nothing of how the nawab came into possession of it. The sapphire was, however, famous throughout northern India for its perfection, and I had long been curious to see it when chance brought me into contact with its owner. The dark glow of the jewel is in my opinion quite extraordinary. I have never seen one the like of it, and you know me for a keen collector of precious stones.

Thomas looked up from the dry words to the portrait of his young grandmother with the sapphire on her finger put there by her father. Wearing the ring had made Thomas's mother feel close to her own mother, but the jewel he held in his hand now felt foreign and dangerous. This heirloom passing down the generations had brought no luck to the Sackvilles who had owned it.

Thomas turned back to the letter:

I had been posted to the northwestern frontier and found clear evidence that the local nawab had been conspiring against the British. There was no alternative but to act quickly and decisively, and I led a small troop against the nawab's palace, as he called his rather ugly fortified house. He was mortally wounded in the short skirmish that followed and I had in fact taken him to be dead when I entered his quarters and found the famous sapphire. The old rascal had, however, more life in him than I thought and followed me into his private rooms. He had an ornamental dagger in his hand, but I am relieved to say that he lacked the strength to throw it very far. The effort was too much for him and he died soon after, although not before he had seen the sapphire in my hand. His last words were to curse me and all my descendants, but I paid this no attention. Some might say that I should not have taken the jewel, but I have always thought that I had a right to it, having risked my life to deal with its owner's treachery.

I also draw a sense of justification from the four years of hard service to my King and country in the trenches of Flanders that followed my return from India. I certainly have no doubt that the Sultan's sapphire sits better on your beautiful finger, my dear, than it would in the back of some dusty case in the British Museum.

You should therefore feel no qualms that the jewel is rightfully mine to give and yours to receive and the sapphire's romantic history should make you value it more and not less.

I asked Cartier in London to set the jewel in a golden ring, and I hope that you will agree that they have made excellent work of the commission. Our family's name is engraved on the inside, and I hope that the ring will become a Sackville heirloom.

Thomas read the letter two more times, and each time he was more struck by the self-justifying tone of the writer. The document was not the romantic history that it purported to be but rather an unsuccessful attempt to defend actions that clearly still troubled his great-grandfather more than thirty years after they had occurred. It was surely significant that Sir Stephen let slip in the first paragraph that he already knew about the sapphire before he met its owner. Was the nawab's alleged treachery just a pretext for murdering him and stealing the jewel? If so, setting the sapphire in a golden ring did not change what had happened.

Thomas walked over to one of the high windows that looked down toward the sea and held the ring up to the sunlight. Sure enough, SACKVILLE was engraved on the inside in flowing script, but the engraving did not make the sapphire the property of Thomas's family. Murder and theft did not create property rights, whatever old Sir Stephen might say to the contrary.

The killing of the nawab on the other side of the world almost a hundred years before and his mother's death on the landing outside became connected in Thomas's mind. He felt as if there were a purpose behind his discovery of the jewel and the letter. It was as if they had been left there by his mother for him to find. The great blue stone was a test. He saw that now. It was for him to choose what to do with it.

Thomas tried to imagine the scene described by his great-grandfather in his letter. For some reason he thought of the nawab as a handsome young man dressed in a crimson tasseled jacket and white baggy trousers, perhaps because that was what the sultan of Baghdad was wearing in Thomas's old copy of *The Arabian Nights,* given to him by his mother for his seventh birthday. The nawab had dark, almost olive skin, and his hair was concealed under the folds of a turban. There was a yellow canary in the palace that sang while the nawab ate Indian delicacies served by girls with long black hair and high breasts. Outside there was a fountain of stone dolphins where foaming silver water splashed down onto the marble paving stones of the nawab's courtyard.

Into this scene of lazy luxury painted by Thomas's imagination burst a younger, crueller version of the man who smiled down so benevolently from his portrait in the drawing room downstairs.

Sir Stephen was no knight then. He was plain Stephen Sackville, three years out from England, with a fortune to make and a pair of black revolvers in his pockets to secure it with. This Stephen Sackville was a young man consumed with a lust for jewels. He had listened greedily to all the travelers' tales until his attention narrowed and became focused on the sultan's sapphire, the gem that contained all the mystery of the subcontinent within its deep, dark blue interior. Stephen Sackville could not rest until he had made it his own.

Thomas had no idea how he knew all this, but he was nevertheless certain of what had happened on that afternoon, almost a century ago, on the other side of the world. His great-grandfather had had no right to do what he did. There had been no British interest involved. The justification for the action had been manufactured after the event, and the nawab had not been alive to contradict the lies told about him.

Thomas imagined the murder. He thought of it as a hot day with the nawab resting on his divan after lunch while two servants moved the still air with palm-tree fans. Thomas did not know if the yellow canary was singing, and he could not see the servant girls. He did not know if the nawab was asleep or just had his eyes closed in meditation, but he saw him rise up from the divan when he heard the horses' hooves on the stones in the courtyard and the sound of shots and cries. Perhaps they were the cries of the servant girls. Thomas could only see the nawab running on his silver-slippered feet through the palace until he came face-to-face with his assassin and looked for a final moment into the cold blue eyes of Stephen Sackville of the House of the Four Winds in the county of Suffolk, come upon the King's commission to kill and steal. Two shots and the Englishman stepped over his victim, just like the killers had stepped over Thomas's mother as she lay on the landing, bleeding her lifeblood out onto the carpet.

The parallel did not stop there, of course. Sir Stephen had come to steal the sapphire just like the killers of Thomas's mother had come for the Sackville jewels and had taken them all, all except the sapphire. It had remained in the drawer of the walnut desk, waiting for Thomas to find it so that the Indian's curse could continue on down through the generations, until there were no Sackvilles left.

=

Thomas put the sapphire in his pocket and looked out of the high east windows of the bedroom toward the sea. It was a view of the elements—sun and sky and water stretching out to the horizon. Suddenly Thomas knew what he was going to do.

He put the letter and the other documents back in his mother's desk. He glanced once up at the portrait of his grandmother, thinking of the conflict between her free spirit and the grasping hand of her father. Thomas wondered if she had ridden her horse on the beach below the house where he was headed now. She must have, although his mother had never told him where she met her death.

At the bottom of the stairs he paused, wondering whether to tell Aunt Jane where he was going. He could hear her voice in the kitchen. She was still talking to the policeman, who would insist on accompanying Thomas if he went outside, and Thomas needed to be alone. He grabbed a towel from the downstairs bathroom and set off across the lawn toward the north gate secure in the knowledge that he could not be seen from the kitchen windows.

He turned the key in the lock and stepped out into the lane. There was no one there, but Thomas felt suddenly vulnerable. It was the first time he had been outside the grounds in a week. The sun shone through the trees whose branches overhung the lane, creating a natural canopy, and Thomas found himself walking through dappled dancing shadows as he made his way down to the beach. The crash of the still invisible waves on the shore grew louder, and Thomas remembered how excited Barton would become by the sound, torn between the need to keep his owners in sight and his longing for the wide open spaces awaiting them beyond the final turn in the dirt road. There was no Barton now; he was buried next to little Mattie back behind the north gate, and Thomas was all alone in the world.

The sudden force of the sunlight made Thomas blink almost in pain as he came out onto the beach, and he put his free hand up over his eyes to protect them. His other hand was held deep inside his trouser pocket, clutching the sapphire ring hard in his palm.

It was one of those rare summer days when the omnipresent clouds had been chased away by the hot sun from the wide Suffolk sky, leaving it a pale blue heaven. The only sign of humanity was a high-flying airplane that drew a white pencil line across the blue as it passed overhead.

Thomas thought of his mother. She always became almost childishly excited by days like this and would bully Aunt Jane into accompanying them to the beach, where the old lady would sit on a folding chair with her long black skirt coming down to her ankles. She would make no concession to sand and sun except for a pair of rather terrifying sunglasses that made her look like a member of the Sicilian Mafia. Thomas and his mother would swim out beyond the waves and then come running back over the sand to eat the sandwiches that Aunt Jane had packed in a hamper she kept under her chair so Barton couldn't get at them. Afterward his mother would lie in the sun and talk to Aunt Jane about the past while Thomas built sandcastles and peopled them with the knights that his mother bought for him at the toy shop in Flyte.

Thomas walked across the deserted beach and put the memories of his childhood out of his mind. Near the water's edge he stopped and took off all his clothes, leaving them in a pile weighed down by his shoes. He stood for a moment naked under the sun before he plunged into the breaking waves, clasping the sapphire tight in his hand.

The day's sunshine seemed to have had no effect on the temperature of the North Sea, and Thomas felt the cold water pressing against his chest like shards of ice as he stood on the sandbank just beyond the waves. He opened his palm and looked at the sapphire glowing in the sunlight. Turning it over, he read his family's name engraved in the gold. It was a beautiful thing, a most precious stone, but it had attached itself to his family like a millstone. There was a price to be paid for what his great-grandfather had done, just as there was a price to be paid by his mother's murderers, but their fate awaited them in the future. The Sackvilles had atoned for Sir Stephen's sins with their blood, and now it was time to be rid of this jewel.

Thomas raised his hand in the air and threw the ring out to sea. It was gone in a second, barely disturbing the surface of the water as it was swallowed up. The sea, like the earth, was indifferent. Pebbles and precious stones were all the same. It was human beings who distinguished between them, murdering one another for the sake of small inanimate objects.

Thomas swam back to the shore filled with a sense of release. He felt the rush of a new beginning and ran across the sand forgetful of his nakedness. He thought of his daredevil grandmother galloping her horse across the beach. He felt her blood in his as he kicked up the surf and the sun shone down on his young body.

Dressed again, Thomas climbed the steep cliff path toward the house. His mother had forbidden him to go this way when he was a child as the cliff sand was crumbly and it was easy to fall. But today Thomas felt immune from danger, and he was soon at the top standing by the viewing cairn—a pile of rocks with a smooth gray central stone in the middle, on which a nineteenth-century Sackville had engraved the landmarks visible from this high point.

Behind Thomas across the sloping dunes were the east gate and the house. In front of him the North Sea stretched out as far as the horizon while to his right were the towns of Flyte and Coyne, separated by the River Flyte. Thomas could see the two church spires and between them a tiny fishing boat leaving the harbor and putting out to sea.

On Thomas's left was the larger town of Carmouth, where the road became wider and the cars and lorries sped up on their way to London and the west. That would be the way Thomas would be going the next morning, in the back of an unmarked police car. Sergeant Hearns had said that they would need to leave just after six to be sure of getting to the Old Bailey on time.

Thomas's head dropped as he felt the weight of the trial that he had done so much to bring about descend on his shoulders. With one last look at the great wide sea, he turned for home.

He let himself in through the east gate, hoping that Aunt Jane and the policeman had not noticed his absence. He had no wish to cause them anxiety if he could avoid it, but he need not have worried. They were halfway through their third cup of coffee when Thomas went into the kitchen. Aunt Jane had always been fond of the forces of law and order, but she seemed to have taken a particular shine to this policeman. He was local and shared her interest in Flyte gossip as well as providing a willing audience for her views about Greta and her barrister, which seemed to become more extreme by the day.

It was not a subject that Thomas wanted to talk about. He needed help with moving a picture out of his mother's bedroom and hanging it in his own.

Twenty minutes later the task was done. Lady Sarah Sackville's portrait hung on the wall of Thomas's bedroom between the map of Suf-folk shipwrecks and a photograph of his mother holding Barton.

That night Thomas looked up at his grandmother from his bed, warmed by the smile in her flashing dark eyes. It gave him strength to face the prospect of meeting the glittering green eyes of his adversary across the courtroom the next day.

Chapter 21

───────────────

"RIGHT, MR. LAMBERT, remember the age of the witness and remember what I have directed about the photographs," said Judge Granger, fixing the defense barrister with a hard look as he got to his feet to cross-examine.

It was two o'clock on Tuesday afternoon, and Thomas had already been in the witness box for more than two hours. John Sparling had finished asking him questions at five to one, and then there had been only an hour to walk the unfamiliar crowded streets around the court and try to compose himself for what was to come.

Giving evidence had so far been both better and worse than he had expected. Better because he found that he had been able to shut Greta out of his mind, even though she was sitting only a few yards away, watching him intently all the time. Worse because Sparling had made him tell the jury all the terrible details of what had happened on the landing when he was shut inside the bookcase and those men were murdering his mother on the other side. Telling it made it real and the reality had made him cry. Thomas had hated that. Crying in front of that bitch, Greta, while the little usher woman brought him a box of tissues and a glass of water. Thomas swore to himself that there would be no repeat of such emotion this afternoon, whatever Greta's fat barrister might do to him.

"I want to start with this man Rosie," said Miles Lambert in a friendly tone. "You say you first saw him outside your father's house in London?"

"Yes."

"In the dark?"

"He was standing under a streetlight."

"With his back to you."

"Yes."

"And he never turned around."

"No, he didn't. He'd have seen me if he had."

"So you never saw his face."

"Not that time. No."

"Just the back of his head where he had a scar."

"Yes, it was long and thick too. I saw it because he had his hair in a ponytail."

"Ah yes, the ponytail. Plenty of men have ponytails though, don't they, Thomas? Scars too."

"Not like that one. Somebody must have taken a knife to him to do that."

"Very dramatic. The point I'm making, Thomas, is that you can't possibly say that the man under the streetlight is the same as the man who murdered your mother on the basis of a view from behind."

"I'm *sure* it was the same person."

"Even though you only saw the man in your house for a few seconds through a spy hole in a bookcase?"

"I will never forget his face."

"You saw one man from behind and the other for only a few seconds when you were beside yourself with terror and distress and you jumped to a conclusion, which was based on very weak evidence. That's the truth, isn't it, Thomas?"

"They were the same person."

"You jumped to the conclusion because you wanted to blame Greta Grahame for what had happened."

"No."

"Because you felt guilty that you hadn't been able to save your mother from those men when you had saved yourself, and so you needed someone to blame." Miles went on relentlessly.

"No, it's not true. I couldn't have saved her. She was behind me. She pushed me forward in there. I didn't shut the bookcase—"

"It's all right, Thomas," said the judge kindly. "Try to calm down. I know this is difficult for you. Mr. Lambert, try to be less confrontational."

"Yes, my Lord. Thomas, I'm not saying you were to blame in any way for what happened that night. That's the last thing I'm trying to say. I'm just suggesting that you feel guilty about it. People do feel guilty even though they shouldn't when someone close to them dies. You know what I'm saying, don't you, Thomas?"

"Yes, I suppose so," said Thomas reluctantly.

"And if you feel guilty, then you need someone else to blame, don't you?"

"I don't know."

"You were upset with Greta at that time, though, weren't you? Before your mother died."

"In a way."

"In a way. You were upset with her because she had rejected you."

Thomas said nothing but he blushed deeply. He turned involuntarily to look at Greta in the dock and found her staring at him intently.

"You know what I'm talking about, don't you, Thomas? She took you out in London, and on the way back home in a taxi you told her that she was beautiful and that you loved her, and she rejected you. She said you were too young. Isn't that right, Thomas?"

"Yes," said Thomas almost in a whisper.

"I can't hear you, Thomas," said Miles Lambert. "Was that a yes?"

"Yes."

There was silence in the courtroom. Sparling shifted uncomfortably in his seat. This revelation had come as an unpleasant surprise. There was nothing about it in Thomas's statement. What else had the boy left out? Sparling wondered.

Miles Lambert allowed the silence to build, and with it Thomas's discomfort, before he asked his next question.

"All this happened less than two months before your mother's death, didn't it, Thomas?"

"Yes."

"So the rejection was fresh in your memory?"

"I didn't think about it."

"Are you sure about that, Thomas? You told Greta that you loved her."

"I didn't mean it."

"So you told her something that was untrue?"

"No. I meant it at the time, I suppose, but it was just something that happened that afternoon. It was just something that came into my head."

"I see. Love is a strong emotion, Thomas, isn't it? Comes up on you unawares, like hate. Are you sure you didn't start hating Greta because she didn't love you like you wanted her to?"

"No. It wasn't like that."

"But you hate her now, don't you, Thomas?"

"I hate her for what she did to my mother."

"Can you remember not hating her?"

"I don't know. I suppose I didn't hate her that afternoon in the taxi. It seems so long ago now."

"I suggest that's when you did start hating her, Thomas. Then a chance similarity between two men brought your hate and your guilt together, and that's where all this started, isn't that right?"

"Don't answer that, Thomas," said the judge. "Make your questions clear and direct, Mr. Lambert. We're not here to listen to you give us a lecture on psychiatry."

"No, my Lord," said Miles. "Thomas, I want to take you back to the night in London when you saw the man with the scar. You never saw him with Greta, did you?"

"No."

"You can't say that the man under the streetlight was the same as the person that Greta was talking to in the basement?"

"No. I know it was, though. They both went upstairs because they heard those creeps looking for me. Greta thought they might be burglars."

"Did you hear Greta tell the other person in the basement to go upstairs?"

"No."

"Did you see him go up the basement steps to the street?"

"No, I ran upstairs to get away. Like I said before."

"And then you just saw the man standing there. You didn't see where he'd come from."

"I didn't see but I knew."

"Well, there doesn't seem to be any evidence for your knowledge, Thomas. Let's just go back to the man in the basement, whom we can agree about."

But Thomas had had enough of being manipulated.

"Why? *She* didn't agree about it," he said angrily. "*She* lied about being down there. She said she was in Manchester. That's what she told my father the next evening. I heard her."

"Thomas, you've already given evidence about that," said the judge. "Try just to answer Mr. Lambert's questions."

"You've told Mr. Sparling what Greta said to the man," pursued Miles, "and I don't have any argument about that, but I want to be quite clear about one thing. You just don't know whether Greta said 'Can't you see I haven't got *it* yet,' or 'Can't you see I haven't got *him* yet.' Is that right?"

"Yes, that's right."

"Good. Then Greta said she was going upstairs, and you told us before lunch that she said: 'Mrs. Posh won't hear.' I dispute that, Thomas. My client never called your mother Mrs. Posh."

"Yes she did. Just like Aunt Jane heard her saying about Mum after Mattie died. She called her Mrs. Posh then too."

"Did I hear that right, Thomas? Do you agree that you've been talking to Mrs. Martin about her evidence?"

"I talked to her about what happened after it happened. Of course I did."

"You talked to her before she gave her evidence, compared notes. Is that what you're saying, Thomas?"

"We talked, yes. We weren't comparing notes. She heard what she heard and I heard what I heard."

"And they both turned out to be the same thing. Very convenient. Now, Thomas, I want to turn to the day of your mother's death. Let me assure you in advance that none of my questions should distress you too much—"

"I'm glad to hear it, Mr. Lambert," interrupted the judge. "Let's get on and have the questions, though, shall we? We don't need a prologue."

This time Miles Lambert ignored the judge's interruption. He wasn't going to be put off his stride at this—the most important point of the trial—because of old Granger's concern for a sixteen-year-old. Thomas was the one who had gathered the evidence that had made it possible for the prosecution to put his client in the dock. Those were hardly the actions of a vulnerable boy—more those of a determined young man. The case depended on Thomas's credibility, and the jurors were entitled to hear a proper cross-examination of his evidence. Judge Granger's interruptions wouldn't stop Miles from doing his job.

"You have told us this morning that you assumed from what your mother said that the initiative for the arrangement for you to stay with your friend Edward Ball on the Monday evening came from Edward's mother."

"That's right."

"Did your mother say that the Balls had invited you?"

"I think so. I'm not sure of exactly what she said."

"Could your mother have said that it was her idea for you to go to the Balls?"

"I don't think so."

"All right, is it possible that your mother didn't say who had made the arrangement but that you just assumed that Mrs. Ball had invited you."

"I don't know. I suppose it's possible."

"Thank you. Now, you've given evidence that you became anxious when Mrs. Ball told you that it was in fact Greta who had arranged for you to go over there."

"That's right."

"Why did you get anxious, Thomas?"

"Because that wasn't her job. She had nothing to do with my arrangements."

"Fair enough, but it would be different if your mother had asked her to ring up Mrs. Ball, wouldn't it?"

"My mother would never have done that."

"Why not? She had a headache on the Sunday afternoon when the arrangement was made, didn't she?"

"I'm not sure. I think so."

"So why wouldn't she have asked Greta to do her a favor?"

"She'd have asked Aunt Jane, not Greta."

"Mrs. Martin was out on Sunday afternoon."

"My mother would have waited until she got back then, or rung up herself."

"Why not ask Greta though? She was there."

"Because my mother would never have asked Greta for anything."

"Why not?"

"Because she didn't like her."

"I see. And what makes you say that, Thomas?"

"It was obvious. She avoided Greta. She never went to London because of her."

"But she took you to London in April when you made your declaration in the taxi, and she went up for the Chelsea Flower Show four days before she died. Greta was there both times."

"She always went to the Flower Show. She had to because of the roses."

"I see. Did she tell you that she was avoiding London because of Greta?"

"No. I knew it though."

"You knew it. Did she tell you that she didn't like Greta?"

"No. She didn't tell me but she told Greta. After Greta let my dog out and pushed me over. My mother told her that she'd turned my father against us and that she was poisonous, poisonous like a snake."

"That wasn't all your mother said to Greta that day though, was it, Thomas? She went into the study with you and apologized to Greta for those things that she'd said, and Greta accepted the apology. Isn't that right, Thomas?"

"Yes. She didn't mean it though."

"Who didn't mean it?"

"Greta. She hated my mother. No, that's not it. She wanted to become her. That's why she sent me to Edward's. Because she wanted to save me. I was part of what she was going to get."

"Well, thank you for giving us the benefit of your theory, Thomas, but that's all it is, isn't it? You haven't got one shred of evidence to support what you've just said, have you?"

"I saw the way she looked at my mother. She tried on her clothes."

"Yes, she did, but that's not quite the same as arranging to have your mother killed, now, is it?"

"I know what she did."

"So you say. Now, you've told us that you decided to come home from the Balls after you couldn't reach your mother on the telephone. Mrs. Ball drove you home and dropped you off at the front gate. How did you get in?"

"I had keys. To the front door too."

"About what time was this?"

"I don't know. Sometime around half past eight."

"How long after you made the phone call to your mother did you get home?"

"I don't know. Twenty minutes, half an hour. I wasn't wearing a watch."

"Did you leave immediately after you phoned up and got no reply?"

"No, we talked about it a bit and Mrs. Ball's husband called about something."

"So you got home, and you've already told us that you closed the window that you found open in the study. Then you went upstairs and opened the window in your bedroom."

"Yes, I did."

"Because it was a warm evening?"

"That's right."

"Did you keep it open when it started raining?"

"Yes, it wasn't a storm."

"You were lying on your bed and your mother was asleep in her room."

"Yes. I'd just turned my light off when I heard the car drive up. Then I saw them coming across the lawn toward the study window, and one of them was really upset that the windows were all closed."

" 'Fuck. They're all fucking closed.' That's what you told us earlier that the man said." Miles seemed to enunciate the swear words with particular relish.

"Yes," replied Thomas. "He was angry."

"Did you see the man say it?"

"No. I was sitting on my bed. They were below the window."

"So you can't say that the man was outside the study window when he swore. He could have been by the side door or the dining room windows just as easily."

"I suppose so."

"He could have been talking about all the windows on that side of the house in fact."

"Not mine, because it was open."

"On the lower level I mean."

"Yes, he could have been."

"Thank you. Now I've got nothing else to ask you about that night at this stage. I want to concentrate instead on this locket that you found in your father's house last October."

Miles Lambert picked up prosecution exhibit number thirteen and held it for a moment by its clasp so that the golden heart-shaped locket swung to and fro on its chain like a hypnotist's pendulum.

"You have told us that your mother was very fond of this locket."

"She was."

"Did she wear it every day?"

"Not every day, no. She wore it a lot."

"You made no mention of the locket to the police of course until after you found it."

"I had no reason to."

"No. I can see that that might make sense, but it doesn't explain why you mentioned nothing in your first statement about Rosie bending down over your mother and then putting something gold in his pocket. That comes in your second statement, made after you found the locket."

"I was upset when I made the first statement. My mother had just died."

"Five days before. Your first statement is very detailed, Thomas. Sergeant Hearns and you took a lot of trouble over it. You'd think you wouldn't leave out something as important as Rosie taking gold from your mother's dead body."

Thomas didn't answer. Lambert's brutal last words had felt like a punch in the face.

"You left the gold out of your first statement because it never happened. That's the real explanation, isn't it, Thomas?"

"No, it's not. It did happen. He ripped it off her neck. That's why they found a scratch there."

"A small scratch. The locket wasn't broken, though, when you found it in the desk, was it?"

"No. They could have repaired it."

"There's no sign of any repair on the clasp or the chain that I can see," said Miles, making a show of carefully examining the locket as he held it up to his golden half-moon spectacles between two of his fat fingers.

"No doubt the jury will want to examine exhibit thirteen themselves when they are considering the evidence," Miles added casually as he replaced the locket on the table in front of him.

"Now, there's no dispute that you found the locket in the desk, Thomas. What I do have a problem with is what you say that my client said about it."

"Which bit?"

" 'Give that to me. It's mine.' That bit."

"She shouted it at me just as she tried to get hold of it—"

"Yes, so you told us," interrupted the barrister. "And then you pushed Greta over and you shouted at her: 'No, it's not. It's my mother's. That bastard took it from her and he gave it to you.' That was what you told Mr. Sparling that you said when he asked you this morning. Do you agree?"

"Yes. Something like that."

"No, not something like that. Word for word. I wrote it down when you said it this morning, and I wrote exactly the same thing down when your friend Matthew Barne told us what you said when he gave evidence yesterday. You've put your heads together about this, haven't you, Thomas? You and Matthew?"

"Of course we've talked about it. We go to school together and he's my best friend, but that doesn't mean it's not true."

"You both stole a paperweight at school from your headmaster, isn't that right, Thomas?"

"It was a dare. We were going to put it back."

"So, you found the locket and then you made your second statement to Detective Sergeant Hearns."

"That's right."

"And you said in there that your mother was wearing the locket on the night of her death?"

"I saw it when I got her up. There was a V at the throat of her nightdress."

"It seems a funny thing for you to notice at such a terrible moment. You could hear the men breaking in downstairs, isn't that right?"

"Yes."

"What happened is that you found that locket and then you set about concocting evidence to show that my client received it from your mother's killer."

"No."

"You sat down with Matthew Barne to agree upon a false version of what was said in the drawing room before your father arrived."

"It's not a false version. It's a true version."

"You invented this story about your mother having the locket on under her nightdress and seeing the glint of gold when Rosie bent over her on the landing. Then as a final touch you got Jane Martin to say that Lady Anne was wearing the locket at lunch on the Monday."

"I never saw it then."

"Well, thank you for that, Thomas. You can see what I'm getting at. I suggest that you made all these things up because you'd already decided that Greta was guilty and so you had to make sure that she got charged."

"I knew she was guilty, but that didn't make me lie. It made me look for proof. That's how I found the locket."

"And yet your reasons for believing she was guilty didn't amount to much, did they?"

"Mr. Lambert, we've already been over that," said the judge irritably. "Try not to argue with the witness. Cross-examination is about asking questions."

"Yes, my Lord," said Miles. "Let's move on, Thomas. Let's talk about what happened on the fifth of July."

Thomas shifted in his seat but otherwise did not respond. Miles did not carry on immediately but allowed a silence to build before he spoke again.

"Let's make sure I've got the setting right first. Jane Martin left at six, having locked all the doors. You were in the dining room eating your dinner, with all the windows open."

"Yes, it was a warm evening."

"So it was. And you had your panic button next to your plate ready to call the emergency services if the need should arise?"

"No, it was in my pocket. Sergeant Hearns told me to keep it with me all the time. He's the one who got it for me."

"He told you there was a risk of the men coming back, the men who had killed your mother."

"Not exactly."

"Did he put that idea in your mind, Thomas?"

"No, he said it was better to be safe than sorry, that's all."

"I see. So the men came through the north door in the perimeter wall, crossed the lawn, and entered the house, and you stayed in this bench while they were looking for you?"

"Yes."

"You can't have been able to see very much from inside that."

"I could see out through the holes in the eyes, like I said before."

"Ah, yes. The holes in the eyes. They wouldn't exactly have given you a grandstand view of what Lonny and Rosie were up to though, would they?"

"No. Not really."

"And yet you say in your statement that 'they looked around the rooms downstairs for a while but they didn't touch anything.' Were you able to watch them all the time then, see that they weren't touching anything?"

"No. I meant that when I could see them, they weren't touching anything. Rosie did later, though."

"And Rosie just happened to mention my client by name."

"That's right. He said that she'd told him how the hiding-place mechanism works."

"It's very convenient, isn't it, Thomas?"

"You don't need to answer that, Thomas," interrupted the judge. "Ask the witness questions; save your comments for the jury. I shouldn't need to keep telling you that, Mr. Lambert."

"No, my Lord." Miles smiled affably up at the judge. Old Granger's interruptions and instructions seemed to have no effect whatsoever on Lurid Lambert, who carried on relentlessly along his charted course, guiding the witness slowly but surely onto the rocks.

"Was it Rosie who said: 'Fuck, they're all fucking closed' about the windows on the night of your mother's murder?"

"I don't know. I've thought about that a lot, but I just don't know."

"Yet you say in your statement about Rosie's return that you would recognize the voice of the man with the scar."

"Yes. If I heard it again I would, but my mother got killed a year before they came back."

"So you can't say if the man with the scar said the words about the windows but you remember the words clearly?"

"That's right."

"I see. Well, let's go on to the end of your story. You hear the siren. Rosie stops talking in midsentence, and he and Lonny run out the front door. Yes?"

"Yes."

"You get out of the bench and answer the intercom."

"I buzzed the police in through the front gate."

"Having spoken to Officer Hughes through the intercom first. Isn't that right, Thomas?"

"I don't remember."

"He told us what happened when he gave evidence yesterday. He said that you asked him who he was and he identified himself as a police officer. Then you opened the gates by remote control. Do you agree with his account, Thomas?"

"I suppose so. I was in a panic. I don't remember everything that was said."

"Well, I'll take that as a yes. Now, you knew from Officer Hughes that the police were at the front gate. You knew that Rosie and Lonny had parked their car in the lane. You must have assumed that they were running back to their car. You knew all that, and so why didn't you tell Officer Hughes through the intercom to drive down to the lane and cut them off instead of buzzing him in through the front gate?"

Miles had asked his final question with a fierce directness that sparked the jury into a concentrated focus on Thomas, who didn't answer immediately. He looked like a chess player who has suddenly seen his king exposed to a massive unforeseen attack and now looks around desperately but in vain for a move that will stave off inevitable defeat.

"I don't know," Thomas said eventually. "I didn't think. Those men would have killed me if they'd found me. I suppose I wanted to feel safe."

"But you were safe. The men had left. This was your opportunity to catch your mother's killers."

"I didn't think."

"You didn't think. It makes no sense, Thomas. It makes no sense because none of this really happened, did it?"

"Yes, it did. I swear it did."

"Just like it makes no sense that the police found the north door locked."

"They must have locked it when they left because they would have known how it would look."

"Like they'd never been there?"

"Yes."

"It looks like that because that's the truth, isn't it, Thomas? You've made all this up. You didn't think the locket would be enough, and so you invented Rosie's return and a casual reference to Greta and the bookcase just to be sure of getting your stepmother convicted. Isn't that right, Thomas?"

"No! No!" The denial seemed to be wrenched from somewhere deep inside. Thomas's face was contorted with pain, but this did nothing to deter Miles from driving home his point.

"You were the one who opened the front door before the police got close enough to see what you were doing."

"No, they left it open."

"Who?"

"Rosie and Lonny."

"Rosie and Lonny! I don't know where you got those names from, Thomas—unless it was some late-night TV movie—but the point is you made them up just like you made up this whole sorry story."

"No, I didn't. They came for me, I tell you. They'll come again."

"Will they, Thomas? Will they?" Miles Lambert wore an expression of sorrowful incredulity on his round face. He was not looking for an answer to his question, and he sat down before Thomas could give one.

Chapter 22

P ETER SAT IN the back of his official car drumming on the leather top of the briefcase that he held across his knees. In front of him across Ludgate Circus the bright midafternoon sun lit up the magnificent dome of St. Paul's Cathedral, but the motionless traffic on Fleet Street barred his progress toward the Old Bailey and made him oblivious to the beauty of the view. He was already five minutes late for his meeting with Greta, and his frustration boiled uselessly inside him. The rat-a-tat-tat of his nails on the briefcase only echoed a more frenzied pounding in his head, which he held in place even more rigidly than usual so that the thick blue veins in his neck stood out above the tight collar of his shirt.

The week of the trial had not been good for Peter. He had hardly slept, and the strain of trying to do his job and worry about his wife at the same time was showing on his face. There were bags under his eyes, and he had developed a tiny tic on the side of his lip. His mind would begin wandering to the Bailey in the middle of complex negotiations with armament executives, and he sensed the growing doubt behind the friendly masks worn by his civil servants. He felt that it was only a matter of time before he made some appalling mistake that would bring his career tumbling down in ruins.

Peter realized now that he should have booked time off during the trial, but he had thought naïvely that his work would be a distraction; better the Ministry of Defense than sitting outside the courtroom wondering what was going on inside. He consoled himself with the thought that it would all soon be over and tried not to think of the possibility of conviction. Only in his dreams did Peter imagine Greta being sentenced and taken away, and then the horror would wake him up with his heart racing. He'd calm himself in the dark by reaching out to take hold of his wife's sleeping body.

Peter had made his life-defining choice on that cold November day in Ipswich eight months before when that smug bastard Hearns finally got around to charging Greta with conspiracy to murder. That was the day that he had proposed marriage to her. It was his way of telling the world who he was and where he stood, and besides, he had grown to love Greta. He owed her so much, and there was not a day that passed that she did not fill him with a terrible aching desire. Marriage meant that she would never go away. Till death do us part.

Of course, the wedding announcement had caused a scandal, but Peter had been ready for that. He had done well in his job since becoming defense minister nearly three years before, and he had known that the prime minister would stand by him. In fact, Peter had almost welcomed the media circus that congregated on his doorstep at the time of the wedding. Answering the reporters' questions had given him an opportunity to tell the whole world how he felt about Greta.

Then, two days later, a train had crashed in the north of England, killing thirty passengers, and the defense minister's private life had become yesterday's news. The media spotlight had only returned with the onset of the trial, and now it was not Peter but Greta who was suffering under its glare.

Once again Peter cursed the ridiculous legal rules that stopped him from being in court until after he'd given his evidence. Patrick Sullivan had been down at the Bailey with Greta for most of the trial, and this had helped a little because Patrick was Peter's oldest friend as well as his lawyer. However it wasn't the same as being in the courtroom himself sharing his wife's ordeal. Miles Lambert had told him that he'd be giving his evidence on Wednesday or Thursday at the latest, and Peter looked forward to the prospect like a prisoner awaiting his release. He'd tell them what Greta was and wasn't capable of and what kind of person she was. He'd tell them that Anne had worn that locket at dinner after the Chelsea Flower Show and that she and Greta had got on fine in London. He'd tell them that he hadn't seen Anne wearing the locket on the day of her death, and he'd tell them that that sneak Matthew Barne had run away without answering when he'd asked him if Greta had said "It's mine." Peter had not seen Thomas since that October afternoon in Chelsea when he'd come home to find the two of them burgling his house, and he'd not missed him either. He didn't intend to see his son again until the boy came to him on bended knees begging his forgiveness, and Greta's too for that matter, and maybe even that wouldn't be enough.

Peter felt he'd been just. God knows he'd been just. He hadn't dismissed Jane Martin even though the old shrew richly deserved being thrown out on the street. Instead he'd allowed her to stay on in the House of the Four Winds because he knew that that was what Anne would have wanted. He'd been just and loyal, unlike his son, who'd gone through Greta's underwear behind her back, and his son's freckled friend, the Barne boy, who ran away because he was too scared to back up Thomas's lies. Peter wasn't like that. He stood up to be counted when it mattered, and he didn't sneak into people's homes and then tell lies about them to fat detectives like Hearns.

Hurrying from the Daimler as soon as it had drawn up outside the court entrance, Peter ignored the group of reporters who shouted meaningless questions at him as he passed. He took it as a good sign that they were so few in number. Most of them must still be inside feasting on Greta's trial, and so perhaps he wasn't going to be late after all.

In the great hall at the top of the stairs Peter almost collided with Patrick Sullivan, who was coming toward him from the lifts.

"Where's Greta?" Peter asked anxiously. "I said I'd meet her here ten minutes ago. She must be looking for me."

"It's all right. She's on her way down. The court only finished a couple of minutes ago."

"How did it go?"

"Good. No, better than good. Miles did a fantastic job on Thomas."

"About the locket? Greta told me he did well with the Barne boy."

"He did. We've got the locket covered, but Miles did his real damage cross-examining Thomas about what happened two weeks ago. I wish you could have seen it."

"You mean this business about Anne's killers going back to get

Thomas. I agree with Greta: he's made the whole thing up. There's not a shred of evidence to support his story apparently."

"That's right. It's obvious he's made it up because Miles was able to poke so many holes in what he said. The best one was when Thomas said he used his panic button to call the police and then when they got to the gate he buzzed them in through the intercom instead of telling them to go around and intercept these Lonny and Rosie characters in the lane."

"Lonny and who?"

"Rosie. They're these weird names that Thomas has dreamed up for the intruders. Rosie's the main man though. He's the one that Thomas saw under the streetlight and the one who took the locket on the night of the, the . . ."

Patrick's voice trailed away. He always found it difficult to talk to Peter about the central event of the case, and it didn't help that the main prosecution witness was Peter's son.

"Didn't Greta show you Thomas's last statement?" Patrick asked in an attempt to get the conversation back onto more neutral ground.

"No, I didn't," said Greta, coming up on them from behind. "Peter's got enough on his plate without having to read Thomas's lies."

Patrick was puzzled by the irritation evident in Greta's voice. She had seemed so pleased upstairs only minutes earlier when they had come out of court.

"I'm sorry," he said. "I was just telling Peter how well everything had gone today."

"Yes, it did go well, didn't it?" said Greta. "Miles is a genius at what he does." She kissed her husband. The anger had passed so rapidly from her face that it was as if it had never been there at all.

Peter did not respond to his wife's greeting. It was almost as though he didn't notice her presence. He had a faraway look in his eyes, and the deep lines on his forehead were furrowed even more than usual, as if he was immersed in some intense thought process.

"Are you all right, darling?" asked Greta solicitously. "You don't look well."

"Peter's been overdoing it, I expect," said Patrick, filling in for Peter's lack of response.

"No, I'm fine. It's been a long day for all of us," said Peter, summoning up the ghost of a smile that flickered across his lips but never reached his distracted blue eyes.

"And I'm afraid it's not over yet," said Greta. "I'm supposed to have a conference with Miles to make sure we've got everything covered before I give evidence tomorrow."

"When?" asked Peter. "Now?"

"No. Down at his chambers at six-thirty. I need to change first and have a drink."

Patrick had already left and Greta was in the Daimler when Peter stepped back onto the sidewalk.

"I don't feel very well for some reason, Greta. Will you wait for me while I just go back inside and use the bathroom? I won't be long."

Peter did not wait for his wife to reply but walked quickly through the courthouse doors. He wasn't lying about not feeling well, although he had no intention of finding a bathroom. An alarm had been going off in Peter's head ever since Patrick had told him about Rosie. He had made the connection instantaneously with what he had overheard Greta saying on the telephone the night that they had first slept together. It was the day of the funeral; the day when Greta got arrested and they had ended up in Greta's flat, in Greta's bed, and then the telephone rang in the middle of the night and she had said: 'Don't call me that. I'm not your Greta Rose.' Peter was sure that that was what she'd said, and afterward she'd told him that that was her name before she came to London: Greta Rose because Rose was her grandmother's name. Was that the truth, or was Greta connected to Anne's killer? Peter had to know. Greta wouldn't tell him. She hadn't told him about the names in Thomas's last statement. She'd told him not to read the statement in fact because he'd got enough on his plate without worrying about Thomas's lies. Or maybe that was wrong, maybe he'd just never asked to see it. Peter could not be sure now. All he knew was that he needed to ask Thomas about this Rosie character. Had the other man called him Rose or Rosie? Was Rose his first name or his second? Was there a connection or was there not?

Peter did not stop to think whether his son could help him with any answers. All he knew was that there was no one else to whom he could put his questions.

He thought that there must be a chance that Thomas was still in the building. Hearns wouldn't allow the boy to leave on his own, and

Hearns himself might not have been ready to leave immediately. The detective always seemed to be busy with something. Peter had seen him in the courthouse corridors several times since the first morning of the trial carrying papers, talking sycophantically to barristers, looking self-important. It would be unlike Hearns to rush away straight after court, particularly if it had not gone well for the prosecution today.

The problem for Peter was that he didn't know where to look for his son, and not only that: time was against him. Greta could not be relied upon to sit twiddling her fingers in the back of the Daimler forever.

There was no one in the witness waiting room and no sign of Hearns in the police room. Peter had just given up the search and was on his way downstairs when he ran straight into the detective and his son on the first-floor landing. It was the first time that Peter had seen Thomas since the day he'd thrown him out of his house the previous October, and he wouldn't have known how to speak to him if the urgency of his need to know about Rosie had not overcome his inhibitions.

"I have to talk to you," Peter said simply. He stood barring his son's access to the stairs.

Thomas opened his mouth but no words came out. Astonishment seemed to have momentarily taken his voice away, and it was Hearns who responded to Peter's approach.

"You're a potential defense witness, Sir Peter. You should know better than to try to talk to a witness for the prosecution."

"He's my son," said Peter.

"He's also a prosecution witness," said the detective, taking hold of Thomas's arm to lead him away.

Hearns and Thomas walked over to the bank of elevators, and the detective pressed the call button. Peter did not follow. The excitement that had taken him up the courthouse stairs and across the great gulf that divided him from his son drained away as quickly as it had come, and Peter stood silent at the top of the stairs. A few seconds later the elevator arrived and swallowed up his son and the detective.

Peter waited for a moment before going downstairs. The great hall on the first floor was empty. Another day of justice and broken hearts was over, leaving only a litter of soft-drink cans and cigarette butts in the bins for the cleaners to empty that evening.

Peter turned away and began to go down the stairs. He took his time; it didn't matter if Greta came up and found him now. He was halfway

228 · Simon Tolkien

down the last flight leading to the entrance doors when a hand touched him on the shoulder. He turned around to find Thomas with a finger on his lips.

"Mr. Hearns is up on the landing," Thomas whispered. "I've got to go back."

"There's something I need to ask you," said Peter, keeping his voice as low as his son's. "It won't take a moment."

"Not here. Later. I'll be at Matthew's. Call me there."

"But I don't have the number," Peter said, but Thomas didn't reply. He had already turned and gone back up the stairs. Peter followed a little way, and looking around the corner of the stone banister he saw Thomas standing between Hearns and another uniformed policeman.

Outside the courthouse Peter found Greta waiting for him on the pavement.

"Are you all right?" she asked solicitously. "You don't look well."

"No, I'm fine now."

"Were you sick?"

"Yes, I'm afraid so," he lied. "It must have been something I ate."

"I don't need to go this evening if you're unwell, Peter. I can see Miles tomorrow morning."

"Don't be ridiculous. It's vital that you're fully prepared."

"I suppose you're right. It's just that I get so tired sitting there day after day, listening to all those lies."

"Patrick said that Thomas did really badly today though."

"Yes, that went well."

"He said that Miles shot him full of holes over his story about the men coming back."

"Yes, it was obvious he'd made it all up."

"Why didn't you show me the statement he made about it, Greta?"

"Which statement?"

"The one that Thomas made about the men coming back."

"I don't know. I only got it just before the trial, and it didn't seem something that you needed to worry about. I told you what had happened and that it was obvious he'd made it up, and you agreed. There didn't seem anything else that we needed to say about it."

"No, I suppose not," Peter said, sounding as if he thought the opposite.

"Why are you suddenly so interested in all that?" asked Greta.

"I'm not. It's just Patrick was saying that Miles made such a lot out of it when he was cross-examining Thomas today."

There was silence between them. Peter was staring out the window, trying to suppress his consciousness of Greta looking at him, waiting for him to turn around. Eventually she lost patience.

"Did you see Thomas inside the courthouse when you went back just now, Peter? Is that what's got you so upset?"

The insistence in Greta's voice forced Peter to turn around to face his wife.

"No, of course not. I went back inside to throw up. I just told you that." Peter tried to mask his anxiety with irritation. To his surprise the trick seemed to work. Greta sounded apologetic when she spoke again.

"All right, I was only asking," she said. "There's no harm in that. I'm sorry you were sick."

"It doesn't sound like it," he said.

"Don't be silly."

Greta kissed him lightly on the cheek and Peter smiled before turning with relief back to his window, where the stone wall of the Chelsea Embankment was flying past alongside the car. He looked out over the river wondering where Matthew Barne lived. He needed to ask Thomas about Rosie, but would Thomas tell him the truth? Peter felt that there was no one he could really trust. He wanted to believe in Greta, and he was almost sure he did, but asking her about Rose again, telling her about the connection, would make her think that he didn't believe, and that would be disastrous for both of them. Peter felt that he'd already said too much. Greta was looking at him strangely again as they got out of the car.

"I think I'll stay here," she said. "I don't want you to be on your own when you're sick. Miles will understand."

"No, Greta, that's a mistake. I know it is. You'll be rushed in the morning, watching the clock. You won't be able to concentrate."

"It's not that bad, darling," Greta said, smiling. "Perhaps you're right though. I'll feel better when I've had a drink. Be a love and make one for me while I go and change."

Peter waited in the drawing room, listening to the sound of his wife's footfalls on the stairs leading up to the top story. He eyed the telephone, feeling like a snake. It was sitting on top of the desk in which Thomas had found the locket. Greta used the bureau now, and Peter wondered if she had put anything in the secret drawer to replace the locket. For the hundredth time he tried to visualize Anne as he had seen her on the day of her death: at lunch, lying on the sofa, passing him on the stairs. He didn't think she was wearing the locket, but he couldn't be sure. He hadn't known that it was the day of Anne's death; he hadn't known that he was looking at her alive for the last time.

I'm not your Greta Rose. Not anymore. But had she been once? Peter had to know. He picked up the telephone and dialed directory assistance. Matthew Barne's number was unlisted and Peter was about to give up when he remembered the school. He was a parent, a tuition-paying parent. Carstow would give him the number; they had no reason not to.

Soon he was speaking to Thomas.

"What do you want, Dad?" Thomas's voice was wary, but at least the word *Dad* implied a recognition of a relationship between them.

"I want to speak to you, to ask you something."

"About what?"

"About Rosie."

There was a silence at the end of the telephone, and Peter thought for a moment that they had been disconnected.

"Thomas, are you there?"

"Yes, I'm here."

"I can't speak for much longer. Will you meet me?"

"I don't know."

Another silence, and Peter could hear Greta coming down the stairs.

"There's no time. I'll meet you on Chelsea Town Hall steps at six-thirty."

"Where's that?"

"Around the corner from the house."

Peter put the phone down just as Greta came into the room.

"Who was that?"

"Just someone from the Ministry."

"What's he doing around the corner from the house?"

"The House of Commons. That's where I'm meeting him next week."

The lie slipped easily from Peter's tongue, and Greta seemed to accept his answer. She took the drink from his hand and kissed him as she did so, allowing her lips to move over his so that he was suddenly filled with desire.

She caught the look in his eye and moved away from him, smiling. Her power over him was still undiluted.

"Not now, darling, or I *won't* be able to concentrate. Besides, I'm wearing my giving-evidence dress. It's a dry run for tomorrow. What do you think?"

"I think it's perfect." Peter was being no less than honest. The black dress was of a perfect cut and length. Her breasts were high and pronounced, but there was no trace of cleavage. He had never seen Greta looking so beautiful.

The time passed slowly. Peter's mind was in confusion, but he tried not to show it, hiding behind government papers on the sofa. But something must have alerted Greta to his anxiety. Perhaps it was the way he kept glancing up at the carriage clock on the mantelpiece. Several times she asked him what was wrong, and several times she wondered aloud about canceling the conference with Miles Lambert.

At five past six the bell rang and Greta gathered up her papers and went down to the car. On the doorstep she hesitated and took hold of her husband by the arm.

"I can rely on you, Peter, can't I?" she said.

"Yes. Yes, of course you can." He avoided her eyes as he spoke.

Chapter 23
========

P ETER PACED the rooms after Greta had left, checking off each
minute that passed on his watch. His mind was in a ferment. One
moment he was certain that Greta could have nothing to do with the
murder, and the next doubts flooded back as he remembered the words
that he had overheard in the basement a year earlier.

At 6:25 he left the house and walked around to the town hall.
Thomas was sitting at the top of the steps. He was wearing the same
outfit that he'd had on at court: a navy blazer with gold buttons, a pair
of tan trousers and a pale blue Oxford shirt. The only difference was
that the black loafers that had been shiny with recent polishing at court
were now scuffed at the toes, as if Thomas had been using them to kick
the curb in frustration. Peter was suddenly touched by the thought that
Thomas would have had to decide for himself what to wear to court.
He had no parents to advise him. His mother was dead, and his father
had gone away. Peter felt a momentary sensation of guilt, but his nerves
were too frayed for him to retain any emotion for long.

Thomas got to his feet and came halfway down the steps toward his
father. Their eyes met for a moment and then Peter looked away. In his
excitement he had not realized how traumatic it would be to see his son
again. The meeting called for a reconciliation, but that of course was
not why Peter had asked Thomas to come. He needed answers to the
questions that had been pounding in his mind for the previous two

hours, but he could not pay for the answers with soft words; that would be too much of a betrayal, and so he launched straight into his questions without saying anything by way of greeting.

"What did this Rosie say about Greta?" he asked breathlessly.

"He said she had told him how the hiding place opened. It's all in my statement. Haven't you read it?" Thomas had gone back up a step and now looked down at his father angrily.

"No, I haven't read it," said Peter. "I need to know about this from you."

"Why?" Thomas threw out the question like a challenge. It conveyed all his pent-up resentment. He'd come across the city at the bidding of his father, negotiating the subway for only the second time in his life, and his father hadn't even bothered to say hello to him. They hadn't properly seen each other since the day of his mother's funeral, and now his father had nothing for him except questions about Rosie. Thomas felt he'd had enough of questions. He'd heard nothing else all day.

"I'm asking you because you were the only other person there. You're the only one who's met this Rosie."

"Apart from your wife," said Thomas.

"All right, I don't want to argue with you. I just need to know some things."

"What things?"

"What else did he said about Greta?"

"He didn't say anything else about Greta."

"Are you sure he was called Rosie?"

"That's what Lonny called him."

"Could it have been Rose? Could you have heard it wrong?"

"No, I didn't hear it wrong. And he did say it and it did happen. I'm sick of people saying it didn't. Sick of people not believing me. Like you. You don't believe me."

It came to Peter that his son had changed in the year since the funeral. The desperation that he remembered from their interview in the little terrace house in Woodbridge had been transformed into a new, dogged determination. Thomas's defiance was now far more than skin deep.

"I don't know what to believe, Thomas. That's why I need to ask you these questions." Peter realized immediately after he spoke how much he had betrayed Greta by his words. He felt an overwhelming self-disgust, which in turn made him angry with his son.

Thomas, however, thought nothing of his father's concession. He regretted coming. Seeing his father only made him realize how little the man loved him. He was better off not seeing him at all.

"I'm going," he said. "I wish I hadn't come."

Thomas came down the steps heading for the street, and Peter instinctively put out a hand to stop him.

"One more question," he said. "Just one more. Was Rosie his first name or his last?"

"How should I know? The other man just called him that. What is it about his name that's so important?"

The angry tone of his son's voice incensed Peter. Part of him wanted to push Thomas away or even strike him again, like he had in Woodbridge, but the need for an answer stayed his hand. There was nobody except Thomas whom he could talk to about the conversation he'd overheard. He had to know if there was a connection.

"On the night after your mother's funeral, I heard Greta talking to someone on the phone," said Peter slowly. "I just heard the end of the conversation; that's all. She said to whoever it was: 'Don't call me that. I'm not your Greta Rose. Not anymore.' Then afterward I asked her what that meant and she said it was her name, that Rose was her middle name."

"And then today you heard about Rosie for the first time and you wondered—"

"I don't know what I wondered."

"You wondered about Rosie and Greta. You wondered . . ." Thomas stopped in midsentence. He didn't need to spell it out for his father. If he could prove a connection, then he could still win.

"Have you looked through her things?" Thomas asked.

"For what?"

"To see if she's really called Greta Rose. She must have a passport or a birth certificate or something like that."

"I suppose I could," said Peter doubtfully. Talking to Thomas behind Greta's back was a betrayal, but going through her papers would be worse, far worse.

"Where is she now?" asked Thomas.

"She's talking to her barrister."

"Cooking up more lies."

"No, going through her evidence," said Peter angrily. He swung like a pendulum between his loyalty to Greta, which made him feel almost violent toward his son, and the doubts about her innocence that he couldn't get out of his head.

"When's she coming back?" asked Thomas.

"I don't know. Not before eight."

"There's time then. Let's go and look."

They began walking toward the house. Peter's agitation became more evident with every step they took.

"I can't give evidence like this," he said as they turned the corner. "I need to know first."

"When are you giving evidence?"

"I don't know. Sometime on Thursday probably. The prosecution have still got some statements to read, and then there's Greta. I don't know how long she'll take."

Peter was talking in order not to think about the significance of what he was doing as he beckoned to Thomas to follow him into the house.

Thomas expected his father to turn into the room on the right, but instead he carried on up the stairs to the first floor and went over to the very same oak bureau in the corner of the drawing room where Thomas had found the locket the previous October.

"Greta keeps most of her papers in here now," said Peter, opening the bureau.

"Not much point in looking in the secret place, I wouldn't think," said Thomas from behind his father's shoulder. He was right. The recess was empty, but in the drawer below Peter found his wife's passport. It had been issued the previous year, three months before Greta's marriage. There was an unflattering photograph taken just after Greta had had an unusually severe haircut, and next to it the details of the holder. Last name, Grahame. Given names, Greta. Nothing else. Just Greta.

Thomas leaned across his father and jabbed his finger against the name so hard that the passport almost fell out of Peter's trembling hand.

"Look, Dad. No Rose. No nothing. She lied to you about it being her middle name. That's not why she used to be called Greta Rose."

"It's not enough," said Peter stubbornly. "It doesn't mean anything.

Greta told me herself that she stopped calling herself Greta Rose after she left Manchester, and so it makes sense that she'd leave it off her renewal application. It's the birth certificate that's important. It'll be here somewhere."

"Let me look," said Thomas impatiently. "You're taking forever."

"No, I don't want you touching anything," said Peter angrily.

"Look in the drawer where the passport was, then," said Thomas. "She's going to keep all those kind of documents together."

Thomas was right. There was an old black address book held together by a liberal application of masking tape and underneath it a thick brown envelope with the word *certificates* written on it in Greta's neat handwriting.

Peter emptied the contents of the envelope out onto the writing surface of the bureau. At the top was a much newer piece of paper than the others, which turned out to be the certificate of Greta's marriage to Peter. Underneath it was a document headed University of Birmingham, and then a copy of a death certificate for a George Grahame, and at the bottom the certified copy of an entry of birth for Greta Rose Grahame, a girl born on November 17, 1971, at 20 Cale Street in Manchester. Greta Rose had had a home birth.

Peter felt an overwhelming surge of relief flood his body. For a moment it was ecstasy. He was like a soldier told that he's lost a leg who then looks down to find the leg still there. Peter's spinning world righted itself, and he forgot for a moment that Thomas was the enemy.

"Thank God," he said. "Deep down I always knew she was Greta Rose. She dropped the Rose because she had a bad time up north. Just like she said."

"She may be called Rose, but that doesn't mean a thing," said Thomas furiously. He felt crushed by the disappointment that the birth certificate had inflicted upon him. For a moment he had really believed that the nightmare of the last year was going to end. He wouldn't be alone anymore; people wouldn't say he was a liar. But now it was worse. Doubt removed is certainty redoubled. Thomas felt his final defeat approaching. Greta had almost won. He made a last appeal to his father.

"It's not the birth certificate that matters, Dad. It's me and you. I heard Rosie talking about Greta. I saw him outside this house. She had Mum's locket in this desk."

The smile on Peter's face faded and the light went out of his eyes. It was as if Thomas's words had reminded him of who Thomas really was. His son was the enemy. He'd brought all this about. He was the reason why his wife was on trial for murder when she was innocent, entirely innocent.

"*You* saw; *you* heard," said Peter angrily. "It's always you. Not you and me. You and your lies."

"I'm not lying. What do you think I am? Why would I want to make it up?"

"Because she rejected you when you tried to—"

"Tried to what?"

"Tried to . . . I don't know what you did. I wasn't there, but I know what you wanted. Greta told me."

"What did I want?"

"To sleep with her."

"And she said no and I went crazy. Is that the idea?"

"You feel guilty too. That's another reason why you've done what you've done."

"Guilty! You're the one who should be guilty. You left Mum on her own all those years and she never complained. And you left me too even though I was small and would have liked to have had a father. What did you ever do with me?"

Peter said nothing. Thomas didn't know if he was even listening, but it did him good to tell his father what he felt. He probably wouldn't have another opportunity.

"I can't even remember you taking me for a walk. You just weren't there. Your career was too important for you to spend time with your family."

"I was earning money for you and Anne," said Peter defensively.

"No, you weren't. You were suiting yourself. And it got better, didn't it, when Greta came along. Green-eyed Greta. That's what Mum used to call her. You and her in this house. You and her and your brilliant career."

"I never slept with her before . . ."

Peter stopped in midsentence and Thomas finished it for him.

"Before Mum died, but you did on the night of her funeral, didn't you? That's how you heard that conversation that rattled you so badly, wasn't it?"

Thomas's words were pouring out in a flood now. There was no chance for Peter to reply to his questions even if he had wanted to.

"Your first wife spending her first night in the ground and you fucking your secretary up in London. What a picture."

"Shut up, Thomas," said Peter. There was a warning note in his voice that Thomas ignored.

"And somewhere deep down you must know that she sent those men to kill Mummy, but it wasn't enough to sleep with your wife's murderer—you needed to marry her as well. You're a pig, Dad, and this place, it's your fucking sty."

Thomas was shouting now and he had brought his face close to his father's, so he had no chance of defending himself when Peter lashed out. His fist was clenched this time, and he hit Thomas on the side of his mouth with a swinging punch that sent his son crashing against the bureau and from there to the floor.

Peter put a hand out toward his son and then immediately pulled it back. He felt disgusted with himself for what he'd done but at this moment of crisis he wasn't man enough to face his guilt. Instead he swamped it beneath a torrent of self-justification. It was Thomas who had brought all this about with his crazy witch hunt against his stepmother.

"You shouldn't have talked to me like that," said Peter, as Thomas slowly got to his feet clutching the side of his face.

"Fuck you, Dad." The anger had gone out of Thomas's voice, and he spoke the words softly like a curse.

"Here, take my handkerchief," said Peter, but Thomas backed away. The blood had seeped through his fingers and dripped down onto his shirt.

"You don't want my blood on the carpet, do you? You don't want your bitch wife to know I've been here."

"Shut up, Thomas."

"Shut up or you'll hit me again. Is that it?"

"No, it's not. I'm sorry I hit you, but I'm not going to let you say those things about Greta."

"So it's perfectly all right for her to have killed my mother?"

"She didn't kill your mother. I don't want to talk to you about it anymore, Thomas."

"But you did half an hour ago. You thought it was a possibility then, didn't you? It's wonderful what a birth certificate can do."

"I was stupid. I feel ashamed of myself, but that's between me and my own conscience."

"If you've got one."

"This is pointless," said Peter wearily. "We've got nothing to say to each other."

Thomas turned away. He didn't disagree with what his father had said. His objection was that his father had no right not to love him, but there was no point in telling him that. He couldn't make his father feel things if he didn't. At the door, Thomas turned back. The situation called for a parting shot, but Thomas could think of nothing suitable to say. He felt suddenly exhausted. A sense of utter desolation overwhelmed him, and his father's words came to him as if over a great distance.

"You can stay in the house for as long as you like. Jane too. It's just I can't see you. Not after all that's happened."

Down below, the front door opened. Greta had come home early.

Looking back on the moment later in the evening, Thomas wondered why he hadn't walked down the stairs to meet his stepmother. He could have told her that he was there at his father's invitation to search through her personal papers. How could their marriage have survived the revelation of his father's doubt? The only explanation that occurred to Thomas for his decision to hide was that a victory based on doubts that his father no longer felt would be no victory at all. He could only properly avenge his mother by showing up Greta for what she really was. He needed proof. The birth certificate was not that proof. He could not use it against Greta now.

Peter had been talking when the door opened. He had his eyes on his son, and Thomas saw the fear in them as Greta began to climb the stairs.

He stepped back into the drawing room, putting the open door between himself and the landing, and at the same time he motioned with head and hand to his father to go past him.

"Are you here, Peter?" Greta called from the stairs.

Peter went out onto the landing.

"You're home early," he said.

"I didn't stay long. I was worried about you. You looked so awful earlier. Are you any better?"

"Yes, much better."

Peter's voice sounded fraught with anxiety to Thomas standing on the other side of the door, but Greta seemed to accept her husband's assurance.

"Come up and talk to me while I get changed," she said. "But don't talk about the trial. Anything but the trial. I've had enough of it for one day."

Thomas listened to the sound of his father following his stepmother up the stairs to the second story and turned back into the room. So much had happened here. He remembered his mother showing him the secret recess in the bureau on that first morning in London and the day he opened it six months later and found her golden locket inside. There must be something else that would connect Greta with his mother's killers. Something that couldn't be explained away, something that wasn't just his own assertion. The birth certificate was not the end of the line. For his father, perhaps, but not for him. There had to be something or someone in Greta's past that would connect her.

Thomas's eyes fastened on the old bandaged address book sitting on the writing surface of the bureau under the documents that his father had spilled out of the brown envelope. There was no time to lose. He could hear footsteps moving about on the floor above his head. It must be Greta changing out of whatever dress she had worn to charm her fat slippery barrister. She'd be down in a minute ready for his father to mix her a Bloody Mary.

Thomas moved across the room on tiptoes. He carefully put back all the documents, including the birth certificate, in the envelope and replaced them in the drawer. Then he picked up the address book and shut the bureau.

At the door he took a last look around the room as if committing it to memory and then went quietly down the stairs. He let himself soundlessly out of the house and stood on the top of the steps for a moment before he walked rapidly away without looking back. He held Greta's address book concealed under his jacket.

Chapter 24

THOMAS WALKED over the Albert Bridge and on into Battersea heading for Matthew Barne's house, where he was due to spend the night.

Thomas and Matthew had been drawn together from the start of their time at Carstow School. It was partly, as Matthew had told Miles Lambert, that they had been the only two newcomers in a class where all the other students had already been at the school two years. But their friendship was also founded on shared interests and passions. They both loved romance and adventure. They had read the same books by the Brontë sisters and Robert Louis Stevenson. They believed in chivalry and heroism, and Matthew had from the outset adopted his friend's crusade for justice against Greta as his own. Thomas, for his part, was intensely grateful to Matthew for his support. After his own experience with Miles Lambert, he knew that it couldn't have been easy for Matthew to give evidence, but he had agreed to do so without complaint. The two put an intense value on their friendship and were inseparable at school.

The Barne family lived in a rambling Victorian house full of children and toys and pets. Matthew's mother was always cooking, trying to keep pace with the insatiable appetites of her red-haired progeny, while Mr. Barne did something in the financial district. This something seemed to take up most of his time, but when he was home he shut

himself up in a tiny room at the back of the house, which the family referred to for some reason as "the cubbyhole." On Thomas's previous
visits he had only seen the door of this sanctum open on one occasion,
when Mrs. Barne had come out carrying two empty bottles of Smirnoff
vodka, from which Thomas had deduced that his best friend's father
was a not-so-secret alcoholic. There was nothing unfriendly about either of Matthew's parents, however. Mrs. Barne had never criticized
Thomas for involving Matthew in his troubles. She was kind to him in
her way, but she shared with her husband an essential distractedness, so
that Matthew and Thomas were left almost entirely to their own de-
vices.

Matthew was the oldest of the six Barne children by two years, and
this, combined with his status as the only boy in the family, had won
him sole use of the attic bedroom at the top of the house. It was here
that Thomas went with Greta's address book.

Matthew hung a DO NOT DISTURB notice on the door that he had
taken from a hotel in Brighton on the last day of the most recent Barne
summer holiday, and the two teenagers sat down to talk about what to
do next.

Thomas told Matthew about what had happened as quickly as he
could. His mouth and cheekbone hurt him, and his lip had swollen
where his father had hit him.

"Your father's a total bastard," said Matthew, not for the first time.
"My one's not great, but at least he doesn't go round hitting me when
he feels like it. You should go to the police."

"I've already done that," said Thomas, smiling ruefully. "He believes
in her. That's the problem. It doesn't matter if she gets convicted. That
wouldn't change anything except that he'd hate me even more. She'd
still win."

"Is she likely to go down?"

"Go down?"

"That's what they call it when someone gets found guilty. Do you
think she will?"

"No. That fat barrister of hers did a real hatchet job on me, made
everyone think that I'd made it all up."

"I know. Me too." Matthew felt slightly sick as he remembered his
day in court.

"I keep on thinking that there must be something that would prove she's guilty. Not just to the jury, but to my father too. Some document that would do it, something that she couldn't explain away like she did with the locket. That's why that birth certificate was so important. If only she hadn't been called Greta Rose to start with—if she'd become it."

"By marrying Rosie?"

"Yes. That's what got my father so crazy. He was holding that birth certificate like it was one of the Crown Jewels."

"Why does the birth certificate mean that she couldn't have married him? Both things are possible, aren't they?"

"What? Greta Rose marries a man called Rose?" Thomas looked more than skeptical.

"If that's what Rosie's last name is. I'm not saying she did marry him. All I'm saying is that it's worth checking it out. There's not much else for us to do. We've both had our day in court."

"How do you check it out?"

"You go to the Family Records Office. It's up in North London just behind Sadler's Wells opera house. They've got big index books for all the marriages and births and deaths that there've been in England since the Battle of Waterloo."

"Eighteen-fifteen?"

"Well, I don't know what date precisely, but it doesn't matter. The books go back at least a hundred years, and if Greta got married, it's not going to be more than ten years ago, is it?"

"No, I suppose not. How do you know all this, Matthew?"

"We did a project on it at my last school. We spent a day there. Everyone had to find out as much as they could about their family history from the indexes. I got back to my grandfather's birth certificate. It gave his father's occupation as prison chaplain, so he probably got to pray with the criminals who were going to be executed the next day. It was quite exciting really."

"So anybody can go in and look through these indexes?" asked Thomas.

"Yes, it doesn't matter how old you are. They haven't got all the information on the indexes though. Just enough for you to fill out the application for a certificate, and then you have to wait."

"How long?"

"I don't know. We had to wait a week for our certificates, but there's probably a way of getting them quicker if you pay more."

"I haven't got a week. Once the evidence is over they won't let any more in. That's what Sergeant Hearns told me."

"When's the evidence going to be over?" asked Matthew.

"I don't know. My father said he was going to be called sometime on Thursday, and he's Greta's only witness."

"God, that's no time. Why didn't we think of this before?"

"Because it was only today that my father decided to tell me about Greta's late-night telephone conversation," said Thomas. He paused and then went on musingly, "He said Greta told the man 'I'm not your Greta Rose.' Not just 'Greta Rose' but 'your Greta Rose.' She and Rosie are linked up together, Matt. I don't know if they were married or not, but someone's going to have seen them together, known about them. I'm going to go through this address book and see if any of the names spring out at me, and then we'll go to your family records place in the morning."

Matthew was soon asleep, but Thomas stayed up into the small hours puzzling over the address-book entries, all made in Greta's careful handwriting. Thomas wondered whether she would miss the book before the next morning. He doubted it somehow. She had enough things on her mind without looking up telephone numbers.

None of the entries seemed to offer much to Thomas. There was Greta's mother in Manchester, but otherwise most of the names seemed to be for businesses of one kind or another. Dressmakers, dry cleaners, travel agents and a shop selling computer accessories. In between there were a few names with or without last names that Thomas copied out on a piece of paper to try the next morning. Anna, Martin, Giles, Peter, Pierre, Robert, Jane—but no Rosie or Rose. Nothing floral at all. The names swirled about in Thomas's head after he turned out the bedside light and lay looking out the high window at the full moon hanging over the roofs of South London. It was a clear night and the moon seemed very close. He felt the great weight of it and thought of the arid desert that was its surface. He imagined the terrible silence and the darkness of its night and felt despair settling on his spirit like dust. The grand gesture of throwing the sultan's sapphire into the North Sea now seemed an empty foolishness.

Thomas thought of his father's last words: "I can't see you. Not after all that's happened," and he thought of his beautiful mother lying un-avenged in the Flyte churchyard. There was no time left and no one to turn to. He looked away from the moon and drifted into a troubled sleep.

He woke again later and felt as if no time had passed, but the lumi-nous clock on Matthew's mantelpiece showed it was nearly 7 A.M. and Thomas could hear the Barne children beginning to move about on the floors below. He felt as if he had just dreamed something vitally impor-tant, but he couldn't remember what it was. The frustration was almost too much to bear. There was a word or a name on the edge of his con-sciousness that Thomas just could not reach, and he would probably never have done so had his eye not fallen on the list of names and num-bers that he had transcribed from Greta's address book before he'd gone to sleep.

Pierre. That was the name. It took Thomas back to a golden after-noon by the River Thames when he hadn't known who Greta was or what she was plotting. He remembered white wine in a plastic cup, the blanket spread out on the grass while Big Ben chimed the hours, and Greta's head resting on his legs. She'd talked about a boy she knew in school years before. A boy who Thomas reminded her of. A boy called Pierre.

Thomas jumped out of bed and ran down five flights of stairs, nar-rowly avoiding a collision at the bottom with Matthew's father, who was headed for his cubbyhole. Thomas waited for the door to close be-hind Mr. Barne and then dialed Pierre's number on the hall telephone.

It was a foreign country code, and the female voice that answered spoke in French. Thomas said "Pierre" twice loudly for want of any-thing else to say. He couldn't understand a word of what the voice at the other end of the line was saying. Then suddenly the flurry of speech stopped and there was silence. Thomas wondered whether the phone had been hung up at the other end before a deep male voice identified itself as belonging to Pierre.

"Do you know Greta Grahame?" asked Thomas, wishing that he'd given himself a little time to work out what he was going to say.

"Who?"

"Greta Grahame. She says she knew you years ago in Manchester when you were both at school there."

"Greta. Yes, I knew her. I more than knew her in fact. We went out together for a while. It was a long time ago."

"I know it was, but I need to ask you about people she knew then."

"Why don't you ask her yourself?"

"Because she wouldn't tell me," said Thomas, desperately trying to think of a story that would persuade this stranger to give him the information he was looking for. "She wouldn't want me to risk my safety."

"I don't get this," said Pierre. "Who are you?"

"I'm a friend of Greta's. A good friend. There's this man who's threatening her, and I need to find out who it is so that I can tell the police."

"Why would I know anything about it? I haven't seen Greta in more than ten years."

Clearly Pierre didn't know anything about the trial. That much at least was in Thomas's favor.

"I'm calling you because you're the only person who might know who this man is. He's someone bad from her past, someone who's got something on her."

"I don't know anyone like that. We were at school together in Manchester. I left before her and came south. I heard she went off the rails for a while, but then her father died and she got a place at Birmingham University. She wrote me from there a couple of times. She seemed to be doing okay. I don't know what happened to her after that. Is she doing all right? Apart from this man who's threatening her, I mean."

"She's doing great," Thomas lied. "She's married someone really rich."

"Pretty girls have all the luck, don't they?" said Pierre. "Anyway, I don't know your name but I'm afraid I'm a working man. I'll be late for my train if I don't go now."

"My name's Thomas. I won't keep you more than a minute longer, I promise. That time when she went off the rails, did you keep in touch with Greta at all then?"

"A bit. I went back to Manchester a few times. Not many because I didn't like the place much. Too far north for me. And Greta had changed. She was a different person somehow."

"Did you hear about Greta spending time with a man called Rosie when you went back?"

"Rosie. That's a girl's name."

"Rose then. He's got a thick scar running down under his right ear."

"I heard about someone called Rose, but he didn't have a scar. I met him once with Greta, and I'd have remembered the scar."

"Was he the kind of person who would threaten people, hurt them?" asked Thomas, trying to keep the excitement out of his voice.

"He had a reputation as a hard man, someone to avoid. Greta was a fool if she got involved with him."

"What was his name?"

"Rose. I told you that."

"I know, but what was his Christian name?"

"John, Jonathan. Something like that. I've got to go now."

Thomas slowly replaced the receiver and stood motionless and distracted in the hall trying to master his emotions. It was another connection between Greta and his mother's killer, but it was useless unless it was turned into a proof, something that would convince his father and that jury down at the Old Bailey, something that Greta couldn't explain away. And he had almost no time left, the evidence would all be complete sometime the next day. He had to get the proof to court before then, and he didn't even know if it existed.

Matthew and Thomas got to the Family Records Office just before ten-thirty. Inside there was a big, light room with long rows of metal shelves divided by high, sloping desks where the searchers could read the heavy index books: black binders for deaths, green for marriages and red for births. There was a constant repetition of thuds as the books hit the desks or got replaced on the shelves. Everyone using the place seemed to Thomas to be both old and preoccupied, their fingers inky from copying out the entries in the index books onto the certificate application forms, which they then took up to a bored young woman sitting at a pine desk by the door.

It took Matthew no time at all to show Thomas how the system worked. There were seven or eight index books for each year, divided alphabetically. They started with the births and found the entry for Greta Rose Grahame after less than five minutes in the "G–H" book for 1971. Thomas wasn't disappointed; he hadn't really imagined that the certificate in Greta's desk was a forgery. However, he felt his heart beating fast as they moved into the central aisles and began to search through the green marriage books. They started in 1987 and worked their way systematically forward through the years, searching under the name Rose. This was the only way of doing it, given that the index worked entirely by reference to the husband's last name. There was in fact very little other information in the books. Just the last name followed by the husband's first and middle initials, and beyond that the wife's maiden name and the district in which the marriage had taken place. Finally there were the reference numbers that enabled the invisible workers on the upper floors of the building to enter the full details of each marriage on the certificates that had been applied for down below.

Matthew and Thomas searched through every Rose that had gotten married in Great Britain in every one of the previous fourteen years, but there was not one who had married a Grahame in Manchester or anywhere else. There were John Roses and Jonathan Roses, who had married a variety of names, but none bore any resemblance to Grahame.

They searched again and again without success until Thomas got careless and knocked one of the huge index books off a high desk onto the floor. It fell with a great crash, and suddenly there was silence in the records room. Everyone in their vicinity turned around to look at the culprits. They were all old and Thomas and Matthew were young. "Old people wouldn't drop precious index books on the floor," they seemed to be saying. "Old people would be more careful."

"Come on," said Matthew, beckoning Thomas to follow him into the black section. They took shelter in an obscure corner of the great room housing Deaths 1860–1868. Behind them the thud-silence-thud noise of the index books hitting shelves and tables began again.

"It's no good, Matthew," said Thomas in a depressed voice. "There's no point in looking anymore. We're not going to find anything. It was a long shot anyway. She could easily have been his Greta Rose without being married to him."

"Welcome to Death Row," said Matthew, relating their present surroundings to Thomas's mood of resignation.

"What did you say?" asked Thomas, suddenly alert.

"Death Row—or Death Row H to be precise," said Matthew, reading a notice on the wall.

"Leading to Death Row I. Put the two together and you've got Death Rows H and I."

"What are you talking about, Thomas? It was a joke but it wasn't that funny."

"*Rows*. Don't you get it, Matthew? There are other ways of spelling *Rose*. We need to check those out too."

They went back to the front of the marriages section where they had been before, braving the disapproving glances that met them on their way, and started to search again. They found what they were looking for quite quickly. There were no Rows, but one or two bridegrooms did have the surname Rowes, and a Jonathan B. Rowes had married a Grahame in Liverpool in 1989.

"It's them!" said Matthew excitedly. "It's got to be. It's just the right date. She'd have been eighteen. That's when Pierre told you she went off the rails."

"The date's all right but the city's not," said Thomas. "Greta was in Manchester, remember. Not Liverpool."

"They're both towns in the north though, aren't they? Not everyone gets married in their hometown. Maybe they didn't want anyone to know about it."

"Maybe. I'm not saying it's not them. I'm just saying that there isn't enough to know one way or another. We couldn't take this to anyone; we'd need the proper certificate. That gives dates of birth and stuff like that, doesn't it?"

"No. Just the ages on marriage certificates," said Matthew. "I remember that. They have the fathers' names though, and their occupations. Greta can't pretend it's not her if the father's name on the marriage certificate is the same as that on her birth certificate. We'll have her then."

"If it's her and if we get the certificate in time and if we get them to the right people before the evidence is over. We've got nothing at the minute," said Thomas. Underneath his cautious exterior he was as excited as Matthew. It was just that he was determined to keep control of himself. He didn't want to repeat his experience of the day before with the birth certificate.

Matthew refused to share his friend's somber mood.

"But we've got hope, which is more than we had twenty minutes ago," he said. "We ought to get on and order the certificates now. They take twenty-four hours if you make a priority application. That's what it says on that notice over there."

Thomas filled out the application forms and handed them in. The bored young woman at the desk by the door had been replaced by a bored young man, who glanced at his watch before writing the collection time on Thomas's receipt—12:21 on Thursday. Thomas wondered, as he went down the steps of the records building, whether he might find himself tomorrow with the crucial evidence in his hand at last, when it was already too late to use it.

Chapter 25

THE FAMILY Records Office opened at ten o'clock on Thursday morning, and by five past ten Thomas was already well embarked on an argument with a cadaverous young man wearing a plastic badge on his lapel identifying him as Andrew, Applications Clerk. Thomas seemed completely unaware of Matthew's efforts to calm him down and of the disapproving impatience of the people queuing for priority collections behind him.

"I know it's ten-oh-five and the receipt says twelve twenty-one," said Thomas, allowing his exasperation to increase the volume of his voice still further. "I know that. I'm just asking you as a special favor to see if my certificates are ready. Maybe they are, maybe they're not, but it won't hurt you to try, will it, Andy?"

"I'm not Andy, I'm Andrew," said the clerk.

"I'm sorry," said Thomas. "Really I am. I didn't mean to offend you, Andrew. Won't you just do me this favor?"

"I can't help you, sir," said Andrew for the third time. "You'll simply have to wait like everyone else."

"Can't or won't?" shouted Thomas, losing his temper. "You government employees are all the same. Everything's got to be by the bloody rule book, and meanwhile justice goes down the drain."

"All right, Thomas, calm down," said Matthew, pulling his friend away from the counter. He'd noticed Andrew's hand straying toward a buzzer on the side of his desk and feared ejection would follow any minute at the hands of the two burly security guards whom they had passed at the front of the building.

"I'm sorry about all this," Matthew said to Andrew. "He's got big problems with his family. We'll come back later."

"Twelve twenty-one," said Andrew mechanically, ignoring the explanation.

"Twelve twenty-one," agreed Matthew as he shepherded Thomas toward the door to the cafeteria.

=

The court sat late on Thursday morning. It was eleven o'clock when Greta resumed her place in the witness box and Sparling started his cross-examination. The reporters had divided eleven to three in favor of Greta at the end of the prosecution case. Even the three still holding out for a conviction had agreed that Miles Lambert had gotten the better of Thomas. They all thought that the victim's son had made up at least some of his evidence in order to strengthen the case against his stepmother.

The jurors were hard to read. The Italian man in the designer suit had seemed to be a sure vote for Greta from the start, and the reporters had noticed that at least three of the other male jurors appeared to have been won over to the defendant's charms in the last couple of days. The Mrs. Thatcher look-alike sitting in the foreperson's position looked more furious with each passing day, and the general view among the press was that this was due to the growing number of her colleagues deserting the prosecution's side as the case unfolded. A single vote for a guilty verdict wouldn't be enough to stop Greta from being acquitted after the judge had given a majority direction. It wouldn't matter in those circumstances if the single voter was forewoman of the jury or not.

Miles Lambert had taken Greta gently through her evidence on the previous afternoon, and now she stood with a soft smile on her pretty face, waiting for Sparling to do his worst. Her air of confidence irritated the old barrister, making him launch into his cross-examination with more aggression than he might otherwise have chosen to use.

"You told this jury yesterday that you got on reasonably well with Lady Anne," he said. "Did you really mean that?"

"We had a few arguments, but I'd say that was inevitable when I was in her house so often over a period of years. By and large, we got on quite well."

"Didn't you mind when she called you lower-class and told you that you didn't belong in her house?"

"Yes, I was hurt, but then she came and apologized and I forgave her."

"It was that easy, was it?"

"Yes, she was genuinely sorry. I admired her for coming to talk to me. It can't have been easy for her to do that."

"No. And it can't surely have been as easy for you to forgive Lady Anne as you say. She told you that you were poisonous like a snake, didn't she?"

"That's right."

"And it made you say, 'You've fucking had it now, Mrs. Posh.' Isn't *that* right?"

"No, it's not. That's a fabrication."

"Just like it's a fabrication by Thomas that he overheard you referring to your employer's wife as Mrs. Posh in the basement of the house in Chelsea?"

"Yes."

"It seems to be something of a coincidence, wouldn't you say, Lady Robinson?"

"Yes, I would, Mr. Sparling, and not an accidental coincidence I should say either."

"Oh?"

"They've put their heads together and came up with this Mrs. Posh phrase. It's not one I would ever use."

"Even when Lady Anne was insulting you for being lower-class?"

"She apologized."

"Yes, and you admired her for doing so. Isn't that what you said?"

"Yes. She didn't need to say sorry. It was her house."

"You'd admired Lady Anne for a long time, hadn't you? Even when you were a girl living in Manchester, you admired her."

"Don't be ridiculous."

"Just like you admired all those fashionable aristocratic women whose pictures you cut out of those magazines and put in your scrapbooks. I think Sergeant Hearns told us they contained more than two thousand pictures."

"I've always liked fashion. Is it so very wrong to have interests when you're young?"

"No, not at all. But does an interest in fashion justify trying on someone else's clothes without their permission?"

"No, it doesn't. I shouldn't have done that. I just couldn't afford those kinds of clothes, and I wanted to see what they looked like on me."

"There was only one way that you could afford them, wasn't there? To become Lady Robinson yourself."

"What are you suggesting, Mr. Sparling? That I murdered Lady Anne for money? There's no evidence for that, you know. Nothing's gone into my bank account. You've got the records. Whoever's got those jewels has got nothing to do with me."

"I wasn't asking you about the jewels, Lady Robinson. I was suggesting that you wanted what Lady Anne had: her title, her husband, and her husband's money."

"But not her jewels."

"Please don't argue with counsel, Lady Robinson," said the judge, intervening for the first time in the morning. "Just try to answer his questions."

"I'm sorry, my Lord," said Greta, bestowing one of her most winning smiles on the old judge.

"That's all right. Please carry on, Mr. Sparling."

The barrister turned a page of his notes and changed tack.

"What were you talking to your midnight visitor about in your basement apartment in April of last year?" he asked.

"Money. It was a man I owed money to. I was asking for more time to pay."

"So it was in the nature of a business meeting. Why were you conducting business in the middle of the night, Lady Robinson?"

"I wasn't. We went out earlier, and then he came back to my flat and stayed late. I thought that an evening's entertainment might make him more . . ."

"More compliant?"

"Yes. More willing to give me more time."

"Were you right? Was he more willing?"

"Yes. He agreed to wait."

"How much money did you owe this man, Lady Robinson?"

"About ten thousand pounds."

"And have you repaid it now?"

"Most of it."

"How?"

"I saved money, and my husband has helped me a bit."

"Even though you lied to him about meeting this man. You've already admitted that in your interview. You told your husband that you were with your mother in Manchester."

"I lied because I was ashamed of owing the money."

"You lied because you didn't want anyone to know that you had been meeting the man who was going to kill Lady Anne. That's the truth, isn't it?" Sparling's accusation came accompanied with a sudden aggression of voice and gesture, but neither seemed to have any effect on Greta. She smiled at Sparling before answering his question slowly and deliberately.

"No, it's not the truth, Mr. Sparling. I lied because I was ashamed of being in debt. I did not want Sir Peter or Lady Anne to think badly of me."

"Did you say to your visitor, 'Can't you see I haven't got him yet'?"

"No, I would never have said that. I would've said: 'Can't you see I haven't got *it* yet,' about the money. If you recall, Mr. Sparling, Thomas couldn't be sure if I said 'him' or 'it.' I'm sure it'll be in your notes."

"So you weren't referring to not yet having secured Sir Peter. Is that right?"

"I was talking about the money."

"Your visitor was the man who killed Lady Anne, I suggest. Thomas recognized him as such."

"He saw a man from behind. And that man can't have been the man in my flat anyway."

"Why not?"

"Because the front door of the basement was locked when I went up to the main house via the internal staircase. I always kept it locked from the inside because of burglars."

"Why couldn't your visitor have unlocked it?"

"Because I had the key."

"You never mentioned this in your interview, Lady Robinson. Why not?"

"Because I didn't think of it."

"And that's not all you failed to mention, was it? Sergeant Hearns asked you again and again to give the name of your visitor. Again and again you refused to provide it. Why? What had you got to hide?"

"I had nothing to hide. The man's name is Andrew Relton."

Sparling stopped, momentarily taken aback. He hadn't expected Greta's reply, and he had never heard this name before. But it took no more than a second or two for him to regain his composure and return to the attack.

"You tell us now when your trial's almost over and so the information's useless," he said. "Why wouldn't you tell the police when you were interviewed? That's when it mattered."

There was a pause, and then Sparling went on as if Greta's silence was exactly what he had expected.

"You aren't answering because you haven't got an answer, have you, Lady Robinson? You didn't name this man to the police because you didn't want them to investigate your story."

"No, I didn't want Andrew dragged into all this, and what's wrong with that?" said Greta angrily. "My debts are my own affair. They've got nothing to do with this trial. Nothing at all."

"You didn't want to name your visitor because he's the man who murdered Lady Anne. That's the truth, isn't it?" Sparling had drawn himself up to his full height as if to emphasize his accusation.

"No, it's not," said Greta with equal emphasis.

"The same man who went back to deal with Thomas just before your trial."

"Don't be ridiculous."

"The man whom his friend called Rosie."

"I don't know anyone called Rosie or Rose," said Greta firmly. "Man or woman. It's a ridiculous name."

Immediately Sparling regretted asking about the murderer's return to the House of the Four Winds the previous week. He'd thrown away the advantage gained by highlighting Greta's evasiveness with the police and instead concentrated the jury's attention on the weakest part of his case. Now he had no choice but to continue.

"He referred to you by name. He said you were the one who showed him how the hiding place worked."

"No, he didn't. Thomas has made that up. It's pretty convenient, isn't it, that this Rosie character should mention me by name just when he could be sure that Thomas would overhear?"

"Please just answer the questions, Lady Robinson," said Sparling in an effort to keep control of his cross-examination. But he was being beaten back and he knew it. He'd noticed out of the corner of his eye how several of the jurors had nodded in agreement immediately after Greta's last observation. Sparling was in fact half relieved when the judge chose this moment for a ten-minute midmorning adjournment.

=

At the very moment that Judge Granger was sitting back in his easy chair in the privacy of his chambers inhaling the smoke from his first cigarette of the day, Thomas and Matthew were sitting at a table in the cafeteria of the Family Records Office with an array of half-drunk cups of coffee and empty soft-drink cans in front of them. They'd just returned from a third unsuccessful attempt to persuade Andrew the applications clerk to expedite their application.

"Bastard, officious bastard." Thomas spat out the words while giving further expression to his feelings by crushing an empty Coke can in his hand.

"I know," said Matthew. "But if you'd carried on, we'd probably have gotten thrown out and then we wouldn't get the certificates at all."

Thomas didn't answer. He'd begun work on another can.

"We should still be okay even if we get the certificates at twelve-twenty. It's not far from here to the court in a taxi, and then we've only got to find Sergeant Hearns. He'll sort it out, Tom."

"If he can. But it may be too late by then. My father told me that Greta's not calling any other witnesses except him, so once he's given evidence, we've had it. Hearns said that there can't be any more evidence after the defense has closed its case."

"We should have gotten him to help with this."

"I couldn't get hold of him all day yesterday, and he's not going to get the information any quicker this morning than we are. Besides, what we've got out of the index book doesn't really amount to that much if you think about it. Jonathan B. Rowes married a Someone Grahame somewhere in Liverpool sometime in 1989. So what! Why should Rowes be Rosie? Why should Grahame be Greta?"

"Because they are," said Matthew fervently. "Because of what your father heard Greta saying on the telephone. That she wasn't his Greta Rose anymore."

"But she can explain that. Greta Rose is her real name. That much is in the index books."

"*His* Greta Rose. That's what she said."

"All right, Matthew," said Thomas, suddenly smiling. "You're right. We've got to keep our hopes up and stop speculating."

But Thomas's frustration returned as he gazed up at the cafeteria clock for the hundredth time that morning just as the hands came together at noon.

===

The bells of the City's many churches had just finished tolling the hour when John Sparling rose from his chair to resume his cross-examination of Lady Greta Robinson. The courtroom was packed, but there was no noise at all. The world outside seemed a very long way away.

"Let's focus on the events surrounding the murder of Lady Anne Robinson," said the prosecution barrister.

"If you wish," replied Greta in a tone that implied that she didn't mind if they did or they didn't.

"You told us yesterday that you rang up Mrs. Ball at Lady Anne's request to ask if Thomas could go over there."

"That's right. It was on the Sunday afternoon."

"Had Lady Anne ever asked you to do such a thing before?"

"She may have done. I don't recall. It didn't seem a very significant request at the time. She had one of her headaches and so she asked me to make the call."

"Did Lady Anne say why she wanted Thomas to go to his friend's for the night?"

"No."

"Didn't the request strike you as being a bit strange?"

"No. As I said, the whole thing didn't seem very significant."

"But Lady Anne had never asked you to make any arrangement for Thomas in all the two and a half years that you'd been working for her husband. Isn't that right, Lady Robinson?"

"I told you, Mr. Sparling. I don't recall."

"You don't recall. Do you recall lying to Jane Martin about how the arrangement came to be made?"

"No, but I recall Jane Martin lying to this court about what I said to her. I never told her that Mrs. Ball had invited Thomas."

"What did you tell her?"

"I simply told her about the arrangement. I said nothing about whose idea it was. There was no reason to. She didn't ask and I didn't tell her."

"Why wouldn't Lady Anne have called Mrs. Ball and made the arrangement herself?"

"Because she had a headache. I told you that already."

"It must have been a pretty bad headache to stop her making a quick telephone call."

"It was. They weren't really headaches, they were more like migraines that she got. She couldn't do anything when she had them."

"Except that on this particular Sunday she was able to give you instructions about ringing up Mrs. Ball and making an arrangement for Thomas."

"That's right. It didn't take long."

"But nor would it have taken her long to make the call."

"I don't know. Maybe Anne thought that Mrs. Ball would keep her on the phone."

"Where's all this heading, Mr. Sparling?" asked the judge, stirring restlessly in his chair. "We seem to be going round in circles. I think it would be best if you just put your case on this issue and then moved on."

"Yes, my Lord. My case is this, Lady Robinson. You telephoned Mrs. Ball and made the arrangement yourself without consulting anyone and then you told Lady Anne and Jane Martin afterward that it was Mrs. Ball who had called up to invite Thomas."

"Why would I do all this, Mr. Sparling?" asked Greta evenly. "Why would I make this arrangement?"

Sparling did not answer immediately. He made it a policy not to allow defendants to start asking the questions. That meant surrendering control over the cross-examination; it meant surrendering his greatest advantage. However, the situation here was different. He could see the jurors looking at him expectantly out of the corner of his eye. They wanted to hear his answer. The trouble was that this was not the strongest part of his case. Sparling inwardly cursed the judge for his intervention. It had forced him onto his back foot, and now the defendant was trying to push him over.

"You did all this because you wanted Thomas Robinson out of the house on the Monday evening so that Lady Anne would be alone and defenseless when the killers came."

"So I basically wanted to kill the mother but save the son. Is that what you're saying, Mr. Sparling?" asked Greta with a look of bafflement on her face.

"That's right, Lady Robinson," said Sparling. "You had no reason to suspect that Thomas had seen you with your accomplice in London."

Greta was about to respond, but Sparling pressed straight on to his next question before she could do so.

"You left the study window open for them, didn't you?"

"No, I just forgot about it."

"Thomas found it wide open when he got back to the house from the Balls."

"Yes, I opened it wide because it was stuffy in the study when I was working in there. I'm not the only one who says it was a warm evening. Besides, Anne hadn't gone to bed when we left."

"Are you saying you expected her to close it?"

"No, I'm saying I forgot about it. It wasn't dark and I didn't think."

"The men who came expected to find it open though, didn't they, Lady Robinson? That's why one of them said that they're all fucking closed."

"I don't know anything about that."

"And that's why they smashed the glass in the window that you left open. Not the other study window; not the windows in the dining room. They smashed that window because that's the one they expected to get in by if Thomas hadn't closed it." Sparling's voice became more insistent as he pressed his point home.

"I told you already. I had nothing to do with these men. I left the window open by mistake. I admitted it to Sergeant Hearns the same night. I didn't try to make a secret of it."

"You don't admit leaving the door in the north wall open though, do you?"

"No, I don't."

"But the killers came through there even though Jane Martin locked the door at five o'clock. How do you explain that?"

"It must have been Anne who opened it when she went for a walk after we left."

"*If* she went for a walk! I suggest she did no such thing. You got Thomas out of the house, you opened the door in the north wall, and you opened the window in the study. Then you left with Lady Anne's husband, knowing that she would be dead before you got back to London. What do you say about that, Lady Robinson?"

"I say it's a lie. A wicked lie. I'm not guilty of this charge," Greta's voice rang with conviction. Miles Lambert thought she looked quite stunning with her flashing green eyes and two spots of color in the center of her wide cheeks.

"Not guilty, eh? Well, we'll leave that to the jury to decide, shall we? I want to ask you about Lady Anne's locket now. Why did you say to Thomas, 'Give that to me, it's mine' when he first showed you the locket?"

"I didn't. I said no such thing."

"So both Thomas and Matthew Barne lied to this court about that, did they?"

"Of course they did. They'd gotten their story worked out together by then. It was different on the day. That boy Matthew ran out of the house when Peter asked him if it was true that I'd said that."

"And Thomas and Jane Martin are lying about Lady Anne wearing the locket after she came back from London, are they?"

"Yes. Well, Thomas is anyway. I don't think Jane said she did see the locket; just something gold, which she thought was the locket. That's how I remember what she said."

"Thomas saw something gold too though, didn't he, when Rosie straightened up after bending down over Lady Anne's body? That was when Rosie took the locket, wasn't it, Lady Robinson, leaving that scratch mark on Lady Anne's neck, which Detective Constable Butler told us about last week?"

"No. She left it in the bathroom in Chelsea when she was up for the flower show. Then we all went down to the coast together on the Saturday, and so no one was in the bathroom again until I used it in the middle of the following week. Peter stayed down in Flyte after the murder."

262 · Simon Tolkien

"But why did you use that bathroom? It's at the top of the house, isn't it?"

"No, it's on the third floor, not the fourth, and the cleaner was in the downstairs lavatory when I used it."

"Yes, I understand that, but why not use your own bathroom in the basement? That would be nearer, wouldn't it, if you were working on the ground floor?"

"I don't know. I can't explain that. Maybe because the bathroom upstairs is nicer than the one in the basement. Maybe I just felt like a change of bathroom."

"And that made it worth climbing three flights of stairs instead of going down one, did it?"

"I guess so." Greta shrugged.

"You never found that locket in any bathroom, did you, Lady Robinson? You got it from Lady Anne's killer."

"Why would I want it? It's not exactly the most valuable of the Sackville jewels, is it, Mr. Sparling?"

"Because you wanted it as a trophy. The locket and the photograph inside it were a symbol of your employer's marriage, and now Lady Anne was dead and you could marry Sir Peter."

"So I put it in the desk and waited for someone to find it," said Greta mockingly. "That makes a lot of sense."

"No, you *hid* it in the desk in a secret recess. Lady Robinson, I must remind you that I'm not here to answer your questions. It's the other way round. You're here to answer mine." Greta looked away from Sparling toward the jury and smiled. The barrister turned a page of his notes and asked her his next question.

"Why didn't you tell Sir Peter about the locket?"

"Because I didn't want to upset him."

"But it was already a week after the murder when he got back to London. Surely it would have been a comfort to him to have the locket. It showed how much Lady Anne cared about him, didn't it? That she should have been wearing a locket containing a picture of him only a couple of days before her death; that she took it to London with her."

"I didn't see it that way."

"But you thought it was important, didn't you? That's why you put it in the secret recess."

"I thought it would be safe there."

"So why didn't you give the locket back to Sir Peter after he had calmed down?"

"Because I forgot about it. I had a lot on my mind. You seem to forget that I was arrested on the day of Lady Anne's funeral, Mr. Sparling."

"You forgot about it even though you had taken the trouble to put it in such a safe place and had decided not to speak to Sir Peter about it because you thought it would upset him. That doesn't make much sense, does it, Lady Robinson?"

"I don't know whether it makes sense or not, Mr. Sparling. All I can tell you is that last summer was one of the most stressful periods of my life. I got arrested for murder. My employer had lost his wife. And his son was conducting a witch-hunt against both of us, aided and abetted by the Suffolk police. Personally I'm not that surprised that I forgot about the locket."

"But I suggest that you did not forget about it, Lady Robinson. You knew it was there. You just didn't expect anyone to find it."

"I forgot about it."

"Mr. Sparling," said the judge. "I notice that we are fast approaching one o'clock. Do you have much more, or would this be a convenient time to stop for lunch?"

"I have only one more question, my Lord. Perhaps it would be better if I asked it now rather than waiting."

"Certainly, Mr. Sparling. Carry on."

"Lady Robinson, I put it to you that you received this locket from the man called Rosie, who visited you in your flat in April of last year and killed Lady Anne at the end of May. The same Rosie who returned to the House of the Four Winds two weeks ago, when he referred to you by name. You conspired with him to commit murder and to divide the spoils between you."

"I conspired with no one," said Greta. "And what's more, I don't know anyone called Rosie or anyone with a name remotely like that. I've already told you that, Mr. Sparling."

"My Lord, I have no more questions," said the prosecution barrister. He wished he could have done more with Greta, but she seemed—just like Matthew Barne had said—to have an answer for every question. Repeating his questions would only make them sound weaker. Sparling felt the case slipping out of his grasp. It filled him with angry frustration, and he looked down at his papers to ensure that none of the jurors would be able to read the irritation written so plainly on his face.

"Mr. Lambert, do you have any other witnesses?" asked the judge once Greta had resumed her seat in the dock.

"One more, my Lord. My client's husband, Sir Peter Robinson."

"Well, we'll hear from him at two o'clock then. Enjoy your lunch, members of the jury," said the judge, avoiding the eye of the furious forewoman. She looked at that moment like she wanted to attack someone with her black leather handbag. Judge Granger felt grateful that he didn't have to have his lunch with her.

Chapter 26

A FTERWARD THOMAS never knew how they managed to get through the two hours that they had to wait in the cafeteria of the Family Records Office. It was torture watching the second hand of the big clock on the wall making its rounds while the evidence went on at the Old Bailey and Andrew dealt with the priority collections of those sensible enough to have made their applications earlier on the day before. He was visible through the window in the door of the café, and several times Matthew had to restrain Thomas from rushing out to physically attack the collections clerk.

It was in fact 12:17 when their number came up on the screen and 12:19 when Thomas snatched the certificates from Andrew's hand. He and Matthew then left the building almost at a run so that there was no opportunity for Matthew to see if Andrew had finally had to resort to his buzzer.

Out on the sidewalk Thomas opened the envelope with trembling hands. The red birth certificate came out first, but he barely glanced at the document, handing it to Matthew while he unfolded the green marriage certificate and began to read.

" 'Certificate No. 38. Married on the twenty-sixth day of November 1989 at the Register Office in Liverpool. Jonathan Barry Rowes aged twenty-one years, Bachelor, to Greta Rose Grahame aged eighteen, both residents of Manchester.' "

"Give me the birth certificate, Matt, quick," said Thomas. His excitement made both his hand and his voice shake as he compared the two documents.

"Father's name and surname: George Reynolds Grahame. Occupation: Factory worker. Name and surname of father: George Reynolds Grahame. Occupation: retired. They're the same, Matt. We've got her now. We've got the murdering bitch." Thomas's voice was hysterical, filled with all the emotions that he had tried to keep suppressed for so long.

"All we need now is a taxi," said Matthew. But a taxi was nowhere in sight. It took them ten minutes to find one, and it was past one o'clock when Thomas and Matthew arrived at the Old Bailey and went in search of Sergeant Hearns.

The court was locked and deserted by the time they got up to the third floor, so they went back down the stairs and peered around a pillar to look through the door of the restaurant. There was no sign of Hearns, but Greta was having lunch with Peter and Patrick Sullivan over at a table by the window. Their heads were close together, but then Greta leaned back in her chair and Thomas and Matthew could see that all three of them were laughing. A moment later Peter turned to his wife and kissed her on the cheek. Thomas saw the love in his father's eyes, and he gripped the envelope with the certificates even more tightly as he turned away and went down the staircase.

"Look, there he is," said Matthew, pointing excitedly to the other side of the great hall on the first floor. They were at the foot of the staircase and Hearns was fifty yards away talking to John Sparling.

"It's perfect," he said. "We'll give the certificates to Sparling and he can show them to your father in the witness box. That's the way to do it."

Matthew pulled Thomas by the arm, but he stood rooted to the spot.

"No, Matthew, it's not perfect," he said. "It'll get her convicted but it'll make my father hate me even more. It'll be something I've done to him."

"Of course it will. And to be honest with you, I can't imagine anyone who deserves a bad time more. He may be your father and a famous politician, but he's also a major-league bastard in my book. He's got it coming to him almost as much as she does."

"Except that he hasn't killed anyone, Matt. The point is that I've got to give him the chance to change his mind for himself. He's got to have the opportunity to choose between me and her."

"Well, I think you're completely crazy," said Matthew angrily. "He hasn't trusted *you*. Not once. You told him over and over again who killed your mother, and all you got was a punch in the mouth. No, I'm sorry, two punches. He hit you down in Suffolk as well, didn't he, Tom?"

"He slapped me."

"All right, he slapped you. How considerate of him!"

"Shut up, Matthew. You've made your point."

Thomas turned away and began to walk back up the stairs. Matthew felt as if he had been consigned to irrelevance, and it infuriated him even more.

"Don't be a fool, Tom," he shouted after his friend. "Your father's obsessed with her. A couple of certificates aren't going to change his mind."

"Maybe not, but I've got to try. For my mother's sake, I've got to try."

"So what happens if you try and fail and the jury never gets to hear about Greta and Rosie being married? What happens if she gets acquitted, Thomas? Have you thought of that? How would your mother feel about that?"

Matthew's questions pursued Thomas up the stairs. He didn't have any answers and he didn't give any. All he had was the sense of certainty that had come to him as he had looked at his lovestruck father through the window of the restaurant minutes before; the certainty that he had to give the man one more chance to choose.

Thomas watched his father and Greta through the window. Time ticked away. Patrick brought them cups of coffee. They drank them and then they drank more. There was nothing Thomas could do. He had to see his father alone, but even if he could win his father over, it would be useless if Greta had seen them together. She would tell old Lambert not to call Sir Peter. The barrister would close the defense case and then there could be no more evidence. Judging by Greta's laughter and continued high spirits, there could only be one result if the jury didn't see the certificates. Greta would be acquitted and could never be tried again.

Thomas wondered where Matthew had gone. Perhaps he was telling Hearns and Sparling about the Rowes marriage, although Thomas doubted it. Matthew didn't have anything without the certificates, and besides, he wouldn't go against Thomas. He was too good a friend for that. Thomas wished they hadn't split up. Matthew might have helped him to create some sort of diversion. As things stood, he didn't see any way of getting his father on his own.

At 1:55 the P.A. system crackled into action, summoning barristers and defendants back to their courtrooms. Thomas ducked behind a pillar as Peter came out of the restaurant sandwiched between his wife and Patrick Sullivan. Thomas caught the lawyer's last words as the three of them walked over to the staircase leading up to the third floor.

"This shouldn't take long, Peter. It's the support for Greta's character that's most important. The Crown has got no answer for that."

Thomas waited a minute and then followed them up the stairs. He realized now that his only chance was to ambush his father in the witness waiting room after the other two had gone into court. He knew the procedure from his own experience giving evidence two days earlier. Miss Hooks settled the witness in the little room next to the door of the court and then went and got the judge and the jury before bringing the witness in. He ought to have about three or four minutes maximum to change his father's mind.

Everything went just as Thomas had predicted. Once his father was alone, he went straight into the waiting room to confront him. Thomas had had time to think out his strategy beforehand. He had to tell his father what he had discovered at the Records Office. Handing him the certificates would not be enough. His father might refuse to look at them. What Thomas had not reckoned on was the level of his father's hostility. It stopped Thomas in his tracks almost as soon as he had gotten through the door.

"What the hell are you doing here?" Peter shouted, getting to his feet. "I thought I told you to stay away from me."

It took every ounce of Thomas's courage to shut the door of the little room behind him and stand his ground as his father advanced on him. Thomas knew that the shouting would be audible inside the court if the door remained open.

"Look, Dad, I know it's a bad time but—"

"Bad time!" interrupted his father furiously. "It's not a bad time,

Thomas. It's no time. My wife's in that court on trial for murder because of you. You've tried everything, haven't you?"

"No, Dad—"

"Everything! You've perjured yourself, you've gotten other people to perjure themselves and now you're going to try and interfere with *my* evidence. Well, you won't get away with it, Thomas. I promise you that."

A frenzy seemed to take possession of Peter. He seized hold of his son's shirt just as he'd done on the day of Lady Anne's funeral a year before, and he shook Thomas as he spoke.

"Dad, you've got to listen to me. I've found out something—"

"New lies, Thomas. I've had enough of your lies. Now get out of my way."

Using all his strength, Peter thrust his son to one side and wrenched open the door of the waiting room. Then he strode out into the hall, leaving his son in a heap in the corner. The door of the courtroom remained closed, but Thomas knew that Miss Hooks would be opening it any minute to summon his father inside. Thomas's legs felt weak underneath him, and he needed all his willpower to get to his feet and go outside.

Peter was standing by one of the high windows on the other side of the hall. Thomas took the envelope out of his pocket and removed the two certificates, keeping his eye on his father all the time.

"Damn you, boy," hissed Peter as his son approached. "Get away from me." The two of them looked, at that moment, like they were playing some strange but deadly game.

"She's not your wife, Dad."

"Shut up, Thomas. Do you hear me? Shut up. I won't tell you again."

"Sir Peter Robinson," called the shrill voice of Miss Hooks behind Thomas. He did not look around but instead grabbed his father by the wrist. At the same time Thomas used his other hand to force the certificates into his father's grasp, pushing Peter's fingers down over the paper.

"Take these," he said. "Read them before you say anything. For Mummy's sake. Do it for Mummy's sake, if not for mine."

"Sir Peter Robinson," called Miss Hooks even more shrilly than before, and Thomas felt his father move past him toward the door of the court. There was a pause. Then a few moments later it shut with a bang.

=

Thomas might never have known what happened in the court after his father had gone into the witness box if Matthew had not at that moment arrived at the top of the stairs. He found Thomas standing as if turned to stone, looking vacantly up through a high window toward a patch of blue sky. The aftershocks of his encounter with his father were sending shudders through Thomas's thin frame, and Matthew could see the tears in his friend's dark blue eyes.

"Where's your father?" he asked. "Where are the certificates? Talk to me, Tom."

"I gave them to him, but I don't know if he'll read them. He wouldn't let me speak, Matt. I think I've screwed it up. I'm so sorry. I should have listened to you."

"There's no time for that now. Has your father gone inside?"

Thomas nodded miserably.

"Well, we've got nothing to lose then, have we? Let's see what happens. We haven't come this far to miss out on the last act."

Matthew started to pull Thomas toward the door of the court.

"Sergeant Hearns told us not to go back in court after we'd finished giving evidence," protested Thomas weakly, but Matthew took no notice. The fight had gone out of Thomas, and he put up no resistance as Matthew pushed open the door and pulled him down onto a seat at the back of the court.

A ripple of interest ran along the press benches as the reporters turned to look at the teenagers, but then they all settled back into their seats as Sir Peter Robinson took the oath. His voice sounded dead and his face was white, but Greta's attention was concentrated on Thomas. It filled him with a raw pleasure to watch the anxiety growing in her green eyes until finally he could not resist the temptation to bait her any longer. He looked at his father and then he looked back at Greta and smiled meaningfully. The effect on Greta was instantaneous. She gripped the rail of the dock and the color drained from her face. Then she was suddenly writing something on a piece of paper and trying to get the attention of Patrick Sullivan sitting several yards away with his back to the dock. Thomas watched him turn around and get up to speak to Greta while with another part of his brain Thomas listened to the beginning of his father's evidence.

"Tell us your name, please," asked Miles Lambert.

"I am Sir Peter Robinson."

"And your occupation?"

"I am the minister of defense." Peter's voice was entirely flat, without any intonation or emphasis.

Patrick Sullivan put a note in front of Miles Lambert, but the barrister did not look down to read it. There was no reason to. All he was doing was introducing his witness to the jury, getting them warmed up for the glowing character reference that Sir Peter was going to give his wife.

"How long have you known Lady Greta Robinson?" he asked.

"About three and a half years. She started working for me in 1997."

"And it's right to say that you were married last December."

"Right and wrong."

"Excuse me, Sir Peter. I don't quite understand that answer."

"Let me clarify it for you then," said Peter evenly. "We certainly went through a ceremony of marriage at the Chelsea Registry Office on the twentieth of December last year, but it is now quite clear to me in the light of these documents that the ceremony was not valid."

"Not valid?"

"Yes. Because the person I thought I was marrying was already married to someone else, and I have every reason to think that her husband was then, and in fact still is, very much alive."

Miles's mouth opened and closed and opened again, but for the first time in many years no words came out. He glanced down too late at the scrawled note that Patrick Sullivan had put on the table in front of him.

"Miles," it said. "Don't ask him any questions. He'll destroy us if you do. Close the case now. Greta."

She might have told me before, thought Miles bitterly. Before her bloody husband or whoever he is got up there and smashed up all my work.

The judge allowed the heavy silence to build in the courtroom for a few moments before he broke it himself.

"I see that you've got two documents there, Sir Peter," he said in his usual courteous manner. "Perhaps you'd be good enough to tell us what they are."

"This one's Greta's marriage certificate," said Peter. "The certificate for her first marriage, I mean. It shows that she married Jonathan Barry Rowes on November twenty-sixth, 1989, in Liverpool—"

"I'm sorry to interrupt you, Sir Peter, but did you just say 'Rose'?" asked the judge. "As in the flower?"

"Yes, that's right. It's spelled R-O-W-E-S but it's obviously pronounced like the flower."

"Thank you. Please carry on."

"This other one is Greta's birth certificate," said Peter, holding up the red-edged piece of paper. His voice was toneless and mechanical, completely at variance with the extraordinary things that he was saying. "The father's name on it is the same as the father's name on the marriage certificate. It proves it's Greta who married Rowes, and I believe Rowes is the man who killed my wife and tried to kill my son two weeks ago."

"Yes, thank you," said the judge, raising his voice a little in order to quell a sudden outbreak of whispering in the court. "Well, the jury had better see these exhibits, don't you think, Mr. Lambert? They really seem to be quite relevant, particularly given your client's assertion yesterday that she doesn't know anyone called Rosie or Rose."

"My Lord, I request an adjournment," said Miles, recovering his voice but not his composure.

"Why, Mr. Lambert? I can't see the need. This is your witness, you know. You called him."

"My Lord, if you won't grant me an adjournment, will you at least let me address you in the absence of the jury?"

"Yes, Mr. Lambert, certainly you may, but first the jury must be allowed to finish examining the documents produced by your witness. Let's make them exhibits twenty-one and twenty-two, Miss Hooks."

The two certificates had just gotten as far as the Indian juror with the turban when Greta couldn't contain herself any longer.

"Peter! Look at me, Peter!" she shouted to her husband across the courtroom. "It's not what you think. It was just a stupid teenage thing. We got divorced years ago. I had nothing to do with this murder!"

Peter turned to look at his wife for the last time, and his composure cracked. He was suddenly like a drowning man, struggling in vain to swim up to the surface. He opened his mouth but no words came.

Perhaps Greta took his silence for encouragement, but she certainly lost no time in intensifying her appeal. "I made you what you are now, Peter," she cried. "You know that. What did Anne ever do for you? All she cared about was Thomas and that house. I saved you from her. I set you free."

"I'll never be free again. You killed her, Greta. And then you made me part of what you'd done. You and your psychopath."

The words were forced from Peter and came between great gulps. But they enraged Greta. It was as if she realized for the first time that she had lost him.

"You're a fool, Peter. That's what you are. You want it all for free, don't you? The power and the glory *and* the beautiful girl. But there's a price to pay. Just like there always is. You don't get something for nothing, Peter. Not in the real world."

Greta drew breath for more, and the reporters' pencils raced across their notepads. But there was to be no more. The security guard whom Greta had pushed aside at the start of her outburst had now recovered. She tackled Greta to the floor and then manhandled her through the door at the back of the dock.

"Yes, take her down," said Judge Granger in a commanding voice. "And Mr. Lambert, I'll give you your adjournment, but your client will stay in custody until I say otherwise. Perhaps you better take some further instructions. Your client seems to have quite a lot to say."

=

The courtroom emptied very quickly after the judge and jury had gone out. The reporters needed to phone the day's sensation through to their editors. Soon Thomas and Matthew found themselves all alone except for Sir Peter, who continued to sit in the witness box gazing steadily into the middle distance. He looked as if something inside him had irrevocably broken, as if the motor that had driven him so hard for so many years had spluttered and died. Matthew saw Thomas staring at his father and quietly left the court.

Thomas wanted to go over to his father, but he hung back, rooted to his seat. He had the words for confronting his father but none for getting close to him. They had been strangers for too long. It was Peter who finally broke the silence, and his voice came as if from a great distance away.

"I'm sorry, Tom," he said. "I've let you and Anne down all because of some stupid infatuation. I've betrayed you both and dressed it up as loyalty. I wanted to believe in Greta because I couldn't bear the thought of life without her, and so I let all this happen. All this ruin, and now it's too late."

"What's too late?"

"Everything. I don't want to be anymore, Tom. That's the trouble. I don't want to be. If I hadn't brought Greta Grahame into our world, your mother would still be alive. I can't live with that, Tom. I just can't live with that."

"Perhaps you can't at the moment, but it'll be different later. You can't give up, Dad."

"Why not?"

"Because you're my father and you owe me," said Thomas simply. It was the only reply he could think of.

"Perhaps I do," said Peter, smiling sadly. "But you can't get blood from a stone. I'm all out of love, Tom. I'm no good to you."

"You're all I've got," said Thomas passionately. "Mummy loved you. That's why she wore that locket. And she loved me too, which is why she saved me from Rowes. We both owe it to her to carry on, to help each other."

Thomas leaned forward and kissed his father on the cheek, and a strange thing happened. He couldn't remember ever seeing his father's piercing blue eyes close before, but now they did.

=

The jury found Greta guilty by a majority of eleven to one at 4:05 on the following afternoon. The press tended to agree that it was the Italian man in the expensive designer suit who was the dissenting voice, although one or two of them thought that it might be the Indian man with the turban and the inscrutable expression who had held out against the rest. There was no doubting which way the forewoman of the jury had voted, however. She positively shouted the verdict across the courtroom, accompanying it with a mean glare at Miles Lambert, who had known what was coming and looked the other way. Afterward he congratulated John Sparling on his victory, and the prosecution barrister had the good grace to admit that he would certainly have lost the case if it had not been for the arrival of the two certificates at the last minute in the hand of Miles's star witness.

At half past four Judge Granger sentenced Lady Greta Robinson to a term of life imprisonment. She showed no reaction to the sentence, but the reporters all agreed that she seemed to have lost none of her pride and dignity as she was led away. She was certainly a cut above the normal run of defendants.

Chapter 27

THE MAN WAS dressed in a white paper suit. The police had given it to him that morning to replace his clothing, which had been removed for forensic examination. And it wasn't just his clothing that the police had taken. They'd also gotten his passport, travel documents, and a neck brace that he had been wearing at the time of his arrest. When on, it had concealed a thick scar that ran down behind his right jawbone into his strong bull neck.

Every police officer worth his salt knew that the paper suit was a sure way of stripping the suspect of his defenses, making him more likely to crack under questioning. But it wasn't working its magic with this man. He wore the suit as if it were tailor-made, shaking out his thick black hair over its collar. He had his long, muscular legs stretched out in front of him as if he didn't have a care in the world. And he said nothing. Just stared at Detective Sergeant Hearns with a half smile playing across his bloodless lips, while the big policeman asked question after question and got no reply. Jonathan Barry Rowes was exercising his right to silence.

Hearns knew he was having no effect. It was bloody-mindedness that kept him going, and afterward he had no idea why Rowes started to talk. Perhaps he just got bored. Clearly any advice given by the shifty-looking lawyer sitting beside Rowes in the interview room was entirely irrelevant. He was the type of man who made his own decisions.

"What's your name?" he asked suddenly, interrupting Hearns in the middle of a question about Rowes's Mercedes C-class car.

"Detective Sergeant Hearns of the Ipswich Police. I introduced myself at the start of the interview, Mr. Rowes."

"Sure you did. But it's not your fucking surname I'm after, Sergeant. What's the name your parents gave you? Or didn't you have any fucking parents?"

Rowes's voice remained soft and slow. There was no increase in volume or emphasis to accompany the abuse and foul language. He kept his small, dark eyes fixed on the policeman across the table.

Hearns looked away for a moment, twisting his stubby-fingered hands together. He was remembering like a mantra the section in the training manual headed "Never lose your temper when interviewing a suspect." He needed to humor Rowes if he was going to get any answers to his questions.

"Martin," he said after a pause. "My parents called me Martin."

"Marty. Funny name for a copper. Well, Marty, you're trying to tell me something, aren't you? Isn't that the truth?"

"No. All I've been doing is asking you questions, which you've been declining to answer. That's your right."

"Oh, come off it, Marty. You're telling me I'm dead in the water. My DNA matches the blood on the windowsill, and there's fuck-all I can do about it. I've got that moron, Lonny, to thank for that. The idiot pushed me when I was trying to pick the glass out. He's always been in too much of a hurry. It'll get him in trouble one of these days." Rowes laughed harshly.

"Lonny who?" asked Hearns.

"Lonny nothing. Don't ask stupid questions, Marty. It doesn't suit you. Now, what was I saying? Yeah, DNA. The scientists have got the better of us. Not just me. You too, Marty. No need for any of your old-fashioned police work anymore, is there? Just grab a blood sample, send it off to the lab, and hey presto, Johnny Burglar gets ten years. You'll be out of a job soon, Marty."

"I agree that it's certainly changed things. Except that in your case we didn't have your DNA to make the comparison. Not until we found you, that is."

"Until I dropped into your lap, you mean. You didn't find me, Marty.

The kid did. Get your facts right. You screwed up the investigation. That was your contribution."

"You're entitled to your opinion, Mr. Rowes. But the point is you've been arrested and this is your opportunity to give your side of the story."

"Uncle Marty. Always looking after my interests. No, you just want answers for your stupid questions. And you know, thinking about it, there's really no reason not to talk, is there? I'm going down anyway, thanks to this DNA garbage. So ask away, Marty. Let me satisfy your copper's curiosity."

"The murder. Whose idea was it? Yours or Greta's?"

"Mine. I suggested it because I needed her. And she had to have an incentive for getting involved. She wanted to be Mrs. Big Time, and His Lordship was never going to divorce the lady of the house."

"So it was your idea. Good. How long before the murder did you and Greta first start talking about it?"

"Conspiring, you mean. Not long. I saw her picture in the paper leaving some fancy restaurant with that creep, Peter Robinson. I did some research, and then I went and talked to her. I hadn't seen her in over a year."

"What did she say?"

"She didn't like the idea at first. Didn't want to get her hands dirty. But she soon changed her mind when I threatened to tell lover boy about her and me. I've always been one of her best-kept secrets, you know. She wouldn't tell her parents when we got married. We had to sneak off to Liverpool when no one was looking. So anyway, she signed up to getting rid of Her Ladyship, but then she kept on getting me to wait because she wasn't sure she'd got His Lordship hooked. I got bored in the end."

"And whose idea was it to go back to the house before the trial? Yours or Greta's?"

"Mine. She got mad about it afterward. She loves the little runt, or used to anyway."

"So what were you going to do with Thomas when you found him?"

"I was going to make him fucking disappear. Give him to Lonny. He's good at looking after other people's brats."

Rowes's voice was still even, but he had let his anger show through for a moment. It was as if a door had suddenly opened and shut, allowing Hearns a glimpse of something obscene, something he'd never seen before.

"Disappear temporarily or permanently?" he asked.

Rowes smiled and said nothing.

"And Greta had nothing to do with this?"

"Of course she fucking didn't. Didn't you hear me the first time? Thomas was the child she never had. Sweet Greta Rose is a crazy woman, but you know that already, don't you, Marty? Like that locket. What a fucking stupid idea, but she insisted on it. I'd never have given it to her if I'd known what she was going to do with it. Put the bloody thing in a desk and wait for the kid to find it. Lonny could have done better than that."

The idea of Rowes diagnosing anyone as crazy struck Hearns as ludicrous, but he let it pass.

"What happened to the jewels?" he asked.

"Forget it, Marty. I'm not telling you that. Don't be stupid."

"How did you feel about Greta and Peter? Your wife with another man. That can't have made you happy?"

"Ex-wife, Marty. You don't know anything, do you? And you call yourself a fucking detective. God help Ipswich. That's what I say."

Hearns resisted the temptation to hit back. Rowes was getting angry, and he probably wouldn't answer many more questions before he clammed up again.

"All right, ex-wife. It still must have upset you."

"No, it didn't. I loved the idea of Mr. Big Shot shacking up with his wife's killer. And him finding out about it at the trial was the best bit of all. Now he'll have to live with the knowledge of who Greta is for the rest of his life. Serves him right. Fucking creep."

"Why does it serve him right? What did he do to you?"

"He slept with Greta. Isn't that enough?" shouted Rowes, finally losing his temper. "She should have stayed with me. I got her away from her pig of a father, *and* I married her. It's not my fault she took all those stupid drugs and lost the baby."

"But it's never your fault, is it, Mr. Rowes? A woman is dead because of you. A boy has lost his mother. What do you say about that?"

Rowes said nothing, but then again, he didn't need to. His response was written across his face. Hearns had never seen such concentrated rage, such a devouring hatred in anyone. Not in twenty-five years of police work.

"All right, you've got nothing to say," he said. "And I've got no more questions. This interview is terminated. I'm turning off the tape."

Hearns flicked a switch on the wall and left the interview room almost at a run. He needed to get out in the air.

Chapter 28

O N A BRIGHT spring day four years later Thomas drove the Aston
Martin that had once belonged to his mother from Oxford up to
London. The university term had just finished, and he had arranged to
pick up his old friend Matthew from his family home in Battersea.
Then they would go up together to Flyte, arriving at the House of the
Four Winds before dark, if the traffic didn't slow them down. Matthew
had asked to come. Thomas had not seen him for a long time, and his
old friend had just lost his father.

"I'm sorry, Matthew. Really I am," said Thomas as they roared away
with Matthew's suitcase wedged upside down beside Thomas's on the
backseat.

"It's all right. He never spent much time with me, you know. Or
anyone else for that matter."

"Yes, he did seem like a bit of a loner. He was always in that little
room at the end of the corridor that you had a funny name for. What
was it?"

"His cubbyhole. No one went in there except my dad, and then after
he died they opened it up and found all these books of crossword puz-
zles. A few empty vodka bottles and piles of crossword books. What a
life!"

"How's your mother taking it?"

"Great. She's learning Japanese. My sister Dorothy thinks she's got a
Japanese boyfriend. The life insurance paid for a nanny so she can live

it up now. God knows she's got some catching up to do. What about you? How's your father?"

"All right, I suppose. He never comes to Flyte, so I only see him every couple of months, and then we haven't got a lot to say to each other, although it doesn't seem to matter too much. He drinks a lot of whisky and we have companionable silences. Sometimes he tells me about the book he's writing."

"What's it about?"

"Spies. Traitors. People who have betrayed their country."

"Yes, I can see why he'd be interested in them."

"It's good for him to be doing something. He was very lost after the trial when he resigned. He's better now, although he still drinks too much."

"Has he seen Greta?"

"He tried to after the trial like I told you before, but she wouldn't see him, and now I don't think he'd want to see her. She's in a prison up north the last I heard. Perhaps she likes being near her mother."

They made good time on the road and passed through Carmouth just before seven, but then Thomas slowed down as they approached the House of the Four Winds. He had not been home for a month, and he worried as he always did that Aunt Jane's health would have deteriorated while he was gone. The old lady made a secret of her age, but Thomas guessed that she was nearly eighty, and the years since the trial had slowed her down so that she could no longer do what she once did. Grace Marsh came in three times a week to help her in the house and Christy looked after the garden, but the old housekeeper still insisted on dusting the family portraits and cleaning the family silver.

Thomas need not have worried. Aunt Jane wrapped him up in a tight embrace as soon as he came through the door and wanted to feed them a huge tea without delay, but Thomas was determined to walk down to the beach before it got dark. He left Matthew to unpack and walked out onto the north lawn. The red sun was hanging low on the western horizon, and the shapes of the old elm trees were sharply defined in the twilight.

Thomas crossed over to the door in the wall and went out into the lane. He could hear the crash of the incoming waves long before he reached the beach, but the sea still came as a shock when he saw it. He stood with his feet in the surf and drank in the last of the light.

Thomas felt at that moment that there was nowhere in the world except the sand and the sea and the sky and behind him the House of the Four Winds standing high above the cliff. Thomas felt the presence of all the Sackvilles who had gone before him and all those who would come after. He thought of his grandmother galloping across the beach on her horse and his mother swimming in the cove before he was born, and he thought of himself as a child and now a man. He was a link in a great chain stretching back to people whose names he would never know and forward into a distant future he would never see, but for now this small corner of England was his own. It was his inheritance.

ABOUT THE AUTHOR

SIMON TOLKIEN is the grandson of J.R.R. Tolkien, the creator of *The Lord of the Rings*. He studied modern history at Oxford and is a barrister in London, where he lives with his wife and their two children. *Final Witness* is his first novel.

ABOUT THE TYPE

This book was set in Bembo, a typeface based on an old-style Roman face that was used for Cardinal Bembo's tract *De Aetna* in 1495. Bembo was cut by Francisco Griffo in the early sixteenth century. The Lanston Monotype Company of Philadelphia brought the well-proportioned letterforms of Bembo to the United States in the 1930s.

FINAL WITNESS